Emlyn Rees is twenty-six and works in publishing in London.

the book of dead authors

EMLYN REES

review

First published in Great Britain in 1997
by HEADLINE BOOK PUBLISHING

First published in this edition in 1998
by HEADLINE BOOK PUBLISHING

A HEADLINE REVIEW paperback

10 9 8 7 6 5 4 3 2 1

ISBN 0 7472 5721 3

Typeset by
Letterpart Limited, Reigate, Surrey

Printed and bound in Great Britain by
Clays Ltd, St Ives plc.

HEADLINE BOOK PUBLISHING
A division of Hodder Headline PLC
338 Euston Road
London NW1 3BH

For Sophie

ACKNOWLEDGEMENTS

Thanks go to everyone at Curtis Brown: Vivienne for rescuing me from the dole queue; Jane for not putting me back on it; Vicks, Jacks, Phil and Anna for telling me to submit(!); Kate M and Kate C for recommending the book to Jonny Geller; the legendary JG himself for making my decade by doing the deal; and to Gill Harris for being kind enough to allow my publication date to coincide with her birthday.

Huge thanks also to Bill Massey, Paul Copperwaite and Sarah Whale at Headline for all the hard work they've put in.

To the Cheltenham and Southampton survivors and anyone else who's woken up on a Saturday morning with their boots still on.

And last but greatest, to Anne, Richard and Kirsti, for being there for the last twenty-six years.

LIST OF CONTENTS

PROLOGUE

She slid the serrated tongue of the key into the lock and opened the door to the flat. Dropping the jangle of keys back into her pocket, she closed the door quietly behind her and laid the parcel she'd been carrying on the marble surface of the table in the hall. Beside it, the red bulb of the answerphone struck out intermittently from its white plastic mould. She'd given up counting how many messages were trapped there, how many unattended, irrelevant lives she'd refused to let cross over into her own.

She could hear her breath now. It came shallow, uneven, and exhausted. Only her eyes moved. Slowly, mechanically, they scanned the surface of the parcel, as if reading a bar code, taking in the name and address on the label she'd written herself and which had been returned to her. And then there were the stamps. She'd bought those too, wondered if they'd ever be used against her, sent tumbling back through the city's postal depots, as they had been now. Sent back. Rejected. Different words. But the message was the same. Such a deliberate act. And so personal. She imagined how some underling – some secretary or assistant – must have taken the stamps from the envelope they'd been sent in, and drawn a smooth, salivating tongue across their acrid backs, slopped out an involuntary sample of cells, mixed the DNA in with the glue, before rubbing them onto the parcel with the soft, padded bottom of a clenched fist. Such quiet malevolence. So personal. It was impossible to take it any other way.

Her eyes shifted and moved up to the oval mirror on the wall. The glass was patchy, rubbed by the accumulated pollution of decades, shabby in its glint. She stared, first at the glass, then at the patches, and finally, beyond the pastiche of patches and glint, past the boundary between reality and imagination, into the shadowy reflection of herself. The shadow's eyes stared back. And though the lips of this untouchable image of her other self remained sealed, failed to expel an ingestion of air over the contortion of a tongue, she heard the voice all the same. Cold, controlled words came loudly, as if she'd spoken them herself. They told her to open the parcel. They told her that only then would it begin.

And she listened. There was nothing to fear here. The voice didn't belong to some silent schizophrenic partner, lurking there, competing with her will for control. There was no tasty fodder for psychologists here, no teeming demons trapped in her head, waiting to be cast out into the nearest herd, sent spinning in a dust-storm of hoofs over the edge, out of her life for ever. No, there was no therapy-induced cure attending her on a couch in a pleasantly cool Harley Street consulting room; nothing alien or autonomous in these words which told her to act, which reminded her that only action could cause reaction, could lend her definition.

The voice that came had come from inside her, conjured by her desire, laced with intent. It was the voice formed from the words of outrage and craving and bitterness she'd silently hissed for years. All those words she'd wanted to speak aloud now came and demanded that she listen. This, their voice, was inside her, because that was where it belonged, where it had always dwelt. Because it was hers. Because she wanted it to be there. Because it told her to do the things she knew she had to do. And because it fed her the sanest words she'd ever heard: her own.

Her eyes disengaged from those of her reflection, cracking the silent bond of complicity, and she picked up the parcel and walked down the corridor to the study at the end of the hall. The door stood before her, innocuous, constructed of ordinary varnished wood, the perfunctory divide between one section of her habitat and another.

But as she stood there, the parcel nestled in the angle of her crooked wrist, she understood it was far more than that.

The future still held the possibility of fluidity, of choice. All it would take to alter it, to divert it back into the predictable currents of normality, was a change of direction, a change of mind. All she had to do was ignore the voice. She could turn back now and things would stay the same; the Rubicon would remain an uncrossed boundary of intent. Her breathing fell away for a moment, and with it her indecision.

The study was black: black walls, black ceiling, black floorboards, drawn black curtains. It was this, not white, that was the colour of innocence. This was the colour of deepest space, the colour the universe had been before it had exploded into its first dawn. And there, on the walls, were the chosen ones: photographs of men and women, garish wounds bursting out from the surrounding dark. Famous faces, their posed profiles culled from magazines, trapped in black, wooden frames. But she didn't look at them now. Each of them had received her stare before. Each of them lay wrapped like vines around her optic nerves, growing as one with her mind's eye.

Black candles lay stacked in triangles like firewood against the wall. She wedged the parcel into the pit of her arm, leaving both hands free, and took two of the candles and placed them in the cast-iron holders on either side of the door. Then she closed the door, severing herself from the world outside, and cast herself into infinity, into space. Darkness burst around her like a bomb. She felt suspended, weightless. Gravity had left her. If she was to reach out now, who knew what her fingers might touch, what strange skin might be quietly biding, waiting to feel the caress of her fingers? Who knew what was waiting for her here?

Her hand snaked inside her pocket, withdrew with its fingers curled around the cold metal of a lighter. She scraped the wheel across the flint and there was light. A flame rose, flickered, and shadows leapt from her, danced across the walls. She heard the paper of the parcel rustle beneath her arm as she guided the petroleum flame to the candles on the wall; it sounded like burning leaves, the genesis of some great conflagration. Then, as the black wax altered state, made the shift from solid to liquid, she gripped a fistful of candles from the pile and walked the perimeter of the room, twisting them one by one into the holders which protruded from the wall on either side of the trapped, targeted faces.

Only when the room had become a seething nest of shadow and flame did she approach the desk which stood draped in black velvet, an altar, against the wall opposite the door. She placed the parcel upon it like an offering, next to the steel knife and iron bowl. Then she slowly pirouetted, allowing her eyes to flicker across the framed faces on the walls. She watched the shadows shudder across them, fluid and transient, making it appear as if they could lose their form, their very identity, at any moment, slide into things no longer recognisable as human, as images of life.

The lighter was hot in her hand now. She felt her skin beginning to bubble into blisters as she completed her slow survey. Her gaze settled on the last remaining frame which hung on the wall above the desk, directly above the knife. She stretched her arm out and inserted the two remaining candles into the two remaining holders. She lit one, then the next. Wax dripped down like drops of blood. Then, eyes straight ahead, she stared into the centre of the frame, into the mirror which held her own reflection, into the only truly credible image in this cathedral of candles, the only masterpiece in this gallery of deception.

She took the knife and shuddered its mercurial, candlelit tip through the end of the manila envelope of the parcel. Open like a wound, she slid her hand inside and withdrew the stack of papers with all the care of a doctor delivering a child. And make no mistake, this was her conception. More effort than gyrating of loins and an acceptance of sperm had gelled to provide this singular chemistry. A whole life – not just a passing animalistic whim – had been responsible for this accumulation of words.

Still born.

These were the words she heard as the candles flickered and the stack of papers rustled as she laid them to rest on the desk before her. The words on the pages were cells. Over the years it had taken her to write this novel, her words had divided, multiplied and grown into a whole. They'd gestated on the pages before her. And now that they'd lost all hope of being raised into the public eye, they'd died. They lay flat on the page, unread and inanimate, shrivelled and emaciated victims of other authors, the unworthy cuckoos who had crowded them out.

She took the rejection letter from the top of the typescript, hardly bothering to read it. Her mind was already set, hardened, now impenetrable to indecision. This letter, from the fiftieth editor she'd sent her work, did nothing but provide the confirmation she needed. The clichés linked together in the formation of paragraphs beneath the publishing house's letterhead were familiar, standard stuff: cursory comments caring nothing for the work they described. Cribbed from the dictionary of end-of-day, slush-pile-reduction laziness, they maimed from a clean, conscienceless and sanitised distance. Only she was immune to the pain they inflicted now. She understood that there was another way, that this letter didn't signify the end of a quest, but the beginning. This – the last submission she'd ever make through conventional channels – hadn't been her last chance, but theirs. It was they who had spurned her. And it was they who must accept responsibility for the agony which would soon rip them apart.

Pinching the letter in the middle, so that its back arched, flexed rigid, she introduced its corner into the flame of the candle bordering her reflection. The flame tasted, then licked greedily, curling the crisp paper back, reducing it to crumbling carbon. She held it over the bowl, over the cremated remains of other, similar letters, and watched it burn, knowing that soon a hungry phoenix would spring from the ashes, knowing that this signalled the beginning of the regenerative process through which life came from death and purpose from rejection.

CHAPTER ONE

house hunting

Reflected in the tinted lenses of her sunglasses, the smooth blocks of recently sand-blasted stone glared golden, burnished in the fierce June sunlight.

'You ready, Tup?' she asked the huge man who stood by her side on the doorstep.

'Uh-huh,' he grunted in affirmation.

'You remember what I said?'

His cavernous voice correlated to his bulk. 'Yeah, Mrs Skreen, I remember.'

'Tell me one more time. Just to be certain.'

He placed the two cases he was carrying on the ground, props that were apparently unnecessary for the performance that followed. 'Don't speak,' he recited with pained concentration, glancing nervously at her for reassurance between phrases. 'Nod only when you nod. Smile only when you smile. But don't speak.'

She raised her eyebrows over the frames of her lenses, accentuating their plucked curves into taut arches. 'What else?' she asked, sunlight sparking off her sunglasses as she turned to face him.

'Er . . .?' Swallowed alive, his sentence died. In the ensuing panic, his muddy eyes swirled in excruciating embarrassment, then, settled in failure, glazed over, became totally devoid of comprehension. It was the same expression he'd been wearing when she'd first seen him. Death had already been in him.

'Gloves,' she prompted.

He looked at his hands, at the black leather gloves that

hid them, and waited for his brain to decipher their secret. Eventually he looked at her and hazarded, 'I must keep my gloves on . . .'

'At all times,' she said, completing the sentence for him.

'At all times,' he repeated, this time with increased confidence. 'I must keep my gloves on at all times.'

'Good boy,' she said, rising onto the tips of her toes so that her lips briefly connected with his heavy jaw. The smell of the aftershave she'd stroked across his skin after she'd shaved him that morning trailed through her nostrils. She remembered how he'd grumbled, told her that it stung. And she remembered comforting him with lullaby whispers, telling him that the smell made her feel good, and that making her feel good should make him feel good, too.

Without shame, he examined the fine silhouette of her body. 'Love?' he queried, shifting uncomfortably in the abrasively new suit she'd made him wear, scratching where the humidity of the day had made it cling to his groin.

'Soon,' she promised, reaching up and straightening his tie. 'You can have your love soon.' With the elegant tweezers formed by the manicured nails of her finger and thumb, she ceremoniously snipped at a petal of apple blossom on his shoulder. Then she jostled him back a pace, surveyed him, and smiled. 'There,' she concluded. 'What a gentleman you look.'

A flare of pleasure warmed his dim face and he lifted the two heavy cases effortlessly, as though they were constructed of rice paper, not packed leather.

She thought back. She'd first seen the man she now called Tup from the comfort of a café, across the street from the nest of bins and boxes and shopping bags in which he'd made his home. It had been impossible to say how old he was. Too much beard and muck had cowled his features. His limbs had been wrapped in soiled, army-surplus wool. Dead. But then there'd been movement: another man, in jeans and a T-shirt, tattooed arms, swaying down the street, shouting, raising his voice to the sky. He'd stopped in front of Tup, interrupted her view of him. There'd been anger in the other man's gesticulations. He'd finished the lager he'd been drinking, crumpled the can in his fist, let fly, followed it with a boot. Two mistakes in two seconds. Tup had risen, hauled upwards by an invisible rope. She'd watched as the other man had crumpled into a heap on the pavement and Tup had stared around him, before examining his fist, bewildered. He'd then impassively stamped on the other man's head, dropped a bead of spit onto his face and set off sluggishly down the street. She'd left her coffee, followed his six different layers of insulation, watched his shoulders roll inside them, sensed their latent strength, and sensed his loneliness and weakness, too.

'Gentle man,' Tup repeated in a soft tone, bisecting the word with a flickering smile, listening with relish to the sounds the fresh words formed as they left his mouth.

She patted a hand over her thick, shoulder-length blond hair, then donned her gloves. In an effort to quell the tide of adrenalin which rolled inside her, she hauled air into her lungs and trapped it there. She then closed her eyes and waited for the grip of suffocation to approach, savouring the taste of stale, shrinking air, and willing the fear of death to approach. She needed to feel it close, to hold it before she could give it away. She waited for her body to panic and react by gasping at the air. She felt her pulse shudder, her stomach strain. This was what it was like. Inert. Powerless. This was the flavour of fear, the medicine they were going to swallow. All of them. Until they choked. This was their cure.

Fresh air filled the vacated space inside her and she steadied herself, waited while the faintness drifted from her body. Her pulse slowly dropped, feeding contentedly off the fresh supplies of oxygen. She opened her eyes, reached out and pressed firmly on the enamel doorbell.

The silver tip of the thin, black, wooden cane she held in her hand tapped regularly against the stone step, precisely recording the passing seconds as they waited for the door to be opened: one, two, three, four, five, six, seven, eight, nine . . .

Ten: a tall, gangling man in his late forties, adorned with

the theatrical touches of affected English eccentricity – a red cravat, striped waistcoat – opened the door and peered warily out at the two callers through the oval lenses of his spectacles. For a moment he looked as though he recognised Mrs Skreen, but then he noticed Tup and his look turned to one of scepticism. He blinked but made no further move. He waited.

Mrs Skreen took the initiative. 'Adam Appleton?'

'Yes,' Appleton replied evenly, his accent old school, old money. 'And you are?'

'Mrs Amazonia Skreen,' she said, holding her hand out until he reluctantly took it. His palm was moist. She felt his thumb pulse, then released. 'And this,' she said, indicating Tup with an encompassing wave of her arm, 'is Mr Tup Maul, a close friend of mine.' Tup's face remained expressionless until she smiled openly, encouragingly at him. He then beamed at her and Adam Appleton in turn and the moment passed and she spoke again. 'He's lost his voice at the moment,' she confided in Appleton, taking a step forward, listening as the script spun onwards in her head, waiting for her voice to catch up with it, synchronise, become as one. 'Recurrent tonsillitis.'

Appleton folded his arms. His fingers drummed impatiently on the sleeve of his linen shirt as if typing at a keyboard. 'Really,' he said, then added, 'Now, would you mind telling me who you are?' His eyes narrowed suspiciously. 'You're not journalists, are you? Because if you are, you're wasting your time. I don't give interviews without prior arrangement and fee negotiation – and I certainly don't give interviews on Sundays.'

'I'm sorry, Mr Appleton,' she said. 'I'm not following you.'

'Before you go any further,' Appleton interrupted, 'I've got an incredibly efficient agent and an incredibly efficient memory. She'd never arrange an interview without consulting me first. And I haven't forgotten; I never do.'

'I didn't even know that you had an agent.'

Appleton squinted at her. 'So you're a journalist, then?'

'No.'

'Well, that's something, at least.' He regarded her silently for a moment before shifting his glare to Tup. 'And if you're trying to sell me something, I don't want it, understood?'

'I can assure you—' Amazonia began to protest, but got no further.

'What's he got in those cases then, eh?' Appleton demanded. 'Vacuum cleaners? Encyclopaedias? Carpet samples? Not that it matters what's in them. I don't care. I'm not interested.'

'We're not trying to sell you anything.'

Appleton remained unconvinced. 'Is that so?' he asked. 'In that case, perhaps you'd tell me why, on a day as abominably hot as this, Mr . . . Mr . . .' He stammered to a frustrated, open-mouthed halt.

'Mr Tup Maul,' Amazonia supplied.

'Yes,' Appleton said. 'Thank you. Why Mr Maul is lugging those two great cases around with him.' His thin lips sealed into an ungenerous smile. 'I am, of course, assuming that you're not intending to stay the night.'

Amazonia rewarded this brief flirtation with humour with a disarming, languid smile of her own. 'No,' she equivocated, 'not tonight, at least. Though we may want to stay here in the future. That's why we're here: to look round your property. We're not here to sell, but to buy.' A predatory tone of voice accompanied a sharpening of her naturally angular features as she enquired, 'I take it that it's still for sale?' She waited for these words to hit their mark. 'It's just that Sue told us that someone else was looking round it yesterday afternoon. Have you accepted an offer already?'

Appleton studied the two strangers in silence as he digested this information. When he did speak, his voice was more equable. 'You mentioned Sue. Sue from Hawthorn Housing?' Amazonia nodded. 'And she told you that you could look round today?'

'Yes,' Amazonia said with a further nod. 'We arranged it all with her yesterday afternoon. We drove by here earlier,' she went on to explain, 'and we saw the For Sale sign at the bottom of your beautiful garden.' She hesitated. 'I take it that Sue didn't ring you to let you know we'd be round. She couldn't come with us herself, you see, because it was at such short notice. But we just had to see it . . . She promised she'd call . . .'

Adam Appleton's Adam's apple bobbed uncomfortably, fleetingly threatening to puncture the loose, thin skin of his throat. 'Well,' he said, 'she didn't.'

Amazonia removed her sunglasses, releasing her glacial blue eyes for the first time. 'Of course we'd fully understand if you didn't want to show us round today. You're right, it's Sunday; you can't even ring Sue to check that what we're saying is true.' Her brow creased in anguish. 'And you've already mistaken both of us for journalists, and Mr Tup Maul for a door-to-door salesman. And you hear such stories these days. I mean, I could hardly blame you . . .'

Appleton stood motionless, transfixed by the eyes of this woman ten years his junior. She watched as he idly wondered if it were possible that the sunlight might melt her eyes, reduce them to the clear Arctic water of which they were so obviously comprised.

'No,' he finally said, 'it's not your fault.' He managed a lukewarm smile. 'Please accept my apologies. And yes,' he added, stepping back into the sanctuary of the tiled hall, 'the house is still on the market. Why don't you both come in?'

In the cool confines of the hall, the heels of Amazonia's shoes clicked resonantly as she strode swiftly past the turning head of Adam Appleton. Tup's attempted passage was less elegant. He got as far as drawing level with Appleton before they both realised that further progress was impossible. The width of the hall could barely accommodate the breadth of Tup, and the combination of the cases he held and the proximity of Appleton holding the door open proved insurmountable.

'Here,' Appleton offered, flattening himself against the wall. 'Can you squeeze through now?'

Tup didn't even acknowledge him. Instead, he gazed

forlornly at Amazonia, who was intently studying a watercolour at the far end of the hall, entranced, seemingly oblivious to the impasse which had developed in her wake. Tup opened his mouth to speak, then obediently clamped it tight again.

'In that case,' Appleton suggested, 'let me take one of those cases for you and make some space.' He released the door, which swung heavily to a rest against Tup's arm, and sidled himself around so that he was standing in front of him. Now free to move, he selected the more accessible of the two cases, reached forward with both hands, muttering, 'I hope they're not as heavy as they look,' and vainly attempted to unfasten the secure knot made by Tup's fat fingers around the buried case handle.

'It might help, Mr Maul, if you were to release your grip,' he said as he continued to struggle. 'Mr Maul?' he asked once more, before giving up altogether and turning to Amazonia with a look of frustration. 'We've encountered a hurdle in communications, Mrs Skreen. For further progress to be made, it's essential that Mr Maul lets me relieve him of one of his cases. Mrs Skreen!' he said loudly, no longer able to conceal his exasperation. 'He doesn't understand what I'm saying. Can you translate?'

'Do as Mr Appleton asks, Tup,' Amazonia called from the end of the hall. 'Let go of the bag.'

There was a dull thud and simultaneous shriek of anger which succeeded her words and finally shattered her reverie. She turned from the painting to see that Appleton had assumed an agonised stance, his arms cocked at right angles, his fingers splayed, pointing at the lime green ceiling, as if begging for divine intervention.

'The tiles!' he wailed as he turned to face her. 'He's cracked the tiles! That bloody case has shattered the tiles!' His expression was the raw residue of distilled dismay as he demanded of Amazonia, 'Have you any idea what tiles cost these days?' He rounded on Tup with a look of disgust. 'These aren't just ordinary tiles, for God's sake! They're antique. In fact, they're not even just antique tiles – they're the original tiles. Hand made. They date back to—'

And there Tup's face altered, distorted, became grotesque. He took a step forward and Appleton's voice lost its volume, became a mime. He froze.

'We're more than happy to pay for any damage,' Amazonia interjected, suddenly behind him. 'Not that I think we'll have to. If that watercolour is anything to go by, your taste is wonderful. I'm sure that any damage we've caused we'll be more than happy to live with.'

Appleton glanced forlornly at the floor one more time. 'I'm sorry for losing my temper,' he said, undertaking the awkward return journey to civility. 'It's just . . . well, I love this place, I really do. Parting with it is proving more traumatic than I'd ever have dreamt.'

He went to usher Amazonia down the hall. She was already moving, her eyes cameras, recording every detail, missing nothing. Only her ears registered him, idly monitoring his performance.

'I've been here twenty years. I've invested so much in it. It will be a shame to let it go.' They reached the end of the hall. 'Anyway,' he said in a lighter tone, 'shall we begin with the drawing room? It's cool in there apart from anything else. That's it,' he guided. 'Through the door on the right.'

The room she entered exuded an air of academia. A vast bay window stood sentry over the still, orchestrated flora of the front garden. The remaining three walls were screened by darkly varnished bookcases which rose from the floor to the white ceiling, and which fell in pleasant contrast against the light, honey stain of the bare floorboards. The furniture – a high-backed sofa and two austere leather armchairs – was positioned around a walnut-topped table at the centre of the room, allowing unhindered access to the army of antiquated texts which stood in regimented ranks on their specified shelves.

The only furniture given its own space was the writing desk positioned in the bay window. On it stood a typewriter, a half-completed folio protruding from it. Other scattered sheets shone silver in the sunlight which illuminated the desk's surface. She stared at the desk with her back to Appleton, aware that he was addressing her, unable to concentrate, incapable of making sense of his words. His voice became drowned, incoherent, as if it was being transmitted from a radio in a distant room.

'Mrs Skreen?'

'It's beautiful,' Amazonia said. 'Sue said I'd love it, but this . . . It's perfect.'

'Thank you.' Appleton blushed at her reaction, flattered, as if the compliment had been directed at him and not his home. 'As I said, it will be a shame to leave it behind.'

'And the books?' she asked. 'Sue said that most of the contents were going to be included in the sale. Will you be leaving the books?'

'No. The bookshelves, yes – along with the rest of the furniture – but not the books.'

Amazonia walked behind the sofa, trailing her fingers across the leather spines of the ordered volumes. 'They're wonderful.'

'Many of them are first editions,' Appleton informed her. 'Very rare. I've collected them since I was a child. Something of an obsession.'

She rounded on him. 'And you wouldn't consider selling them with the house, not even if the price was right?'

'I'm afraid not, Mrs Skreen. No. To me they're priceless.'

'You're quite sure, Mr Appleton?' she asked, cornering the sofa and standing by the table in the centre of the room. 'Money really isn't a problem.'

His brow creased. 'I'm sorry, though I'm pleased you appreciate their worth. Do you collect books yourself?'

'No. But they look so right here.' She surveyed the bookshelves again. 'Still, I could always buy replacements.'

'You're a keen reader, then?'

'Oh, yes.'

Appleton turned suddenly at the sound of heavy footsteps and stepped gingerly to one side as Tup blundered into the room. He then breathed out with evident relief when he saw that the cases had finally been successfully deposited in the hall without further damage being caused. Looking back at the enamoured face of Amazonia Skreen, he felt his blush return, and said, 'I almost forgot. Drinks. What would you both like?'

A few minutes later, Appleton returned to find Amazonia and Tup sitting silently on the sofa. He placed the jug of iced water on the table and poured out three glasses. 'Such an invigorating drink at this time of year,' he said in passing as he handed Amazonia a glass.

'Not for Mr Maul,' Amazonia said as he held a glass out to him. 'He's fine as he is.'

Appleton looked quizzically at Tup. 'Something alcoholic, Mr Maul? A beer, perhaps?'

'No, nothing at all,' Amazonia said. 'He's not thirsty.'

'Are you quite sure? It's terribly hot.'

Amazonia nodded. 'Quite sure, thank you.'

'I see,' Appleton said, keeping the glass in his hand and sitting down on the armchair opposite his two guests.

Amazonia drank deeply from her glass, erasing half of its contents. 'I hope you don't mind my asking, Mr Appleton . . .'

'Oh, Adam, please.'

'Well, Adam, it's just that I was wondering why you're selling up when you obviously love this place so much.'

'A good question, Amazonia – I may call you Amazonia?' She nodded her acquiescence. 'Such an exotic name,' he reflected. 'Why am I leaving? I'm leaving, Amazonia, because I'm shortly to surrender my bachelor status, and my fiancée has expressed an active disinterest in living in Hampstead Village, or any other part of London.'

'You mean she doesn't like this house?' Amazonia asked, her expression incredulous.

'She's an American. She doesn't even particularly like this country.'

'You'll be emigrating, then?'

'No, not entirely, anyway. We'll divide out time between her homes in Los Angeles and Scotland.'

'And your work? Won't the move affect your work? I'd

rather assumed that you were an academic of some sort. It's this room, the books . . .'

'Some might think of me as an academic,' Appleton said. 'I'm a writer. A critic. A novelist.'

Amazonia's head inclined towards the window. 'The writing desk and typewriter,' she observed. 'Of course. It all makes sense now.' She stared at him intently. 'How wonderful. What have you written? Will I have read any of your work?'

'I don't know. My novels are definitely at the literary end of the market – I'll write the titles down for you before you go, in case you're interested – but that doesn't necessarily mean you won't have encountered my writing. I edit a small magazine, *The Clarion*. Have you heard of it?' Amazonia shook her head. 'Well, if you're interested in my views on literature, that's where you should begin. It's like a crusade – a sort of campaign for real literature. It's my aim to influence the publishers into . . .' He stopped speaking and rolled his eyes. 'I'm sorry. I'm ranting. To return to your original question about how the move from here might affect my work, I really don't think it will. If there's any effect at all, I think it will be a positive one. My fiancée, Caroline, has arranged for wings of both her main homes to be set aside for me to work in. Once we're married, I'll be able to concentrate on my writing full time. I won't ever have to compromise again.'

'Compromise?' Amazonia asked.

Appleton flushed slightly and got to his feet. 'Come now,' he said hurriedly, ignoring her question. 'I think we've put the world to rights enough for one day. Let's take a look round.' He watched Amazonia rise. 'Mr Maul?' he queried.

'He'll stay here,' Amazonia said, leaning her cane against the sofa.

'Very well,' Appleton said, standing by the door and waiting for Amazonia to pass through. 'After you.'

After half an hour, they reached the final room of the house. The master bedroom, situated on the second floor, was large and deliberately simple, an aesthetic showcase. A porcelain basin, supported by a cast-iron frame, stood to the left of an open window, the shutter of which rested against the window alcove, protruding into the room. On the floor to the right of the basin was a large jug, meniscus high with clear, settled water, and behind that a rustic pestle and mortar. Against the left wall was a vast brass bed of continental design, its mattress bandaged by soothing, cool white sheets. On the right-hand wall, two closed, slatted, wooden doors betrayed an alcove which comprised the only available storage space. The floor consisted of stripped wooden floorboards, ingrained with compact veins of grey dust.

'Although I sometimes feel that this room has been like this for ever, I only had it refurbished two years ago,' Appleton confessed. 'Its theme is simplicity. It's inspired by a photograph by Willy Ronis, *le nu provençal*. Do you know it? It's famous; even commonplace. I've seen it in cafés and cheap poster shops all around town.'

She looked at him quizzically for a moment, before prompting, 'Describe it for me.'

'It's of a naked woman standing on a mat – a disc of straw – in a flagstoned provençal room. She's washing her forearms in the basin with her back to the camera. The coarse, wooden shutter is open. Morning sunlight slopes in, illuminating the woman's shoulders and her spine.' He gazed wistfully at the empty basin. 'It's quite beautiful.'

She looked around the room, slowly, waiting for him to join her. 'So, apart from the flagstones, it's all here. And the naked women, of course . . .'

His face reddened and his voice adopted a more studious tone. 'I've never quite made up my mind whether its popular appeal lies in its contrived composition or its sensuality.' She watched him staring at the junction between the top of her thigh-length leather boots and her milky skin. 'Perhaps the one complements the other,' he trailed off, his voice becoming lazy, drugged.

'And you,' Amazonia asked, 'which are you?'

His eyes rose to meet hers and he answered slowly. 'I'm not sure I understand . . .'

She walked to the bed and sat down. 'Which are you?' she repeated. 'Sensual, or composed?'

He tried to hold her stare, but when her legs moved apart in his peripheral vision, his gaze began to drop. 'I don't know,' he said quietly, focusing on the forbidden shadow beneath her black skirt. 'It depends on my mood. I think I have the capacity for both traits.'

'That can't be strictly truthful,' she said. 'In each person, there can only be one dominant trait. Only one.' She removed her jacket and folded it neatly by her side. Keeping her gloves on, she rested her hands on her knees. 'Life's a struggle. People are either constantly fighting arousal, or they're constantly trying to break free from repression.' Her tongue flickered tantalisingly across her lips. 'But deep down, they're one or the other.' She undid the top two buttons of her shirt. 'Which are you?'

He swallowed audibly. 'I don't know.'

She stood, taller than he remembered, walked up to him and slid his spectacles off his head, slowly folded them and placed them on the floor. 'You do know, really, don't you . . .'

He took a step back, half-raised his arms. She noticed they were shaking. 'I think. Er, rather, wouldn't you say it was time we went . . . Mr Maul. Yes,' he blundered on. 'Mr Maul. He'll be wondering—'

'Mr Maul,' Amazonia said, 'won't be wondering anything.' She slipped behind him and closed the door. She stared at his back. 'Mr Maul doesn't even think unless I tell him to.'

'Yes. Qu-quite,' Appleton stuttered to the depopulated area before him. 'I've been meaning to . . . to ask—'

'Never mind what you've been meaning to ask. I *know* what you've been meaning to ask.' Command crept into her voice. 'You may not have guessed it yet, but I know exactly what you want, Mr Appleton. Just like I know exactly what you need.' Behind him came the silken passage of discarded clothing. 'Do you think I haven't noticed the way you've been looking at me?' she asked, her voice now husky, a purr. 'Do you really think I believe you've given one benevolent thought to your fiancée since I walked into this house?'

He spun round, purple-faced and flustered. 'I don't . . .' he began in outraged tones, and then his mouth dehydrated. He became deprived of the power of speech. He was magnetised by the isosceles of brown, matted hair between her legs, magnetised. He shuddered. Then, as he gradually became acclimatised to her almost complete nudity, and his initial disbelief evaporated, his stare dared to consolidate and rise above the inverted point of her belly-button and the faint undulations of her ribcage, flicker across her breasts, and then move slowly, with attention, along the captivating length of her taut throat, to her eyes. Those eyes.

'Now it's just the flagstones,' she said, her words echoing heavily through his ears. She walked over to the jug and cascaded water into the basin. The jug clinked empty as she returned it to the floor. She drew her gloves off, let them fall beside it. Then she leant over the basin, her left arm across its chilled rim for support, her right crooked inside its rippled centre, as though ready to splash fresh water upwards to anoint her hidden face with the purity of baptism. 'Everything else is exactly how it should be. I've become part of your room, part of your art. I am your art. I'm living it.' She adjusted her body slightly beneath the light from the window, so that her arched spine became freed from shadow. She sighed contentedly. 'Just like the photograph, I've become the moment.'

She watched over her sloped shoulder as Appleton stared in confusion at his quivering hands. Tick-tock. Tick-tock. She registered the thoughts swinging back and forth through his head with the predictability of a metronome. Written on his face. So easy to read. Old man, young woman. Beauty as he only remembered, could normally only praise in print. Just to touch again, peel back the rotten layers of time, feed off her youth and become young once more. But fears, still fears. Mr Maul waiting downstairs. But she was right; he'd never dare. She wouldn't even let him drink water . . . And of Caroline, his fiancée? No one could deny him possession of this sight before him. Caroline's money and devotion would still be there afterwards. She need never know.

First fell his cravat, next his waistcoat. He stripped to the waist, removed his shoes and socks. Not Caroline, not anyone. No one was worth that. Just like the photograph, hadn't Amazonia said? But photographs were art, detached from reality. They had no motion or narrative. Here was the chance to explore that very narrative, to take it beyond temptation into abandon. He unbuckled his belt. The muscles in her back stiffened as he approached her. She was panting. He could hear her clearly now that his own mouth was almost touching the skin of her inclined neck. He wiped the perspiration from his palms across his thighs, then pressed his splayed fingers across her posed hips and gripped tightly.

'Now!' she gasped, tensed grotesquely, pushing back against him, feeling his skin-and-bone pelvis clawing at her through his trousers, starting to grind.

He began to lick her neck and released his hands, fumbling instead with his flies. 'Now?' he panted deliriously, needing that one last gasp of confirmation from her to allow him to shake the insecurity that dogged him even now that her desire was so apparent.

'Now!' she said, just as he successfully freed his trousers from his waist and shuffled them to the floor.

There was a crack and a scream and the sound of a floundering body. She turned from the basin to see that Appleton was performing a tortured mime, half-collapsed, clutching at the knee of his left leg, jerking feverishly as he tried to free his foot from the case which Tup had brought crashing down onto the side of his leg. She leant down and efficiently pulled her gloves back on, watching as Appleton craned his neck back.

He begged between gasps, 'Help me! For God's sake, help me!'

She walked towards him and he clenched his eyes tight, though not tight enough to prevent the tears streaming free to dilute the involuntary ejaculations of spittle on his lip and chin. On reaching him, she knelt down behind him, so that his heaving back was against her, and gently ran her hand through his thinning hair. It smelt musty, old and decaying, like the books downstairs.

'Lift the bag carefully from his foot, Tup,' she said as she continued to stroke. While Tup reached down, she took Appleton's hand with her free hand. 'That's right,' she said, grimacing only slightly as Appleton's sweaty fingers clawed at her own for relief. 'You squeeze as tight as you like.'

'Aaaaarrghhh!'

Amazonia peered over his shoulder as Appleton's foot was released. 'I think it's best if you keep your eyes closed for the time being, Adam,' she advised. 'Your ankle really does seem to be at an extremely odd, even perverse angle. Though I must admit, it's rather hard to tell what with your trousers being down there. What could have caused them to fall like that, I wonder? And look, there's some sort of secretion in your underwear. Are you hurting there as well?'

Appleton lunged forward in a struggle to see his leg, then screamed again. 'It's broken!' he whined, sinking back again. 'I can see the bone! That fucking lunatic's broken my ankle!'

'Now, now, Adam,' Amazonia admonished. 'There's no need for that sort of language. I'm sure Mr Tup Maul didn't mean to hurt you so much. He's just a bit clumsy sometimes, that's all. Besides, we don't know for certain that it's broken. It might just be the shadows in here making it appear distorted. Appearances, as you're probably beginning to realise, can be shockingly deceptive.'

She slipped her hands under the pits of his arms and began to haul him across the floor. He was light, insubstantial, getting lighter still, fading closer and closer to nothing, more ghost than human, already more dead than alive.

'What are you doing?' he screamed as his injured foot trailed stickily across the tiles. 'Where are you taking me?'

'I'm just moving you back a bit so that we can have a good look at you,' she explained. 'First things first, eh? It might be nothing at all.' She heaved again, the jarring motion sending Appleton into mumbling spasms. 'There we are,' she said. 'Now, Tup, if you'd be so kind as to place the offending bag on the floor over there and join me here, you can carry Mr Appleton to the bed where he'll be much more comfortable.'

'No!' Appleton begged. 'Keep him away from me! Call an ambulance! Please!' he screeched. 'Just call an ambulance!'

'All in good time, Adam,' Amazonia said. 'Let's get you comfortable first. Then we'll see just how bad it is. With a bit of luck, you won't need anything more than a good long rest.'

'Don't! Please don't!' Appleton raged as he caught sight of the bloody pulp of his foot once more. He gripped her wrist, excavating frantically with his nails. 'Don't let him near me!'

She ripped her hand free and slapped him hard across the head. The sharp noise silenced him, echoed off the wall, reverted to her. 'Pick him up, Mr Maul!' she barked. 'Pick him up this instant and put him to bed!'

'Oh God . . .' Appleton managed to gargle, before he was snapped up into the air and a wave of debilitating nausea and anaesthetising pain heaved across his frame.

As she watched Tup dump Appleton on the bed and strap him down, sounds filled Amazonia's inner ear: *clack, clack, clack* – dead moments from the past, hunting one another down in chronological order, following their path of predestination, leading here; leading, inevitably, to now. They came clacking like dominoes, their velocity increasing with the accumulated momentum of each connection made. *Clack*: waste can only be made good if it's recycled. *Clack*: the only way to remedy the past is to purify the present. *Clack*: life must learn from death. *Clack-clack-clackclackclackclackclack* – faster still, becoming a blur – railroading into a fist of conviction, punching the air from her lungs.

It was inevitable that Appleton would be the first. If anyone had brought her here to his room, instructed her to stand over his inert body now and stoically await his horrified awakening, it was him. Careless talk costs lives. He was well versed in history, or so his reputation would have it. He had no excuse for forgetting a perennially bandied soundbite like that. Careless talk costs lives. Especially when the talk concerned the life of the speaker.

Back then – maybe a year ago – as she'd sat at a table parallel to his in Qualdo's off Piccadilly, it would have been well for Appleton to have remembered that. But he'd been too stupid for that. Discretion then might have saved him. But hypocrites always gave themselves away. Eyes like hers – cheated eyes – would always see the deep sickness manifest itself on their faces. And if anyone deserved the dishonour of being the first exposed, consigned to having his persona deconstructed by her, then reconstructed, cast afresh in a semblance of truth by the media, it was him – sick, hypocritical piece of filth that he was. He'd been the first to show her the symptoms of his diseased mind. And, likewise, it was he who'd made her realise that, of all people, it was her who should be the one to administer the cure.

That day in Qualdo's, living alone, she'd dined alone, too. She sat there at the table the waiter had shown her to and draped her napkin over her thighs. And as she pondered the menu and felt the bustle of business and humanity clash in animation about her, she reminded herself that this solitude was hers by choice. These people had nothing she wanted. She'd cut them off. Businessmen and women. Product pushers and buyers. Shallow, worthless nobodies, achieving shallow, transient success. She should have been above them all by now, raised high, a string of published books to her name. Their guru. Their God. Hers was the face they should have turned their own from in awe, hers the altar at which they should all have now been worshipping.

She didn't set out to eavesdrop on Appleton's conversation. In truth – until he batted a hovering waiter away with an agitated swish of his arm, and an aggravated, 'I'll tell you when I want you to clear,' – she hadn't even noticed that he was sitting there so close to her. But when she did glance across, her glance slid immediately into a stare. Recognition was immediate. Resentment cracked like an egg inside her, slopped its rotten contents through her mind. He was famous, iconised, had engineered things that way. His voice – those practised, clipped intonations – and the contrived sophistry his whole being seemed intent on projecting were things she already knew. She'd watched him on television, listened to him on the radio. Prizewinner. Editor. Critic. All these accolades belonged to him. False prophet. His was the tongue her own voice should have silenced by now. His was the voice the publishers had chosen over hers.

She continued to stare at him. No doubt his voice was still being listened to, his words being consigned to people's memories, quoted by dolts at dinner parties and in superficial undergraduate essays across the country. Pathetic. She'd been like that once. She'd studied his work, even considered it competent. But an immeasurable distance had been travelled between where she'd observed him from at the start of the path she'd set out on – believing it would lead her to a glittering literary career – and where she coldly observed him from now. He'd become dwarfed, no longer someone she wanted to grow up to be, just someone who'd stolen what should have been hers, someone she could only despise as she sat here in the crowd with all the other nobodies, without voice, suffocating in her own failure.

'It's still essential, Raymond,' Appleton said to the plump man in the loud suit across the table, as he smeared butter across a water biscuit and applied a wedge of ripe, dripping cheese, 'that my identity should be protected.' He dipped his lips into the rim of the glass of red. 'Rumours have a habit of becoming headlines; you know that as well as me. And I hardly need to remind you quite how detrimental that type of exposure would be for me.' He ground his teeth, swallowed. 'For me of all people.'

'Relax,' Raymond said, sliding a manicured nail into a clogged crevice between his front teeth and clawing free a scrap of fish. He didn't take his eyes off Appleton for a second, seemed to take pleasure from watching the other man's involuntary wince betray his evident physical disgust. Raymond held the finger before his close-set eyes and examined the morsel in silence for several seconds before inserting his finger into his mouth and sucking it clean. Laying his hand on the table, he smiled. 'There's nothing to worry about, Adam. We've had this arrangement for – what? – five, six years?' Appleton nodded. 'And, apart from the two of us,' Raymond continued, 'no one's got a clue. So why worry now? I've never let you down before. Why should I start now? What makes you think anything should change?'

Appleton cleared his throat, stared at his plate. From her table, she watched his fingers patter in agitation across his thigh. 'Precisely because things *have* changed,' he finally said, his voice hollow, its customary arrogance evacuated.

Raymond poured wine into their glasses. After taking a sip, he sat back in his chair and waited for Appleton to face him. 'Now why do I get the feeling I'm not going to like this?'

'I'm sorry,' Appleton said, 'but it's got to stop. Now. I want to put an end to this.'

'You're not being very precise, Adam,' Raymond chided. 'What exactly do you want to stop?'

Appleton took a slug of wine. 'These books,' he said hurriedly. He pointed a thin, long index finger across the table and stabbed at the Harrods bag that lay next to Raymond's elbow. 'This whole deceit. I want it to finish.'

Raymond frowned, leant forward and rested his forearm on the bag. 'But we've got an agreement, Adam. Admittedly, we haven't exactly got a written contract. But, then, I'm not someone who's ever needed any more than a man's word to go on.'

'I'm sorry, Raymond, I really am.'

Raymond moved back again, taking the bag with him, placing it on the floor by his feet. 'It's a done deal now. You know that, don't you?'

Appleton nodded his head slowly. 'I know. I know I agreed to write it for you. And I have. I did what I said I would, what we agreed. But circumstances have changed.'

'How so?' Raymond asked, lighting a cigarette, and exhaling across the table.

Appleton coughed gently, flicked his hand before his glasses, cleared the air. 'It's no smoking in this section,' he said, pointing to a nearby sign.

'You let me worry about that,' Raymond said, exhaling again. 'You concentrate on explaining to me what's changed.'

'I don't want to run the risk of exposure any longer.'

'But I've already told you: there isn't any risk of exposure.'

'I'm engaged to be married.'

'And?' Raymond asked without pause.

'And I don't want her to find out about this. I don't want anyone to find out. We've been lucky so far. I don't want to risk it.'

Raymond sighed. 'Again, Adam, we've come in a circle. You don't have to worry about her finding out. She won't. No one will. So why the cold feet?'

Appleton looked around the room, fleetingly causing her to look away, glance back at her menu. Then he turned back to Raymond, leant across the table and lowered his voice. 'The woman I'm engaged to is very wealthy.'

'Ah,' Raymond said with a thin smile. 'Money. It all boils down to money in the end. Money and sex.' He crumpled his half-smoked cigarette onto his side-plate. 'So let me put two and two together. Now that you're about to get her money, you no longer need mine. Is that it?'

'Yes.'

'I see.'

There was silence for a minute and the two men stared at one another. 'So what happens now?' Appleton finally asked.

'I can't force you to write for me, Adam. Couldn't interfere with your creativity like that. It just wouldn't work. I suppose we'll have to call it a day.'

'Good,' Appleton breathed out. 'Good. And what about this one?'

'What about it? I paid you to write it. You wrote it. And now it's mine to publish.' He held up a hand. 'I'm a businessman. True to my word. So you needn't worry; no one's going to find out you wrote it. Same as before, OK?' He peered with glinting eyes at Appleton's worried expression. 'What's the matter now? You've got what you wanted – our partnership is dissolved as of now.' He looked across the room and caught a waiter's attention, then faced Appleton. 'End of story.'

'There's something else,' Appleton said once the waiter had gone to fetch the bill.

'What?'

'The typescript. I want it back. I'll pay. I'll buy it back.'

Raymond glanced at the floor by his feet. 'Is that a fact?'

'The money you gave me to write it. You can have it.' Appleton slipped his hand inside his jacket pocket and produced a pre-written cheque. He pushed it across the table. 'Take it. Please . . .'

Raymond made no move. 'I don't think it's that simple. This is book ten in a series I've invested a lot of marketing in.'

Appleton's face was flushed now. 'I'll pay more. Whatever it takes,' he hissed across the table seconds before the waiter appeared with the bill and drew the negotiations to a temporary halt.

Then her own waiter arrived and she hurriedly ordered, wanted this distraction dealt with, already captured by the events unfolding at Appleton's table. When she looked again, the two men were standing, shaking hands across the table. The green plastic bag was gripped firmly in Appleton's free hand, as if it had the potential for autonomous animation and he feared it would slip from his sight the moment his concentration wavered. They followed the waiter between the tables to the glass doors and then she glanced across at her own waiter disappearing through the wooden swing doors which led to the clanking kitchen and, before she could reconsider, she was on her feet, swinging her bag onto her shoulder, walking quickly past blurred, chewing faces to the doors, out onto the street.

Raymond was standing nonchalantly on the pavement. Before him, a doorman strode into the street and summoned a black cab with a professional salute. Her head twisted, surveying the street, searching amongst the shopping-laden pedestrians for Appleton's lanky frame. Then she saw him, standing by the traffic lights a hundred yards up the street, waiting for the green to flick through amber into red, signalling his escape from whatever it was he was so desperate to leave behind. She checked on Raymond. He was squeezing into the cab, barely a yard away. The cab window was open and above the growling traffic she heard him answer the cab driver with a destination. And even if she hadn't heard of the company the building he was going to was named after, the cab driver's leering grin would have tipped her off as to what sort of business it was. Looking up the street now, she saw the lights had stabilised on red. Appleton was crossing and so she stepped out into the street herself, behind the winking indicator of the cab which housed Raymond, then stop-started through the lanes of traffic to the other side.

She wove quickly through the people between her and her target. Target. Already she was thinking of him in this way. That's what he'd unknowingly transformed into the moment she'd risen from her table and followed him from Qualdo's. She knew it was right, that this intense curiosity expanding inside her, pressing against her lungs, leaving her breathless, had to be satisfied. Appleton had the answer. She was certain of that. She crossed another road, directly behind him this time, close enough to hear the click of hardened leather soles on the tarmac.

It was only once they reached Soho that his progress became hesitant. Next to the sex tourists, this didn't look unusual. Only he wasn't looking up at the ostentatious neon signs of the strip joints, or studying the faces of the hookers who poked their tightly bound chests and make-up draped faces out of the various dingy open doorways which led to bed. It was the alleys his gaze was surreptitiously searching as he passed them. Here, in one of these, was what he'd come here for.

And then he found it, the one he'd been searching for: a thin, greasy way dividing two rearing, black-bricked buildings. He stopped, adjusted his glasses and studied it closely. She'd drawn up alongside him now and, sensing his apprehension, walked a couple of feet beyond and stared into a news-shop window, past the handwritten cards offering or requesting employment and accommodation, into the reflection of the street. Her heart was stuttering now. She'd become the hunter. Appleton, for all his brains and words, couldn't hide from her. He was weighing the green bag in his hand, shifting his own weight nervously from one foot to the other. Then he pirouetted, performed a double-check on the disinterested people around him, and slipped off the street into the alley.

She turned and crossed the pavement and entered a phone box which stood sentry over the alleyway. Taking the receiver in one hand, not bothering to insert any money or think of any number she might want to dial, she peered between the cluster of lurid prostitute's business cards on the perspex window at the bespectacled, suited man, so comically out of place as he walked hesitantly down the unswept alley, over the fast-food tins and beer cans. When he was about halfway down, next to a stack of sweating bin bags, he stopped. He crouched down, putting the green bag he'd been carrying on the ground beside him, and stretched two clawing hands out to rip one of the bin bags open. He then wedged the green bag forward into the bin bag, left it there to rot. Remaining at her vantage point as he made his way back to the street, she felt her lips twitch into a grin.

The sound of Appleton coughing filled her ears and she looked down at where he lay on the bed. When he opened his eyes and the room came zooming back into view, his first action was to vomit down his bare chest. And when he automatically attempted to lean forward to redirect this effluent, he found his neck snapping backwards after an advance of no more than three inches. The instinctive attempts of his arms to release his neck met with equal failure. Cords bit in, gnawed at his tendons. He coughed violently. Fever burnt across his skin. Sweat bubbled up. Unable to focus through his tears, he closed his eyes and forced the vomit from his mouth.

'Don't ever make the mistake of confusing the aesthetic with the sensual, Mr Appleton,' Amazonia said. 'It doesn't become you. It doesn't become any true artist. Not, of course, that either of us believe that you can be clasped in any honesty by that bracket.'

Appleton looked with despairing eyes at the beautiful woman sitting beside him on the bed, naked but for gloves, and croaked, 'Why me?'

'Come now, Adam,' she said, 'even Adam, the first man, must surely know the answer to the first, innocuous question.' She watched his eyes close and, rolling her own, complained, 'Pain is such a bore. You're obviously too distracted by the flesh, so let me vocalise your intellect: the reason for its being you is because you're here, we're here . . . and because there's no one else who deserves it quite like you.' She ground her teeth and forced a woeful smile in Tup's direction. 'Pathetic. But what did we expect? Do your thing, Mr Maul. Empty the contents of the first of those cases on Mr Appleton. Shower him with the words he's written.'

Tup, who'd been standing with his continent of a back resting against the wall next to the head of the bed, released one case to the ground, and fumbled with his ungainly fingers over the clasp of the case he still held until it gave with a satisfying click. His lips freed an inane grin and settled into rictus as he launched his arms into the air above Appleton's body. His lungs articulated a gurgle of excitement and he ripped the ribcage of the case apart. An avalanche of hardbacks, periodicals and paperbacks pummelled down on Appleton's spreadeagled form.

'Books, Adam, so many beautiful books,' Amazonia announced as his convulsions following the impact subsided and the books settled. She picked through them, holding each before his horrified eyes, before tossing them across the room, their pages fluttering like the wings of shot, crippled birds. 'Lit-er-a-ry Fic-tion,' she commentated, her delivery staccato. 'And all written by you, each one a product of your lit-er-a-ry mind. Just listen to these reviews: *'A staggering achievement'*; *'A novel of revelations, both funny and sad'*; *'A new voice, resoundingly authentic'*; *'Adam Appleton reveals his love affair with words, beauty, and truth with every sentence he writes'*; *'An uncompromising artist.'*

'And articles, too,' she continued, slapping a magazine across his face. 'Lit-er-a-ry articles.' She sifted unhurriedly through the other magazines. 'Polemic and opinion, Mr Appleton. The opinions of a lit-er-a-ry man. The thoughts of, some might say, an artist. And such clever titles: *'The Afterbirth of the Author'*; *'Postmodernism and Pastiche'*; *'The Architecture of the Void'*; *'Responsibility in Art'*; *'Pulp Publishers: Intellectual Criminals'*; *'Editors not Marketers'*. And so, so many, many more.'

She sighed. 'An impressive oeuvre, Adam. Yes, indeed. You must be proud of your achievements.' She tossed the copy of *The Clarion* she was holding onto the floor and leant her face in close to Appleton's, so that she could feel his rasping breath glancing off her face. 'Tell me Adam, are you proud?'

'I don't know . . .' he muttered, his eyes flickering between Amazonia and Tup. His voice bubbled weakly through the phlegm and bile he found himself unable to swallow or spit free. 'I don't know what you want me to say . . .'

'Come, come, Adam, there's no need to be modest now. You're among friends here. You just tell it like it is.'

'I don't—'

Amazonia jerked away from him and nodded at Tup. Appleton, making his own interpretation of what this signal would precipitate, panicked, his neck wrenching at the cord in an effort to look where Tup stood, to see what he was preparing to do. Amazonia, watching the cord, which was tightly criss-crossed over Appleton's throat, strip the skin in raw red lines, slowly shook her head. At the limit of Appleton's vision, Tup took his jacket off, lay it carefully on the bed, and began to roll the thin material of his sleeves up over the hulked meat of his forearms.

'Tell me!' Appleton gasped through his contracted trachea. 'Anything! I'll say anything!'

'That's always been your problem, Adam.'

Tup's fist swung twice with rapid precision, expertly detonating rabbit-punches in Appleton's face. Appleton turned a paler shade of grey. His eyes clenched tight like fists. Amazonia examined him with grim resignation. It was difficult to equate the arrogance of the quintessential Englishman who'd stood guard at his front door earlier with the miserable specimen who lay before her now. Reversion to type. Ashes to ashes, muck to muck. It was only natural. But still, it was amazing how quickly pain cut through pretence.

'Now you know that's not the point,' Amazonia counselled, placing a soft leather palm onto Appleton's swelling face, tenderly feeling the pulsing chamber of barely-contained blood beneath the skin's surface. 'I want you to be honest with me. I want you to tell me that you believe in yourself. I need to know. I really need to know if all this – all your books, all your words – really means something to you.' She hesitated and a stoical expression settled on her face. 'I need you to justify your life to me, because that's what this is all about, you understand. We're here to judge you, Adam.' She flicked her index finger towards Tup. 'And if needs be, we're here to punish you as well.'

Appleton opened his eyes and muttered incoherently.

'You'll have to speak up, Adam,' Amazonia said, as Tup watched her keenly.

Appleton's lips moved again, this time managing no more than a hoarse groan. Stinging sweat sank down his brow, seeping through the guard of his eyelashes. His eyes flashed briefly with concentration and he uttered, 'My leg . . .'

'Your leg's fine for the time being. I had the courtesy to wrap a tourniquet around the wound. Only a temporary measure, of course, but the flow of blood has been significantly reduced.' She smiled benignly. 'After all, you're not dead yet, are you? You may wish you were, but you're not.'

She clenched and unclenched her fists, the leather creaking lightly, then crossed her arms and hugged her shoulders. 'So, in the light of that medicinal information, perhaps you'd be so kind as to repay the courtesy by sticking to the subject in hand, which, unless I'm very much mistaken, is whether or not you believe in yourself, in your writing.' She waited a couple of seconds for Appleton to reply. 'I'm growing impatient, Adam,' she reminded him when he failed to speak, 'and I fear that Mr Tup Maul is growing bored; and I'm sure that no one – particularly you – would want Mr Tup Maul to have to find new ways to alleviate his boredom.'

As Amazonia stood, the muscles of Appleton's body contracted, anticipating the next blow. It never came. Instead, his pinned perspective allowed him to see Amazonia's bare back recede into the blurred distance beyond the bed. He heard her gasp and simultaneously heard the splash of cold, relieving water. A shadow moved near him and his eyes sealed instinctively. Next came the renewed pressure of a body resting on the bed beside him. Then he flinched, as if electrocuted.

'Many believe that water possesses curative properties, Adam,' Amazonia said, her voice in his ear, as his mouth suckled compulsively on the damp leather fingers that she'd thrust between his lips. 'I don't, though I do believe that it's essential for the power of speech to function adequately. All gone,' she chimed, pulling her fingers free. She clamped his vomit-encrusted chin in her hand. 'Now tell me!' she snapped. 'Tell me what your writing's worth. Convince me whether you should live or die.'

'Yes . . .' Appleton grunted with a surge of desperate adrenalin. 'Yes – I believe in my writing. Have pity. For God's sake, let me live.'

She sighed. 'Oh Adam. All I wanted was a little honesty. A little purity . . .'

'I do,' Appleton whimpered, tears welling out of the

puffy craters of his eyes. 'You've got to believe me. I believe in my books, my words—'

Amazonia continued her diatribe, unaffected by Appleton's appeal, '. . . A little truth. A little . . . artistic integrity. Is that too much to ask from a writer?'

'Why don't—' Appleton wheezed, his voice collapsing feebly in on itself once more.

'Why don't I believe you, Adam?' Amazonia interjected. She snapped her fingers. 'Show him, Tup. Show him why.'

The contents of the second case thundered down. Amazonia swept a typewritten piece of paper from Appleton's quivering face, and waited for the spines of the glossy books and the other typewritten pages which had spilled from a green plastic bag to slide to a rest. 'I wonder,' she asked, 'do you think your words have anything to teach you now?'

Appleton gurgled, his tongue lolling limply over his lower lip.

'I know you don't know, Adam. And that's why we're here. We want to help. We want you to realise the error of your ways before it's too late.' She picked up one of the books at random, waved its cover, which depicted a naked girl licking the tip of a half-peeled banana, before his face. '*Head Girl*, by Ranald Sky. Now what kind of book is this? A guide to eating fresh fruit, perhaps? Ah, here's the blurb:

> *'The first book in the Master of Erotica's Dawn Mist series. Dawn is seventeen and has just entered her final year at Shaftesbury College, an exclusive English girl's boarding school. Her father, an American oil millionaire, expects her to be appointed Head Girl by the end of the year. And, although Dawn's academic record isn't as good as it could be, she soon discovers that it's not necessarily her mind that her teachers are interested in . . .'*

She exchanged the first book for the green plastic bag and shuffled through the loose typed pages. 'This one hasn't actually been published yet, but I'm sure you'll be familiar with it anyway. You hid it in a bin, remember? No? OK, then, let's choose a random page and see if that jogs your memory.'

She plucked a page from the pile. 'My reading voice might not be up to the standard of the people who record your other – let's call them mainstream – novels for the BBC and audio publishers, Adam,' she apologised, 'but I'll give it my best shot. We'll start with a blurb of our own, filling in the background for you. It's entitled *The Crack of Dawn* and is book ten in the Dawn Mist series by Ranald Sky, Master of Erotica, the very same man who, according to the back cover of book five in the series, was single-handedly responsible for putting the tit back in titillation. Anyway, here's the blurb:

'The happy-go-sucky days of Dawn's pulsating rise to the coveted position of Head Girl of Shaftesbury College are now ten years behind her and her millionaire father has died in a plane crash. Dawn now controls his considerable portfolio of stocks, as well as his floundering oil empire. We join the action on page fifty-seven, where Dawn has to secure the backing of Slick Silo, the middle-aged President of a New York venture-capital corporation.

'Dawn slowly got to her feet, leant forward and pushed her splayed fingers across the smooth surface of the huge desk behind which Slick slouched in his chair. She then moved her hands until her thumbs touched and her breasts squeezed tantalisingly together. She watched him survey the dark line of her cleavage and the lace of the top of her bra which showed through the gap left by the open V of her shirt.

' "There are two ways we can play this, Slick," she purred.

' "And those are?" he asked, not taking his eyes off her chest for a second.

' "Your way or mine. You can either screw my company for good by not giving me the money I need to save it . . ."

' "Or?"

' "Or . . ." She climbed up onto the desk and crawled towards him, stopping only when her mouth was inches

away from his. ". . . You can sit back there and let me screw you into a stupor." She slid her shapely, stockinged legs round and lowered them over the edge of the desk, so that a stiletto heel rested on each of Slick's thighs. "And if we do it my way, then you agree to lend me the money," she whispered huskily, peeling her short skirt up over the tops of her thighs, revealing her knickerless state. "So Slick," she said, spreading her legs and slipping down onto his lap. "What's it to be?"'

Amazonia grimaced and let the offending piece of paper drift down onto the bed. 'Pseudonyms. It's not pseudonyms per se that I despise; just the way they're sometimes used. You can see that, can't you, Adam? After all, you've been writing under a pseudonym for years now. Parading the literary avenue one minute, honourably fighting the corner of high culture in this ugly post-modern world; and then masquerading as Ranald Sky the next, watching your bank balance, amongst other things, bulge.'

Her breath fell regularly and she looked at the two separate messes which constituted Appleton's leg and face. The more time that had passed, the less easy it had become to identify them as distinct bodily parts. Now they would have looked more at home on a butcher's rack. There was only satisfaction to be found in this sight: the enactment of belief and conviction. And conviction was powerful, more powerful than emotions. This was the oldest truth: ideas had always had the upper hand in human affairs. She peered into Appleton's eyes. *Clack*: sometimes creation requires destruction. *Clack*: the end of one life can signal the beginning of another.

'Tup, hand me the knife.'

Tup lifted his jacket from the bed and walked round to where she sat, rummaging through its inside pocket as he did so. Appleton's eyes flickered in their sockets. A thin stream of cracked air strained from his lips. By the time Tup reached her, the knife, its wide blade honed and polished, was in his hand. He flipped it in the air, with surprising agility and speed, and passed it to her handle first.

'You probably realise that death is inevitable now,' she said, turning her attention back to Appleton. 'You are, after all, a reasonably intelligent man. That's never been in dispute. It's what makes your crimes all the more heinous.'

She wedged a hand over his mouth, patiently waiting for his exhausted body to enact its final agonised protestations before realising the futility of it all. 'And don't worry, your life isn't fading in vain: they'll catch me one day. Capture and the platform it will provide is part of what I desire. I'm here to spread the word of truth, Adam, to pluck the cataracts from the public's eyes. Their sight will be restored. They'll see that the adulation they've spent on you has been wasted. They'll look to others for their wisdom. They'll look to those who've waited in your shadow up till now to succeed you. They'll look to me.'

She lowered the knife and stroked it with incongruous sensuality across the stubble beneath his snorting nostrils. His teeth ground weakly against her glove. He didn't need to speak; the language in his mind was now hers.

'It's all right,' she accommodated, holding the blade to her lips. 'You still want to know why me. We now know why it has to be you. But you still don't know why it's me that has to do it. It's because I write too, Adam. And because, as I told you before, I am my art, I live it.'

Her expression hardened and she flipped Appleton's chin up with one hand, with the other placing the tip of the blade against his throat beneath his ear.

'There's something I want you to think about as the darkness descends, Adam. It's writers like you, not me, who really wield the knife. It's you and your kind who are responsible for pinning other writers' talents like butterflies in the dirt. Think of me as an angel, Adam,' she whispered as she sank the blade deep into his throat and drew it across. 'Think of me as the one who's going to set them free.'

His mouth blew like that of a landed fish, fragile bubbles of blood bursting at its corners. His body twitched. She pulled the knife free and closed his eyes for the final time with the tips of her gloved fingers.

'Dead wood has to be cut down so that something fresh can grow in its place. That's why killing you is the only decent thing to do. It's a sacrifice and, like all sacrifices, its intention is to make people believe again.'

She arose, her gloves drenched in fresh blood. Everything was clear to her; everything was pure. Holding the dripping knife before her like a torch, she made her way to the basin and cleaned herself and it. She then walked up to Tup and handed him the knife, which he secreted with a suddenly clumsy, agitated arm in the depths of his jacket pocket.

'Love?' he asked, dropping the jacket next to Appleton's body.

'Yes,' she said, reaching up and loosening his tie, running her hands over his chest, the memory of his first release becoming solid in her hands. 'You can have your love now.'

Afterwards, as Tup descended into a deep, post-coital sleep on the sofa in the sitting room downstairs, Amazonia Skreen sat down at the writing desk, tore the unfinished folio from the typewriter and scrumpled it up into a ball. She listened to Tup's contented sighs. Then other sounds claimed her. *Clack*: the conversion of ideas into language. *Clack*: the noise of a typewriter. *Clack*: the conversion of language into print. *Clack*: ideas must be worthy of language. *Clack*: language must be worthy of print.

She inserted a fresh sheet of paper into the typewriter and her gloved fingers began to type.

CHAPTER TWO

life begins at forty

His life had crashed again.

It had happened right there, in the middle of the Antidote Entertainments building, in the middle of London, in the middle of the day, in the middle of June, in the middle of his fortieth birthday.

The middle, Jack reflected uncomfortably, as he moved from the lift towards the glass doors, of a life: what a cynical observer might choose to view as the fulcrum; the point from which movement in any direction could only lead down.

He smiled at the security guard as he left the building for the last time. It was a perfunctory gesture. He didn't feel good about himself, or about the recent turn of events. He hadn't enjoyed his behaviour towards Leonora Smiles any more than she had. Sure, she'd seen a man of power, an equal, exit her office with a straight back and a swinging gait. But the exertion, the discipline required to summon up that unnatural charisma, had taken their toll the moment the lift door had sealed him out of her vision. And now he felt drained, hungover. Her eventual acquiescence to his demands had been a small triumph. It meant nothing in the greater scheme of things. He'd spend the money soon enough; just like he always had. Money meant nothing to him compared to luck. And – he exited onto the pavement and allowed himself to be borne away by the bustling bodies and accompanying babel of voices – he was convinced that his luck had run out again.

He covered several Soho streets before he finally ground to a halt, his body purposeless, immobilised, his brain a sponge, soaking up the chaos which engulfed him, trying to filter some kind of sense out of it all.

A couple of tourists hesitated, momentarily confused by the unforeseen obstacle he'd suddenly become, then side-stepped into the road and negotiated their way beyond. He watched them continue on their way, felt himself forgotten. They were young, maybe half his age. A boy and a girl, in love for all he knew. The happiness in their voices seemed alien, inexplicable. Behind him, somewhere near, an engine gunned towards them. Jack's breathing cut shallow. Then a motorbike snapped past, dodging the couple by the width of a brake cable. They leapt over the safety zone symbolised by the kerb. The biker turned to look, raised an angry finger at them, ignorant that he could have sent them limb-flipping, spine-cracking across the road. The boy shook his head and took the girl's hand, secure once more. And then the girl looked beyond her partner, into Jack's face, into his eyes.

'I don't believe it,' she said, a smile bursting, dismissing her boyfriend's hand, her backpack shuffling on her shoulders as she walked towards Jack, as if it contained something live. She stopped in front of Jack, thrust her face up close to his, then turned. 'It's David Jackson!' she called back, her antipodean accent becoming more pronounced. 'Jee-zuz!' she said, leering at Jack. 'I can't believe it's you.'

'You're wrong,' Jack muttered, starting to walk.

But the boyfriend had moved, blocked his path. A thick grip jutted out, grasped Jack's flaccid hand, pumped his arm to the horizontal. 'Rupert Savage,' the boyfriend introduced himself.

Jack pulled his hand free. 'Listen, I'm nobody . . . nobody you know.'

The girl was rummaging through her backpack now. Behind her, cars growled by. The boyfriend stood still, an inane grin chiselled into his youthful face. He started to speak, undergraduate sincerity flexing his tongue. 'We're such big fans of yours. I mean, it was your writing that inspired us to come to Britain. You made it sound so perfect . . .'

But Jack's eyes had switched from him, back to the girl and, in the absence of visual targeting, the boy's voice had effectively ceased to exist, subsumed by the infinitely complex sound pattern of London. A gust of air breezed beneath Jack's shirt, then faded, leaving the cotton to settle back against his skin, pasted like glue.

'See!' the girl declared, holding the battered, train-weary hardback before her boyfriend, flipping it open so that its paper cover threatened to slide down its spine, leaving it naked, exposed. The boy's mouth started to transmit words once more, and then the girl sidled up to Jack, thrusting the inside of the back cover before him, demonstrating her discovery, producing the evidence for the prosecution, resting her case before his eyes. The photo of the book's author, David Jackson, was there: profound eyes scrutinising the camera; furrowed brow, rapt in thought; lips half-parted, the gateway to wisdom; the archetypal novelist's identikit. But physically, it was Jack's face. Aside from the tracks of time that had left their mark on the face since the photograph had been taken, it was identical. 'Could you sign it?' Jack heard her imploring. 'Please. It would mean so much to me.'

And then – heat beating down, sounds pounding his ears, exhaust fumes condensing on his tar-marred lungs – something inside him snapped.

That he snatched the book from her hand and flung it into the street was stupid. That the book ruffled through the air and landed on the bonnet of a car, forcing it to a blistered-rubber halt, was unfortunate. That the car was a police car and contained a young, uniformed policewoman who was keen enough and fit enough to catch up with Jack and slam him up against a dusty brick wall before he'd managed to run more than ten paces, was just typical.

Minutes later, safely corralled in the back of the police car, the sequence of events that had led Jack here had become a blur, as erratic as the beat of his panicked heart. But even blurs became coherent once you slowed them down, dissected them, analysed them frame by frame. And sitting here – with an incommunicative policeman next to him, a policewoman sat in the front, driving – there weren't many options other than analysing the blizzard of events that had settled into the drift which was currently smothering him. He glanced down at his shaking fist, remembered the first flake falling.

Leonora Smiles had fired him.

The air conditioning of her office had been broken. Somewhere beyond her door a keyboard clattered, and (he imagined) a typist sighed. The closed, translucent blind in the open window behind her head flapped in the gusting, swirling thermals that swept up sporadically from the Soho street four floors below. Scents permeated his nostrils (fast-food grease, slow-food spices) as he watched her lips kiss sounds. He knew the combinations. Food was, after all, meant to be his business. And mingled with them, her perfume: No 5.

He continued to quietly fry in his jacket and trousers as she spoke, locked in a wet suit on dry land, still unable to bring himself to listen to her. Sweat bled self-consciously through the pores on his upper lip, glazing the stubble that he'd forgotten to shave that morning. He imagined how she must see it: an embarrassed sheen; a biological mirror, reflecting the impact of her managerial words on his employee psyche. Mistress and servant. Her scrutiny of his physical condition, he understood all too well, would only serve to endorse her opinion that he was scum.

She'd just fired him from his position as manager of the Covent Garden branch of the David Jackson Book Bar, the overpriced theme restaurant, with its shelves of freshly published books, its regular readings and its self-consciously literary clientèle. Decked out in stylised Fifties décor, it was a place where people could listen to performance poets as they dined, flick through novels as they drank, or simply ask for recommendations on which books to buy from the arts undergraduates who staffed the bar and tables. The charges that had been levelled against Jack, and which he'd not even attempted to deny, were false accounting and gross mismanagement.

'Is there anything you feel you want to say?' Smiles asked.

'Well . . .' he said, then lost his momentum, succumbing once more to the oppressive, colonial clamminess which pervaded her office.

'Well, Mr Jackson?' she repeated. '*Is* there anything you wish to say?'

This time Jack not just heard, but *understood* the question. It was rhetorical. She didn't want him to say anything. She simply wanted him to understand that she'd already said everything that needed to be said about the matter in hand. He could see it in her eyes, hear it in her voice, and smell it in her predatory perfume. It was obvious that, as far as she was concerned, there was no defence, no matter how convincing, and no advocate, no matter how zealous, capable of altering the facts as she saw them.

'I'm curious,' he slowly articulated after a moment's studied reflection. He observed a look of condescension settle like a shroud on her face. 'I'd like to know why you haven't called the police.' He wiped the back of his hand across his damp forehead, then pushed his black fringe back over the receded territory it normally guarded, tucked its unkempt length behind his ears. It felt good, wiping the sweat away, acknowledging its seedy presence without any inhibition like that. He leant forward and lowered his voice conspiratorially. 'I thought that it would have been the first thing to do in such . . . such *circumstances* . . .'

'Normally, yes,' she conceded, apprehension staining her voice for the first time since the interview had begun five precarious minutes previously.

'And abnormally?' he pursued, revelling in the sense of control that playing the interrogator lent him.

'I would have thought that was apparent.'

'David Jackson,' he suggested, his words sounding distant to him, sounding strong, as if they'd been uttered by another. 'Your boss. Antidote's owner. The individual you're accountable to.'

'Yes,' she said, stiffening in her chair with evident discomfort.

'And publicity, of course,' he reminded her. 'I imagine that the last thing he'd want is for it to surface that his brother – his identical twin – isn't quite as clean-cut and moral as people would assume.'

'Quite possibly,' she said, placing a hand on the desk before her and edgily splaying her fingers.

He paused theatrically – longer, he realised, than was strictly necessary. 'Which brings us to money,' he began. 'I'm afraid that even brotherly love has its price these days. So do excuse my bluntness, but what money do I get? Fiscal remuneration, I believe, is the euphemism currently *en vogue*.' The pretentiousness brought a sparkle to his eyes. 'I take it that you wouldn't be thinking of sending me out into these grey economic times without some sort of severance package to add a little colour to my wallet.'

'If I had it my way, Mr Jackson . . .'

'Jack,' he said, immune now to the implicit threats imposed by her voice and body language. 'Let's not pretend we don't know one another.'

'Quite. If I had it my way, Mr Jackson, that's precisely what I'd do.' This time it was she who hesitated. He felt himself smile at the reversal of roles, unable to resist the irony. 'Your brother, however, is a man of great compassion.'

'How much compassion?'

Her disdain darkened. 'Three months' salary.'

'It's not enough.'

'I think it's extremely generous and—'

He raised his hand in visual interruption and dictated, 'I said it's not enough. I have expenses . . . debts . . . I'm quite sure you understand . . .'

'I really don't feel you're in a situation to bargain, do you?'

He stared back with a calculated lack of emotion. 'Six months.'

'What?' she asked.

'Six months' salary. In my bank today. A cheque won't do. I need immediate access.'

'I'm afraid that's not possible.'

'You're quite right to be afraid,' he said, casually oblivious to her growing fury. 'The papers would have a field day. I have a friend I can ring right now. I'm quite sure she'll make it worth my while, if you don't. And as for whether it's possible or not . . .' He raised his eyebrows and let them conclude his sentence for him.

In the police car, the policeman, not bothering to look at Jack as he spoke, linking eyes instead with the policewoman in the mirror, asked, 'So what are we going to do with you, then, Mr Jackson?'

Jack turned to face him and the policeman reflected the motion. They stared into one another's face. He was about the same age as Jack, seasoned, stoical. He wasn't the type who'd take kindly to self-righteousness. Now was neither the time nor the place to launch into a verbally articulated justification of the actions which had brought him to this hot sweaty car on this hot sweaty day. Reality had bitten once. Chances were, it was more than prepared to do so again.

'I'm sorry,' Jack said. 'I lost my temper. It was stupid.'

'Good,' the policeman said with a nod as the car drew into the police station, 'that's good. Speaking without swearing every second word can definitely be construed as progress.'

After an hour of questions and answers and form-fillings, they released Jack with a caution. Even they hadn't bothered to take him seriously. Outside the police station, he tapped his jacket insecurely and relaxed at the reassuring solidity of the wallet in his inside pocket. The money it contained – some hundred pounds – had been transformed between the moment of his entry into the Antidote Entertainments building and his recent exit from reserves to loose change. For the time being, at least, there was more where that came from. But the bank transfer wasn't going to last for ever. And then what?

One thing was certain: David wasn't going to fix Jack up with a job a second time round. Not that Jack would take it. Not that the arrangement between himself and his brother had ever really had anything to do with business the first time round. It had been personal, right from the start. Sure, ostensibly, David had offered Jack the position as a result of their mother's final cancer-riddled request. Ostensibly, David had done it out of the kindness of his heart. Ostensibly, David had done it to give his failure of a brother a crack at making a steady living. And sure, ostensibly, David was a hell of a great guy. Personally, though – and Jack had no doubt on this score – David had employed him for no other reason than to humiliate him. David had known that Jack had needed the money and stability. And he'd known that, because of this, Jack would, in time, have become his – beholden, an employee, a kept man. David would have got him on a leash, just like all the other people in his life.

Only it hadn't happened like that. Jack had conned David, not the other way round. Jack had run the David Jackson Book Bar well for a number of months, long enough for the initial close scrutiny that had accompanied his appointment to drift into complacency and, eventually, into trust. And then he'd set his real plan into motion. It had been little things at first: free drinks slid across the counter to his friends; cigars and packets of cigarettes slipped into people's outstretched palms; the odd meal bill waived. Each such act of generosity had given Jack pleasure, though not for reasons of altruism, but because he'd known that each such act had denied David income, had hurt him the only way Jack knew how.

But successfully burying these discrepancies in the maze of mathematics that made up Antidote's accounting system hadn't been enough for Jack. Sure, he could have made some money for himself. But he wasn't a thief. He wasn't a bad man. He hadn't been in it for the money. His motive had been simple and pure: revenge. He'd wanted to inflict pain on David. He'd wanted to pay him back for the accumulation of misery he'd thrown down on Jack's shoulders over the years. So Jack had raised the stakes. Forget free drinks. Free parties had been the way forward. And not just once in a while, either. First every month, then every week and, in the last few weeks, almost every night. That was where the real pain for David had lain. For the first time in its five-year history, as the recent investigation that had ended Jack's run had clearly demonstrated, the Covent Garden branch of the David Jackson Book Bar had made a loss. Jack's mission had been accomplished.

So why this sense of failure? Why, even now that he'd succeeded at what he'd set out to do, did he still feel that it was David, and not him, who'd won? He knew why. David had stolen his moment of triumph by failing to attend the meeting. He'd swept Jack aside like an insect, left Smiles to finish him off. No matter how much Jack thought of the severance money, David had won. It was Jack, not David, who was left walking the streets with nowhere left to go. That smug son of a bitch had rolled him over again. Jack felt his skin flush, threaten to burn. If David thought that that was the end of it, that Jack was just going to lie down and let him get away with it, he could think again. Jack visualised turning the tables, sending them slamming into David, crushing him cold. He visualised it over and over again.

He followed the iron railing which curtained the pavement for a hundred yards or so up the street. Where it broke, he cut through into the grounds at the front of a church. There'd probably been a graveyard here once upon a time. But it was gone now. The gravestones were at any rate, replaced by swept stone paving slabs. He sat on a bench near the church wall, facing the sun, and watched an old man casting showers of breadcrumbs up into the air for the pigeons to squabble over. And then, with his skin pulsing in the heat, he closed his eyes.

His mother's hadn't been his first encounter with death. He knew as well that it wouldn't be his last. He'd reached the age where death didn't always come in conveniently packaged solemn phonecalls like it had done with his father. It came close now. Immediate. There wasn't anything abstract about it. It was the touch of dying skin. That's how it had been with his mother in her last few days. He'd felt her skin die in his hand, wrinkle and collapse on itself, begin the degenerative process without even waiting for her last breath to be wheezed. But she hadn't been the first he'd watched, knowing that the end, in spite of the remaining light in her eyes, had already arrived, feeling powerless in the face of something infinitely more powerful than himself.

It had been after he'd finished his A-levels, as he'd dawdled at the junction between gaining the qualifications to swing himself into adult life and putting those qualifications to use. He'd been in love, complete. There hadn't been any reason to look forward or back. There hadn't been any point in moving because he'd already arrived at where he'd wanted to be. But it had become the place he'd lost his direction.

That morning, he'd been with Emily, the girl he'd fallen for during his final term. He'd been in her parents' holiday home in Devon. He – they – had decided to go for a walk. There was a path leading from the back of the house to the beach. Huge, solid jellyfish – opalescent blue, like melted Frisbees – were scattered along the sand, dead and solid to the touch. The tide was coming in to reclaim them, suck them out to their watery graves. They'd probably been stranded here for hours.

'Emily,' he said, distress chewing him up as they walked along the edge of the beach where the water was seeping up the sand, staining it like filter paper. 'We need to talk.'

The phrase he'd chosen was as good as an alarm bell, but she just quickened her pace, walked onto the jagged rocks which formed the foot of the cliff. 'In a minute,' she said, her shoes crackling across the mussel-beds. 'There's something I want to show you.'

'It's important,' he said, the strain in his voice becoming increasingly evident, catching her up, continuing to climb. 'We need to talk now.'

'This will only take a couple of minutes,' she said, reaching the top of the rock slope and peering over the edge.

He joined her and looked down. Below them was a bay, little more substantial than the mouth of a cave. It was hemmed in by steep rock on either side, the only other exit being the sea itself. The cave was impressive: deep, stretching back into purple darkness, the heart of the cliff.

'A cave,' he said, moving to sit. 'Big deal. Listen—'

'No,' she said, tugging him back to his feet and beginning to clamber down. She looked up at him and smiled. 'I used to come here with my cousins when I was a kid. We carved our names inside.' She dropped down into the thigh-deep water and laughed and started wading towards the cave. 'It's freezing!' she shouted back. 'Come on. I want to see if they've stood the test of time.'

Jack looked out across the grey sea, then at the place the waves spat against the rocks. 'What about the tide?' he shouted out. 'I think it's coming in.'

'Don't be pathetic,' she yelled from inside the cave. 'This won't take long.'

By the time they'd inspected the carved names and reappeared in the sunlight, the water had risen. Adrenalin rose inside him like the tide. He told her to stay put and forced his way out. He managed to get as far as where they'd initially climbed down. The water was up to his chest, heaving, sucking him out a couple of feet one second, shoving him back towards Emily the next. He tried to keep his footing and shouted for her to come. She got waist-deep, then got thrown. She vanished beneath the dark, heavy water for seconds, before bursting free, spluttering, terrified, her mouth flapping, unable to scream.

It was just water. He'd never realised how uncompromising it could be, how insignificant he really was. When she disappeared for a third time and didn't come up, he gulped air and dived. He thought he saw her once: a swirling ghost, her hair spinning towards him. But when he tried swimming towards her he became disorientated. There was so much sand and muck. Everything was clouded. When he came up, he was crying, desperate. He knew she was gone. He tried again and then he tried dragging himself along the rock, but every time he got a grip, the swell ripped him free, slicing his fingers across the barnacles. Eventually, he managed to haul himself up out of the swell. Even then, he kept looking for her, hating David for having taken her from him, for having cursed him with this sick confusion where he couldn't even mourn her death, because he knew she was no longer his.

Everything had changed the night before. He and Emily weren't the only ones staying in the house. There were eight of them altogether, friends from school. And David. Already Jack's silent rival. Already the person Jack found watching his back, waiting for him to stumble. Already someone whose insidious comments were designed to push Jack down one side of the seesaw and raise himself up the other. The drinking through till dawn had been Jack's idea, so in a way it had been appropriate that he'd been the first to collapse in a stupor on the living-room floor. His memory of the evening was splintered. He vaguely remembered arguing with Emily about something, vaguely remembered David defending her, telling him to can it, telling her to ignore him, saying that he couldn't handle his drink. The last thing Jack remembered before he woke the next morning was Tim and Mark supporting him up the stairs to bed. But after he woke and rolled across the bed to reach for a glass of water only to find that the glass was empty, he remembered everything.

Weak dawn sunlight drifted across the landing where he stood at the top of the stairs. There was the sound of movement downstairs. He checked his watch. He was impressed. Someone had managed to ride the alcohol train all the way to morning. He yawned, felt the skin inside his throat crack as it stretched. There was bottled water in the fridge downstairs. That would do the trick, sort him out, allow him to return to bed and sleep this monster off. He walked slowly down the stairs, conscious of the need not to jar his brain with any sudden movement.

He reached the bottom of the stairs and turned left for the kitchen. The door to the living room was ajar and he nudged it quietly open and squinted across the room, mildly interested to see what state whoever had made the distance was in.

He saw Emily first, or rather, he saw her head; the rest

of her body was blocked by the sofa which lay between them. She was sitting down on the floor on the far side of the room. She raised a hand to her head, brushed her hair back from her face with her fingers. She was speaking to someone he couldn't see. Her voice was low, a whisper; he couldn't make out what she was saying. He stepped forward into the room and then froze, gripped in the shadows. He could see her body from the waist up now, naked, cloaked in the golden glow of the dawn. And then, feeling his tongue collapse in silence on the floor of his mouth, he watched Emily's arms reach forward and her body shift back as David reared up from beneath her and placed his mouth on hers. The muffled sounds of moans and sighs cut through Jack's ears. He turned and walked back to the foot of the stairs.

He stayed there, watching the cave fill, watching the water slosh round it, feeling the wind blow across his heavy clothes. Everything had changed. A darkness had settled in his mind. All he could see was Emily and David. All he could think of was Emily and David together.

David found him walking across the beach, back towards the house. It was raining now. Jack's hair was plastered across his forehead, trailing down before his eyes. Water channelled down his bare forearms, pouring onto his wet denim shorts, mixing with the salt water already trapped there. He ground to a halt as David reached him and placed his hands on his shoulders.

'Where've you been?' David asked. 'What's happened?' He shook Jack's shoulders. 'What is it? For Christ's sake, Jack, tell me what's going on.'

Jack spun his shoulders, tore free and stared into his brother's eyes. Words filled his head, words he couldn't speak.

David stared across the beach in the direction Jack had come from. 'Where's Emily?' He stared back at Jack. 'Where the fuck is she?'

'Don't!' Jack heard his voice release itself in a scream. 'Don't you mention her fucking name!'

And then he was on top of David, pounding his fists repeatedly into his face, hearing David's head thud against the sand, feeling the beach shudder against his knees. There was blood streaming from David's nose, mixing with rain on his face and trickling onto the sand.

Jack's eyes returned to the old man feeding the pigeons. His knuckles were now buried in a supermarket bag, burrowing for crumbs. Then they emerged and he flung the food free in a final cast. The man crumpled the bag into his pocket and walked. The pigeons stabbed their crippled limbs around, desultory for a minute, then flocked and rose, applauding themselves into flight in a blur of grey wings across the thin blue sky.

Jack had never told anyone what he'd seen that morning in the living room. Not even David. And David's arrogance had blocked his sight, never allowed him to guess. He, like everyone else, had put the attack on the beach down to grief, to rage over Emily's death. They'd thought that David had been the one he'd chosen to take it out on for the simple reason that David had been the one who'd been there. But it hadn't been that way. Jack had taken it out on David, not because he'd been the only one there; not even because he'd managed to find some perverse way of blaming Emily's death on him; but because it had been David, not the sea, who'd swept Jack's life away. And it was this, over all David's sick behaviour he'd witnessed since, that Jack would never be able to forgive.

Jack spat on the ground. No matter what you gave, life, like death, took its own course regardless. You might as well have never existed in the first place.

But enough. Enough. He walked back to the street and lit a cigarette. Enough self-pity. That had never got him anywhere; that was precisely what had got him to where he was now. He needed to think. He took in his surroundings: familiar restaurants, clubs and pubs – his personalised A-Z. He hit a junction and took a left, quickened his pace, keeping the paralysis at bay. Yes, he reassured himself as his feet set off on autopilot, he needed to relax and clear his mind. He needed a drink.

He docked at his destination not long after, and ducked inside. The SlipSide Club was owned by Tommy Rhodes. Tommy and Jack went way back into the narcotic sludge from which Jack had helped Tommy emerge. In the wake of Emily's death, Jack, too, had allowed the waters to close over his head. He'd gone to university and it was there, in hall, that he'd met Tommy for the first time. Ex-army, Tommy had been older than Jack. And ex-army, he'd taken his new-found freedom seriously. For a while, thanks to Tommy's contagious appetite for living, Jack's own life had become bearable again. Tommy had been hard and Jack, weak as he'd been, had been able to draw on the other man's strength, had found himself able to switch off in his presence, relax.

Tommy had been dealing back then, small time, soft drugs to his fellow students. They'd entered the acid patch together, Jack for the escape from memory that it offered, Tommy for no better reason than that it was there to be explored. Within a couple of months – though, Christ knew, Jack could hardly be accurate – if someone had stuck some litmus paper into their heads, they'd have witnessed that their brains had been well and truly acidified. All Jack now remembered from this time was swirling shapes and colours, a kaleidoscope with him and Tommy suspended at its centre. But that hadn't been enough for Tommy. The effect of the acid had dropped and reality had begun to encroach on the dream he'd been living. Where Jack had chosen to straighten himself out, Tommy had pined for more. And that had been when the real nightmare had begun. One night when Jack hadn't been there to apply the breaks, Tommy had accepted a needle, a high he hadn't wanted to come down from. Within a month, he'd jumped ship, packed his bags without a word to anyone and set off for London to self-destruct.

It had been two months before Jack had succeeded in tracking him down. But by then, the track marks had got to

Tommy first. Jack didn't even want to think about what state Tommy had been in when he'd taken him away from there, sorted out a flat back near the university and locked the door. He didn't want to know how long he'd kept vigil over Tommy's feverish, writhing body. He'd stayed until Tommy had come down for the last time, until his feet had landed back on the ground and he'd learnt to walk alone again. The cement that still existed between them had set solid then.

Somehow, saving Tommy had temporarily chased Jack's own black dogs over Emily away. And when they'd returned, snapping at his feet, hounding him down, Tommy had been there for him. Guitar, the band that Tommy had formed at university subsequent to his return to normality, had gone on to claim the Seventies as its own. And throughout this purple period, Tommy had kept Jack close, had kept him busy, given him sanctuary from himself. Jack had trotted the globe with him, as Guitar's chief roadie. Just as Jack had rescued Tommy's life, in those crucial years, Tommy had given Jack life, a purpose. Without him, Jack suspected, he would have had neither.

Jack knew SlipSlide's history like his own. It consisted of three floors of conflicting calm and hedonism, descending downwards: SlipSlide, Level 2, and The Basement. Tommy had opened it in 1980, following his retirement from the music business. Jack had been here when Tommy had first inspected it in 1979. It had been through the tunnel-vision provided by an industrial flashlight and to the accompaniment of a property developer's apprehensive sales pitch. The building had been a wreck. Gutted by fire. Skeletal. But it had been a skeleton that Tommy's vision had led him to patiently feed with wisdom and money.

And just look at it now, Jack thought to himself, as he paused at the top of the stairs which descended to The Basement. This floor was the size of two tennis courts and was bisected by a soundproof glass wall. Beyond that lay a continuation of the bar and a dance floor, its walls and ceiling patterned with cinema screens, speakers, lights and black-grilled air-conditioning ducts. And this side, the perfect contrast: furniture, fittings and ambience more suited to a gentlemen's club. The six-by-six notice board on the wall behind the bar testified to SlipSlide's popularity. Autographs. Messages. Thanks. The various tributes of the various personalities who'd requested (had never *been* requested) to add their reputations to the reputation of the club.

Jack spotted Tommy, alone at a table, at ease. He was turning the tip of his cigar against the rim of an ashtray. Its smoke curled tantalisingly across the dimly-lit room. Jack watched as he dispersed it with a long, contented blast from his lungs. Then, following the smoke's lead, Tommy rose and walked to the smooth, varnished bar and plucked a nut from a bowl.

'Can I fix you a drink, Tommy?' the barman was asking as Jack reached the bar.

'Thanks, Sean,' Tommy answered.

Jack added, 'Yeah, and you'd better make that two.'

'Jack,' Tommy said, recognition breaking through, turning from Sean to shake Jack's hand warmly. 'Happy birthday, mate.' He took in his friend's countenance and his own expression fell in empathy. 'Or maybe not . . .'

Minutes later, Sean raised the bar-gate and, ice clinking like chains inside the whisky glasses, crossed the room to the table where Tommy sat talking with Jack. Sean placed the glasses on the mats before them, filled them and put the bottle between them. Before he'd turned to go, Jack had already drunk and replenished the contents of his glass.

'You got the pay-off. It could have been worse,' Tommy was saying.

'How?' Jack asked. 'I'm out of work. I'm back at square one for the millionth time. What could be worse than that?'

'Well, if you'd been working for me and ripping me off like that, I'd have had you in prison by now. How's that for worse?'

Jack's tone relented. 'Yeah,' he mumbled, fumbling for a cigarette. He swirled the golden liquid round his glass, allowing its meniscus to surf the rim. 'But that money sitting in the bank is convenient, that's all. Once it's gone, I'm totally screwed.'

'Everyone gets screwed from time to time,' Tommy said. 'People get screwed every day. Don't take it so hard. You'll bounce back. It's no big deal.'

Jack looked at Tommy's shirt, his tie, his lustrous brogues and the tailored suit that projected them so well, then beyond him at the mirror which trapped them side by side on the wall. For a moment, he found himself externalised. He saw himself as a stranger might. His figure was slight next to Tommy's wrestler's frame. His face was weary, flushed with stress and heat. His suit, like Tommy's, was made of dark material. But that was where the similarity quit. It was obvious he had no pride in his appearance. His brick-dusted jacket was draped uncaringly over the arm of his chair. His inappropriately loud tie hung in a loosened noose across his classic, striped shirt, the sleeves of which were rolled lazily up above his elbows. It was as if the only things keeping him from falling apart altogether were his blood red braces. He was a wreck.

'We're from the same background,' he told Tommy. 'Look where it's got you.' He stared across the room to illustrate his point and found himself confronted by his diminished, blurred reflection in the glass divide. 'Now look at me,' he said, staring at his friend, 'and try telling me I've got an excuse.'

Tommy held Jack's belligerent stare unflinchingly as he lit a fresh cigar. 'Have you finished?' he challenged as the initial smoke-burst obscured his face.

'Do I need to go on?'

'If you do, you do. And if you do, I'll listen. But I can't see much point in it myself, not if you really believe all this shit you're spouting. If it's all therapy, spitting out your anger, getting all the phlegm off your chest, then go ahead. Just don't expect me to swallow any of it.' He pointed his cigar at Jack's face. 'I *know* the truth, which means that I'm not going to get suckered in by this crap.'

'And what truth's that?'

'That you're a good man and a good mate.'

'You're as big a fool as me.'

Tommy shook his head dismissively. 'You trust me, don't you? You trust the word of an ex-junkie?'

'Yeah,' Jack said. 'You know I do.'

'Then trust my judgement now. Listen to me when I tell you that it's your fortieth birthday and you've lived more than most people twice your age. And trust me when I tell you that things will work out.' He sat back in his chair. 'My offer still stands, you know. There'll always be a job here for you, if you want it. I mean, why the fuck not? Thanks to that prick of a brother of yours, you've even got the relevant experience now.'

The corners of Jack's mouth turned down. This was turf they'd trodden over time and time again. 'You already know why not.'

'Because you want to stand on your own two feet. Because you reckon you're too old to be relying on me for work.'

'Correct.'

'So how come you worked for David? You'd rather rely on him than me?'

'I did it to piss him off. It was a laugh at his expense.'

'So do the same at mine.'

Jack smiled. 'What, and end up in prison? You've got to be kidding.'

Tommy's eyes rolled. 'No, I don't mean rip me off, you soft git. I mean help me run this place. Don't tell me you didn't like managing Jackson's, because I know you did. So have a crack here. It can't hurt and if you don't like it, you can quit. It's your call.'

Jack looked away. 'Do you know what I want to do next?' he asked. 'What I want to do more than anything else?' Tommy raised his eyebrows. 'What I really want is to go down to Wales and let David know just what I think of him. Give him the truth. Spell it out to him. Break the fucker's nose.'

'What good's that going to do anyone?'

'Who cares what good it'll do anyone? It'll make me feel better. He's laughing at me. I can hear him from here.'

'You don't need him to make you feel better. Anyway, you know what he's like. He'd treat it as an opportunity for a power-play. Same as giving you the job in the first place. Same as firing you. He'd love watching you lose control. Do yourself a favour,' Tommy finished, 'and put him out of your mind – for good this time. It's time you moved on.'

A still of David with Emily flashed into Jack's mind. 'You don't understand,' he said. 'You don't know half the stuff he's done to me. And you don't have a brother. Let alone an identical twin. You don't know what it's like. Putting him out of my mind would be like you standing in front of a mirror with your eyes sealed tight, trying to will your reflection away. It wouldn't work. The moment you opened your eyes, you'd find yourself staring back. You've no idea what it's like seeing some shit like him with everything he's got, knowing that it could have been me, knowing that if he hadn't consistently fucked up my life the way he has, it probably would have been.'

Tommy's eyelids lowered wearily. 'Fine,' he said. 'You go to Wales. David answers the door. Then what? Just what are you going to say that's going to make you feel so good? That he's a manipulative, two-faced piece of shit?' He stopped for breath, then heaved at his cigar and blew smoke antagonistically into Jack's face. 'Is that what you're going to say? Because if it is – if that's the truth you're going to tell him – then let me tell you this: there's no fucking point. He already knows it himself, and he already knows that you know. It won't make any difference. Not to you, and definitely not to him. And if you want to do him over, knock some sense into him, then save yourself the effort. I can fix that for you. All you've got to do is ask and it's sorted.' He pulled the bottle off the table and sloshed drink into their glasses. 'But if not, just forget him, OK? He's not worth it. Just forget him, and let's drink. Let's drink to your birthday.' He held his glass up to Jack. But Jack remained unmoved, his eyes glazed, impenetrable. 'Here,' Tommy said hurriedly, delving into his pocket. He passed an embossed, cardboard jeweller's box to Jack. 'I nearly forgot.'

Jack flipped the lid of the box open, and lifted up a leather-bound, silver hip-flask. 'Thanks,' he said.

'Thought you'd like it. Now let's drink to you.' As Jack began to lift his glass, Tommy placed a restraining hand on his wrist. 'Not with that, you cretin,' he said, removing the flask from Jack's other hand and unscrewing its top, 'with this.' He ditched his cigar into the ashtray and, kissing the flask's neck with that of the tilted whisky bottle, began to decant. 'Don't know if there's enough left to fill it,' he grumbled playfully, his eyes narrowed in concentration. 'Don't know how you do it on an empty stomach.'

'I couldn't give a flying fuck what your policy is, you bog-dwelling Mick!' an angry voice shouted from the other side of the room, shattering the ritual mid-flow. 'I want to buy a round of drinks and you're going to fucking well serve me!'

'Typical,' Tommy said, downing his task and getting quickly to his feet, striding off towards the bar, his voice suddenly rough, capable of dealing in fear. Without thinking, Jack stood and walked pace for pace behind him until they were standing behind the four young men who were glaring belligerently across the bar at Sean.

Jack knew what was coming next. He'd seen it all before, time after time. Something had happened to Tommy in the months after he'd kicked the drugs. He'd imposed a rigid control on his life. Nothing and no one was ever going to mess him up again. It was like he'd reverted to the way he'd been in the army, taken the strength and discipline he'd known then and made it his. In some ways, this had been good. Without this determination and self-belief, Guitar probably wouldn't have ever got off the ground, and the same went for SlipSlide. But there'd been a down-side, too. To Tommy, being in control meant more than self-control. It meant stamping out opposition, killing it quick before it got the chance to threaten the status quo. This siege mentality had brought with it violence. Just as Tommy had become ruthless in business, he'd become ruthless in the flesh. Jack knew – everyone knew – how Tommy had learnt to deal with people who crossed him, the methods he employed to keep SlipSlide's profits his in Soho's gangster economy.

'What's your fucking problem?' Tommy barked.

The man opposite Sean turned slowly and his friends in series did the same, executing a clumsy section from a dance routine. Jack felt Tommy's calm filter through to him, dilute the adrenalin and allow him to see clearly, cool his head and assess the situation clinically. The men were drunk and stoned. Of the four of them, only two – the one who'd turned first, slick-back, leather jacket, standing opposite Tommy, and the one on his left, grade-two shaved head, gold stud through his lower lip, standing opposite Jack – looked like they might want to take this any further. The other two flanking them were already acting sheepish, avoiding eye contact, looking like they might quietly peel off at any moment and slip away. The smell of hash filled Jack's nostrils.

Sean nodded at the stacked cigarette paper snip-gripped between Slick-Back's fingers. 'I told him no drugs in here.'

'Put it out,' Tommy told Slick-Back. He glanced at Sean, saying, 'Phone upstairs.'

No one spoke for a couple of seconds and Jack watched Sean scuttle away into the room behind the bar.

'What's it to you, old man?' Slick-Back eventually said, making no move to douse the spliff. 'Why don't you piss off and mind your own business?'

'House rules. Put it out.'

'Hear that, lads?' Slick-Back asked as he surveyed his ranks. He faced Tommy again. 'Whose rules, old man? Yours? 'Cos if they are, they don't mean shit to me.' He held the spliff up to his lips and sucked briefly before passing to Grade-Two.

'I'm not going to tell you again,' Tommy said, his stare burrowing into Slick-Back's face. 'Now do it. Put it out and get out.'

Slick-Back's nostrils flared. 'Carry on talking to me like that and I'm going to give you a slap.'

'Fact,' Grade-Two said, resting the spliff on an ashtray by his side. Jack watched Grade-Two's fist clenching up, felt his own muscles tightening in response.

'I reckon you should fuck off,' Slick-Back said.

The moment Slick-Back's hand appeared at his side, Tommy hit him. His fist caught him on the bridge on the nose, cracking the bone and sending blood cascading down his nostrils. Jack watched Slick-Back stagger back against the bar, a knife which Jack hadn't even clocked falling from his hand to the floor. Then Jack felt himself hurled onto the ground, Grade-Two sprawled on top of him, his throat forced down by one arm, Grade-Two's other rearing up above Jack's head, ready to come flashing down into his face. Jack reached up, gripped Grade-Two's wrist and wrestled against its will to move forward. Then there was a clatter of footsteps somewhere to his left and suited limbs were shunting around him. He felt Grade-Two's hand being torn away from his throat. He groped for air to fill his aching lungs.

When he managed to get to his feet, he saw that events had accelerated in his absence. Two bouncers were strutting up the stairs, frog-marching Slick-Back's and Grade-Two's partners away, whilst another bouncer efficiently herded the other customers from the room with a minimum of fuss. A further two bouncers stood stationary in front of Tommy, Slick-Back and Grade-Two locked in their arms. Blood ran from Slick-Back's nose, down over his lip and onto the floor.

'All right!' he was shouting at Tommy. 'Just fucking leave it, all right! We'll go. OK? We'll fucking go.'

'Too late,' Tommy told him, touching his lip with the back of his hand, looking in disgust at the blood smeared across his skin. 'You should have listened the first time.'

'We're sorry, OK? Is that what you fucking want? An apology?' Grade-Two demanded.

'You cut my lip, you arrogant little shit,' Tommy said. 'You pulled a knife on me and cut my lip.' He stared down his front. 'You got blood on my shirt.' He looked at Jack and then stepped across to Grade-Two. 'And you, shithead, you attacked my friend.' He was taking his jacket off now, walking to a nearby chair and hanging it over the back. 'You came into my club and attacked my friend.'

'I'll pay,' Slick-Back said. 'I'll give you the money for your shirt.'

'You'll pay all right,' Tommy said, rolling his sleeves up to his elbows.

'What?' Grade-Two said, panicked now. 'What the fuck do you want us to say?'

Tommy walked up to him and punched him in the face. Jack watched the bouncer holding Grade-Two tightening his grip.

'I don't want you to say anything, prick,' Tommy said, punching Grade-Two in the gut and watching impassively as he doubled-up.

Jack stood there dumbly. He didn't want any part of this, couldn't deal with Tommy when he got this way. He wanted to tell him to leave it, tell him that the kids had learnt their lesson and he should let them go. But this wasn't his business. This was Tommy's. He could see the bouncers' eyes. There was nothing personal here. These were just minutes from an hour that they were being paid for. He looked at Tommy's eyes. This was management. This was what Tommy thought people management was all about. And then he looked at the knife on the floor, pathetically brittle and fragile now that it lay outside the animation of a hand, and barely managed to recollect the menace that had been in Slick-Back's voice only minutes before. Grade-Two was still struggling for breath. Slick-Back had begun to shake. Jack looked away. This was nothing to do with him. Nothing at all.

He turned and walked back to the table, lifted the whisky bottle from the table and concentrated on filling the flask, watched the liquid trickle through its neck, focused his mind on monitoring the change in tone emitted by the flask as it approached full, cut away at the other sounds which came from behind him until he couldn't hear them at all.

When Tommy returned to the table, he sank into his chair with a sigh and lit a fresh cigar. Stoicism descended.

'Happy birthday, Jack,' he said to the empty chair next to him. 'Wherever you are.'

One swerving, talkative taxi and several hours' sleep later, Jack awoke in his bed in his rented flat in West London, fully clothed, a leather-bound, silver hip-flask gripped in the drunkenly stubborn rigor mortis of his left hand. One impulsive decision and several gear changes after this, he found himself behind the wheel, queuing through Kew and cutting out onto the M4 and heading due west.

'Cuckoo!' he chimed out of the wound-down window into the fast lane of hot summer sales-executive exhaust fumes. Maybe that was it. That would explain it all. Maybe David wasn't really his brother at all. An alien, demon, cuckoo, perfectly placed at the moment of birth, with Jack's real twin surreptitiously disposed of in a carry-cot on a doorstep, buried in a basement, walled up in a well, slung in a sealed hessian sack into a disused, flooded slate mine; a nameless bag of bones. 'Cuckoo!' he called again. 'Cuck-ooooo!'

He focused back on the motorway which carved through the undulating hills and valleys of the counties before him, then lifted the hip-flask from between his thighs and took a swift, illicit swig. Click, scan, and the radio was on. Rock music. Heavy on sentimentality. Blood-bubbling. Emotive. Just what the witch-doctor ordered. Then an interruption. The hourly news. Unemployment figures. The heatwave continues. The hideous murder of a famous author. A chilling calling card: a callously typed piece of prose left for the police in a typewriter at the London home of the deceased, a copy leaked to the press, describing in excruciating detail the exact circumstances leading up to Adam Somebodyorother's ignominious death. Other evidence found at the scene of the crime. Questions raised about Somebodyorother's sexual inclinations . . . Followed by the travel news: all quiet on the westbound front. No usually ubiquitous ten-truck pile-ups.

No more than a weak wheeze of wind on the Severn Bridge. Then back to the music. A regular beat. A regular beat.

Jack clawed behind his neck, adjusted the headrest, flexed his legs, once, twice, and settled the engine's revs down to a steady, stealthy pace. Thoughts strobed through his head like passing streetlights.

According to Tommy, he shouldn't be doing what he was doing now, driving to Wales, a recent defector from the dream state, neither sober nor drunk, dozing, a danger to himself, a criminal to others, with the expressed intention of instigating a fierce, bloody row with David. But Tommy was wrong. By not being there to fire Jack in person, David had denied Jack the confrontation he'd spent the last few months working towards. He'd stripped Jack's purpose from him, left him cut loose without meaning. And that wasn't right. David had taken enough from him already.

And there were other, darker reasons driving Jack on this insane journey. Tommy knew nothing about what had happened with Emily, about how that event had hobbled Jack's life. And neither had he ever uncovered Jack's other deep secret. The name that flashed neon through his coldest and loneliest moments had remained hidden. Rachel. The face he saw every time his eyelids drooped. Rachel. The face of the woman he loved, the only woman he could conceive of loving now. Rachel. The same woman who was married to David.

Taboo, a drunken voice inside his head said. To covet one's brother's wife. Intimations of incest. Not quite. But close enough, all the same. Immoral. Jack glanced furtively at his reflection in the mirror. Tiredness hung like war-paint in sore, grey streaks beneath his eyes. He turned away, back to the road, back to the matter in hand. But still the voice persisted. Evil. Shameful. Pitiful. Hating his brother for the way he treated people – that was reasonable. Hating him because his own life was so dire – that was understandable, too. Even envying David's lifestyle could only be deemed sad. But nursing this smouldering desire; stepping beyond his brother's personal possessions to covet his emotional life too: that was just sick. Too sick to be simply sad.

He switched on the headlights, adjusted to the altered environment with a narrowing of his sodden eyes. But that wasn't the way it was, in spite of how it might look. He didn't love Rachel because she was David's wife. He loved her because he loved her. Not because of what she was. 'No,' he mumbled aloud, remembering one of Tommy's lyrics, 'not for her role, for her soul.' Because he couldn't help it. He smudged his eyes with sweeping, whitened knuckles.

But that wasn't why he was going to see David. Not to see her. She no longer lived with David. She'd set herself up in a flat in London. Away from David. Sick of the sight of him. But not with Jack either. Perhaps because he looked the same. Perhaps, he still hoped, because she'd never guessed the way he felt. No, he wasn't going to see David just because of her, but because . . . because David had this coming. Because David had taken everything Jack had ever wanted. Because there was no one else for him to blame. Whatever anyone else might think – Tommy, or whoever – they'd be wrong. They knew nothing. Nothing about what David had done with Emily the night before she'd died. Nothing about what Jack had felt for Rachel since the first day he'd met her. Nothing about the sick way David had treated her before she'd left him. Nothing about how the only two women Jack had ever loved had turned to his brother instead of him.

He turned the music up, took a series of swigs, applied a notch more pressure to the accelerator, and remembered the last time he'd visited David's home, the night of Rachel's birthday party, shortly after Jack had accepted the job at the Book Bar.

Of course, Jack had witnessed David's releases of hatred before, but never like this, never at the risk of his pristine public image, never in front of other people. Previously, it had always been one on one, or from a sheltered distance. David had always been left disassociated from the mental violence he'd wielded. His superficial benevolence had remained intact. But on this night, his caution had deserted him. His malevolence had shone for all to see and he hadn't given a damn. Something had happened to him. That much had been apparent. It was as if the sickness that he'd always nursed inside himself had burst like a boil, exploded into the open, and he'd no longer cared about disguising what he really was.

David was laughing at Rachel. His behaviour had progressively soured over the last hour. Persecution was in his eyes. 'So tell me. Name one thing you've done in your life that means something.'

'I married you.'

'Something real. Something of worth.'

'That is real,' she said, her voice weak.

'No. Getting married is nothing. Thousands of people do it every minute. Just the same as thousands of people defecate and urinate.' He paused to survey the other guests at the table, savoured the social taboos he was shattering, the pain he was inflicting. 'It's nothing unusual, nothing extraordinary. Something as common as that has no meaning in itself.' He stared back at Rachel. 'So tell me. What have you ever done? When you die, what are people going to look back and say? What will you have achieved?' Rachel looked down at the table. 'Tell me,' David persisted.

'I don't know.'

David's mouth curled in disgust. 'Nothing.'

'Leave it,' Jack said.

David ignored him. 'You've done nothing. Therefore, you are nothing.'

Tony attempted to intervene, 'Come on David, you don't believe that.'

David glared at him. 'I believe everything that's real.'

'You think my life's meaningless,' Rachel said, her voice louder now, beginning to crack.

'Yes, but you're not the only one. You, Jack – all of you – you're just the same. That's your fate. It's normal. And that's your problem. You're normal. Unexceptional. Worthless.' He waved his hand across the dining table. 'I'm surrounded by mediocrity.'

'And what about you?' Jack demanded. 'What makes you so special?'

'Don't ask me, Jack. Ask the countless nobodies who've bought my books. They'll tell you. They'll tell you what you already know – that I'm someone whose opinions matter; someone who has the capacity to affect their lives.'

'And if they could hear you now? If they could hear you slagging them off, what then?'

David shrugged. 'Who knows? Maybe one day they will. Maybe that's the laugh I'm saving till last. But failure,' he continued, pushing his plate away from him and resting his elbows on the table, 'is something you should all be familiar with by now. It's unwise to ignore something so obvious. All that's likely to achieve is making your lives even more miserable than they already are.'

'You can't say that,' Tony said. 'You can't pass judgement on us like that.'

'Why not?'

'You just can't,' Jack intervened.

David sighed and mimicked, 'You just can't.' He stared into Jack's eyes. 'That's been your problem throughout your adult life. Just can't. Just can't get a decent job off your own back. Just can't find a decent woman. Just can't make enough money to settle down and make a life for yourself.' He reached for his glass of wine. 'Just can't. You're a loser, Jack. Always were. Always will be.'

'Leave him alone,' Rachel said.

'Why should I? He's weak. It's only the strong who've earned the right to be left alone.'

'Leave him.'

'I don't need you to defend me,' Jack said.

'Ah,' David said with a smile, 'but you do. You're hopeless, Jack. Left to your own devices, you'd sink without a trace. You need the misplaced generosity of people like Rachel. And people like me to give you a job. Without us, you'd have nothing at all.'

'Don't talk to me like that.'

'I'll talk to you any way I like. You may not have

noticed, but this is my home. I'm the master here. You're my employee and tonight you're my guest. Correction: you're my wife's guest. If it wasn't for her and the fact that it's her birthday, you wouldn't even be here. If it was left to me, you'd be spending the night in whatever squalid little dump you currently call home.'

'You piece of shit,' Jack spat.

David slowly nodded his head. 'An interesting choice of words, Jack. Base, of course – not that I'd expect anything else from you. But still, interesting. When a piece of shit like yourself describes me that way, I suppose I should take it as a compliment, an acknowledgement of equality of status. And that would be fine if it were true. Only we both know it isn't.'

'Arsehole.'

'If I am, Jack, I'm an arsehole that shits money and intellect, and one whose born right it is to shit on you.'

'Stop,' Rachel said. 'Both of you. Can't you just stop?'

'Keep out of this,' David snapped.

'What is it with you?' Jack demanded. His mind was locked onto David now. Hatred filled him. 'Look at her. Look what you're doing to her. Look at your other guests. You think this is funny?'

David looked at Rachel and the other people at the table in turn and then smiled. 'You couldn't possibly understand, Jack. So don't even try.'

'She's your wife, for Christ's sake. You can't treat her like this.'

'I can treat her any way I like. She can walk. I'm not stopping her.' He looked at her. 'Do you hear that, Rachel? You can walk. You can walk out on me right now. I won't give a damn.'

From the opposite end of the table, Alice spoke up, 'I can't believe you're speaking like this in front of her.'

'What do you know?' David asked, spinning round to face her.

'I know that you've got no right to—'

He released a bitter laugh. 'Got no right? She's my wife.

For better or for worse. I've got every right in the world.'

'Ignore him, Alice, Rachel pleaded, a tear at her eye. 'He's drunk. He's trying to bait you. Just ignore him.'

'Far from it,' David told Alice. 'I'm merely speaking the truth. Do you know who I married, Alice? I married a bright woman, a strong woman, someone I thought I could respect.'

'She *is* a strong woman,' Alice stated. Her shoulders were quivering. 'Or she would be, if you didn't keep putting her down.'

'She had a breakdown, for Christ's sake!' David mocked. 'She quit her job and hasn't lifted a finger since. She's useless. Her whole life's useless. What's so strong about that?'

'She's been sick,' Alice said.

'Rubbish! She's not sick. She's just weak. She should snap out of it and get a bloody grip.' He shot Rachel a glance. Tears were flowing freely down her face. 'It's pathetic. Didn't your shrink tell you that, Rachel?' he demanded. 'Didn't he tell you that tears never solved anything?'

'You disgust me,' Alice told him.

'Good.'

'Right,' she said, getting to her feet, 'that's it. I can't stomach this any more. Come on, Philip. We're going.'

Rachel had risen, too. 'Wait—' she started.

'Go on, Philip,' David taunted. 'Be a good boy and piss off like your wife says.' The chairs of the remaining guests began to scrape backwards. 'Good idea,' David continued. 'You can all fuck off. Piss off and don't come back.'

But it wasn't the torrent of abuse that had followed them out of the room that Jack remembered most. It was the look that had accompanied it – the smile, the pleasure of a job well done engraved on David's face.

It was still warm when Jack got out of the parked car and stood staring at the looming silhouette of the farmhouse crowned by the cobweb of wood on the hill behind and framed by the luminescent night sky. A fresh breeze fed his nostrils with the sweet scent of the sea which lay barely two miles away. This peaceful place. This place whose tranquillity he'd driven all the way from London to taint with his frustration and anger.

The curtains were open in the drawing room and two rectangles of light beamed out into the courtyard in which Jack stood, picking him out like the headlights of a car, leaving him feeling utterly isolated, as if he was standing in the middle of a road waiting for a car to come rushing through the darkness to meet him.

He blinked and abandoned the concept of surprise being the best form of attack, just as easily as he'd originally plucked it from his swirling, confused imaginings during the last few winding miles of deep indigo, hedge-hemmed lanes, when he'd entertained the idea of marching in on one of David's public relations soirées and laying down the law, spitting out a few unpleasant home truths to the assembled agents, critics and authors about the real nature of their starchy host, about the sort of behaviour he was capable of exhibiting at other parties, parties where the guests were of no use to him other than cheap amusement.

But there was no soirée occurring here tonight. Through the lit panes of glass, he could clearly see that no gathering sat talking their way towards the witching hour. And no incongruous convertibles cluttered up the courtyard. Aside from Jack's own car, the only other vehicle was David's battered Land Rover (a vehicle whose carefully cultivated, decrepit appearance, Jack sincerely suspected, was the perverted suggestion of some PR firm or another), the same charmingly traditional car that David had posed next to in tweeds in a photograph which had accompanied a feature article in the *Sunday Post*, entitled, 'David Jackson's Rural Renovations: A Simpler Slice of British Life.' Jack considered scratching the length of the offending object with his car keys, but realised the pointed futility of such an action. Borrowing it for a few days, repairing it, and restoring it to its former glory with a fresh skin of paint would probably have caused David far more grief.

He released his keys into his pocket as he passed the car, lifted the latch of the wrought-iron gate and approached the front door with his heels clicking firmly and ostentatiously on the flagstoned path which led through the beautified herb garden. The bright light from the drawing room rubbed at his eyes as he drew nearer. Surprise *was* out of the question. In all likelihood, his arrival would already have been noted. The front-door key might very well have been turned in the lock even before he'd stepped from his car. He stopped in front of the door, emptied the flask into his throat, breathed in the loitering fumes, breathed out, and pulled the bell chain.

'David!' he shouted two infuriating minutes later, after repeated ringings and hammerings had solicited no response. 'David! I know you're in there!' he slammed the sole of his shoe against the locked door, jarring his knee. 'David! Open the fucking door before I kick it down!'

A startled pigeon clattered into flight somewhere in the woods. But apart from that, nothing.

'Right, you bastard!' Jack fumed, drunkenly removing his shoe and walking up to the nearest of the drawing-room windows. He gripped the shoe by the toe and swung it against the window pane, sending splinters of glass onto the carpeted floor inside. 'Still think I'm playing fucking games?' he demanded, wedging the shoe back on. He methodically snapped off the remaining shards of glass and reached through the window frame, grasping for the latch. Simple. Traditional. No security lock. No problems. Jack cackled at how easy it all was. 'So much for rural renovations, you stupid bastard,' he gloated, pulling the redundant window frame open and clambering inside.

It was hot inside; hotter than the night. The thick stonework, of which every wall in every room in the ancient building was comprised, was in the process of slowly surrendering the heat it had stored during the day, and – upon his tumbling, stumbling entrance onto the carpet by the window – was quick to stoke Jack's already raging fury.

'Shit!' he growled, picking himself up off the floor and

getting unsteadily to his feet. He rested against a marble-topped table and his eyes fell on a framed photograph of David the day he'd received his OBE. 'Other Buggers' Efforts,' Jack muttered. He then stared closer and the curl of his lips straightened into doubt. The face was the same. The clothes and haircut different. The expression, one that Jack had never worn: contentment. But the physical features: identical. His brother. His twin. His face. His doppelgänger. He looked closer, and chagrin swept over him. There, in the background, out of focus, was a blurred image that haunted him every day, tugging him back from the future, forcing him to face the lost opportunities of the past. There she was. Rachel. His brother's wife. Standing behind David, the man she'd once loved. 'Oh Jesus,' Jack whispered, knowing that it could so easily have been him instead.

He swept the silver frame onto the broken glass on the floor and lurched out the room into the hallway. Here, he halted by the towering Welsh dresser and his eyes fell on the fax machine and telephone system. He counted the flashes of the red message indicator of the answerphone: four. Tut, tut, David, he mentally admonished, pressing the wipe button with a degree of relish. Not listening to your messages when you get the chance . . . He looked at the single transmission hanging lifelessly from the fax machine, then ripped it free, recognition raising a rash in his cheeks immediately. He read, his lips muttering the words, his brain pouncing on certain phrases, certain names: 'TO: David Jackson, FROM: Leonora Smiles. RE: Today's meeting with Jack Jackson . . . went much as expected . . . incredibly mercenary and grasping . . . the termination of his contract was concluded with a minimum of fuss and financial inconvenience . . . I trust this arrangement is satisfactory . . . He finished reading and screwed the paper up in his fist.

He marched through the hall, through the empty sitting and dining rooms, through the kitchen, then back and up the spiral stone staircase to the first floor. It was here that the renovations described in the *Sunday Post* piece sprang to life. Jack hadn't set foot in this place since the night of Rachel's birthday. But the memories of the evening became fuzzy now, disconnected from reality, dreamt.

The room the staircase terminated in, once the home of a snooker table and all its accompanying paraphernalia, was now a period showcase, some interior designer's contrived interpretation of a fifties family room. Period furniture and fittings. A stack of period board games. Even a ridiculously archaic gramophone. A technology-free zone. A snug shrine to family values, conversation and civility. It could have been hauled straight from one of David's novels, conjured from the kind of Britain that no longer existed, that had probably only ever existed in David's head. But this was what David's readers loved: this tourist-board Britain, the same mythological country those two backpackers had crossed the globe to experience for themselves. They'd discover the truth soon enough, assuming they didn't get mugged and hospitalised first, that is. But they wouldn't discover the real David. He'd never give them the opportunity to see behind the humanitarian mask, into the elitism beneath. Jack stared round a final time. The hypocrisy of it all made him want to vomit.

He spun from the sight and stormed down the corridor, ignoring the guest rooms, knowing from the various articles that had chronicled David's lifestyle that the only place still unexplored that he could possibly be in was his bedroom, his study, one and the same. He'd be in there now. Ignorant of the phone messages. Ignorant of the fax. If these articles were to be believed, he'd currently be sitting before his computer, headphones on, his creativity being fuelled by Wagner. Ignorant of his unwelcome guest's rapid, rabid approach. Ignorant of the truths he was about to be forced to listen to. Ignorant that he was about to pay his debts in full. Ignorant.

Jack threw the door of the bedroom open in triumph, only to collapse to his knees in tragedy.

David hung suspended by a bright red rope from a shiny brass hook in the ceiling, the tips of his bare toes touching the carpeted floor. Inches away from his feet was a tiny footstool, eternally out of reach. One arm hung loosely at his side. The other was crooked at a right angle, its hand clawed uselessly beneath the tightened noose around his contorted neck, frozen. The women's underwear that clothed him – suspenders, laced knickers and bra – matched the deep red of the rope and the deep red of the lipstick which covered his lifeless lips.

Hyperventilating uncontrollably, as if his accelerated consumption of oxygen might reverse the result of asphyxiation before him, Jack stared through streaming eyes. At his brother. At his brother's face. Beneath the make-up. Into the horror. Into his own face.

CHAPTER THREE

sold out

It was night in the West End of London.

From the back seat of a black saloon car, she watched the twenty-eight-year-old Mick Roper, dressed in club gear, swing the black cab door shut, jam a note into the driver's outstretched hand, step across the swept section of pavement and nonchalantly stroll between the two immaculately-attired bouncers who stood solidly like classical statues either side of the entrance to SlipSlide.

She rattled off some instructions to her driver, then exited the car and watched it blend into the slow procession of vehicles moving as if in tribute up the street on which SlipSlide was sited. She put on her spectrum-tinted Soulsearcher shades, gently patted her gelled, Twenties-style hair, crossed the street, and sauntered past the turning heads of the bouncers who surveyed this hermaphrodite of fashion with the body of a woman and the clothes and demeanour of a man.

SlipSlide was Mick's preferred nocturnal haunt of late. Aside from a two-week trip to Amsterdam one month previously, he'd indulged himself with the many amusements offered by the club and its self-consciously metropolitan clientèle on at least one evening each week since he'd made his inaugural visit between Christmas and New Year.

He flexed his way through the throng of city slickers, media types, wannabes and minor celebrities towards the back bar, pointedly ignoring the barely concealed gestures of recognition aimed in his direction, as well as their accompanying stage whispers. His observers didn't seem to mind.

Since they obviously knew who he was, they would have been just as obviously disappointed if he'd spun uncharacteristically to face them and gone on to introduce himself with a self-deprecating smile and beckoning arms. No, the brooding show of sullenness was Mick's predominant public trait, his social signature. They turned back to one another in his wake, loaded with fresh fuel for conversation. He hadn't disappointed them. He'd acted just like one of the streetwise protagonists from his books, thrown off the same enigmatic aura his screaming fans adored when he fronted his band, Ego, or appeared on television promoting one or other of his many product lines.

If truth be told, SlipSlide wasn't populated by Mick's kind of people. Mick's kind of people featured in his books, his records, and his videos. They were junkies, prostitutes, criminals: the kind of people who took him at face value and rarely looked any deeper. The kind of people he could afford to relax in front of. The same disenfranchised social set he'd encountered, known and dumped in Amsterdam.

But SlipSlide's nocturnal tribe were a different brood altogether. They were either the type of people who actually bought his books, records and associated merchandise or they were the type of people who had it in their power to manufacture and promote the stuff. And the defining difference between the two categories in Mick's mind? Serfs and royalty. Treat the former like dogs. Feed them carrion and wait for them to come panting back for more of the same. But treat the latter like dogs and wait for them to bite your hand clean off. That was what Mick's manager, Link, had warned him. And when Link spoke, Mick listened. Yes, he had to be careful in an establishment such as this. One way or another, his whole career depended on it.

And what a career it was. Way too meteoric to burn out just yet. Mick smiled. Way too meteoric to burn out just yet. He liked the sentence. It was one of Link's. Mick had used it in an interview on Radio 1 the previous week. It had been quoted in the press the next day alongside Mick's name. Not that Link had minded that Mick had passed it off as his own.

Link was good about stuff like that. He had a soundbite for every occasion, a whole dictionary of the damned things. He was clever with words, so he could afford to give them away. Like the lyrics he wrote for Mick's songs. Mick didn't understand half of them himself and he was the one who sang them. But the critics loved them. What was it that guy in the *Guardian* had said? That Mick's lyrics were enigmatic, that he was a master of paradox? Something like that. Shit, he'd even gone on to compare him to Jim Morrison and Bob Dylan. But that was cool; Mick didn't understand their lyrics either. 'Without you,' Link had told Mick, the one time Mick had been worried about someone guessing that he hadn't written the lyrics himself, 'my lyrics would just be words on a piece of paper. You're the one who breathes life into them.' Just words. Link had been right. It was the same with Mick's books. What did it matter who'd written them? Without him, they were nothing.

He'd been discovered four years earlier by Link. Link was his mentor, his manager, his agent. And unlike his distant, long-lost relative, he wasn't missing, was always there: solid, unbreakable, a reassuring constant in the fluid world of currency and fashion in which Mick lived. It was Link who'd always provided the connections Mick had needed. It was Link who'd formulated the strategy that had brought Mick his success. It was Link who Mick owed everything to. And it was Link who Mick was here in SlipSlide to meet. Business, of course. Where Link was concerned, all social interaction was business. As far as Mick could tell, Link knew no other way.

Mick reached the bar and flipped his Soulsearcher shades – the trademark of which he shared ownership with Link – like a visor up onto the top of his shaved head. The studied, idiosyncratic gesture of professional impatience identified him as a thirsty consumer to the nearest bargirl. As she approached him, he lowered them again, so that she was faced with dual rainbow reflections of herself as she took his order and mixed his suitably esoteric cocktail. He remained unforthcoming and monosyllabic throughout the transaction. This was something else Link had taught him. The only way that people might end up suspecting that you're not all you're cracked up to be is if you say too much. Keep what you say short and keep it vague. Let them read into it what they want. Don't go shattering their illusions by saying too much. And it worked. It had got Mick through all his interviews unscathed. The bargirl handed over his drink and his change and he lit a St Moritz, walked away from the bar and down the stairs to Level 2.

The music was louder here, the people wilder. As a result, he drew fewer stares. Fewer, certainly, than he would have wished. Because one thing Mick Roper not only craved but demanded was recognition. Call it a habit. Call it an addiction. It was something he'd grown used to, something he took for granted when it was there – forgetting quite how high it was getting him – and something he only missed when it was . . . missing. Halfway down the stairs, he stood like a god and observed the Brownian motion of social creatures for a moment. Raised above the masses, he waited for those who believed in him to bear witness to his arrival, his coming.

His eyes probed the crowd, assessing the bright young things, any one of whom might be fortunate enough to experience a night of passion they'd never forget if that was what he chose. Aside from a twentysomething, coyly bespectacled hunk of Iberian extract, there was no one worth more than a cursory inspection. And the Iberian boy was with a girl, hand slipped into the back pocket of her black synthetic trousers, knuckles sporadically flexing in the motion of surreptitious, sensual massage.

Not that this public show of affection bothered Mick. He'd always found that those already captured were the most eager to escape. On another night, in another city, he was certain, the boy could have been his. But he wasn't in a position to become involved. Not this night. Not in this place. Not somewhere so public, so far from the anonymous backstreet brothels of Amsterdam. Boys were off-limits now that he was in the UK, had been so officially for the last two years, since an in-depth market research investigation instigated by Link's Policy Unit had shown that seventy-eight per cent of his end-users were heterosexual teenage girls. Of course, he'd learnt to cope with the situation. It just limited his choice by half. As a temporary measure, until the research stats changed – and Link reckoned it was only a matter of time before bisexuality was hip in the mainstream again – it was no big deal to put up with.

He forced his eyes from the boy to the girl he was with. She turned and Mick noted that, beneath the spray of red hair, her profile was passable. But combined with the clothes, the make-up, the hair . . . she did nothing for him. Unoriginal. Dressed by the magazines she read, the shops she frequented. Way too normal. Way too suburban. Getting photographed with her would be nothing short of embarrassing. He shook his head in disgust. She didn't deserve the Iberian, didn't even deserve to be in the same room as him. And likewise, she didn't deserve Mick's attention now. He turned his head, straight ahead, and walked the last remaining stairs.

'Mick!' a conventionally ecstatic female voice called as he reached the bottom of the stairs. 'I know this is totally embarrassing,' the female voice continued into his ear, 'but—'

He noticed a familiar face at a table near the bar and waved a dismissive hand in the direction of the unseen owner of the voice – a mosquito-swatting motion. 'Sorry, love,' he mumbled as he walked towards the table. 'I don't do autographs. No one does these days, you know.'

The sharp contours of the wrinkles on Link's face flattened beneath his thick, ponytailed hair as Mick moseyed through the mingling bodies towards him. The grey, carefully unkempt stubble on his cheeks and chin seemed to align in recognition. His grey eyes sparkled, like wet slates framed in a burst of sunlight. Their pupils shrank. His lips withdrew across his capped teeth, the photogenic diamond, embedded there for all to see by a Harley Street specialist, sparked once, twice, then vanished as his lips slunk down.

His swollen body remained impassive throughout this brief social flirtation, right down to the fingers whose habitual position perpetually threatened to cut off the life of his diminishing cheroot, but never quite got round to delivering the *coup de grâce*.

Mick watched Link's recognition ritual with the same familiarity that he recognised the man. He'd witnessed it countless times before. Up and down the nation. Out and about throughout the media industry boardrooms of the globe. A glimmer of warmth, a taste of generosity, flashed in the face, then swallowed deep, hankered after, always there to be striven for, like a grail. The promise of something deeper, something worth fawning for. A guard-dropper. It was what Link was all about. Mick sat down opposite him and decommissioned his St Moritz in the ashtray.

'You're late,' Link said, pirouetting his wrist from beneath his jacket sleeve and scanning the luminous face of his watch.

Mick retired his Soulsearchers onto the top of his head, pulled his pack from his pocket and threaded another St Moritz between his lips. 'Late, but still great,' he said, winking disarmingly as he torched the end of the cigarette.

The column of ash on the end of Link's cheroot collapsed silently onto the table. He brushed it away onto the floor. The diamond glinted once more as he smiled. 'You're looking good, Mick.'

Mick searched the bar for the Iberian, but bodies blocked the view: nobodies. 'Guess so,' he said, looking back at Link. 'Guess I should do after a morning spent working out and an afternoon of massage and steam baths.'

'How's the new batch of steroids working out?'

Mick ran his hand across his cheek. 'Tops. As the acne advert goes: vanquish spots, stay velvet smooth.'

'And the headaches?'

'Better. Less often. Nothing a few pills won't take my mind off.' He rested his hands on the table and clenched his fists. He looked down at the textbook definition of his bare arms, their veins taut, like buried cables. 'And the weight gain's running according to schedule. Adding fresh meaning to perfection every day, Louise says.'

'Louise?'

'My new trainer.'

Link examined his buffed nails and enquired, 'You fucking her?'

'On and off.' Mick smirked. 'Got to give all my muscles a fair share of the workout, haven't I?'

'Nothing serious, then?'

'No.'

'Good. You know what I think about you and relationships.'

'You don't, yeah? You don't want to think about them at all.'

Link stared at him. 'That's right. And I don't want you wasting time thinking about them either. There'll be time enough for that kind of crap when you're an old fart like me. And more to the point—'

'Yeah, yeah,' Mick sighed. 'And if I go getting hitched record sales will drop to rock bottom and the people who buy my books will think I've sold out and become a boring piece of shit overnight.'

Link sucked on his cheroot. 'That's good. At least you've been listening to what I've said. You're getting used to thinking business. Keep on doing that and you'll get everything you want.'

'Just like you.'

'Spot on, son. Just like me.'

'So who's this bloke then?'

'What bloke?' Link said, looking round.

Mick clicked his fingers for attention. 'The one you want me to meet. The guy who works for Murphy.'

'Ah,' Link said, his tongue darting out reptilianly to moisten his lips. 'You mean my illustrious acquaintance, Pete Gott.'

'That's the one. What's his story? What's he offering?'

'Excuse me, gents,' Sean interrupted. The barman was holding a tray with two fresh drinks on it. He nodded in the direction of a nearby table, where a woman, dressed in a dinner jacket and black tie, with hair plastered down like a monsoon victim, sat facing them, her expression unwavering, a challenge waiting to be taken up. 'The lady over there asked for them to be sent over.' He smiled reservedly at the quaintness of the notion as he placed a double vodka before Link and a fizzing green broth before Mick.

Mick held the glass before him, examining its colour in the dim, calculated atmospheric lighting. He sniffed at it with the same tentativeness another man might reserve for the finest wine, then sipped, padding his tongue on the roof of his mouth as he swallowed.

Sean, sensing his satisfaction, recited the ingredients, 'An iced citrus cocktail: two parts lemon isotonic, two parts bitter lemon, laced with a single gin charger. The lady was quite specific about the proportions. Does it taste right?'

'Whoever she is,' Link said, squinting over his shoulder at the woman, 'she seems to know what your taste buds are into. Even got our Soulsearchers on the top of her head.'

Mick flirted with addressing the anonymous drink donor, but dismissed the idea. It wouldn't look good. More to the point: saying nothing would look better. His eyes flicked from her to Sean. 'I don't recognise her. Who is she?'

'She didn't say. She said she'll be in The Basement later on, if you want to find her.'

'Might be a fan,' Link ventured, still squinting.

'Nah,' Mick said, studying her again, keeping his voice clear, letting her listen. 'Too classy. Too hot. I can feel her from here. She's *someone* all right.' A thought burst in his mind. 'Not foreign, is she? Not Dutch by any chance?'

'No,' Sean said. 'Definitely British.'

Link gave up and turned his attention back to his drink and cheroot. 'Well, I don't recognise her.' He snorted derisively. 'No one in the business, that's for sure. I mean, Christ, what's she wearing?'

'A tux,' Mick said, ignoring the snub, slipping Sean some cash and raising his cocktail to the woman. She raised her glass in return, unsmiling. 'She looks kind of cool. Twenties hair-fix. Can hardly tell if she's a guy or a girl.' He continued to examine her, muttering to himself, 'Best of both worlds.'

Link coughed intrusively, unhooking the invisible nylon of Mick's psyche from her ice blue eyes. 'Anyway, that can wait. For now, just concentrate.'

'Sure. What were we talking about?'

Link rolled his eyes, exasperated. 'Pete Gott. Murphy's man. The one we're here to do business with.'

'Yeah. Pete Gott. What's Gott got? What's he got for us?'

Link balanced his cheroot on the ashtray. 'You're gonna like this one,' he said with a smile, interweaving his fingers and flexing his knuckles. They crackled like distant gunfire. 'A neat piece of work. All the joints fix exactly into place. Just like nature intended.'

Mick drank. 'So what's the score?'

'Gott's being moved in to head Boast Records along with the rest of Clover Group's UK operations. It'll hit the papers next week.'

'What about Saunders?' Link indicated Saunders' fate with a downturned thumb. Mick shrugged. 'Who cares? He was a tosser, anyway.'

'Gott's American. A troubleshooter. Rumour has it that Murphy's lining him up to head Clover Group International a few years down the line when he retires. Saunders isn't anyone any more. Finito.' He gave Mick a few seconds to take this information on board, then moved on. 'I had lunch with Gott yesterday. Sharp guy. Fed me a load of PR crap about Clover's expansion and then spun his pitch.'

'Which is?'

'The way he sees it, we're happy with our recording contract with Boast Records. Phenomenal sales. Good back-list promotion. The works.'

'Tell me something I don't know.'

'OK,' Link said, the wrinkles on his face hardening like a geographical relief map, becoming rough terrain. '*He*'s not happy with things as they stand.'

'You what!' Mick scoffed. 'That's bullshit. Sales are

phenomenal. That's what he said, yeah?'

Link's voice remained steady. 'Calm down. He just means that things could be better, that's all.'

Mick lowered his Soulsearchers and clawed his fingernails across his scalp. 'How so? My last three albums have cashed in straight at Number One. Countless awards. The crits can't get enough.' His top lip curled unpleasantly. 'Fuck it. I don't need to justify myself. How the fuck could things possibly be better?'

Link stretched across the table and placed a placating hand on Mick's bare shoulder. 'He's not just interested in your music. It's the books, too. Music and books. The double whammy. Music *and* books.' He leant back, smiling broadly, smoke funnelling from his nostrils in a victory signal. 'Like I said, Clover Group are expanding. Aggressively so. You probably only know about their music interests: Boast, Stylus, Xen. And their TV and newspaper companies. And so did I. Until yesterday, that is.'

Mick was smoking furiously now. 'Come on,' he encouraged. 'Quit with the details. Get to the point.'

'Another prediction for the financial pages in next week's papers: Clover Group Completes Successful Acquisition of Thomas Prandle Publishers Ltd.'

Mick shrugged, lighting a new St Moritz from its dying predecessor. 'So Murphy's getting into books. So what?'

'Think about it,' Link said with a sigh. 'You've got one more book left to deliver to your editors at Renaissance House; the second in the two-book deal. And thanks to some skilful negotiating by me when we drafted it, there's no option clause in the contract. Not that that would have stopped us for long anyway. But as it stands, if we want to move you from Renaissance to another publishing house, there's nothing to stop us from doing just that.'

'To Thomas Prandle, for example.'

Link smiled. 'Good. Now you're with me. But it's not just for example. It's for fact. Gott talked figures. The advance he's offering for a three-book deal is fantastic.'

'How many zeroes?'

'Six. The million. Up front. All on signature. No bullshit.'

Mick sucked air in. 'Big money,' he eventually got out.

'Exactly,' Link said, clinking his drink against Mick's. 'Welcome, once again, to the big time.'

Mick smoked and drank, overawed beneath his Soulsearchers. 'How come so much? What did you say to him? You hold a gun to his head, or what?'

'Much as I'd like to claim otherwise, I didn't say anything. The offer was flat, up front, non-negotiable. Pure. And who am I to argue with a perfectly rounded number like that?'

'But why so much? Renaissance paid us peanuts next to that.'

'The way Gott sees it, it's a bargain. The massive amount of money Clover Group are already spending on Boast Records' publicity campaigns for your albums can now work twice as hard. If they sign you up as an author as well as an artist, then the publicity generated through your music will be able to give you the sort of exposure no author has ever had. Rationalisation. Pure and simple.' He chuckled. 'Shit. Who knows where it will stop? The marketing possibilities for an author with a fan base like yours and the corporate support to stage international advertising campaigns makes the mind boggle. A few suggestions Gott made:' he continued unabated, 'book stalls at your gigs; extracts distributed via the Ego web-site; symbiocity – the simultaneous release of thematically complementary books and albums. And this is just the beginning . . .'

'Big money, then,' Mick deduced.

'Yes,' Link said patiently. 'In other words, big money.'

Mick called for a waiter, ordered duplicates of what they'd just finished. 'Just the beginning,' he toasted when the drinks arrived. 'My name in lights, twice as bright.' Then his expression fell.

'What is it?' Link asked.

'That guy,' Mick replied, preoccupied, facing the bar where a suited man was interviewing one of the bargirls whose head was bowed in deference. 'Fat bastard over there.'

'Tommy Rhodes,' Link informed him. 'I'd watch your mouth if I was you. Bit of a hard man. Owns the place. Ran the gangsters off the turf when he opened it. Used to front a band back in the Seventies. Unimaginative title: Guitar. Quit while the going was good. Pretty much finished off Seventies culture when he did.'

'Best thing he ever did,' Mick said without irony.

'Maybe,' Link said, rapt in his study of Mick's troubled face. 'So what's bugging you? What's your problem with him?'

Mick's brow furrowed. 'You know those autographs behind the bar downstairs?'

'Sure. Who doesn't?'

'Well fat lad over there wouldn't let me sign it. I asked a few weeks ago and some flunky told me no.'

'Did he say why?'

'No, but after I'd asked him about ten times, Rhodes came and spoke to me himself. Said I was a puppet. A nothing with connections. Said I sold my fans shit and laughed about what suckers they were.' He faced Link. 'Told me I was only in it for the money, or what money other people could wring out of me.'

'So what? Ignore him. The way I remember it, he made a packet. How else could he have afforded to set this place up? Hypocritical piece of shit.'

'He said his motives were different. Said he did it for the music as much as the money. Said he respected his fans.'

'Fuck him,' Link spat. 'What does he know? He'll be paying you to put your name up there once this deal's taken off.'

Mick shook his head demonstrably. 'No. He'll beg. No one talks to me like that and doesn't live to regret it.'

'Forget Rhodes,' Link said sharply, raising his substantial body and waving in the direction of the stairs. 'They're coming, so think about the money and get that smile back on your face. And remember,' he said, fixing his eyes on Mick, 'keep your mouth shut unless I tell you otherwise. Concentrate on looking sharp and leave the sharp talking to me.'

Mick craned his neck and saw a man walking towards them. It was, he noticed as he drew nearer, Rupert Savage, Vice President of Boast Records. Boast Records had Vice Presidents like mice. Notoriously so. During their brief lifespans, they scurried around frenetically for a year, maybe two, until the next whizz-kid stepped in. Then the trap snapped shut and they weren't worth their weight in cheese. Mick made a mental note of this state of affairs, a flag designed to periodically pop up in his mind signalling red, lest the alcohol, and accompanying chemical compounds, which the night would surely serve his way, should confuse his brain into concluding that this no one was in fact a someone whose opinions and very presence should be, for reasons of potential financial gain, tolerated at the expense of his mood.

As he reached the table, Rupert Savage creaked forward on his brogued feet and raised a manicured palm into the air. Mick, still sat, high-fived him, vaguely uncomfortable that this was, perhaps, yesterday's greeting. Link shook hands and pulled Savage a chair. Mick slumped back without so much as a syllable of sociability and lit a St Moritz. He drew deep and exhaled, listening to the idle laundering of gossip between Link and Savage, waiting for the real players to arrive and remind him what an incredible star he really was.

Mick saw the woman in the dinner jacket later, downstairs, through the wall of glass which bisected The Basement. She was dancing with another woman, three or four inches shorter than her. They weren't touching, just teasing. The other woman swayed slowly, high, unconcerned about the sex or sexuality of her dance partner. The combination of alcohol and soundproof glass cast the situation out into the surreal, their movements and those of the assembled dancers making them appear to be in various stages of suffocation. His eyes connected with hers over the distance and he watched her leave the girl, move to the staging door and enter the main bar. He caught glimpses of her moving in his direction, but then the crowding bodies buried her, so that he couldn't tell if she was inches or yards away from him, whether she was in earshot or had shot off altogether.

He was sitting at a table with assorted members of his future business personality portfolio. There was Rupert Savage. And there was Pete Gott, an American abroad, beautiful and articulate; everything you'd expect from someone who'd been given a free hand in orchestrating the economic and strategic future of an international corporation. Accompanying Gott, from the moment he'd joined them in Level 2 a couple of hours ago, was Kate Johnson, Clover's International Marketing Coordinator. Gott and Johnson were sharp. Even Mick could tell that much. Maybe they were even as sharp as Link. Mick hadn't taken any chances on this score. He'd done exactly as he'd been told. He'd sat back and listened, let them peer into his Soulsearchers and assume that something profound was ticking over in his brain.

Over the past hour, the double act of Johnson and Gott had reiterated their pitch. Link had smoked his cheroots, drunk his vodka and flashed his diamond encouragingly throughout. Mick had got a kick out of it for the first half-hour or so; he could listen to people talking about him all day. But then they'd moved onto a lot of talk about royalties and other details that Mick wasn't too interested in. He'd concentrated instead on Link, nodding whenever Link nodded his assent to the various proposals and projections put before them, leaning back in his chair whenever Link had objected to something. At one point, though he couldn't be sure, he'd even dozed off for a couple of minutes. But now the business was over, and the conversation, like most conversations over the last week, had turned to the murder of Adam Appleton. Mick didn't read the papers much, only the reviews that Link cut out for him, and all he really wanted to do now was kick the night off with a wrap of coke in the gents, move on from here and have some fun.

'What I'd love to know,' Link was saying, drunk in the aftermath of the deal, 'is how much the *Chronicle* paid for the copy of the typescript found at Appleton's house.'

'The way I understood it, it was leaked to them anonymously,' Johnson said.

Link sighed. 'Of course that's what they'd say. They'd have to, wouldn't they?'

'Either that or be forced to give the name of the cop who sold it to them,' Savage agreed.

'Exactly,' Link continued. 'And they'd hardly do that, would they? That typescript, or confession – which is basically what it is – is the only evidence they've got to work on. Apart from that and the bloody mess of Appleton upstairs, the place was left spotless: no fingerprints, no witnesses, nothing. The police must be livid. With stakes like that the *Chronicle* would have to protect its source.'

'There's one witness,' Johnson interjected. 'There was the estate agent. She met the killer. She was going to take her round to Appleton's on Monday. Only the killer brought the appointment forward a day . . .'

'Yeah,' Link said, 'but she wasn't much use. Said the killer was wearing shades, might even have been wearing a wig. No, all they've got now is the typescript.' He stared at the glowing end of his cheroot in meditation, eventually saying, 'They haven't got shit to go on. That's why no one's been arrested.'

'It might not have been a cop who leaked it at all,' Johnson said. 'And it might not have been done for money.'

'Who else could it have been?' Link scoffed. 'The police were the first on the scene. Amazonia Skray called them from a phone box and told them the score and they were there in minutes. And as for it not being done for money . . .' He laughed encouragingly at the others: 'What the fuck else is there?'

'Skreen,' Johnson said. 'Her surname's Skreen.'

'Whatever,' Link said. 'What does it matter what her name is?'

'So what's your theory, Mick?' Johnson mediated with professional ease.

Gott and Savage turned to look at Mick and Mick glanced at Link for guidance.

'Yeah, Mick,' Gott encouraged. 'Give us your view.'

'Some pig sold it on,' Mick muttered. 'Like Link says. It makes sense, yeah?'

'But what if Skreen leaked it herself,' Johnson suggested. 'That makes sense, too.'

Mick was confused. He regretted not having followed the conversation more closely. He looked to Link again, who nodded slowly at him. It was a signal Mick knew of old. It said, *Don't commit to anything. Keep things loose. Keep them open.* 'Everyone's entitled to their own opinion, you know,' Mick settled on. Link smiled at him, so Mick went on, 'It's tough to be certain about anything these days. You've got to be sure before you go committing yourself to one particular view.'

'But if you had to commit yourself to one view . . .' Gott said, his clear eyes shining, his California-ripened skin wrinkling.

Mick adjusted himself in his seat, stared across the room, so that his profile could be admired by the new players who were here to observe their recent acquisition – Gott on his left and Johnson on his right. 'No one ever has to commit themselves to anything.'

'OK, then,' Gott said patiently. 'But let me put a question to you. Why did she kill Appleton? What was her motive?'

'Maybe she's just a nutter,' Mick hazarded. 'Probably doesn't even know why she did it herself.'

'But what about what she's saying about art? I'm interested to know what you think about that. You're a writer. Do you agree with anything she's saying?'

Mick clicked his tongue. 'Like I say, she's a nutter, so it's not like I'm going to go agreeing with her, is it?' Mick stared at Gott, realised he wanted more. 'Look, so she's into art, right? Prepared to cut some bloke up over it, right? Well, that's just bullshit, you know.'

'You feel strongly about your writing, though, don't you?' Gott persisted.

Mick shifted uncomfortably in his chair. 'Sure.'

'Strong enough to kill for it?'

Mick didn't know what to say to this. All this stuff about art and murder was doing his head in. He felt his skin beginning to burn. This guy Gott was getting on his nerves. He foraged about desperately for a reply, let slip the first of Link's soundbites he came across and hoped that Gott hadn't read the *GQ* interview it had appeared in only a week before. 'My art comes from inside. It comes from life, not death.'

Gott nodded slowly and Mick sat back. In the corner of his eye, he saw Link smile.

As the conversation moved onto speculation over whether Skreen would be apprehended before she struck again, Mick excused himself and moved off. He'd done his bit: made the right noises, smiled the right smiles. And as for that soundbite. Just perfect. He'd done more than enough. Besides, the deal was sealed and Gott and Co. were boring him senseless. He was now off duty. Off with the old persona, on with the new. It was time to relax and have some fun. It was time to get high and get laid. He'd earned it.

His nose aflame with the afterburn of powder, Mick located her on the other side of the glass partition. She wasn't dancing this time, but was sat on a high metal stool at the bar, her back straight, her clothes, in spite of the dancing he'd witnessed earlier, immaculate. She watched him approach, staring him down every inch of the way, almost in chastisement, as if she'd been waiting for him all this time and he was now intolerably late. The intensity of the stare intimidated him, even through the armour provided by his Soulsearcher lenses. It was a signal his erratically wired brain was unable to translate. Aggression or lust. Maybe both. Maybe neither. He sat on a stool on her left, ordered his unusual usual, and turned to her and said with all the dispassion he could summon in the face of those stinging blue eyes, 'Name your poison. We'll come to your name later.'

'Water.'

He raised his eyebrows in mild surprise at the unexpected

reply her low, sensual tones had emitted, his Soulsearchers shifting slightly on the perfectly straight bridge of his nose. 'Ice?'

'No. Just water. Still water.'

'Runs deep,' he muttered, pleased with the thought. 'Water,' he told the barman. 'Plain water.' The barman brought the drink. 'Put that and mine on Clover Group's tab,' Mick told him. 'And take a tip,' he added magnanimously. 'Whatever you think right.'

The blue-eyed woman sipped the water, then raised her eyes. 'Clover Group?' she queried.

'They own the record label I'm signed to.' He smiled arrogantly, the same smile he always imagined millions of teenage girls weeping over in their sleep. 'I doubt they'll mind a few freebies taken on a bar tab. Besides,' he added with a conspiratorial lowering of his voice, 'we've just concluded some business. They'll be pleased to pay.'

'Congratulations,' she said, returning his smile.

He lit a St Moritz, offered her the packet. She shook her head. 'Very sensible,' he said after a deep inhalation. 'They'll be the death of me.'

'Everybody's got to die some time. It's probably preferable to choose the method yourself than have someone else take the choice away from you.'

'Yeah, whatever.' He removed his Soulsearchers and placed them on the bar next to where her pair lay. 'Snap,' he said, then peered without inhibition into her eyes. 'That's incredible. They're real.'

'What are?' she asked, unblinking. 'The Soulsearchers?'

He shook his head. 'Your eyes. When I saw you upstairs when you sent the drinks over – and thanks, by the way – I kind of assumed you were wearing coloured lenses. I mean, that blue's just so . . . bloody blue. It doesn't seem natural.'

'I'll take that as a compliment.'

'Christ, yes,' he laughed. 'And I don't pay them often. Only when I mean it.'

'That's good to hear. Honesty's such a rare attribute nowadays.'

'Your name,' he said. 'I still don't know your name. I'm Mick,' he added with an outstretched hand. 'But I guess you already know that, because of getting my drink right upstairs, and because . . .' The arrogant smile resurfaced. 'Well, everyone seems to know who I am these days.'

'I'm no exception,' she admitted. 'You can call me Diana.'

'*Can* call you Diana?' he queried. 'You make it sound like it's not your real name.'

'Does it matter whether it's real or not? We hardly know each other yet. What difference is a name going to make at this point?'

He shrugged, puzzled. 'Dunno. None, I suppose.'

'Anyway, I like Diana. I like strong names.' As if to emphasise her point, she slipped her white gloved hand into the one he'd proffered her and squeezed with a force which surprised him, then released him, leaving him with the aftermath of pressure on his palm, the aura of her touch. 'I remembered the drink from some article I read in one of the Sundays. When I saw you upstairs, I wanted to see how you'd react to one being sent over.'

'And did I react as expected?'

'Yes: you didn't react at all.'

He laughed again. 'So, are you a fan, or what?'

Her mouth slid into the beginning of a smile. 'I've read your books and listened to your music. Does that make me a fan?'

'Depends on what you thought of them.'

'I thought about them. They made me think long and hard.'

He flexed his arm muscles subconsciously, let the soundbites flow. 'That's why I write them: to make people think. If my writing helps people to make sense out of their lives, then I feel that I've achieved something. It makes all the effort worthwhile.' He looked at the two pairs of Soulsearchers. 'You've got to have what it takes to want to wear these.' He picked her pair up and examined them. 'Class design.' He returned them to the bar. 'They suit you.'

She stared into her glass. 'Am I to take that as another compliment?'

He waited for her to look up, then held her eyes, contentedly this time, thankfully accustomed to their strength. 'Like I said, I only pay them when I mean them. Take it as read: I like what I see.'

She held her glass to her lips and tilted it back. When she'd finished, she dismissed it to the bar with a blink of finality and put her Soulsearchers on. As her eyes disappeared from view, he felt somehow as if the lights had been turned off, as if a meeting had been concluded successfully and the time had now come to move on. She ran her tongue over her lips, absorbing the gloss of moisture the glass had left behind.

'Well, Mr Roper,' she said, sliding off her stool, and taking his Soulsearchers and threading them onto his head. 'I think we both feel the same way about what we want to end up doing tonight.' She took his hand and led him away from the bar. 'But for now, let's just dance.'

With his hand grasped firmly in hers, she took the lead into a neglected corner of the dance floor. It was almost as if it had been designed for intimacy. The lights which swept, strobed, or fried the rest of the social arena, somehow missed the small area she now stopped in. It was a blind spot, an escape route highlighted by its lack of lighting. It felt safe, out of sight, out of mind, as comforting and secure to Mick as his Amsterdam haunts. He stood for a moment, observing the relaxation on her face. The reflection on her Soulsearchers transmitted silent films of shifting limbs, torsos and heads, shuddering, swaying, and pumping like automatons in the concentrated styles of the times. But there, behind the chaos, was her face, constant and assured.

The music throbbing from the carefully sited speakers was hardcore postmodern, a mix of television and film samples, coupled with contemporary rhythm and anti-melody. It left the body with no option but to translate into motion what was going on around it, to signal its allegiance to the familiar through its movements one moment, only to be left hanging, deserted and confused the next.

'Yesterday's sounds!' Mick shouted as the track began to fade down to zero.

Another track of the same genre began and he screamed, running away from Diana to the hole in the wall that housed the hidden DJ. Then his angry gesticulations subsided to familiarity and he removed his Soulsearchers, thrust his hand through the gap, threw his head back in laughter, and jammed the Soulsearchers back in place. With the dialogue completed, he headed back to her. Just before he reached her, the music cut to an unprofessional audio vacuum and an announcement, cramped by reverb, echoed through the ears of the suddenly self-conscious crowd which found itself deprived of aural camouflage and its implicit motivation towards motion by the unnatural silence which now enclosed it.

'Due to popular request!' the DJ boomed. 'Or rather, due to a single request by a friend of mine whose popularity knows no bounds . . . I give you the latest club anthem from . . . Ego!'

The screaming was deafening. But the link between the switch in music that followed and the presence of its singer went unnoticed. The people just danced, ignorant of their animator's locality. Entranced, they didn't have the will to look further than the immediate space in which they moved.

When he began to dance again, everything about him was fluid. Seamless. It was impossible to identify the moment one complicated series of steps flowed into another. Her own movements bowed to his technical superiority. She took second place to him, kept her steps to an instinctive interpretation of the sounds that filled the room, leaving the limelight to him alone in this dim corner of the dance floor. He sang the words live, overwhelmed by the recording that played, drowned out by his own fame.

Several tracks later, the tempo of the music descended to something more intimate. She placed her white gloved hands on to his arms, seeing the shadows alter on his skin as his muscles tensed. She gripped his cosmetic strength, running her hands down over his biceps and elbow, eventually settling with a knitting of her fingers between his. Apart from a gentle swaying of his hips, he remained a statue, enjoying her enjoying him. Real pleasure filled him: the pleasure of being worshipped. She moved in closer, released her left hand, clamped her right hand tighter around his left. Her left hand stroked down his waist onto his thigh and slid behind, pulling him powerfully into her, so that they joined, his hips still swaying, beginning to grind against hers. They moved tightly like this, cemented to one another, for an electric period of time, and then she let go of his hand, and broke the seal between their waists. Unzipping his flies, she thrust a rummaging hand inside. Pushing hard against him once more, she grinned and took his hand from where it gripped the small of her back. Their Soulsearchers sparked off each other, absorbed, and she led his hand through her own flies, guided it inside.

'You should always let the left hand know what the right hand's doing,' she said into his ear, letting the rhythm of the music encourage the natural motions of their bodies.

He said nothing, enjoyed.

When the next song died, she separated them. 'Shall we leave?' she asked. 'I'm ready to move on now if you are.'

He nodded, fumbled with his trousers, and then she set off with him around the perimeter of the dance floor to the staging door. In the brief moment they stood inside the soundproof chamber, while a bouncer shut the door to the dance floor behind them and another opened the hermetically sealed door to the main bar of The Basement, he said, 'I've just got to say goodbye to a few people. They're pretty boring, but you can meet them if you want.'

'No,' she said, as they entered the bar. 'I've already met the person I want . . .'

He took her wrist. 'All right, then. I'll meet you outside in five minutes.'

Diana was standing several yards from the entrance to SlipSlide when she saw Mick Roper walking down the street towards her four minutes later. She gesticulated wildly, slammed her hand onto the cool steel bonnet of the car and waited for Mick to sprint to her aid.

'What's the problem?' he asked, breathless beside her.

'Unlicensed cab,' she said. 'He says twenty, I say ten.'

'Where are we going?'

'My place. Fulham.'

He nudged between her and the car. 'Ten,' he said, dropping his head to the level of the car window, and nearly lifting it straight back up again when he saw the vastness of the driver.

'Fifteen,' the driver said. 'No less.'

'Done,' Mick said, opening the door. Diana climbed inside and shuffled along the back seat, feeling the pressure of his body next to hers. 'But at that price, I get to choose the music,' Mick stated, handing over an unmarked demo tape.

'One of yours?' Diana asked.

'Just something I was playing around with in the studio at the weekend. Let us know what you think.'

'That's the reason I'm here.'

The driver grudgingly took the demo tape, inserted it into his machine, flicked a switch, and pulled away from the kerb. 'That's good,' Mick said, stretching his arms across the back of the seat, nodding his head appreciatively to the music, draping a greedy arm across Diana's shoulders. 'Make me proud. Nice and loud.'

They drove through the streets of London for twenty minutes, no one speaking, listening to the music and staring out of the windows at pedestrians who only saw their own reflections in the tinted glass. They were sealed in, totally severed from the world through which they drove.

She looked at the side of his head bobbing a stunted interpretation of the music. The music which filled her ears was generic, a compound of other sounds around. It was original only through its ruthless lack of originality. It was corrupt, infected by the stench of popularity. There was nothing admirable or pure about it. There was no art, merely artifice. It was just like his books, just like him. It was diseased.

'Next left. By the off-licence,' she told the driver. They rounded the corner. 'Right. To the end of the street and then take a left.'

Houses flowed by on either side of the car. Mick felt good, alive, like he was in one of his videos.

'Next left,' she continued. The car slowed for the turn and drove down a wide, unlit alley which ran between the backs of two streets of houses. The headlights bobbed over the rough surface, picking out stones, picking out grit. 'Here. Into the yard.'

The car scrunched to a halt and Mick peered out at the assorted urban detritus that had been dumped in this uncared-for place: old mattresses, broken pallets, festering, swollen black bin liners. To the left was a brick building, its windows boarded over. Above its door a sign, reading DANCE HOUSE, hung at a crooked angle. Totally uninhabitable. He turned to Diana, unable to control his surprise.

'You live here?'

'No, Mick, I don't live here.'

He sensed motion in the front of the car. The music collapsed into silence. 'Then why?' he laughed.

'I don't live here,' she repeated, her voice, like her face, swept of emotion. 'This is where you die.'

The driver spun round, a silhouette Mick had seen a thousand times in a thousand movies extended from his hand, the barrel pointing into his face. He looked at the driver. The driver just smiled stupidly back at him.

'What the fuck is this?'

'Haven't you guessed yet?' she asked.

'Guessed fucking what? Do you know this head-case? What kind of crap is this?'

'That's no way to talk when someone's pointing a gun at you, Mick,' Diana advised.

Mick looked back at the driver, at the gun he held unwaveringly – professionally. Loathing was rising inside him. This bitch had stitched him up from the first. It was a shake-down. Pure and simple. They'd featured in his books enough times. And now they were leaving the page, striding towards him, ruthlessly seizing him and splitting his skull in two. He held his breath, counted to five. He exhaled, trying to keep it calm. He inhaled, trying to keep it cool.

'You want money?' he asked. 'Is that it?'

'No,' she said, 'what I want is going to hurt you far more than money ever could.'

'If it's not money, then what?' Mick demanded, suddenly aware that the charisma in his voice was waning, like a muscle that had been flexed in an unnatural position for too long. 'Look, I can get you as much as you want. Just tell me. How much?'

Her voice flatlined. 'I want you dead, Mick. Dead, buried and forgotten all about. I want you exposed for what you are, pegged out in the sun to dry.'

His voice faltered. 'But why? What have I done to you? What the fuck is this all about?'

'It's not what you've done to me, Mick. It's what you've done to the world. It's what people like you and the people who control you do to the world every day. I've got to set an example. You've got to be taught a lesson.'

He reached for her arm and gripped it viciously. But in spite of his strength, the action was a feeble one. His voice pitched into a whine. 'But I don't understand. Be reasonable, for fuck's sake . . .'

'Let go,' the driver said, prodding the gun roughly into Mick's temple. 'Do it now!'

Mick slumped back, mumbling.

'That's all right, Mick. Don't let it get you down. There's no need for you to speak any more. It's not like it was with Appleton. People had to hear what he had to say, hear it from his own lips, because his was the voice they'd believed in the past. But you're different to him, Mick. No one's going to care about your words once they find out you didn't write them. It's your image that they'll be forced to look at, the extent to which they've been suckered in. Hype, Mick. Hype and greed. A scam. That's all you've ever been. And once I've got rid of that, nothing's going to be left. They're going to hate you, Mick. Just like they're going to hate themselves for having believed in you in the first place.'

'Appleton?' Mick coughed out. His stomach had slumped, a landslide. Nausea had risen with his pulse. It couldn't be. No. Never. Not him. Not . . . her . . . His eyelids flapped beneath his Soulsearchers. Keep it cool. Jesus Christ. Make it go away. Keep it cool. He spoke slowly: sickening syllables, sounds tumbled out. 'Appleton?' he asked again, even though he didn't want to say the words, didn't want to hear the answer, but knowing now that their expulsion was inevitable, just like he knew that saying them meant that the situation was real, the game over. 'Adam Appleton?'

Diana slowly clapped her hands and watched Mick push back against the door and fumble desperately for the handle. He tugged pointlessly at it, his breathing irregular, adrenalising into hyperventilation.

'Locked,' Diana said as he gave up and turned shaking to face her. 'Child-locks.'

'You're her,' he wheezed, pointing an arm at her. 'Amazonia Skreen. You're her.'

'Yes, Mick. Different name. Same nightmare. And you're over.'

'Fuck you!' he gasped at her, then rounded on the driver, his voice exploding into a scream: 'And fuck you too! Let me the fuck out of this car!'

'Congratulations, Mick,' she said over the hissing of breath which followed his outburst. 'You've caught up with the action for the first time this evening. You want out of the car. I want you out of the car. We've reached a concord.' She turned to Tup. 'If he so much as looks in the wrong direction once we're outside, shoot him in the head.'

'Uh-huh,' Tup said, his finger flexing eagerly over the trigger.

'You heard that, didn't you, Mick?' she checked and once he'd nodded, told Tup, 'You can let Mr Roper out now and escort him over to the Dance House. And remember what I said. If he gives you any trouble, kill him.'

Tup opened the door and backed slowly out of the car, not relinquishing Roper from the sight of the gun for a second, mesmerising him with it as he circled round the metal hull to the passenger door up against which Roper was wedged.

'No fucking way,' Mick said. 'I'm not going out there. I'm not going out there with him.'

The door clicked open behind him. 'You don't have a choice,' Diana said.

'He's going to kill me.'

'He will if you don't do as you're told.'

'He'll kill me!' Mick shouted.

Diana shifted across the back seat, grabbed Mick by the shoulders. 'You shut it. You shut it now or the last thing you're going to hear is a bullet entering your head.'

'He'll kill me! You want me dead. He's going to—'

Diana pulled her head back, then released, butted him in the mouth. She watched the blood break free, flood the gullies of his teeth. A silver slither of tear trickled down his cheek. 'We all want things, Mick,' she said, once it was apparent that her action had defeated his voice. 'All it comes down to is what we're prepared to do to get them. Now get out.'

'Move,' Tup growled, jabbing the gun into Mick's spine.

'If you want to live a second longer,' Diana warned him, 'you'd better just do it.'

Mick shifted in his seat and, with his chin lolling against his chest, shuffled out of the car and stood next to Tup.

'That way,' Tup said, jolting him with the cold metal of the gun and pushing him in the direction of the Dance House.

Diana joined them at the door to the building. 'This place should interest you, Mick. It's an old dance studio. Quite exclusive in the early Eighties, before the recession hit. Or maybe you're too young for that. It doesn't matter. You'll be able to relate anyway. They specialised in pop video routines. Boy meets girl. Bright clothes. Dull lyrics. Standard, superficial stuff. You should feel right at home.'

She switched on the torch she was holding and, keeping her body close to smother the burst of light, traversed its beam across the chapped and blistered paint of the warped wooden door, until it picked out the starlight glint of a padlock. Her thumb rolled across the wheels of numbers until they aligned into the correct combination, and then she slipped the loop of metal free and forced the creaking hinges of the door back.

'Inside,' Tup grunted.

She followed Mick and Tup through the doorway and, flipping the door shut with her heel, continued down the hall, the torch beam skittering along the dusty ground by their feet, a sheepdog marshalling its flock. They passed doorways leading to changing rooms, the jock-strap scent of which not even the best part of a decade of neglect had managed to fumigate.

'Walk to the centre of the room,' she told them when they reached the end of the corridor, showing the way with the torch into the wooden-floored gymnasium. 'That's it, Tup. Sit him down at the table. Tell him to be good.'

'Shut it and sit,' Tup interpreted, placing his weight on Mick's shoulder, squashing him into a chair at the heavy wooden table, holding him still.

'That's good,' Diana said, placing the torch on the floor and striking a match, walking the perimeter of the room, stroking the long match across candle wicks which lay on trays around the room, melting them into life.

In her wake, light burst across the room, illuminating first corners, then the whole. The floor stretched forty foot square. In the centre was the table at which Mick sat. Tup stood sentry at his back. Above them were metal beams, locking the damp plaster in place, stopping the rotting roof from tumbling down and revealing the cold night sky. And across the walls were mirrors, bordered by exercise bars, so that no matter where she looked as she pursued the circle of illumination, she saw herself, flickering and surreal . . .

When the candles were lit, she returned to the table and sat down opposite Mick. She looked above Mick's head, where two looped wires hung from pulleys attached to the roof's supporting beam on the ceiling above the table. Then she looked back at Roper. His mouth was open, a thin crack. Spittle was clumped in sticky patches in its corners.

'Look at the table, Mick,' she said and watched his head obediently tip down. 'Look at the mirror on the table and tell me what you see.'

'Can't you just—'

'I don't need suggestions, Mick. Just accuracy. Observation. I just want you to tell me what you see.'

'Nothing,' he said, staring into the mirrored surface. 'Nothing but my own reflection.'

'Good. That's what you're meant to see. An image. That's what I see when I look at you. That's all there is.'

His head didn't move, didn't dare address hers. 'Are you going to let me leave?' he mumbled. 'I've done everything you said. Are you going to let me go?'

'Not yet Mick. All in good time. The night's young. There's plenty of fun to be had before the dawn.' She reached beneath the table and lifted a small plastic package, placed it on the table before her. 'Look up, Mick. Look up and tell me what you see.'

He raised his head. 'I see a bag.'

'Not just a bag, Mick. A life. There's enough in there to take you as far away from this place as your mind can travel.' She pulled a penknife from her pocket, snapped a blade free and drew it across the surface of the plastic. She licked the tip of her forefinger and dabbed it inside, then reached across and held it in front of him. 'Would you like to taste?'

Something inside Mick's mind began to itch. She sensed it wriggling its body through the bars of the cage of pressure which held him taut, scratch at the lens of his Soulsearchers, push itself flat in an attempt to burst through. His hand flexed into a spider. 'I'll take that as a yes,' she whispered, stretching her arm further forward until her finger touched his lips and his tongue flicked out and met it, leaving a sheen of saliva and blood where the powder had been. 'That's good. Get it in your blood. It's the only way forward left for you to take. It's the only way to ease your fear.'

He stared across the room at the mirrors on the wall and she took a packet of Rizlas from her pocket and licked them into a parcel which she filled with powder and sealed with a stroke of her tongue.

'Now take it and swallow,' she said, pushing it across the table.

He stared at the parcel. 'There's too much. It'll—'

'Your choice, Mick. That or the gun. Name your poison.' She gazed at him patiently. 'Surely it's better the devil you know.'

'An overdose or a bullet,' he said slowly. 'You call that a choice?'

'A bullet's final. Believe me. With this, who knows? You might get lucky.'

'My throat's dry.'

She reached across the table and nudged the parcel forward a few inches. 'So find some spit.'

Mick picked up the parcel and inserted it between his teeth, clamped his jaw shut. She waited for his throat to bob and his mouth to open, his breathing to become stable again.

'All we have to do now is wait.' She sat back and stared. 'And then we'll see just how high someone as low as you can get.'

It wasn't long before whatever light had previously burned inside Mick slowly began to power down and graduate towards the shut-off point. She watched it in his face, as all expression faded, leaving nothing behind but shadow and space. She looked across at the mirror on the wall, at the other her and other him that existed on the other side of the glass. And she remembered another mirror in another time in another place.

The moment she'd stood in that alley and read the first page of the typescript that Appleton had secreted in the bottom of a bin, she'd known that he was only one of many. It was back in her room that night, as she'd finished reading the typescript, placed it next to her own already many-times rejected work, and stared into the mirror on the wall, that she'd heard the voice for the first time. It had told her that if there was one, there would be others, and that if she wanted to find them, she only had to look. It had told her that if anyone should be the one to hunt them down, it should be her.

Roper had as good as targeted himself. With his face frozen on billboard posters and magazine covers, fluid on TV and videos, his voice squealing from radios and venues across the nation, he couldn't have called to her any more clearly if he'd tried. His hype had acted like a perfume: she'd known that something so potent and artificial could only have been there to disguise something base.

It hadn't been difficult to track him down. A quick survey of the events columns in the music press had pointed to the Power Record Store, where he'd be performing a three-song set, to be followed by a major book signing and promotion.

'So lemme hear ya!' Roper had shouted through the microphone at the pack of bobbing teens and twentysomethings wedged up against the small stage constructed at the back of the ground floor of Power, blocked from encroaching any further by a leather-jacketed security crew armed with muscle to pin them back and water sprays to cool them down. 'Fast-track it!'

And, as the mixer had upped the pace, they'd matched Mick's gesture of punching his fist into the air and called back as one, 'Fast-track it! Far-strack-it! Farstrackit! Farstrackit!'

She extricated herself from the crowd and pushed her way to the back, no longer able to stomach the hypnotised generation in whose midst she'd been swamped, sickened by their ecstatic belief that being here in Roper's presence made them part of a legend, and that by being part of a legend they too were part of something historic, something that was going to pass the test of time, something truly great.

'Books!' she shouted over the noises at a man in an Ego T-shirt who was standing behind one of the cash tills.

'What?' he shouted back, not taking his eyes off Roper, not dropping his raised, clenched fist from the air.

'Books! I'm here for the book signing! Where is it?'

He reluctantly leant forward, lowered his arm. 'You say you wanted books?'

'Yes. Mick Roper's books. He's meant to be doing a signing.'

'Yeah, yeah, I know,' the man said, looking back to the stage. 'Over there,' he said, pointing vaguely to the left. 'Through there at the back. They're setting things up for him now.' Then his attention switched, his fist flew triumphantly upwards again, and he bellowed out, 'Farstrackit!'

She walked round to the section he'd pointed to. There were racks upon racks of books, displayed cover-up like compact discs, ordered alphabetically. Most were music orientated: biographies covering icons from jazz to jungle, collections of lyrics, anthologies of rock journalism and the like. But there were novels, too. Mostly the kind you'd expect in such a store – an eclectic mix of post-war cult works by various photographers, designers, hipsters, beatsters, drug addicts and alcoholics. She walked from Z to C and there the alphabet cut short. A and B were missing. In their place a space had been cleared and jammed with a spectrum of Roperesque paraphernalia: a Soulsearcher stand, posters, T-shirts, badges and Ego tour jackets. There were also books, about four hundred copies of Roper's new novel, *Doing Nothing Well*, ordered in stacks on either side of a wide desk. On the wall, the fluorescent lettering of a sign read, LIFE SUCKS, SO SUCK IT BACK.

A young, smart-dressed woman and an older man with a ponytail were sitting on the front of the desk, their legs gently swinging, quietly conversing. She recognised the older man's face from an interview she'd seen him orchestrate on TV, where he'd sat next to Roper and blocked any unrehearsed questions the interviewer had asked, cut Roper short whenever he'd begun to flounder. He went by the name of Link. It had been watching that interview that had confirmed in her mind that Roper was a phoney. Link had acted more like an intellectual bodyguard than a manager. As she'd watched the recorded footage again and again, it had become obvious that it was Link and not Roper who was the brains behind the operation. Roper was a marketing tool, nothing more. Yet people worshipped him and publishers promoted him more than almost any other writer alive. It made no intellectual sense. She'd read his books and lyrics. At best they were mediocre. This wasn't what people were buying when they handed over their money. They were buying Roper himself, they were buying into the image they'd been sold. It couldn't go on like this. She wouldn't allow it. It was the sustenance of people like Roper that edged people like her into the unread margins of the page. With Roper exposed and eradicated and the realisation forced on the public that this wouldn't be tolerated any more, the centre of the page would be left to others more worthy. She moved along the row of C books, observing the man and the woman over the top, then halted and made a pretence of flicking through a book of S&M photographs.

By the time the music in the next section had halted and sustained screaming and applause had broken out, she'd discovered all she'd needed to know. The woman talking to Link was Roper's publicist from Renaissance House. And it was her, not Roper, she'd come for.

'Get ready!' a security guard shouted from the end of the section, standing aside as Roper was shuttled through by a unit of leather jackets.

She returned the S&M book back to the rack, turned and fought her way in the opposite direction to the people flooding the room. She secured herself a space at the back and observed the obsequious circus, her eyes focused on the publicist throughout.

Later, she'd tracked the publicist across town to Renaissance House and then it had only been a matter of sitting in a café opposite and waiting for her to re-emerge. She didn't want to think about the details of what had happened in the woman's flat later that night. They weren't important. The woman had been a minor player in this deceit, an insignificant soldier in a wider war. At least it had been quick. Faced with Tup and the barrel of a gun, the woman had confessed within seconds that one of Renaissance's editors was the real author of Roper's books and that Roper himself was as good as illiterate. She'd paid the woman back for her honesty by cutting the interrogation short. The police had found her body the following afternoon floating down the Thames, a bullet lodged inside her skull.

Before her now, here in the Dance House, Roper's metamorphosis was nearing its completion; his mental weakness had manifested itself in his physique. He was slumped forward across the table. His fingers twitched involuntarily, and his breathing came in short, asthmatic pants, framed by a mouth stretched into an agonised yawn. Drool lay in a pool like glue, locking his chin to the table's surface. The rest of his body was flaccid. It was as if someone had slit the skin of his back, delved a powerful claw inside and stripped his spine free from his flesh.

Diana looked into the mirrored surface below her and examined the ceiling's reflection. Her eyes followed the path of the two hanging wires, up over the pulleys on the beam directly above Roper's head to where they stretched down through the air and joined at a single pulley fixed to the exercise bar screwed to the mirror on the wall behind Mick's back. In the candlelight, the wires shimmered like spider's threads.

'Put the gloves on,' she told Tup. 'The heavy ones I gave you. Then fix the wires around Mick's arms.'

Tup took a pair of industrial gloves from his pocket and slipped them over his hands. He then reached into the air and pulled the first wire down. He lifted one of Mick's arms and drew the wire noose over its wrist and adjusted his grip to tighten it.

'No,' Diana said. 'Put it above his elbow and pull it tight behind the bone.'

Tup loosened the noose and shifted it up Mick's arm. He glanced at Diana to check that it was correctly positioned and then drew it close. The wire bit into the skin, breaking the surface, leaving a circlet of blood to seep from Mick's muscle. Mick's head briefly spasmed on the table, then became still again.

'That's enough for now,' Diana said. 'Do the same to the other arm.'

Diana reached below the table and produced a piece of white card. There were two punched holes in its top corners and a piece of string ran through them. She put it on the table before her and reached her gloved hand across the table and wiped her forefinger through the pool of blood that had collected around Roper's elbow. Pulling her hand back, she carefully smeared the blood across the card until a letter was formed, and then she repeated the process a further five times, until a complete word was constructed. She got to her feet and placed her hand over Mick's scalp, lifted his head and hung the freshly painted sign around his neck. She looked up at Tup.

'He's ready now,' she said. 'String him up.'

Tup crossed the floor towards the pulley on the exercise bar and leant down and picked up a thick length of rope which was tied to the end of the wire. He pulled it round his waist, gripping it on either side of his body and began to walk slowly back towards the table. The slack collected quickly and then Tup flexed his legs and began to take the strain, moving back slowly now, as the weight at the other end of the wires began to shift.

Behind him, Diana watched Mick become animate. His elbows leapt to the perpendicular and his head bobbed. Then he began to rise, the blood that had seeped from his arms before, now running freely, splattering down onto his front and legs as he was lifted to his feet, a force that was nothing to do with him suddenly in possession of his body. The wires behind his elbows had disappeared from sight now, sunk into the flesh, coiled around the bone. And still he continued to rise, his elbows now above his head, his whole body dancing as Tup continued his progress backwards.

When he drew level with the table, he stopped and simultaneously Mick's ascension ceased. Tup slowly slid the rope free from behind his back and set about tying its end to one of the table legs. When the knot was tight, he released the rope, and the table shifted loudly an inch or two across the floor. Then it stopped and the only motion came from Mick's feet, which performed an erratic series of kicks as the blood dripped from his shoes through the air and onto the floor below.

And there, suspended in the air, Mick's senses returned, revolted against the draining of blood, and his voice rediscovered projection. First it came in incoherent mumbles, and then it rose into a sustained growl, then pitched higher and higher still until the dying thoughts hidden beneath his Soulsearchers, stabilised into a note, a scream that wouldn't stop.

'Puppet,' Diana said, reading the sign around Mick's neck. 'The show stops here.' She glanced at Tup, clicked her tongue and listened to the hydraulic phut of the gun as it was fired. Then she examined what was left of Mick's head. The left lens of his Soulsearchers had been reduced to a single shard. The gulf left in its place was bloody and raw. As with Appleton towards the end, Mick's appearance did little to recommend the human condition. Perhaps the legion of ingenues who'd read his words with open eyes, heard his music with open ears, would now comprehend that they'd been deceived into idolatry. Roper's beauty had been transient. And now it had been dissolved into the base elements from which it had been formed, all that remained was revelation, all that remained was truth. *Clack*: art is beyond marketing. *Clack*: art is the god that can only be feared.

Tup grinned at her and said, 'Dead meat.'

'Yes, Tup,' she confirmed, putting her Soulsearchers into her pocket. 'Now put the gun away and let's get out of here. Even the sight of this man makes me sick.'

After a final look at his handiwork, Tup did as instructed and followed Diana from the gym, down the corridor and out to the car.

'Computer?' he asked, once he was at the wheel, looking keenly back at where she sat in the back.

'Yes, well remembered.' She took the laptop from him,

opened it up on her knees, and booted it up. 'Now drive,' she told him, the fluorescent screen casting a shimmering halo around her head.

Ten minutes later, as they drove through sleeping, sober suburbs, her fingers began to clatter across the keyboard:

She watched from the back of the black saloon car as Mick Roper arrived at the right place at the right time. It was what she'd expected. People like Roper had no autonomy. Their intelligence was artificial. They ran according to their programmers' wishes. They'd continue to run this way until someone had the sense to pull their plugs. Just like the clothes he was wearing, just like the shades that hid his drugged eyes and the drugged mind behind, he was a construct, an image, the product of a sick designer's imaginings. Personality accessories, designed to fool the casual observer into believing that these trinkets were stimulating parts of a stimulating whole. Only she wasn't fooled. She saw the superficiality of this creature. She saw the trinkets and muscles and clothes as they truly were: a shell. And she saw what the shell was there to conceal: emptiness. She watched him walk into SlipSlide. Shells were fragile. They were the simplest of things to smash.

CHAPTER FOUR

grave decisions

The pungent aroma of earth, carved like cake in sodden slices from the ground the previous evening by cold steel spades, and left to bake and crumble throughout this day, the hottest of this summer of legendary temperatures, perforated the membranes of Jack's nostrils. It was a smell that, predictably, would always remind him of death, and of regeneration, too.

He looked at the freshly dug grave one final time, and turned to walk to the hired car parked on the other side of the small South London cemetery. He wanted to slip his jacket off, allow the light breeze to evaporate the slick of sweat which clogged his cotton shirt. Anything to alter the environment he found himself trapped in, give him a temporary parole.

Elderly and distant relatives swayed like scarecrows at staggered intervals. They trickled out commiserations, tears and occasional, tentative touches on the shoulders and lapels of his sombre black suit. The friends of the deceased kept to themselves.

As he covered the final few yards and watched the chauffeur extinguish his cigarette with the absurdly polished heel of his polished black shoes and swing the back door open in rehearsed preparation for his arrival, Jack saw his reflection, stretched and unfamiliar in the waxed black paint. He felt as though he was staring into a stagnant pond and remembered himself the day before, before he'd left the house and driven up to London. He'd shaved carefully, as he'd shaved for the last few days, always remembering not to harvest the defined area reserved for the idiosyncratic, strictly rectangular sideburns which now adorned an exact two inches of his jaw line. And he'd plucked his eyebrows remorselessly, divorcing the united front of his monobrow into two distinct, thick curves.

When he reached the car, he ducked inside and pulled the door into him with a thud, forgetting for the first time that day (that month, that year) the woman behind him who, left stranded beside the chauffeur, began to walk around to the other side of the car. Inside, Jack breathed in the luxurious conditioned air. It felt like water pouring down his throat. He craned his neck and stole a glance at his head, or, more precisely, at the top of his head. The fringe was gone, the length of black hair substantially severed from front to back. Totally conservative. He remembered the prior reservation and subsequent regret that had accompanied the snapping of the scissors. But he'd gone through with it anyway, knowing how important, even vital, it was that he looked presentable for inspection. He remembered the chauffeur's cigarette. He craved nicotine. Just one drag – one utterly selfish, disconnected moment of relief. But again, it wouldn't have been right. Like removing the jacket outside, it wouldn't have been appropriate. More to the point: it wouldn't have been him. And appearances were everything. Especially today.

Hearing the click of the door on the other side of the back seat, suddenly exposed by a burst of sunlight, scolded by a sauna of heat, he sat back and stared into the uniform leather upholstery of the passenger seat before him.

'You haven't lost any of your vanity, then,' the woman said as she slid into the car beside him and heaved the door shut after her. 'Still checking the mirror to see if you're still there and not too good to be true.'

He didn't turn to face her, didn't deign to reply. No matter how he felt, he knew it was the right thing to do. Instead, he listened to her breathing until the chauffeur got in. And then, as the car set off, he leant his clammy forehead against the window and closed his eyes.

★ ★ ★

He'd stayed there on the floor, staring at his brother's dangling corpse, for seconds, minutes, maybe hours. He didn't know how long. Time had been relegated by circumstances to irrelevant detail. It had passed him by completely.

Eventually, his breathing became regular, a hissing metronome in his ears; and time imposed itself once more. He got to his feet, the excessive movement, after so much immobility and introspection, causing his guts to violently somersault. He lurched forward and vomited on the carpet by the footstool adjacent to his brother's bare feet. Doubled-up, he vomited again, the acrid whisky and bile burning his throat and nostrils, reminding him of the turning point of a thousand bachelor evenings. He continued to retch long after his stomach had been fully evacuated. He vomited gulp after gulp of air.

He stared at the technicolor gruel which curdled on the carpet, and then lurched from the room, stumbling down the corridor, clawing at the walls on either side of him for support, until he reached the bathroom. Flopping over the edge of the bath, he turned the cold tap on and stuck his head beneath it, letting the liquid wash his face clean, waiting for the warm water that had been trapped in baking pipes all day to be sluiced away, waiting for the cold subterranean stream to surface and shock him out of inertia, wash him away with its current into sobriety.

He turned the tap off and stood upright. The water which had crept through the gap between his collar and his skin trickled down his spine. Too much had happened for it to cause him to shiver. He walked to the basin and stared at the mirror. He looked like a drug addict. Worse, he looked like an actor camped up to look like a drug addict: he looked too bad to look real. Black circles enclosed his eyes. Fresh phlegm, generated since the baptism provided by the tap, filled the pit between his lower lip and his chin. It shone like plastic in the weak bathroom light. Its message: overdose. He looked like a corpse. He looked worse than David.

He'd read of such things in the papers . . . a politician

here, a judge there. In these voyeuristic articles, there'd been accompanying diagrams, pictorial descriptions of how the dead had been found. Like David. It was as if the scene Jack had just encountered was a three-dimensional display, the emotive centrepiece from a psychology seminar. A cliché leapt to prominence in his mind: *always those you least expected*; always those you considered impervious to perversity. That's what the public would think when they found out. And though Jack had always known of David's darker side, his wildest imaginings had never led him to dream up a scene like this. David was a hypocrite. Jack knew that. Puritanical on the outside, rotten at the core. A writer of novels stacked with moral integrity, but a man who indulged in destructive manipulation at every opportunity. But not this. Never this. David's destructiveness had always seemed to stem from his desire for self-elevation. Not self-debasement. Never that.

But that was what this was. David hadn't committed suicide. His feet were too near the ground. They'd been cheated of their safe landing by miscalculation. The red rope had been tied too short. Less than an inch. But enough to end a life. Or it had been too strong. It was meant to have snapped and had failed in its purpose. Or the knot had been too tight; it hadn't slipped when David had.

But whatever the reason for the bungle, the climax of the thinking that had brought David to this end hadn't been misery. The climax had been climax itself: orgasm. Jack remembered more from one of the articles: how it was possible to induce orgasm via semi-asphyxiation. He remembered the accompanying trivia, how orgasm was often the last action of those hanged, how even at the moment of death the urge to reproduce raged on. He hadn't believed it at the time, had asked around his friends for validation. But he believed it now. What had probably been the orgasm of David's life had brought with it that same life's climax: death.

Accidental death. The underwear only served to confirm this conclusion. Jack had read about that too in the papers. People had told cheap jokes about it. Journalists had realised political capital and drawn moral and ethical conclusions on the state of the nation. He'd repeated the jokes, sneered at the political analysis which hadn't interested him. Then there was the make-up: cheap, vulgar, sluttish. The perfect anti-ideal. It was the vehicle of disgust in which cleansing could be guaranteed, orgasm achieved. Had things gone according to plan, David would have achieved orgasm and simultaneously killed what he despised. He'd have been left clean, without blame.

An automaton, Jack returned to the bedroom and drew back the thick purple curtains, reaching for the window and pushing it wide open, hoping for a breeze, cold and clean, finding nothing but the unsympathetic silence of a sleeping world. It was to be expected. Normal. Why should it be otherwise? What was one more death to the outside world?

He turned quickly, employing the determination of the motion to puncture and deflate the horror which threatened to balloon inside him once more. But then his eyes locked on David and his mind took off and, before he could stop it, tapes inside his head were reeling back over the years. He found himself thinking of David as a child. Not the antithesis he'd become. A brother. A fellow human being. Stills from photographs he remembered swept into motion. Memory reasserted itself as having really happened. Days at school. Afternoons with Mum and Dad. Weekends with David. Moments long before he'd seen David's lips seal against Emily's. All the episodes that time had eroded into incomprehensible sand, indigestible solids lodged in his gut, now came swelling up. A trap-door opened somewhere inside him and his emotions fell out. He began to cry. Just tears. There was no noise. He had nothing to say; there was no one to speak to. Suddenly, beyond the view he held of his brother, deeper than what he knew he should feel, there was grief. It was instinctive, built into his circuitry, like pain. The power to dismiss it wasn't his.

And in that moment, he made his choice. He wasn't going to let David be found in this state. He'd make it look like suicide. He'd make sure no one ever found out what

David had been doing when he'd died. David was dead. It was Jack who was going to have to live with this. It wasn't about revenge any more. If he left David like this, Jack wouldn't only have become as sick as him, he'd have become worse. He'd have become scum. He'd have become everything David had always said he was. No, Jack couldn't run from this. If he did that now – if he ran to London and waited for someone else to find the body – he knew he'd be running for the rest of his life.

He surveyed the room and settled on the chair by David's writing desk. It was strong, secure, capable of holding his weight and giving him the added height and platform he'd need. He carried it to the centre of the room and put it down next to the footstool, repeatedly glancing up then down again, making minute adjustments in its placement until he knew he could procrastinate no longer.

Standing on the chair, beside his brother, Jack's head nearly touched the ceiling. Fighting the claustrophobia that gripped him, dismissing the thoughts of giants in fairy-tales, trapped in tiny rooms, dwarfed, he looked around. From where he stood, he had a clear view of the brass hook and the tight loop of red rope which girdled it. He pinched it between his fingers and flexed his muscles, channelling his strength to the tips of his fingers. It wouldn't budge. He dropped to his knees for added leverage and pushed upwards, trying to slide it free again. It moved this time, slightly. With the dead weight working against him, he continued to push, shifting it upwards gradually, then quit; his strength was sapped.

Straightening up, his arm brushed lightly against David's body. He flinched, pulling his arm back as if he'd suffered a bite or a burn. He turned his head and felt the now familiar swoon of nausea rise up against him. The touch of his arm had been enough to animate the suspended weight, so that it now spun slowly to face him. Again, he found himself face to face with David. But there was nothing in the eyes but flesh. There was nothing to fear.

Shuddering, he pulled David into him. They embraced.

Lowering his shoulder, he hauled his brother onto it. Warily, he straightened his back, cautious not to overbalance, until he could reach his free arm up to the brass hook. The rope slid easily now that the slack with which it had originally been attached had been restored. It flipped off the edge of the hook and dropped down over David's back, so that it swung like a pendulum beneath Jack's hypnotised eyes. With steadily directed coordination, he stepped from the chair and carried David to the bed, where he lay him down and released his dead arm which clung pointlessly at his dead neck. He then sat on the edge of the bed, waiting for the relative clarity of five minutes previously to return.

He found what he was looking for in one of the drawers of the dressing table. As soon as he'd seen the key sticking out of it, he'd known that this was the place. Inside was the make-up. Like the underwear, it was cheap. Make-up remover and tissues were there, too. He returned to the bed and began to clean David's face with remover-soaked tissues, wiping relentlessly, sucking in the petroleum fumes, until all that was left was his own reflection. He touched his hand against the cold skin of David's cheek, then unfastened the noose and slung it across the room.

David's limbs were stiff, naturally inanimate and consequently unhelpful, as he stripped him. He carried the soiled underwear to the bin. A pile of discarded clothes lay on the floor on the other side of the bed. These were what David must have been wearing before he'd changed his clothes and his life for ever. They were, therefore, what Jack would tell the police his brother had been wearing when he'd discovered him and got him down.

The thought stopped there. The police. He dropped the sock he'd just picked up. What the hell had he been thinking of? The police, for Christ's sake! He'd have to call the cops. They weren't stupid. They didn't just accept what they were told. They'd carry out an investigation, scour the place, search for clues, piece it all together. And if they did, they'd know. They'd know something wasn't right . . .

He wheeled round and pulled at David's chin. There,

below the jaw, was the bruising: black, swollen, and violent as an eel. Who was to say that it hadn't been caused by manual strangulation? He looked at the untied noose on the floor. It wasn't even a noose any more, just a piece of rope, a rope that could have been used to . . . The police would draw their own conclusions, reconstruct events as they saw them. He thought of the broken window and picture downstairs, of the forced entry and betrayal of rage. His own hands appeared before his face, as the police would see them . . .

He looked back at David's contorted face. What would they think? What would anybody think? That David Jackson, at the height of his fame and success, of renowned sound mind, had committed suicide? No way. Or that his brother, Jack Jackson, on the day he'd been fired from a company owned by his twin, and been arrested for throwing one of his brother's novels at a police car, was a murderer, a strangler, someone who should be put away for the good of society, for the good of himself?

So where did that leave him? That left him with the truth. He could tell the police the truth. He could tell them exactly how he'd found David, exactly why he'd interfered, exactly what David had been wearing, let them deduce for themselves exactly how he'd died. But who was going to believe the truth? Who was going to believe that David Jackson was a pervert, a closet transvestite? No one, that's who. There was even less chance of the police believing that than there was of them believing that David had committed suicide. And as for putting the underwear back on, attempting to reapply the make-up, recreate the whole scene and then run . . . It was hopeless.

Jack opened his eyes and lifted his forehead off the car's window. He glanced at the chauffeur and then turned to face Rachel. Her head was leant against the opposite window, as if asleep. But her eyes were open. She was looking over the driver's shoulder, letting the London streets and traffic wash over her, embalm her like a drug.

She was still beautiful. Her hair, the colour of stripped

pine, was tucked behind her ears and curved across the skin of her neck, jutting out below her chin. He watched her long eyelashes sporadically sweep together, mesh.

Perhaps she was even more beautiful now than the evening he'd met her, the same evening he'd watched impotently as David had flirted with her at the publication party for his first novel, *Marriage Vows*. It was a party that Jack had been invited to along with his mother. David hadn't wanted him there for company, but alongside the novel – with its emphasis on the sanctity of marriage and family life – the presence of David's family had been a matter of pragmatism. Rachel had been David's editor. Jack couldn't have spoken to her for longer than five minutes. But even now, though he'd forgotten the words she'd spoken, he could remember the event with intense clarity. He could remember the way he'd felt – the way she'd made him feel. He could remember the hope she'd opened inside him. He could remember the beginning of love.

Back then, before David had destroyed her, she'd been an idealist. Young. Bright. Burning. Someone who the future had been beckoning impatiently with open arms. She'd believed in David's writing. She'd taken his words – his insistence on a return to strong moral values – at face value. She'd seen a man who was going to help to steer the world in a better direction. And Jack couldn't blame her for this. She hadn't been one of the family then. She hadn't yet learnt to distinguish between genuine articles and fakes. How could she have guessed that David couldn't have cared less about the values contained in his book? How could she have known that the only direction David had wanted to steer the world in was towards himself?

Getting published was the worst thing that could have happened to David as far as Jack was concerned. Publication had been the endorsement that he'd been looking for. His right to influence the minds of others had been confirmed and with it his ego had been unleashed, freed from the confines of his social circle, sent snapping into the public domain. His first novel had, according to the critics, been art, and had contained a remedy to moral decline. But Jack had known different. David had never been a moral creature. His first novel had been pure cynicism, a way in, a camouflaged crowbar, nothing more noble. David had given them what they'd craved, a philosophy of nostalgia, an escape from the misery and pressure of the modern world. He'd given them honest characters, performing honourable deeds and receiving just rewards, because he'd known that they'd then turn to him, that they'd then begin to worship and adore. In just the same way that they still did.

But nobody close to David stayed stupid for ever. Rachel had finally left him a year ago. Jack had met her a few weeks later in a London restaurant. She'd been a mess. Broken. On medication. She'd told him that she wasn't going back, that David made her sick to the core, that she couldn't believe she'd let him trample over her for so long. But she hadn't given up on herself. She'd told him that she was learning to cope. In time, she'd said, she'd become strong. In time, she'd find her life again.

And looking at her now, Jack didn't doubt for a moment that she'd done just that.

She turned her head from the car window, caught him staring. 'Look at you,' she said. 'You're pathetic.'

Jack was suddenly excruciatingly aware of the driver glancing at him in the mirror. Then he remembered where he was, who he was. He cleared his throat, concentrated on projecting a crisp, clear accent, and asked with exaggerated pomposity, 'Is that so?'

'Tell me,' she said, lowering her voice, 'do you feel anything?'

'About us?'

'No. About your brother. About the man we've just buried. Or have you forgotten about him already?' She closed her eyes, as if just looking at him induced revulsion. 'You don't feel anything, do you,' she stated, opening her eyes once more, the emotion neutralised.

'What would you know?' he muttered in reply.

'With someone like you, it's not hard to guess.'

'You don't know the first thing about me any more.'

'So tell me,' she said. 'Tell me you're not glad he's dead.'

'I'm not a monster.'

'Since when?'

'I said I'm not a monster.'

'Just tell me.'

He stared at her. 'He was my brother.'

She shook her head. 'He's dead now. It's too late. He can't hear you any more.'

Jack dropped his eyes to the floor and, although he knew he shouldn't ask, he did. 'You cared for him, didn't you?'

'More than you'll ever know,' she told him, tilting her head back and closing her eyes.

Aside from the muffled white noise of the air conditioning, the remaining five minutes of the journey passed in silence, leaving Jack isolated. The present held nothing for him. He had nowhere to look but into the past.

By the time he'd fortified himself with whisky from David's drinks cabinet and got David's naked body into the back of his car and covered it with a blanket, he was ready to quit, to call the police and pray that they'd listen to him. But he knew he couldn't risk it. He started the car and crunched down the drive. No way. He wasn't going down for this. He should have left David hanging. What had he been thinking of? He should have left him hanging and called the police there and then. If he'd done that – if he'd stuck with his hatred – he'd be fine. Better than fine, he'd be happy, that's what he'd be. Against all the odds, he would have triumphed. It would have been the perfect end to a perfectly shitty day.

But it was too late now. He'd blown it big time. No point in even thinking ifs and buts. That kind of talk had never convinced anyone of anything. Least of all the police. No, what he had to do now was continue down the road he'd irreversibly committed himself to: he had to get rid of the body and deny everything.

He turned right at the bottom of the drive and headed

into the night. Doubts competed with the speed of the car, tailgating his conscience. The body might be found. Then what? David would be transformed from a missing person to a murder victim in a single newspaper headline. And with his connections and fame . . . The search for the killer would be both relentless and legendary. They wouldn't stop looking. They wouldn't be given the option to quit. Suspects would be sought. And who was more suspicious than Jack, the brother of the deceased? Not just murder either. Nothing so simple. Nothing so decent. Fratricide. A journalist's wet dream. A lake of copy waiting to be tapped, waiting to burst the dam and flood the nation.

So it was essential, then, that the body wasn't found. Not today. Not tomorrow. Not ever. Wasn't there a law about that? Some Latin tag? No body, no crime. Or was that just in America? Had he just watched too many imported movies? Dump it in the sea. That was the only idea that had occurred to him so far. But it would get washed up, surely. What about weighing the body down? Make sure the truth never surfaced in any shape or bloated form. But weigh it down with what? With rocks? He had no ropes. And even if he had, ropes rotted. Especially in the sea. And what if the fish didn't get to David first? So stick to the traditional method of disposal. Bury him. Where? The whole county was farmland. They'd dig it up in no time. Or notice the fresh earth immediately. Or it would get churned up and harvested with the rest of the crop, only to appear shrink-wrapped in the supermarket vegetable section in bite-sized portions. Or, more likely, some farmer would shoot him as a poacher in the process of burying the corpse.

He shivered. What chance did he stand? The only way he was likely to get away with this was if there wasn't a body at all. Just the same as he wouldn't be in this situation if David hadn't gone and died in the first place . . .

An idea prickled over his skin, settling like the afterglow of massage, leaving him numb. Passing the entrance of a drive, he slammed his foot on the brake pedal, jammed the car into a whining reverse, swung it backwards into the gap in the hedge, slew to a halt, changed gear and shunted forwards, aiming the front of the car in the direction he'd come from.

He eventually located the main road and a twenty-four-hour garage, pulled to a halt and filled the car to the point where the petrol spat from the top of the tank onto his trousers. He pulled his wallet from his pocket, checked for a valid credit card with his name proudly embossed on it, and entered the shop. He grimaced at the in-house closed-circuit television, gave it his best side, for posterity's sake. And then, as he covered the final few yards to the bored girl in the baseball cap who was chatting to a friend on the phone, he tapped the well of tears he'd still not emptied.

Sensing a situation, the girl stunted her conversation. Seeing that the tears were for real, not just some allergy, she placed the phone on a shelf before her, not risking a potentially dangerous disconnection, not just yet. She glanced from Jack to the forecourt, then back, and punched a few keys into the computer pad. 'Number seven, yeah? That'll be fifteen forty-two.'

Jack handed the credit card over. 'What's your name?' he asked.

The girl eyed him warily over the machine that was spewing the receipt out. When the shunting stopped, she ripped it free, and passed it back to him along with his card. He ignored it, left her holding it uncertainly. She pointed to her badge. It read, Zoe. 'Why do you want to know?'

'Because you're the last person I'm ever going to speak to.'

Her eyes pinched, and then she smiled waveringly. 'For real?'

'For real.'

'I don't understand.'

'You don't need to.' He snatched the card from her, then thought better of it, handed it back, saying, 'Just remember my name. No one else will.'

'Wait,' she pleaded, staring at him in confusion.

But he was already halfway to the door.

He reached the coast, a cliffside carpark, as much of a

place for love as a place for death. He knew this place. He'd been here years before. He remembered how the cliff gave way to a plateau of rock and rubble some hundred feet below. The kiosk which guarded the entrance through the fence to the carpark was closed. No sweets or polystyrene cups of hot sweet tea were going to be administered to breathless, windswept tourists tonight. He cut the lights, suddenly conscious of the regular sweep of the benevolent beam from the nearby lighthouse, wary that some bearded insomniac might be taking duty one step too far, conscientiously holding vigil over a mug of malty broth at this strictly antisocial hour.

As the car rolled on, his eyes strained to assimilate the available light. Before him, the horizon was clear, the place where the cliff cut to hollow air precise. He dropped out of gear as he neared the edge, let the momentum carry the car recklessly forward, watched impassively as the front of the bonnet teetered over the edge. Then reaction. He jerked on the handbrake and cut the engine. Silence saddled his mind.

He waited fifteen minutes, just to be sure that no one was around, heading to investigate, then got out. Dropping onto his belly beside the car, he slithered slowly forward until the world dropped away beneath his eyes. Carefully, he moved back, then stood and opened the back door of the car.

David's foot had slid out from beneath the blanket during the ride and now pointed accusingly at him. It didn't do any good. Jack was beyond guilt now. Beyond grief too, for that matter. The self-preservation override had set in. The sooner this was over the better. He grabbed the foot with both hands and unceremoniously heaved the body out of the car until it slumped onto the grass with such a force that Jack wondered if it might leave a dent, an impression from which police artists could reconstruct the man's identity.

He crouched beside the body and began to strip. Once he was naked, he forced David's legs together and threaded his boxer shorts onto them. Next went the trousers. He jerked them up to David's waist, but couldn't get the button done up. Either David's gut was minutely larger or something had happened since his death. Gases, perhaps, were expanding in his digestive system . . . But what was a button between brothers? He peered at it. It was plastic. It would probably melt anyway. If not, so what? Socks next. The shoes fitted perfectly, though tying the laces from this unfamiliar viewpoint proved awkward. He had to crank the arms like a car-jack to loosen them in order to get the shirt on. He snapped the braces into place, tugged them tight. Then he pulled the jacket on. That just left the tie. Off with one noose, on with another. He jerked it high.

Getting David into the driver's seat proved nearly impossible. It was as if David had suddenly changed his mind and no longer wanted to go, like he was having one final, arrogant tantrum. Limbs poked out unhelpfully, creaked like they were about to crack when he forced them into positions they were no longer used to. But finally, the legs were down by the pedals, the arms either side of the seat. He adjusted the headrest, pushed David's neck back so that it lolled, staring carelessly through the sunroof. He considered the logistics of the impact and fastened the seatbelt. The last thing he wanted was for the body to get catapulted from the car, live to tell its own story . . . He looked again. Things were as satisfactory as they were going to get. The thought occurred to him that the overall impression was one of a drunk sleeping it off. He could think of worse ways to go.

He took the blanket from the back and wrapped it round his body, more for comfort than for warmth. In the front seat, next to David, he switched on the map-light and rummaged around in the jacket that his brother was wearing, until he found his pen, diary and hip-flask. He tore a page from the diary and scrawled:

No job. No life. No point any more. Do as you think best, Tommy. All my earthly goods are yours to dispose of as you wish.

See you on the other side.

He read the words once. They sounded glib, insincere. But

what else were they? He opened the flask and rolled the note up and slid it inside the protective shell, screwing the lid down tight afterwards and returning the flask, along with the pen and diary, to the jacket pocket, next to his wallet and all his identification.

He checked the car was out of gear and started the engine. He looked at his brother one final time and thought that maybe he should say a few words. But none came.

He released the handbrake and scrambled out of the car, managing to swing the door shut as a parting gesture just before the car tipped over the edge of the cliff towards oblivion on the rocks below. The explosion, when it came, caused him to throw himself instinctively onto the ground. Seconds later, the smell of death and burning leapt up over the cliff in a tidal wave. He wiped his forehead with the back of his hand and stared at the tacky grime before smearing it across his bare thighs.

Swept with sweat, suddenly feverish, he pulled the blanket tight round his shoulders, like a cape, a shroud, and ran. The earth beneath the grass beneath his bare feet was still warm. He stumbled the two miles to David's house without stopping, keeping off the lanes and in the cover of the country, sacrificing his feet in nettles, streams, woods and fields – anything to minimise the chance of his being seen. Pain gnawed at him like a cannibal with each step. By the time he reached David's house, the skin on the soles of his feet was raw, as inflamed as the sunrise that would shortly stain the sky.

The car swung a wide left and Jack's eyes focused on the world outside. It was the road where Tommy lived. A thousand different taxis had brought him here on a thousand different nights. No amount of dislocation could scramble those memories.

'Red brick building on the left,' he absentmindedly instructed the driver.

'You're remarkably well informed, David,' Rachel commented.

The mention of his dead brother's name resounded like a curse in Jack's ears. He still wasn't used to it. People had been addressing him as such all day, all week, but it still rang like an accusation. Give it time, he told himself. You'll learn to cope. Just give it time. 'I heard someone mention the address at the funeral,' he lied. 'A friend of mine lives further down the street.'

The car drew to a stop and Rachel opened the door. 'Well maybe you should go there instead,' she said, slamming the door shut after her and walking round to the front door of the Georgian block that Tommy lived in.

Jack stayed where he was, silent for a moment. The idea that had detonated out of nowhere like a mine as he'd gunned the car through the Welsh lanes on the night of his birthday, had mushroomed upwards ever since. Its fallout had buried his former life alive. But it had been the antidote he'd been seeking. It had saved his life. Better than that, it had saved him from a lifetime of alienation and captivity in a maximum-security prison. It hadn't been a matter of choice. Morality hadn't even got a toe-nail in the door; it had been that desperate. His stupid sentimentality over obscuring the sordid reality of David's death had left him open to abuse. The idea might have even been David's. He'd always claimed to be into family values like religion, hadn't he? Maybe when he'd died, he'd actually started to believe them for real. And with that in mind, it wasn't beyond the realms of possibility that he'd repented, witnessed Jack's selfless actions, and sent a message back from the dead to help him out in his hour of need. But whether or not it had been David who'd sent the message that had popped up in Jack's brain was immaterial now. Jack had listened. He'd listened and he'd acted accordingly. He'd faked his own death. He'd used David as a fall guy, sent him tumbling over the cliff like a crash-test dummy. And he'd taken on his identity for then, for now, for evermore. If there was a price to be paid, he was paying it now. It was the price of learning to live with what he'd done. It was revoking David's death, taking on his life, his personality, his everything, as his own.

Tommy, who'd been the first to leave the funeral, and Rachel were the only people in the sitting room when Jack walked through the open door. Rachel was sitting in an armchair, a drink in her hand. She didn't look up. Tommy was standing by the window, staring out at the street below where a couple of kids were playing on skateboards.

'Drink?' he asked Jack, his voice unfriendly, uncaring whether he got a reply or not.

Jack walked to the drinks cabinet and looked inside. He selected a malt whisky, poured it liberally into a glass. He looked from Rachel to Tommy, remained silent. It was too late for confessions now. Better not to think about them at all. He drank the whisky, filled the glass again. Then the taste of the alcohol and the pressure of the atmosphere became too much to tolerate. He felt weak, needed a crutch. 'Have you got any cigarettes, Tommy?' he asked.

'You don't smoke,' Rachel said, staring at him strangely.

'People change.'

'You hate smokers.'

He didn't want to get into this, didn't have the energy to concoct some vague justification. He chose instead to ignore her. 'Tommy?'

'I think there are some in the kitchen,' Tommy said with a glare, leaving the room. 'I'll check.'

'You're serious, aren't you?' Rachel asked.

Tommy returned and handed Jack an open packet of Silk Cut. 'Jack left them here a few weeks ago,' he said. 'They're probably a bit stale.'

Rachel watched with fascination as Jack pulled a cigarette from the packet, lit it with a designer lighter from the coffee table in the middle of the room, and sucked smoke down into his starving lungs. She waited for the pretender's spluttering cough. There wasn't one, just an expression that epitomised relief and completeness, fresh from the advertising billboard. Jack continued to smoke hungrily, only pausing occasionally to lubricate his dry throat with whisky. A temporary high gripped him. He felt good, more himself than he'd done all day. It made him want to walk right now to some quiet bar, forget all about this. He looked at Rachel and, unable to help himself, smiled. She just turned away, revolted by the habit or him. He wasn't sure. It hardly mattered which.

The other mourners began to arrive over the next half-hour or so. Standing by the door to the sitting room and thanking them, one by one, for attending, the permanence of the choice Jack had made on the Welsh cliff encased him. It left him cold, an ice sculpture. He understood that each sterile handshake he performed was a callous, unacknowledged farewell, not the greeting and gesture of warmth it feigned to be. The truth behind the façade was that he was saying goodbye to his friends, people who thought he'd already left them for good.

Eventually, the room became filled with smoke and conversation, and Tommy left his post at the front door and walked past Jack into the sitting room. Jack watched him slide with ease through those gathered, cigar in hand, guiding those in need to drinks, stopping to laugh with some, frown with others. Jack knew he couldn't follow this time. Tommy wasn't here for him any more. None of these people were. He looked around at the assembled faces whose friendships had insulated him against the world over the years, named each of them in his mind, remembered stories in which he'd featured with them.

The relatives were to be expected, but far more of his friends than he'd imagined had made the pilgrimage to stamp the full-stop on the end of his life. He was flattered and it made him sick. He wanted to join them, get drunk, be himself again. Just one last time. He wanted to thank them properly, let them know how much this meant to him, how this was the kind of moment that made life worth living, the kind of moment that was even worth dying for.

But his voice was gone now. All he had left was David's tarnished tongue. And they wouldn't listen to that. Alcoholic decryings of the magnitude Jack had gone into didn't drop from memory just like that. Even now, he could feel certain people eyeing him strangely, their faces closing in, focusing on his through the magnifying glass of his discomfort. He was uncertain whether it was because he reminded them of his dead self, or whether it was for darker reasons, because they knew of the animosity that had existed between David and himself. And then, of course, there was always the possibility that word had flown from Tommy's grieving mouth over his last conversation with Jack. Anger – no, loathing – was in his eyes. Chances were it had been in his voice, too. Perhaps the others knew why he'd gone to Wales, had extrapolated why he might have turned instead to the sea.

Whatever their thinking, one thing was certain: they didn't see Jack any more. Only David. Jack was dead in their eyes. A memory: sharp for now, becoming a blur. He was a shadow of his former self, no more. It was how he had to learn to see the situation, too. The ropes that had bound him to them had been cut. He'd cut them himself. If he tried to pull at them now, all he'd get was slack.

'At least try and look connected,' a voice said.

He looked at Rachel. 'I didn't think you were speaking to me.'

'I never said that,' she told him, walking with him round to the drinks cabinet where he poured himself another whisky.

He lit a fresh cigarette and spun the whisky round the rim of his glass habitually. Catching himself in the act, he steadied his hand, sipped slowly, demonstrated control, like David would have done. 'So, let's talk,' he said, assertion dropping like a brick from his mouth. 'How have you been?'

'I don't want to talk about me.'

'What then?'

'Jack.'

He smoked for a moment, taking comfort in the knowledge that silence was safe. 'What do you want to know?'

'What he was doing in Wales. I want to know what you said to him before he died.'

'I didn't say anything to him. I didn't see him.'

'You're lying. I know Jack. He'd have seen you before

he did it. He'd have let you know why.'

'I said I didn't see him. The police believed me, so why don't you?'

Her head dropped. 'You're sick.'

'When are you going to grow up?' he asked her. He knew he had to bring this to an end. He had to be David, couldn't cope if he was Jack. 'Surely you know me well enough to know for certain that you're never going to get a reaction out of me?' He remembered something of David's he'd read, paraphrased as best he could, 'I've evolved. Can't you get that into your head? I'm here to do things, not waste my time listening to people whine.' He looked down at her. 'And you're above this kind of thing, too. You know there's no point in arguing for the sake of it.' He stared at her, words swam out. 'It doesn't become you.'

'You don't fool me, you know,' she stated. 'I know you. Remember that. I know everything about you.'

He felt the arrogance he'd pushed forward begin to recoil. He fought off the urge to dissemble, become himself again and apologise. He wished she'd go. He wished he didn't have to treat her like this, that there was another way. His voice wavered as he spoke: 'I told you before: you don't know the first thing about me any more.'

Her lips contracted, rolled inwards, became shadow, a line. She turned away from him and he watched her walk through the crowd to the door and into the afternoon. He quelled his inclination to follow. If he was to catch her up, what was there to say? Her preconceptions weren't something he was going to eradicate with a few charming words. She hated what he'd become, just like she'd hated David. It was one and the same now. And as for honesty, telling her the facts? Impossible. His honesty was long gone, ingrained in the rocks of a Welsh seashore – strata, history. He could forget that. Just like he could forget her. He must start afresh. Wasn't that what rebirth was all about?

He blanked her out of his mind and paced through the crowd, avoiding the faces of his friends, hunting down decrepit relatives, familiar from photographs, people who'd take him at face value, probe no deeper. He sank into their conversations with garbled pleasantries, amplified their uncomfortable mutterings with his own, waited for a decent enough amount of time to sift by so that he could leave this place, leave them all behind, forget.

'Where's Rachel gone?' Tommy asked, suddenly at his side.

The familiarity of his voice brought Jack transient relief. 'Outside,' he told him. 'Somewhere else . . .'

'I know that,' Tommy said. 'I heard what you said to her. I saw her go.' He sucked on his cigar, chugged smoke into Jack's face. 'You just can't help yourself, can you?'

'What do you mean?'

'Don't be a bigger prick than you have to.'

Jack looked at his friend, recognised the symptoms, diagnosed the condition. He'd seen him like this before: drunk, emotional, looking for a fight. He watched him watching him. There wasn't any fear. Just malevolence. It was like he was willing it to happen, like he wanted something to start that only he could finish. Like it would make him complete. Jack checked his fear. This wasn't SlipSlide. It wasn't Tommy's turf. It was a wake. Tommy wasn't going to go swinging for anyone right now. And David would have known that.

'You shouldn't have been listening to what Rachel and I said. It was none of your business.'

Tommy's countenance darkened. 'But Jack is.'

'And what's that meant to mean?'

'What do you think?'

'I'm not a clairvoyant.'

'Don't fuck me about,' Tommy warned.

Jack glanced around. The conversations about them were teetering towards silence. People were beginning to stare. 'I don't think this is really the time to—'

'This is the *only* time to talk about it,' Tommy snapped. 'You read the suicide note, didn't you? So don't you fucking stand here acting like nothing's happened!'

'And you blame me, I suppose?'

'Who else am I going to blame? You knew what that job meant to him. You gave it to him, then you took it away again. Playing God like you always have. You pushed him too far.'

Jack closed his eyes, collected himself. 'I didn't push anyone,' he spelt out loudly enough for the whole room to hear. He looked them over as he spoke. 'He was fired. He did it to himself.' His voice collapsed, his final words ill-channelled air: 'You know what he was like.'

Outside, he walked by the car, ignoring the friendly nod of the chauffeur, and moved swiftly on to the end of the road. He didn't bother to look back over his shoulder to see if Tommy was following. He didn't look back at all. It was over. He wasn't going to think about it ever again. Like the emotions he'd suppressed all day, he'd suppress this memory, too. Like the rest of his life, it was behind him now.

He flagged down a cab and got in.

'Where to, boss?' the driver asked.

'A bar.'

The driver grinned at him in the mirror. 'A bar. Any one in particular?'

'Any bar. Just get me the fuck away from here. I need a drink.'

Jack downed the first whisky at the bar, the second one, too. It was only once the third had been poured and he'd lit a cigarette that he walked to one of the alcoves and sat down.

After Rachel's guests had left on the night of her birthday, Jack had sat with her in the sitting room, away from David. Neither of them had spoken. And then they'd listened to the sound of David's feet climbing the stairs and creaking away down the corridor to his room. A door had slammed and then there'd been silence.

Jack looked across at Rachel. Her bowed head stared down at her lap. 'I'm sorry,' he said. 'I'm so sorry. I shouldn't have let things go so far. I shouldn't have let him say those things.'

'It's not your fault.'

'It is. I should have stopped it. I should have dropped the conversation before it went so far.'

'He was going to say it anyway. That's what he wanted.'

'But why? Why would someone want to do that? Why would he want to do that to you?'

She looked up at him. 'Because it entertains him.'

'What do you mean?'

'He finds it amusing.'

'How can he find hurting you amusing?'

'It wasn't just me.'

'I don't understand.'

'He wasn't just trying to hurt me. That's just part of it. It was you as much as me. It was everyone. Can't you see that?'

'No,' Jack said. 'No, I can't. What he said about you—'

'About the fact that I'm useless, that my whole life amounts to nothing?'

'Yes. That. Why?'

'Because he wanted to see your reaction. Just like he wanted to see mine.' She leant forward and drank from her glass. 'He was playing with us, Jack. Playing a tune and watching us dance.'

'He can't do that.'

'He can and it works. What do you think we're doing now? He's not even in the room and we're still dancing. We're talking just how he imagined we would.' She looked at the ceiling. 'He's probably sitting up there now writing this very conversation down. He doesn't even have to be here to see it. He knows he's in control.'

'That's ridiculous.'

'Is it? I don't think so.'

'But we're real people, not characters from one of his books.'

'Sometimes the distinction can get blurred.'

'No, it can't. You're believing what he tells you. It's not true.'

'There are times when I'm here alone with him and I feel that every word I say is a word he's written for me.'

'That's not possible.'

'Why not? He's spent his life writing about people. You think he doesn't know how they work – how we work? What's to stop him from putting ideas in our heads, making us speak and think how he wants us to?'

'Because it's crap, that's why.'

'It's what he believes,' she stated.

'That doesn't mean you have to. You mustn't think like that. If you do, then you're right, he is controlling you. You mustn't let him get in your head like that.'

'It's too late for that. He's already here.'

'Then leave him.' He waited for a reply, but in its place silenced thickened. 'He's a shit. He doesn't deserve you. Not if he treats you this way. Why don't you leave? I don't understand. You can leave now. There's no reason for you to stay. Why don't you just leave?'

'Because there's nothing out there for me. I'm nothing.'

'There's life. There's everything. How can you say there's nothing?' Jack held his hands up. 'This is nothing. What you've got now. Just leave. Leave with me tonight. You've got nothing to lose.'

She stared into Jack's eyes, then got to her feet and walked over and placed a hand on his shoulder. 'I'm tired, Jack.' She leant down and kissed his cheek. 'I'm going to bed. If we stay here together, we'll just be giving him what he wants.'

'Oi, mate,' a voice said and Jack looked up across the table at the barman standing there. 'Watch the furniture. We only got these in last week.'

Jack followed his gaze to his hand which was resting on the table, the untouched cigarette poised against the wooden surface, ending in an ash-flecked burn mark. 'I'm sorry,' he said, putting the butt of the cigarette into an ashtray and sweeping the ash off the table onto the floor. 'I was somewhere else.'

CHAPTER FIVE

exorcism

The morning sunlight had broken in through the gap in the curtains and stamped a pale block on the grey wallpaper above the closed door. Louise Elliot's eyes moved from this to the clock on her bedside table; it was just gone eight.

As she rose, the anarchic tapestry of her long, ash-blond hairs gathered, cloaking the curve of her cotton-clad spine to her waist. She got up and walked to the window, opening first it and then the pale varnished wooden shutters. The humming weight of heat at this early hour surprised her and the sunlight made her squint. As her eyes grew accustomed to the glare, she stepped out onto the small balcony, leant on the cast-iron guard, and looked down at the courtyard below.

Mr Hardy sat, as though stunned, at the sturdy oak table with his back to her and his front to the sun. His shadow fell like an oil slick across the graph paper of cobbles. An empty wine bottle stood before him, next to the candle and the solidified tears he'd watched it shed as he'd ponderously eaten his dinner with Louise and his sister the night before.

'Good morning, Louise,' a woman's voice called out.

Louise saw Mr Hardy's sister, Cleo, standing near the front door, basking in the sun. Her long, pale yellow dress was barely distinguishable from the mustard-coloured Cotswold stone wall of the courtyard against which she leant. She looked as though she belonged, was relaxed, as though she'd lived here all her life, not just come down from London for a weekend break. But as Louise had reflected the previous evening, Cleo was one of those people who could probably fit in anywhere.

'Good morning,' she called back. 'I'll be down to fix you both breakfast in a few minutes.'

Cleo walked nearer, so that she stood between Mr Hardy and the balcony. Her shadow blended with his, became one. 'No rush,' she said with a broad smile. She glanced up at the cloudless blue atmosphere. The rush of sun filtered through her dark red hair, casting it strawberry. 'I feel like I've got all the time in the world today.'

Louise stepped back into her room, removed her nightshirt and walked carelessly down the corridor which led to the bathroom. She trailed her fingers along the wall as she went. It was a ritualistic action she'd performed every morning since she'd bought the property some ten years before. Even now, the thrill of it filled her. It was hers. Every atom of every stone. Like pinching herself to escape a dream, touching this now made it real.

As the bath filled, she stood in front of the mirror, straining through the clouding condensation, and the screen of familiarity which shrouded her blurred reflection, in an attempt to recapture the beauty she'd once possessed. But all she saw was herself as she was now. She smiled. There was nothing wrong with that. Familiarity, like its parent, solitude, was something she'd chosen. Pangs of chagrin for something greater, like the one she was suffering from now, were transitory. That was one of the many things living here alone had taught her. Whenever she came back to her senses, the house was still here for her; it was the thought of the house and its surrounding land that brought her back. With so much beauty around her, she didn't need anything else.

She glanced into the bath. The water was still only inches deep. The pressure in the pipes was poor, she'd been told when she'd moved in. The only way to improve it would have been to instigate a complete overhaul of the plumbing system. Out with the encrusted old, in with the gleaming new. But she'd declined then and her reason for doing so seemed no less valid now.

The house had a soul. She was convinced of it. She'd

fallen for it as soon as she'd seen it. Not in the conventional way of simply desiring it, wanting to own it and do it up to suit her purposes and lifestyle. She'd fallen in love with it. Quite literally. Her feelings had soared to a greater intensity than she'd ever felt for another person. She'd wanted not just to live in it, but to live *with* it. And when, years before, after driving past, she'd enquired in the estate agent's in the nearest town if it was likely to come up for sale and had been informed that the occupant was an octogenarian spinster, she'd left her number with them, telling them to call her, day or night, the moment it became available. The ensuing wait had been like a courtship. Every day that had passed without her being in the house had left her empty. And when the phone call had finally come – some eight months later – she'd penned her agreement to the price asked immediately. She hadn't bothered to haggle. In all truth, the thought hadn't even entered her mind. What price love? The danger of losing the property had nagged at her too hard. Instead, she'd leapt into debt, knowing that she could work her way free. In a labour of love, any amount of work, no matter what it entailed, was a small price to pay.

So the plumbing had stayed slow to begin with; she hadn't been able to afford to make it otherwise. And looking now, as the thin stream of hot water – more a leak than a stream – laboriously filled the bath, she wouldn't have had it any other way. Even now that she had the money, she never seriously considered following the plumber's original advice. The house had a soul. It was haunted by beauty. She didn't feel she had any right to have it gutted just because, like herself, it was getting old.

Her gaze moved from the bath and traversed the room, looking for something to occupy herself with until the bath filled. On the floor by the window was a magazine. She walked over, intrigued, knowing that it wasn't hers, suspecting that Mr Hardy, in all probability, couldn't read, wondering what a metropolitan beauty such as Cleo indulged her intellect with. She picked it up. It wasn't anything of any note, simply a supplement from one of the Sunday papers.

Not the fashion or media-orientated magazine she'd been expecting. She glanced at the bath again and sat down on its edge. It didn't really matter what it was; she hadn't read it before. It would help to pass the time. It divided exactly in two as she opened it, the centre pages flapping down over her thighs like exhausted wings.

THRILLER KILLERS WRITE SECOND CHAPTER
The serial murderers, dubbed the 'Thriller Killers', by the tabloid press on account of their apparently literary motivation, struck for the second time this weekend.

Two photographs straddled the upper quarter of the page. One was of a late-middle-aged man in a striped blazer and Panama hat; the other was of a young man holding a microphone to his face on stage.

Less than two weeks after the novelist and critic Adam Appleton's corpse was discovered at his luxurious home in Hampstead Village, Mick Roper, front man of the dance band, Ego, and author of a string of bestselling street-culture novels, was found strung up from the ceiling of a disused dance gymnasium in Fulham. He had been drugged, tortured and shot in the face at close range.

Although the two men had been killed in different ways (Appleton had been tortured before having his throat cut), there was never any doubt that they had been murdered by the same people. Similarly, despite the fact that neither of the victims knew one another, or ostensibly had anything in common other than that they were published writers, the motive for the two murders was identical: art.

The female killer, known variously as Amazonia Skreen and Diana, has provided detailed confessions of her actions, as well as those of her mentally submissive and physically imposing accomplice, known consistently as Mr Tup Maul. Two unemotional confessions (one for each of the murders) have been given, not just directly to the police, but to the public as a whole.

The first appeared following the death of Appleton. It was a document of some 8,000 words which was sent anonymously to the Chronicle. *The editor, James Peters, chose to publish it in full the next day, and will shortly appear before a House of Commons Select Committee to defend this action. The second confession came shortly before Roper's body was found. Perhaps realising that no newspaper would dare to publish again, several popular public-access electronic noticeboards on the Internet received an account of the murder. The equipment through which the Internet was accessed has not been traced, and according to computer experts is not likely to be.*

There was a colour photograph of a young man smoking a cigarette in a night club. The caption beneath it ran: *Mick Roper: SlipSlidin' Away.*

The authenticity of the two confessions is not in doubt. Although, in both cases, the confessions were stylised, presented as chapters from a work of fiction, attention being given to characterisation and dramatic structure, the writing is far from fiction; it is nearer fact. The locations described – from Appleton's residence to SlipSlide, the Soho club where Roper unknowingly danced the night away with his soon-to-be nemesis, Diana – are real places. The characters portrayed – from the victims themselves to Sean O'Connor, the barman in SlipSlide who presented Roper with a drink from his murderer – are real people. The narration of the events that occurred is accurate, tallying closely with what witnesses remember.

Louise suddenly remembered the bath, and turned to see that it was nearly full. She turned the hot tap off, started the cold running and returned the magazine to where she'd found it on the floor by the window.

Some time after, once she'd bathed and dressed, she was standing in the flagstoned kitchen, gazing absentmindedly at the discarded, imperfect lilies she'd left on the table when she'd arranged a vase a few minutes earlier. Away from the limited territorial glow of the stove, it was cool in here, untouched by sunlight, a cave. She shook some coffee beans into the hole at the centre of a wooden grinder and began to turn the handle, enjoying the simple efficiency of the task. When the noise of the grinder's activity finally subsided, she opened the machine's drawer and lowered her face to it. Her nostrils flared at the heavy aroma the rich, dark brown powder released.

'Nothing quite like it, is there?' Cleo said, suddenly beside her, a beautiful ghost who'd entered the room without her knowledge.

She looked at her and smiled openly in the way she always felt obliged to with people she didn't yet know enough to simply declare her mood. 'No, I suppose not,' she said.

'It's funny, though. I can never be bothered to make it at home. Tend to stick to instant. Stupid, really. I mean, we've even got one of those machines. A Christmas present, I think. There just never seems to be the time.'

Louise smiled hospitably. 'As you said earlier, you've got all the time in the world now. Besides, there's no such thing as instant anything down here.'

She removed the small wooden drawer from the grinder, walked to the stove, and set about straining the coffee with boiling water from the kettle into a blue metal pot. She listened to the water trickling through the wire gauze of the strainer, aware of Cleo observing her. It left her feeling vaguely uncomfortable, self-conscious. She wondered what someone like Cleo must make of her secluded life down here. She struck Louise as intuitive. Perhaps she could guess her thoughts. Perhaps she could sense her easy comfort at the familiarity of the routine and was, even now, imagining how she must have performed these identical actions, day after day, alone, week in, week out. Maybe she found it quaint, endearing. Or just sad.

When she turned back to face Cleo, her brow was glistening from the heat that the stove emitted. Cleo watched a bead develop, threaten to fall. Louise felt it too and swept the encroaching moisture away with a languid stroke of the back of her hand and moved further from the source of the heat. Cleo continued to stare at her.

'What is it?' Louise asked.

'Nothing. Just that you seem so content.'

'I am. I'm happy here.' Louise walked to one of the cupboards and started to take the crockery from it for breakfast.

'I do hope you don't think I'm prying,' Cleo said, 'but how do you afford to keep such a large place?' She blushed. 'I'm sorry.' She looked around the room. 'It's just that everything here's so perfect.'

Louise smiled. 'It's all right. Don't be embarrassed. It's a reasonable enough thing to want to know. Anyway, there's nothing to it really. I lead a very simple life. I grow a lot of my own food. And then there are the chickens and ducks.' She went to the fridge, crouched in its weak light. 'Would you and your brother like eggs for breakfast? Scrambled or boiled? The duck eggs are excellent boiled. Very rich yolks.' She indicated a steaming saucepan on the stove with a nod of her head. 'The water's just about boiling.'

'Yes, boiled eggs would be lovely.'

She took the eggs to the saucepan and slipped them into the boiling water one by one. 'And then, of course, there's the bed and breakfast. I've been doing it for a good few years now. The income's irregular, I suppose, but every little counts. Toast?' Cleo nodded in reply. 'This summer's been particularly good. I don't think I ever remember it being this hot in Britain. There have been a lot of people like you coming down from London.' She slotted four slices of bread into the toaster, wedged them down and watched the filament begin to glow. 'It must get terribly stuffy up there, what with all the pollution.'

'Yes, it's grim. I can't believe the difference in the air quality here. You tend to forget just how fantastic fresh air can be. It's intoxicating. Like the dreams I had last night: they were so vivid. I'm sure it's got something to do with the air. Or the silence. I still keep expecting to hear car horns and police sirens . . .'

'I don't notice the silence any more,' Louise commented. 'Once you've lived here for a while, it ceases to exist. Your ears become more sensitive. Insects, animals, streams – you hear them all. I probably don't appreciate it as much as I should.'

Cleo sat down at the table, pressed her fingers together pensively. 'Doesn't it get lonely here on your own all the time? I mean, you don't work, do you?'

Louise thought for a moment, then said, 'There's a big difference between loneliness and solitude. Besides, I do work. Quite hard in fact. But it doesn't affect my solitude. I work from home. In one of the outbuildings.' A spring twanged and the toast popped up. She glanced at her watch. 'The eggs will be ready in a minute. I put three in for your brother. He's a big man. Will that be enough?'

'Plenty.'

'You're very close to him, aren't you?'

'Yes, I have been ever since his accident.'

Louise turned to face her and noticed that her mouth was drawn, her smile gone. 'I'm sorry,' she said. 'I didn't realise . . . What happened?'

'It was when we were children,' Cleo explained. 'He nearly drowned. That's why he's kind of slow now. Brain damage. It was caused by oxygen starvation. There wasn't anything that could be done about it.' She ran her hand through her hair, frowned. 'It could have been a good deal worse. His conversation's not up to much, but he can do a lot of things. He can fend for himself, really. He can even drive. Only he's used to me doing most things for him now, so he doesn't really try. I don't mind. He has a good quality of life. That's the main thing. I've got more than enough money to take care of him. And I think he's happy most of the time. I try to make sure of that.' She stood up and walked to the kitchen doorway, hovered there, looking down the corridor through the open front door which framed a rectangular view of the courtyard and the fields beyond. 'But enough of that,' she said, spinning round, smiling once more. 'Tell me about your work, what you do in the outbuilding. Please. I'm dying to know.'

Louise checked her watch again. 'You wouldn't believe me if I told you.'

Cleo came closer. 'Try me.'

'Very well, but I know you won't believe me.' She curled her fingers up, studied her nails, and said, 'I'm a ghost.'

Cleo laughed. 'What do you mean?'

Louise smiled, infected by Cleo's surprise. 'Exactly what I said. I told you you wouldn't believe me.'

'I don't understand.'

'Don't worry,' Louise said, beginning to scoop the eggs from the saucepan with a teaspoon and bed them down in egg cups, 'it's not what you think. I don't go round haunting people, or throwing vicars off steeples, or whatever it is that ghosts are supposed to do these days.'

Cleo's eyes shone with amusement. 'I'm relieved to hear it.'

'No, nothing like that at all. I'm a writer. A ghost-writer. People pay me to write their books for them.'

Cleo's eyebrows darted up. 'That's incredible. What people?'

Louise nodded at the cups, saucers and plates next to the stove. 'Can you give me a hand by taking those outside?'

'Of course. But tell me about the books. Is it autobiographies you write?'

Louise finished loading a tray with the coffee, eggs and toast. 'No, that's not my speciality. I write novels.'

Cleo lifted the crockery and walked with Louise down the corridor. 'I don't think I'm following you. You write novels for *other* people. I don't get it. Autobiographies I could understand. But novels?'

They stepped out into the brilliant light of the courtyard. With the sun now higher, dappled shadows filtered through the tree which reared over the table, patterning the varnished wood. Tramp, Louise's mongrel dog, lay drowning in the shade beneath the table. She wheezed irregularly in her sleep, dreaming, her paws paddling frantically, going nowhere.

'I really don't get it,' Cleo continued as she sat down next to her brother. 'Why don't they write them themselves? I thought that was the whole point.'

'Put simply,' Louise said, laying the tray she was carrying on the table, 'it's because they can't write.'

Cleo decapitated her brother's eggs for him, slicing the tops off with clinical strokes of the spoon she held, and then arranged them before him. He acknowledged her attentions with a grunt and began to eat. Cleo frowned at Louise and nibbled at a piece of toast. 'So what you're saying is you do *all* the work and—'

Louise warned a wasp off with a wave of her arm. 'And they take *all* the credit. Yes, that's about the sum of it.'

'But why?'

'Because they're famous and it's easy for publishers to market them.' She filled their cups with coffee. 'I'm not famous. I can only write. And writing's not always enough on its own these days.'

'Whose books have you written?'

Louise slowly shook her head. 'One of the conditions of the work is that I'm not allowed to take any credit for the writing. It's in the contracts . . .'

'And that means you're not going to tell me now, I take it?'

'Sorry.'

Cleo sat back and drank her coffee. 'Can you tell me what sort of people they are?'

'Television and film celebrities, politicians . . . People who are universally known. That way publishers are happy to pay them a fortune. Who they are pretty much guarantees the publicity required to generate substantial sales.'

'Does it pay you well?'

'Well enough. It depends on who I'm writing for. Depends on how famous they are. Or how greedy. I usually get a cut of the advance the publishers pay them. Sometimes a cut of the royalties, too.'

Cleo leant forward and chewed on her toast for a moment. Her brother had finished eating and was watching Tramp out of the corner of his eyes through the razor-thin slats in the table, unblinking.

'Doesn't it bother you not getting credit for your writing?' Cleo eventually asked. 'It would get me down. I don't think I could stand it.'

Louise reached across the table and refilled their cups with coffee. She smiled warmly. 'I've got everything I want here. The money from the writing gives me security to keep my lifestyle. It's paid off my mortgage. If you want to know the truth, I think that's worth far more than any amount of credit and fame.' She waited for Cleo to comment, but she was now staring into her brother's inscrutable eyes. Louise got to her feet. 'I'll go and get that guidebook I was telling you about last night. It is Cheltenham you're planning to visit, isn't it?'

'Yes,' Cleo said, peering over her steaming coffee cup. 'Thanks.'

Later, after Cleo's BMW had faded down the driveway in a cloud of dry dust, Louise was sitting at the table, gazing into the distance. She was unaware of time passing, unaware of anything but the pleasant sensation of the sun slowly baking her forearms.

Tramp twitched in her sleep, lifted her bearded, square muzzle from her mistress's feet, stretched idyllically, and finally slouched sleepily from the shade beneath the table. She sniffed the sunlight in the courtyard with transient interest, then slumped next to Louise's chair and turned her oily, olive-black gaze lovingly up towards her mistress' face. Her tail swept the cobbles clear of dust immediately behind where she patiently lay.

Tramp's movement pulled Louise from her reverie. 'Another morning,' she said, 'of talking to myself through you. But even you . . .' She reached her palm down to caress the dog's head. '. . . Even you, old friend, sometimes get bored of listening to me.'

She slapped her thigh and rose. Tramp needed no

further encouragement. It switched from listlessness to alertness in the way that only an animal can, its limbs snapping upright, darting for the point which signalled the end of the courtyard and the beginning of the zone of olfactory exploration. Just past the gatepost it momentarily checked its mistress' compliance before marking the berried hedge with its scent and setting off along the territorial patrol route which it undertook beneath her guidance every day.

Louise crossed the swollen pasture of long grass, intermittently sprinkled with wild flowers, that separated her from the shallow, sun-studded stream at the centre of the valley, avoiding the heaps of dried, cracking sheep dung, and their attendant soporific clumps of insects which Tramp seemed so frantic to animate and draw her attention to. Above her the sky was vast, a panorama of unclouded blue, an image of contentment as old as life itself. Beneath her she felt the burgeoning grass scratch the skin which her sandals failed to cover in an unrewarded, clawing quest for moisture. When she reached the stream, she watched for a while as Tramp plunged her paws into the water and shook her muzzle insincerely before plunging it back to the surface again to placate the dryness of her exercised tongue. Louise turned her head to survey her demesne, her life, each overlapping the other, perhaps the equation she'd striven for from the first.

It was a view she'd described on many occasions, from many perspectives, in different styles in different novels over the years, a view she could conjure up in intricate detail, if she so chose, from memory alone. The field in which she stood sloped gently upwards to the drystone wall which enclosed the courtyard. Above the wall, the flaking whitewash of the first floor of the main house was cast in relief, and the dark, greasy slates of the roof reflected the brightness of the day in glinting patches. She followed the straight line of the rooftop to the right, and her eyes dropped a floor to the similarly slated roof of what had originally been a barn, but which now, with the addition of skylights, provided her studio. A house martin, commuting from its grizzled home beneath the guttering, sailed the air, hooking her attention, and she traced its arcing flight to the left where the jumbled outbuildings lay next to the main house.

She closed her eyes; imagined the view; opened them again; saw it was real. What she'd told Cleo had been the truth. Fame and reputation meant nothing in comparison to what she already had. She clapped her hands. Tramp looked up, wagged her tail, casting off a spectrum of water. Together, they set out across the fields.

In London, Clare Carrier stopped in front of the dressing-table mirror with her back to the young man. She pulled her dressing gown in tighter around her shoulders. Her tongue flickered as she performed an instinctive polishing of her lips. He was grinning at her. Her reflection reacted, flashed him the kind of perfectly capped smile that was only usually witnessed in toothpaste advertisements.

'What are you grinning at?' she asked.

'You.' His eyes swooped up and down. 'Your body.'

She took her eyes from herself for a full ten seconds, studied him. Fresh from a poster, his muscles, even at this sleepy hour, looked swollen. Energy packed every inch of him, in spite of what he'd achieved the night before.

'I didn't know morning-after compliments were part of the service,' she said, her expression neutral, allowing him to conclude whether she was being serious or not.

He rolled over, mumbling, 'They're not,' and pushed his classical, symmetrical features into the pillow.

She smiled at his equivocal reply and took in the rest of the impersonal atmosphere of her bedroom. It had about as much character as a hotel room. It wasn't the décor. That, like the rest of the house, had been designed at great expense. It wasn't what was here at all – antique furniture, oil paintings, flowers – but what was missing that unsettled her. The intricate pattern and the price of the rug which covered most of the stripped-pine floor failed to disguise the sterility of the air that hung here. What you saw wasn't what you got. The décor was a promise that the atmosphere devoured. Since her divorce, this bedroom had never aspired to anything greater than the visually ornate and perfunctory. It was the place where she went to bed, where she achieved orgasm and where she slept. It would never be anything more.

'What are you doing today?' he asked. He was sitting up now, his athletic legs crooked over the edge of the bed, locked.

'Working.'

He stretched his arms and spoke through a yawn, 'Acting?'

'No, not today.'

He stood up and looked critically down his body. His stomach muscles tensed into an undulating grid in reply and his face relaxed. 'What then?' he asked, hooking his thumbs into his shorts, striking the kind of pose a fashion photographer would kill for.

'Writing.'

'So many talents,' he said, starting to collect his clothes from where they'd been discarded during the early hours of the morning. 'I don't know how people like you find time to do it all. I have enough trouble just getting up in the morning.'

'That's because you work so hard at night.'

He watched her walk to the bed and sit down. 'Maybe,' he said with a wry smile, pulling his trousers on.

When he'd finished dressing, she told him, 'You can let yourself out. You'll find an envelope on the table in the hall.' He smiled at her, unabashed. She felt herself blushing. 'I've given you a little bit extra – just like you gave me.'

He grinned broadly and touched his brow, as if he were doffing an invisible cap. 'Thank you, ma'am. I hope I can be of service again,' he said as he ducked out of the room.

'You can,' she called after him, listening to his sure-footed progress down the stairs. 'And tell your boss you were the best yet . . .'

Later, still in her bedroom, Claire continued to mimic the orchestrated motions of the tanned supermodel on the exercise video, pumping the weights in her hands up and down in time with the beat of the music, riding the arterial thrust of adrenalin which raged through her blood-stream in a torrent of cellulite-eliminating fury. Then, following the series of exercises with her memory alone, her gaze surreptitiously shifted from the television, out through the large rectangular pane of glass which captured her aerobicised figure like a television screen, and across the street to the upstairs window of the house opposite.

To the uninitiated, the curtains were drawn, the occupant unaware that morning had arrived. But Clare, armed with the esoteric knowledge of having witnessed occasional, but telling, impulsive twitches of curtain fabric and diamond flashes of telescopic lenses over the preceding months, knew otherwise. Suppressing a smile, feeling both flattered and wanted, she looked back at the television and continued her performance, her mind in no doubt that the young man who lived in the house opposite was going to be late for college again.

Minutes later, with her eyes closed, self-consciously statuesque as she listened to the supermodel bidding her a superficial farewell until the next session, she was thinking that there'd been a time when her ex-husband, Patrick, would have paid excessive rent for a room with such an exclusive view of her. He too, like her secret admirer, would have stretched out through the chink in the curtains with the arm of his fantasy, claiming her for his own. Like the insatiable craving of an addict, the vision of her would have haunted him throughout the following day and night, cursing him with the burden of intolerable impatience, incessantly cutting into his concentration, leaving him perpetually gibbering and salivating over the thought of his next fix. But that was before his success and fame had infected him with arrogance and complacency. And that was before she too had undergone a similar transformation. The only thing, she suspected, that really haunted either of them now was the shimmering, already opaque memory of the way things had once been, a memory that, more and more each day, was fading from reality into the transparency of dreams.

As she opened her eyes, her gaze and her thoughts returned to her current admirer. He would, right now, be anticipating the climax of her repeated morning performance: the very moment he lived for. And like the fans of her television series, the moment the performance was over, he'd find himself wishing the next episode was already here. She felt no pity for the inevitability of his daily tragedy. As with her work, she maintained a professional attitude. Leave them begging for more. She understood that. No matter what they thought, it was the agonising wait that made it so worthwhile in the end.

She placed the weights on the floor and stood upright. There was no need to turn away from the window to consult the mirror on the wall to her right: she already knew that she looked good, that she had the kind of body that would shame most women ten years her junior, and the kind of face that the paparazzi still loved to capture on film. Even the escort who'd spent the night with her had made that perfectly apparent.

Crossing her arms, as if she were giving herself a narcissistic hug, she freed her shoulders from the confines of the straps of the leotard she always wore for exercise. She peeled it smoothly down to her waist, her arms still crossed so that her breasts rested on her forearms. After a moment of deliberately tantalising hesitation, she straightened her arms and leant forward towards the window – towards him – pushing the leotard, and the cotton knickers beneath, down to her ankles, stepping out of them, and standing upright once more. She felt herself rising to the occasion, and was, for the brevity of that transient moment, his and his alone to worship.

In the shower, as the downpour of warm water channelled the conditioner from her hair into foaming streams which formed a delta across the plain of her skin, she thought again of her young man across the road. She'd seen him on a hundred occasions, venturing to and from college in the mornings and evenings, stumbling back drunk through the early hours of weekend blackness. He was in his early twenties, about the same age as Charlotte, her only child. He was handsome. She idly wondered, had the years been different and their youth coincided, if she would have found him attractive then, and if she might have chosen to make a life with him instead of Patrick.

She interrupted herself. Such futile speculation didn't stand up to scrutiny. She was where she was now because of the decisions she'd chosen to make, and the decisions, beyond her control, that Patrick had made. Undertaking fantastical odysseys through the cross-roads of the past would only hinder her further, in just the same way that fantasy was currently hindering her young man's initiation into adult life. Anyway, even now she was uncertain if she would change her choices. Somewhere, before the emotional haze of cocaine, alcohol and lovers that had permeated her career, was a place where she'd loved Patrick with an intensity that had only been equalled by his own reciprocal emotions. Somewhere, she concluded bitterly – but not here, not now.

She finished showering and returned to her room. Standing in front of the mirror, she unwound the white dressing of towel from her body, clasped it round her head in a makeshift turban, and massaged the moisture from her night black hair. As she shed the towel onto the floor and began to rummage through her make-up bag for the first shade of the day, she looked out through the window.

The curtains across the street were now open, the room empty; and so she dressed alone. Her clothes for the day were laid out neatly on the chair next to her dressing table. This ritualistic organisation, like the daily exercise, was one of the many products of her regular discussions with her therapist. Such things helped her occupy her time, stopped her from yearning for the easy comfort of a bottle, or the confidence represented by, and embodied in, a line of white powder. For the last two 'dry' years, this organised existence had helped to empower her, allowed her to increase her control over the blank spaces which occupied the suburbs of her life, and which still threatened to invade and conquer her once more the moment she dropped her guard.

Downstairs, in the kitchen, she opened the window. An ancient, uncompromising heat had settled in the back garden. The leaves of the apple tree were still. Motionless but for her pulse, she played the reptile for a few moments, absorbing the energy that would power her through the day. She peered up at the sky: blinding blue. It was an auspicious day to be leaving London.

It was just gone noon when Clare pulled off the high-hedged lane and began to drive slowly along the winding, uneven half-mile avenue which led to Louise's house. Opposing parades of trees flanked either side of the drive, their branches reaching out towards one another, their tangled meeting forming a natural tunnel. The roof of green and yellow leaves filtered the sunlight into flickering, maddening patches, causing her eyes to strain as she attempted to negotiate the vehicle safely through the minefield of pot holes which the now unimaginably distant winter of howling winds and cracking ice had swollen into existence.

She made no move to leave the car once she'd found a shady space to park it in. Instead, her eyelids snapped down over her astonishingly bright blue eyes, and the dictaphone on her lap clicked into life. Her thoughts roamed, returned to the lascivious antics of the night before. But she'd already recorded that, along with the rest of the morning. She concentrated, cleared her mind, and continued to fill the tape, employing the same clear tones she'd used for much of her journey down from London.

She said: 'Beautiful yet brooding, looking strong to a stranger but feeling fragile inside, she sat in the driver's seat and looked out at a butterfly that had landed on the bonnet of her car and now swayed in the warm summer breeze that fluttered through the green leaves of the green, green trees cuddling comfortably against the beautifully blue sky. The butterfly was just like her. It was fragile and could so easily be squashed by something else. But it could be loved too. And so could she. She, too, could learn to fly high in the blue sky.'

Clare found Louise in the courtyard, dozing. The creak of the gate woke her, and she turned and smiled. 'Good journey?' she asked, getting to her feet and exchanging kisses with Clare.

'I kept myself busy,' Clare said, holding up the dictaphone.

'That's good. How are you finding it?'

'I don't think I'll ever feel fully comfortable with it, but it's getting easier with each book we do.' She shrugged her left shoulder slightly. The leather bag hanging from it by a strap bobbed. 'I think there's about eight hours' worth of recordings altogether. And I've been more selective than last time. I've only done the interesting bits. Specific events and memories, you know?'

Louise sucked air in between her lips. 'Eight hours. I'm impressed. That should give us plenty to work on.' She glanced at the front door. 'You must be thirsty. Let's get ourselves a drink and then get straight down to business.'

Outside again, the scents of the courtyard and garden beyond seized Louise's attention, fumigating her imagination, leaving her settled and at peace. Clare followed her in apprehensive silence. These sessions always left her awkward, as if she was back at school. She could never quite follow the process through which Louise could take her thoughts and weave them into a story. She was never sure where her contribution ended and Louise's began.

Beneath the baked blue glaze of sky, Louise turned left and trailed the stone wall of the main house with the habitual glide of her fingertips, then descended the step onto the marginally lower level of cobbled plain which spread out from the foundations of the outbuilding she called the Studio. She reached the door of the Studio and slid the key into the well-oiled mechanism of the ostentatiously decrepit and rustled lock.

Shafts of sunlight from the window opposite and the skylights above spread outwards as they neared the floor, their angles revealing the hour of the day and illuminating gently swirling spirals of dust which the draught of the open door had stirred. Louise closed the door behind them and their feet began the brief pilgrimage across the cold, uneven flagstoned floor. They walked beneath the dusty wooden planks of the mezzanine floor above where grain had once been stored, past the spectre of the sheet-draped easel without even so much as repressed curiosity. They weren't here to paint, though lessons in that particular art could also be taken here. They settled themselves at the table which housed Louise's typewriter and other working paraphernalia. Outside, Tramp, who'd tracked their scent, scratched at the door in frustration.

'Let's start with the tape you've done for me today,' Louise decided, flipping the tiny cassette into a machine and pressing the Review button. 'It'll be more immediate in your mind.'

Some time afterwards, as the recorded words gave way to static, Louise opened her eyes and pressed the Stop button.

'Well?' Clare asked. 'What did you think?'

Louise nodded her head. 'Good. Very impressive. I enjoyed the way you wove the memories of Byron into the narrative. You're obviously starting to feel comfortable with him as a character.'

'I am. I did what you said. I tried to relive the emotions I felt about my ex-husband, Patrick, and then fed them into Byron.'

'And the rent boy. He was good, too. His presence in the flat in the morning told us a lot about our protagonist, Clara. It conveyed her sensuous nature extremely efficiently. And . . .' She noticed Clare's blush. 'Oh,' she said. 'He was real, was he?' Clare raised her eyebrows in affirmation. 'No matter,' Louise said. 'It's good to see you're not afraid to mix reality and fiction.' She scribbled something down on the notebook of her lap. 'I liked the description of the house, of the bedroom particularly. Is that what your house is really like?' she asked, still writing.

'Yes, pretty much.'

'OK. I think we can use that. We'll change it a bit so that

your friends won't pick up on it. The scene will work very well, combining Clara's discomfort in her own bedroom with the rent boy and her strip for the voyeur across the street.' She stopped writing and looked up, half-smiling. 'And don't worry, I won't ask you whether that's fact or fiction. We can use it anyway. The combination keeps her mysterious. Sexy and vulnerable. Very neat indeed. That one tape alone gives me plenty to work on. You should give yourself a pat on the back.'

'Thank you,' Clare said.

'Aren't you pleased?'

'Yes.' Clare frowned. 'It's just that when I'm speaking into the tape, I really feel like I'm creating something. But whenever I try to write it down myself – and I have tried – it seems so useless.'

There was a movement in the rafters above and both women looked up at the small cloud of dislodged dust which was drifting down.

'Don't worry,' Louise said. 'Mice. They're everywhere this summer. Too much food around.' Her head tilted sympathetically as her eyes met Clare's once more. 'And don't feel that you're useless. You're not. The books *are* yours. Nearly all the ideas and characters come straight from your imagination. You're providing the building materials from the foundations up. Without you, I wouldn't have anything to work with.'

'I suppose so,' Clare said.

'Anyway, I think you could write if you invested the time. You must have noticed yourself how fluent your audio tapes are becoming. The voice already seems to be there. Do you make notes before you record things?'

'No. But it's like acting. Once the words have swilled around your head for a while, and you've had a chance to toy with them, they fit into place. I find it comes naturally to speak the words. It's just the thought of putting a whole book together without someone to guide me, not just following your advice about what sort of things I should be thinking about, not just doing bits and pieces. It's too complicated even to begin thinking about.'

A short, tortured yelp came from outside the door and Louise tensed, half-rising. There was no more noise and she relaxed again. 'Tramp's got bored of waiting for us,' she said with a smile.

Clare said nothing.

'You could write without my help if you tried.' Louise sat back in her chair and put the notebook on the table. 'All fiction really is is the application of imagination to reality. There's no great secret about it. And you don't just have to think about the things I've suggested. Writing can come from anywhere. From the simplest of places, too. It's there to be realised wherever we look. Here. Let me give you a demonstration.' She stood up, picking a different notebook from the table and holding it gravely before her, as if she were about to give a sermon. 'Would you agree with me that this room is real?'

'Of course,' Clare said.

'Right, well this is a simple place. Beautiful, yes?'

'Lovely.'

'But not particularly dramatic?'

Clare looked slowly around. 'No, not really.'

'It's hardly the kind of place where anything wildly romantic is likely to occur, is it?'

'No.'

'Well, actually, yes,' Louise said. 'All we have to do is inject a bit of imagination, then capture it in words. And then arrange those words to suit our purposes. Put our characters in them. That's all fiction is. And that's exactly what we're doing with your novel. You remember how we decided last time that the man who was going to win Clara's heart and mind, save her from herself and those around her, was an artist?'

'Yes,' Clare said. 'An older man. Maurice. Strong, but unafraid to show his love for her.'

Louise nodded, pleased. 'That's it. Well think of Clara, how she'd be feeling on the day she decides to risk everything and give herself to him.' She looked at Clare. 'Now think of her in this room, and listen.' She flicked through a couple of pages and read aloud:

Clara stopped in front of the mirror on top of the battered tea-chest in the corner of the room, and tilted its wooden frame so that her reflection stared back into her eyes. She picked up a brush and repeatedly drew it through her hair, watching the waves she created subside time and time again. Then her fingers turned from the brush to her dress, unfastening the buttons and drawing the garment over her head and placing it on a nearby bench. She walked into the shower of sunlight provided by one of the skylights, imagining its warmth to be the languid touch of a lover on her pale skin, the touch of Maurice on her naked body. She closed her eyes and stood motionless as the passing seconds grouped into minutes. Then, her intuition anticipating his approach from across the fields, she moved to the bed and slowly crawled to its centre, willingly curling up in the soft tangle of sheets, knowing that he would come to release her soon.

Before Louise had time to look up from her book and attend Clare's reaction to her creation, another sound came from the floor above. This time the dust came in a downpour. Footsteps crossed the creaking boards.

'I take your point, but feel I have to point out that the reverse is equally true: characters from fiction can also step out into reality. Nevertheless, a most inspirational seminar, Louise,' Cleo said as she appeared at the edge of the mezzanine floor and stared down at them. 'You're wasted here. You should be lecturing creative writing at night-school. Who knows how many Nobel winners you'd mould.'

'What are you doing here?' Louise asked. 'I thought you'd gone to Cheltenham . . .' She looked across the room in confusion, at the door. 'And how did you get in?'

'Do excuse the cliché,' Cleo said, dropping from the rafters and landing in a crouch on the ground, 'but fact is often stranger than fiction.'

Clare watched her get to her feet, then turned to Louise, uttering, 'Who—'

'Who am I?' Cleo asked. 'Well now, that really is a question.' She waited until Clare turned back to face her. Her skin had turned sallow, its customary television glow gone. 'Louise knows me as Cleo Hardy, as I'm sure she'd have told you herself if I hadn't rudely interrupted. But what's in a name? People use false names all the time.' She bowed dramatically in Clare's direction, waited for a response. But the equation in Clare's head was still incomplete: no answer came. 'So Cleo Hardy it is,' Cleo said, holding up her hand. 'No, no, don't tell me. I already know who you are, Clare. I watch your television show. I've read your books. Knowing your name's the least of your problems.'

'How long have you been up there?' Louise demanded.

'Long enough.'

'I don't know what you think you're doing, breaking in and sneaking around and eavesdropping,' Louise said, striding forward and taking Cleo by the arm, 'or what gives you the right to act in this insane way, but I won't tolerate it.' She led her briskly across the room. When they reached the door, Louise opened it. 'I think you should go up to the house and pack your things. I don't want you as a guest in my house any longer.'

'Is that a fact?' Cleo asked, making no move to leave.

Louise glared. 'Yes it is! I'll come up now and sort the bill out for your brother and you.' She peered with severity around the room. 'I take it he's not hiding in here as well?'

'No.'

'Well where is he?'

'Why, outside the door, of course.'

Louise wheeled round to see Mr Hardy standing there. His face was as blank as ever. He was pointing a gun at her chest. Next to him, on the ground, was Tramp. Blood and drool clung to her muzzle. Louise lunged down towards the dead animal, but Cleo grabbed the back of her neck and snapped her to her feet. She felt Louise shaking. Rage?

Fear? Perhaps she hadn't yet established in her mind that the first was irrelevant to her circumstances, the second inevitable.

'You'll notice that Mr Hardy is holding a sawn-off shotgun. You'll both, particularly Clare, be familiar with it from television. As you can see for yourselves, it's got two barrels. One for each of you.' She released Louise's frail, quivering hand from her arm. 'It would be prudent at this stage for you to return to your seat.'

Mr Hardy and Cleo, Mr Hardy closing the door behind him, crossed the room and waited for Louise to join Clare at the table. Cleo smiled. It was good to see the two of them together in public at last, united, even if it was in such adversity. Still, looking at them now, she could almost sympathise with the publicity department of Clare's publisher. Louise was hardly a photogenic beauty. Maybe when she was younger. But then, maybe if when she'd been younger she'd had the honesty to match her face to her words, she wouldn't be looking quite so appallingly unphotogenic now. Yes, she could almost sympathise with the publicity department. But almost wasn't going to be enough. *Clack*: decisions made in the past must be seen to affect the future. *Clack*: accountability is essential to art.

'So,' Cleo said, putting one foot on the table and leaning forward, 'here we all are.' She smiled encouragingly at the two other women in turn. 'Now, does anyone know why we're here?' There was no reply. 'Cat got your tongues? Come on, Louise, let's start with you. Why do you think we're here?'

'I don't know what you're trying to do,' Clare said. 'But you won't get away with it.'

'Spoken like the cheap television actress you are,' Cleo said. 'Now shut it, slut!' 'You don't speak unless I tell you to!' She leant down towards her. 'Understand?' Clare covered her face with her hands, amplifying her hissing breath. Her shuddering became more pronounced. 'There's a good girl,' Cleo said. 'We wouldn't want to have to get the therapist in just yet, would we?' Her head flicked round.

'Now, Louise, answer the question.'

Louise looked Cleo straight in the eyes, spoke evenly. 'I know who you are, Amazonia, or Diana. And I know he's Tup Maul.'

There was a moment's silence before Cleo finally replied, 'Well, well. Someone who recognises the face of death when she sees it.' She turned to Mr Hardy. 'What do you think of that, Mr Hardy? Louise here has guessed who we are and, I think we can safely infer, why we're here.'

Mr Hardy swung the gun, which he'd been swinging idly between the two seated women, at Louise. 'Now?' he asked.

'No, Mr Hardy. Not just yet. We don't want to go breaking the narrative off just yet. Not before the dénouement.'

Clare's hands were on her lap now. Thin white scars ran through her mascara where her tears had trailed. Her breathing was imperceptible, her blue eyes dull. Cleo walked up to her and waved her hand in front of her face, peering keenly into her eyes. There was nothing to be read there now that the moment was nearly here. Not one thought. Not like it had been with Appleton. If Clare was the only one she'd come for, then she'd wait until she snapped out of it, even nurse her back to health for the satisfaction of snatching it away from her once more. After all, what was the point in taking the time to demonstrate to someone that they were wrong and you were right when they weren't paying attention? What was the point in telling someone that their stolen time was over and your overdue time had begun when they weren't even aware what time it was? But Clare wasn't the only one. She was part of a pair, meaningless alone. There was Louise still left, eyes and ears wide open. And wasn't it just that things had turned out this way? Clare had never been anything but an inert body, a face to be photographed. It was Louise who held the intellect. It was Louise who needed to be taught. *Clack*: progress feeds off victims. *Clack*: the establishment of the new necessitates the destruction of the old.

'Remarkable,' she finally said, stepping back a pace. 'Clare appears to have gone catatonic on us. Sedated by events. Free drugs, no less. What do you think of that, Louise?'

'Does it matter what I think?'

Cleo's mouth dropped open in surprise. 'Of course it does. We're here to hear your opinions, to let you have your say, and then show you where you've been going wrong. But you know that already. You've read the article. That's how you know who we are.' She tilted her head to one side. 'I couldn't resist leaving it there for you in the bathroom. Call it an excessive desire for irony. I'm surprised you made the connection, though. My research had led me to believe that you weren't that interested in the goings on in the world outside the boundaries of your precious land.'

'You don't have to go through with this, Amazonia,' Louise said.

Cleo hissed. 'Now, now,' she reprimanded. 'Let's keep in character, shall we? Amazonia was Appleton's nemesis. Cleo's yours.'

'This can end now. All you have to do is choose for it to be that way.'

'We all have choices to make. You and Clare made the wrong one. What I'm doing now is correcting that error.' Cleo walked to Mr Hardy and took the gun from him. 'Move their chairs to the centre of the room. Back to back.'

Mr Hardy strode to the seat Clare was sitting in and picked up both her and it and walked across the floor and placed the chair back on the ground. He turned to Louise, but she'd already risen, and was carrying the chair towards him.

'Cooperation is good,' Cleo said, as Louise positioned the chair with its back to the one Clare occupied and resumed her seated position. 'Have you got the bag, Mr Hardy?'

'Outside. By the dead dog.'

'Well, go and get it. The bag, that is. The dog's not going to be much use to anyone any more.' Mr Hardy grunted in agreement and left the room. When he returned, he dropped the bag at Cleo's feet and she told him, 'Take the rope. Tie them up. Not too tight. Enough to hold them, but not enough to crush. I want to be able to hear them.'

Mr Hardy unzipped the black canvas bag and slipped his hands inside and withdrew a bundle of rope. He walked to Clare and adjusted her arms so that they hung at her side, then did the same to Louise. He then tied a loop and dropped it over their shoulders, onto their waists, and jerked it tight, so that the chairs they sat in creaked back against one another. Clare's head lolled forward and Louise exhaled, her ribcage shrinking beneath the strain. Mr Hardy glanced at Cleo for reassurance and once she'd nodded, he circled the chairs, holding the rope low to begin with, coiling it first around their legs, then rising, sheathing their waists with white fibres, working his way up to their necks.

'When you've finished that, tie the knot and take the sheet from the bag and drape it over them,' Cleo said, crossing the room and sitting down at the table, closing her eyes.

As her memory asserted itself over present events, the noises of Mr Hardy's activity slipped further and further from her mind.

The office of the literary agency which represented Clare Carrier hadn't been difficult to track down. All it had taken to find the agency's name was a quick call to the publicity department at Clare's publisher. And then a call to the agency to discover the name of Clare's agent. What could have been less innocuous than a fan who'd recently watched Clare discussing her latest novel on prime-time TV now wishing to write to Clare in person and press her further on some of the fascinating topics she'd broached? What she hadn't mentioned over the phone was that Clare's televised comments on her own novel had demonstrated one of two things in this particular viewer's mind: either Clare's memory was so poor that she should be forgiven for having forgotten a pivotal moment from her own novel, or that that novel hadn't been hers to begin with.

Breaking into the office had been simple, too. It had

taken her two minutes of one morning, standing next to the lifts on the landing outside the door to the agency, watching one, two, three people arrive and initiate their nine-to-five day by stabbing a four-digit code into the keypad on the wall. And with this so-called security compromised, it had then only been a matter of choosing a night to suit her.

At ten, she'd entered the building which housed the agency. The security guard raised his TV-sedated eyes and observed her.

'Hi,' she said, her head bobbing, embarrassed. 'My husband left his house keys in his office.' She dropped the agency's managing director's name and the security guard nodded in recognition. 'He's waiting in the car outside.' She watched the guard crane his neck and peer out through the glass doors at the shadowed car whose exhaust exhaled into the night air. 'OK if I pop up and get them? I'll just be a minute.'

The guard looked her over, took in the designer cut of her clothes, her open, honest face, and nodded. 'Sure, go ahead.'

'Thanks,' she said and walked to the lift.

The lift door opened on the fifth floor and she walked across to the keypad and entered the appropriate code. A buzzer sounded somewhere inside and the door clicked. She pulled it open and stepped through into the reception. Opposite her, Clare Carrier stared out at her from a promotional poster, her brilliant white teeth locked together in a grin. To the left of the poster were shelves displaying the latest publications of the agency's authors' new releases. She ignored these and walked round to the back of the reception desk, listening all the time for betrayals of late-night dedication – the sound of a boiling kettle, fingers rattling a keyboard, voices and footsteps – none of which she heard. She leant across the desk and studied the phone systems. There were forty or so rectangular bulbs, each signifying a phone on someone's desk. None of them were lit, none of their receivers gripped by a hand. She searched the desk until she saw, taped to the side of the computer monitor, a sheet of paper listing the members of staff and their extension numbers. She read down until she found Clare's agent's name and number, then walked round the desk, out of reception and down the short, symbolic section of corridor which led to the office proper.

The extension number on the phone in the fourth office she tried matched the agent's name she'd read at reception. A glance at the bookshelves confirmed the discovery: various editions of Clare's books lay wedged together. She glanced at her watch. Three minutes had ticked by since she'd turned her back on the security guard downstairs. That left her another two – three at most – before he might start wondering what was taking her so long. She walked to the filing cabinet and hauled its drawers out into the light until she found Clare's files. A cursory inspection of the first one she pulled out revealed that it was recent correspondence. She returned it and removed the one slotted behind. This was the one she was looking for: contracts. She flicked quickly through them, checking their top pages, dismissing those between Clare Carrier and her publishing house. If she'd had time, she would have checked out the advances Clare had been paid, seen just how much money she'd taken for nothing, but she didn't. It wasn't publishing contracts she was here for. Something else. Something detailing an agreement between Clare and . . . and there it was. She pulled the stapled wad of paper, headed Collaboration Agreement, clear from the folder.

'Got you,' she said, ripping some paper from a pad at the desk and writing down the name of the ghost-writer named here who'd been contracted to write Clare's books for her.

She returned the contract to the filing cabinet. Then she picked the diary off the desk and flicked through the weeks until she found Clare's name next to that of the other woman in the Collaboration Agreement. A final search, through the address rotadeck this time, and a few scribbled lines on the piece of paper, and she was done.

She glanced at her watch as the lift door opened in the lobby on the ground floor. Six minutes in and out. Easy. She smiled at the security guard on her way to the door.

'You find them?' he asked.

'Oh yes,' she said, pulling a bunch of keys from her pocket and shaking them at him. 'Just where I thought they'd be.'

Cleo heard Mr Hardy's breath falling close by. She opened her eyes and saw he was now standing in front of her. He was staring. Not at her. At the gun. The gun was all he saw.

'Here,' she said, placing it in his hands, watching him swivel and train it on the centre of the room.

His sculpture was now complete. A Gothic masterpiece. The two heads that belonged to Clare Carrier and Louise Elliot were now concealed beneath the white sheet. Their individual characteristics – facial features, hair and bodies – had been ironed out by the starched cotton which now shrouded them. With the single sheet stretched over their scalps, it was impossible to tell where Clare ended and Louise began. Nothing remained to distinguish them from one another. Their separate lives had slid together, gelled into a two-headed ghost. They were bound in this parody of death, as they'd bound themselves to one another through their association in life.

There was silence for a moment, and then a muffled voice came from the ghost. 'I'm not going to do it.'

'Do what, Louise?' Cleo asked, walking towards the voice. 'At least I assume it's Louise talking. I can't tell for sure. Not any more.'

'Give you the pleasure of watching me beg and trying to justify the way I make a living. I don't need to. I don't have a problem with it. Nobody does. Nobody but you.'

'What do you know?' Cleo flared, forcing her hands down on the two heads of the ghost, clamping them in her grip and twisting their necks around. 'What do you know about problems, you ignorant bitch?' She lifted her hand from Louise's head and brought it smacking down in a fist. There was a muffled groan from below the sheet. 'You're going to learn all about problems and suffering. You don't have a problem, because you *are* the fucking problem. I'm going to teach you. I'm going to teach you what suffering's all about.'

She pulled her hands back and walked the length of the room, stopped by the door. Her breath fell heavily for several seconds.

'So be it,' she suddenly announced. 'If you won't play it by my rules, we'll play it by yours.' She began the walk back. 'We won't go through the rigmarole of persuading you that the level of deceit involved in your partnerships with people like Clare is immoral, and that it makes a mockery of the essential accountability of writers for their works. And we won't bother mentioning that people like you are responsible for diverting the available financial resources from writers of quality to writers of crap. And we won't even venture near the issue of your revolting formulaic writing being responsible for dropping the level of published literature to something that a schoolchild would comprehend fully at a first reading.' She reached the bag and leant down. 'No, we won't do any of that. We'll do it your way, OK? How's that for fair?'

'It doesn't matter.'

'You're wrong,' Cleo said, shaking her head violently, lifting a petrol can from the bag and getting to her feet. 'Justice is everything. Justice is why I'm here.' She unscrewed the cap of the can and walked around the ghost, the can now tilted, letting the petrol pour out.

'What are you doing?' Louise shouted, her head twisting from side to side.

'What does it smell like? Revenge?' Cleo asked, lifting the can above her head and drenching the sheet over Clare's head, neck and shoulders. She walked around and lifted the can again, this time letting a controlled splash spatter across Louise's shoulder. She watched the sheet act like a sponge, suck the splash across itself, drain from white to grey. 'It smells like baptism, like cleansing.' Cleo threw the empty can across the room, watched it skitter across the ground and come to a rest. 'Go and get the other cans from the car,' she told Mr Hardy. 'Then come back here and drown this place.'

By the time Mr Hardy had doused the mezzanine floor along with every flammable part of the building, seven empty cans had joined the first on the ground. The place stank like a refinery. Cleo took the last of the cans from his hand and trailed petrol from Louise's and Clare's bodies to the door. She then recrossed the room, paused to empty the last few drops of fuel onto Clare's head, and then deposited the empty can on the table and picked up one of the notebooks.

'I need one of your books for a prop,' she said. She bowed around the room at an imaginary audience. 'I'm going to attempt the artistic equivalent of alchemy: the conversion of fiction into fact. So pay attention. It's a one-off.'

She walked purposefully to the far side of the room and stood by the open doorway, beckoned Mr Hardy until he joined her, stood by her side. The sun beat down on her back, threw her shadow across the path of petrol, so that, when she raised her hand, her shadow stretched out and clawed across Louise and Clare's ashen silhouette. Cleo steadied herself. When she spoke, her words came out in a monotone.

'Would you agree with me, Louise, that this room is real?' Silence followed her words. 'You'll fucking answer me now!' Cleo screamed.

'Yes,' a voice mumbled from beneath the sheet.

'Good. Better.' Cleo paused briefly, regained her composure. 'Right, well this is a simple place. Beautiful, yes?'

'Yes.'

'But not particularly dramatic?' Again, there was no reply. This time, she let it go. 'It's not the kind of place where anything wildly violent is likely to occur, is it?'

Nothing.

'Well, actually, yes,' Cleo said, her voice still wooden. 'All we have to do is inject a bit of imagination, then capture it in words. And then arrange those words to suit our purposes. Put our characters in them.' She lowered her hand

and flicked through the pages of the book in a perfunctory fashion.

Clare was catatonic by this point, the realisation of her imminent punishment for crimes against literature and the reading public enough to induce an altered state of mind. She'd become the death-row victim, destroyed by the wait, just wanting it over. Louise was sitting back-to-back with her, strapped to her silent partner. Beneath the sheet, her eyes were closed against the burning fumes which settled in her nostrils and throat. She knew there was nothing she could say that could erase or atone for the sins she'd committed. She understood that Cleo would never agree with her that ghosting the books of talentless public personalities was justified by her love for the house she lived in. In her heart, she now comprehended the destruction of one form of beauty was not justified by the preservation of another. Cleo looked at Mr Hardy and raised the hand that held the notebook above her head. Mr Hardy transferred the gun to one hand and pulled a lighter from his pocket. He glanced back eagerly at Cleo, knowing that when she released the book he could spin the wheel across the flint and watch a flame grow tall. He could then bend to the ground – without hesitation – and let the flame lick the tip of the petrol trail. He'd then stand up, move back, and watch the flame sprint away from him. Nothing happened for a moment. Cleo waited for Louise to set the screams inside her head free. She waited longer. Still, Louise kept her silence. Cleo dropped the book.

CHAPTER SIX

taking notes

The phone had clocked up its eighteenth ring and Jack his eighteenth muffled curse when he finally tore the pillow off his head and slung it across the room. He rolled across the bed, sheets winding round him, leaving his legs and torso mummified, and fumbled frustratedly for the receiver, determined not to open his eyes, and by so doing capitulate to the day.

'What?' he as good as belched into the mouthpiece.

'Hello?' a voice enquired through the oscillating static of a mobile link. 'Hello?'

Jack sighed. 'Yes,' he said, shifting with agonising effort, so that he sat with his back against the wall at the head of the bed. 'Hell-Bloody-O. Who is this?'

'Is that David Jackson?'

Jack looked at his bare wrist and wondered where he'd left his watch. 'Yes, it is. What do you want?'

'My name's Toby Still. I work for Probe TV.'

'Where did you get my number?' Jack asked, sliding a cigarette from the packet on the bedside table and clamping it between his dry lips.

'We've got it on a database here at the office, Mr Jackson. We produce *Answer Time* for the Network.'

'*Answer Time*?'

'Yes, you appeared on it last year in the debate on abortion . . .'

Jack didn't have a clue what Still was talking about. A vague memory surfaced about David being involved in some television debate along those lines, but he couldn't clarify it in his mind. 'Quite,' he said noncommittally. He scraped a match into life and singed the end of the cigarette. He inhaled deeply, immediately regretted it, and launched into a coughing fit, shuddering like a car with a dying battery. He needed to rehydrate, sluice the previous night's lonely excesses into oblivion. The back of his throat was screaming for chilled juice, fridge-frosted water. He opened his eyes and jerked the glass of stale water from the bedside to his mouth. It had been there for days, maybe weeks. It tasted of dust, dead skin. He controlled the urge to retch and asked, 'What time is it?'

'Nine.'

'Middle of the bloody night, then.'

The phone crackled for a few seconds. 'I'm sorry if I woke you up.'

'Sure,' Jack grunted, testing his lungs with a second tentative pull on his cigarette. They warmed to it this time, the nicotine kicking in. His head swam. 'What did you say your name was?'

'Toby. Toby Still,' the voice said with apparent relief. 'You may remember me from the last time you were on. I was a runner back then. I made sure—'

'Yeah, I remember,' Jack lied. He untangled his legs from the sheets and dropped them over the side of the bed. He located his watch, slipped it onto his wrist. 'How are you?' he asked absentmindedly, getting to his feet and stretching his shoulders.

'Well.' The tone of voice was surprised. 'Thanks.'

Jack tapped his cigarette over the full ashtray. 'So what's the score – the situation – this time? Do you want me to appear on another debate, or what?' Jack glanced at his slack body in the mirror, attempted to flex his stomach. It remained dough and he turned away in disgust. He thought about breakfast.

'Yes.'

'When's it going to take place?'

'Tomorrow night.'

'Ah,' Jack said, taking another swig of water, following

it up with two swift drags of smoke.

'Yes, I know it's short notice, but—'

Jack laughed. 'The other guy couldn't turn up, right?'

'No, not at all,' Still responded quickly. 'We had a different subject scheduled, but after yesterday's murders . . .'

Jack's eyes sparked. He hadn't read a paper in days. 'What murders?'

'Louise Elliot and Clare Carrier. Their bodies were discovered this morning in Elliot's house in Gloucestershire. Police were alerted when an account of the killings appeared on the Internet.'

A connection snapped into place in Jack's mind. Information found its way to his tongue. 'Clare Carrier? Isn't she the woman off TV, off the *Candy Shop*? Good-looking, yeah? Quite funny.'

'Yes.'

'Shit,' Jack exhaled. 'And who's the other woman?'

'Louise Elliot.'

'Never heard of her.'

'Don't worry. Not many people have. Led a pretty quiet life by all accounts.'

'So what happened?'

'They were burnt alive. Tied up in an outbuilding. The whole place was torched.'

'Christ!' Jack gasped, collapsing back onto the bed. 'And you want me to come and talk about that? What the hell am I meant to know about that? You need a shrink, not a writer.'

'It's more the literary connection we're after.'

'I'm not following you.'

'Louise Elliot was a ghost-writer. She wrote Clare Carrier's books.'

'You're kidding,' Jack said. 'What a con!' He wormed his cigarette butt through the legions of others that filled the ashtray, eventually locating the glass beneath and twisting the final glow of tobacco into ash. 'Glossies, weren't they? Pretty hot stuff.' He halted, then added, 'At least that's what I've heard.'

'Yes,' Still confirmed. 'Bestsellers.'

'Only you're telling me she didn't write them at all?'

'No.'

'Jesus.' Jack shook his head. 'So who killed them?'

'The Thriller Killers.'

'Come again?'

'The Thriller Killers. The same people who killed Adam Appleton and Mick Roper.'

Jack remembered an article. Roper had been killed by someone he'd met at Tommy's club. He'd cut the piece out, kept it, thinking that maybe one day it would provide him with a neutral subject to start a conversation with Tommy, that maybe it would stop Tommy going for his throat, give him a chance to be human again. Uncertain how long the conversation was destined to last, he lit another cigarette. 'Who else is going to be on the programme?'

'It hasn't all been finalised yet. We're aiming for a panel of four, along with Dick Middleton.'

'Yeah, he's the host right?'

'Yes. Can we count you in?'

Jack thought for a moment. He wondered if he should just say no. Since he'd been David, he'd declined everything that had come his way. Flatly. Bluntly. The phone had become an enemy, the answerphone a bodyguard. He'd been a wall without a door. He'd turned down the offer of editing a collection of pre-war short stories, refused to become one of the judges of some literary award. The only thing he'd accepted was an honorary degree from a South African university, and the only reason he'd done that was because Sally Scott-Thompson, his literary agent, had said that she'd deal with it, negotiate him out of having to fly out there. But Sally hadn't been happy about any of this. She'd told him he couldn't go on hiding like this, that it wasn't healthy, that it wasn't good for his career. And he'd known that she was right.

'OK,' he answered Still. 'You're filming in London, I take it,' he hazarded. Another commitment snagged his conscience, spurred him on: he had to go to London today anyway. And if he had to be there today, what was the harm in staying the night and being there tomorrow, too? 'What time do you need me there?'

'It'll be the same arrangements as last time.'

'Right,' Jack said. 'Remind me what they were.'

A short while later, he was lying in the bath. He'd been right to follow Sally's advice. He couldn't put his life on pause indefinitely. Even though he hadn't taken on David's life out of choice, but desperation, he was going to have to turn his eyes to the future at some point, so why not now? Yeah, trust in Sally. She was, after all, meant to be one of the best agents outside of Los Angeles. And what's more, she was charismatic. She was someone he felt a need to please. He submerged his head beneath the water, curled up on his side, imagined the water as amniotic fluid, searched for the reassurance of the womb. He'd be OK. In his time at the Book Bar, he'd heard enough literary opinions. And he'd watched enough TV in his time. It shouldn't be any big deal fitting in, should it? He spun and burst to the surface.

Back in the bedroom, he selected one of David's shirts and a suit and tried them on in front of the mirror. The material was austere, not something Jack would have chosen himself; it was altogether too square. But it was what David would have worn to appear on television. Jack new this instinctively.

He walked to the chest-of-drawers and rummaged through the cardboard box of photographs which stood on top. There must have been a thousand in there, a pictorial chronicle of David's public life. Jack had collected them from the attic and various drawers and photo albums around the house in the days following David's death. It had been a matter of bloodshot, pulse-flushed urgency.

He'd realised then that if he was to impersonate his brother successfully he'd have to start with emulating his physical appearance. That, at least, would allow him to pass cursory inspections with a degree of confidence. With this in mind, he'd arranged the photographs into chronological order, had reconstructed David's life from initial flash right through to exposure, the photographic process which had metamorphosed him from anonymity into an icon. He'd then selected certain photos and grouped them inside themed envelopes. He took one from the box now. It was labelled 'Media'. He knelt down on the floor and placed the thirty or so photos before him as if he was playing solitaire. His intuition had been right. The suit was there, in a photo of David shaking hands with the presenter of a rival show. He flipped it over. The date was good, too. Six months earlier. Fashions hadn't changed much. He looked the photo over again, then went to the wardrobe and pulled out the right tie. He studied the mirror again, felt satisfied; he'd look just right in front of the camera.

After he'd packed the clothes and dressed again, he went downstairs to eat. Swallowing the final bite of his breakfast, he watched Gellet eyeing him suspiciously from the corner of the room. The dog still didn't trust him, wouldn't come near him. Whenever he put food out for him, he ignored it. It was only after he'd left the room that he would go near it. The one time he'd waited outside the kitchen door and, hearing the clank of shaggy muzzle and teeth meeting metal bowl, had sprung in in surprise, the dog had turned from his food, bared his teeth, snarled, and sloped off to his usual corner in disgust.

Jack had only discovered his name when the woman who cleaned for David once weekly had come round with a commiseration cake baked in the wake of the news of the discovery of the burnt-out car. The woman had greeted Gellet like a child, softly repeating his name in comforting tones, ruffling the thick black hair on his back.

And, with this dog, Jack knew now: loyalty was something that stretched past life into death. It was going to take more than a change in appearance and attitude to fool this creature. He was going to have to become David, concentrate on achieving the spiritual transition, assume David's internal qualities as well, until they seeped out of the pores of his skin and Gellet sniffed the scent and recognised his master once more. OK, so before that was accomplished, the cigarettes might have to go. But they weren't going anywhere just yet. He needed them too much. It was the one vestige of his own personality he'd refused, or been unable, to leave behind, and he would cling to it right up to the point where he was so certain of his new self that he wouldn't need crutches of any sort any more.

He cleared away the dishes and washed his hands with fastidious care at the sink, until the tips of his fingernails were bleached, as sterile as David's ever were. He then sat down in the chair by the window and gazed out across the garden. There were signs of creeping neglect: the grass grew above regulation length; the rose bushes needed tending to. Perhaps gardening should be the next thing. He'd already tried the clothes on. They'd even felt strangely comfortable and – dare he think it? – his. But that could wait. He hadn't had anyone to stay yet and wasn't planning to in the foreseeable future either. He could deal with his private life after he'd successfully constructed his public persona.

He picked the small tape machine up and placed it on his lap, loaded the audio book and sat back, closing his eyes and listening to David's voice reading his third novel. He let the voice cradle his mind for five minutes or so, succumbing to the therapy provided by the sequence of words he already knew. As with his favourite songs, he'd reached the point where he could anticipate the next word and, more than that, the exact pitch and tone of the enunciation. He switched the tape off and continued the story with his own voice for a few paragraphs, slyly observing Gellet with his peripheral vision, searching for signs that the animal, with its superior hearing, could distinguish flaws in the performance.

Deep down, though, this was a perfunctory exercise. He was convinced he'd been tone perfect for some time now. But still, his confidence was incomplete. Despite the preparation he'd put in, he still felt hubris lurking demonically in the background, waiting for the most inopportune moment to declare itself. He understood that Gellet, not himself, was the real judge. And he'd only be absolutely sure of himself the day that he passed the examination that the animal had unwittingly set for him, the day that Gellet viewed this ritual as a strangely narcissistic exercise on his master's behalf and not an imperfect attempt at deceit.

After a further half-hour's practice, which failed to elicit a positive response from the dog, Jack returned to the bedroom and sat at David's writing desk. He took a pen and a sheet of paper and then practised David's signature until the paper was covered with the idiosyncratic scrawl, as regular as print. He checked it briefly against the back of one of David's credit cards and then downed the pen and picked up a diary.

He'd been lucky with David's financial life. After poring over the diaries that David had unfailingly written every day since he'd left home and gone to university, Jack had armed himself with a working knowledge of David's dealings and, implicitly, his duplicity. Financial details were meticulously logged here, income and expenditure, and these black and red figures went a good way to colouring in the blank spaces in David's life.

Jack had been staggered to discover the extent of David's wealth. Even putting his literary earnings aside (alone enough to provide security for the rest of his life), those of Antidote Entertainments (the three David Jackson Book Bars and the first-editions book club – 'Turn back the page to the lessons of the past') were fantastical. And there, beneath today's date, a meeting with Leonora Smiles was pencilled in for lunch. Notes lay beneath this, detailing the purpose of the meeting (the renewing of Smiles' contract as managing director), as well as key phrases to be used and an increased salary to be offered. Jack packed the diary, along with financial reports faxed by Smiles, which he'd read the previous afternoon, into David's briefcase.

If David had been in the habit of logging in his diary the events of his personal life, and recording his emotions, the picture would have been complete. But he hadn't. Possibly out of fear of them being used against him, there wasn't a single item of this sort in any of the diaries. This would have concerned Jack. Without a torch to shine through the murk of David's inner life, he would have been blind. The most he could have hoped to achieve was a mimicking of David's voice and appearance and mannerisms. And how long would that keep him safe from prying eyes? What kind of half-life would that leave him to lead? It was the brain behind the face he needed to probe, the heart behind the ribs. And if he hadn't had a scalpel with which to slice through the armour of David's media-hardened exoskeleton and study the workings of the flesh beneath, he would have had every right to be concerned. But he did: the metaphorical scalpel was his to wield. He had something more revealing than any diary. Forget diaries. What David had left behind was far better than that. And, better still, it hadn't been difficult to find; it hadn't even been hidden.

He reached beneath the desk, lifted a typescript and notebook and put them on the desk before him. That David had been writing an autobiography wouldn't have come as a surprise to anyone, least of all Jack. David was prime for such self-adulation. And the public would have been a willing partner in the enterprise. David could have sated their demand, supplied them with the explanations behind the enviable facts that grouped together to form his curriculum vitae. If he'd chosen to share his knowledge concerning the route to success in business and the arts, who but a fool would have chosen to block their ears? People would have queued outside the bookshops to secure their copies. But if these same people had known the revelations that this typescript actually contained, they wouldn't have just queued, they'd have broken down the door. The typescript before Jack chronicled the events of David's life over the preceding months. Jack recognised many of the names and places as real, not products of David's imagination. And where the typescript ended, the notebook continued. It laid out in detail other experiences David had intended to undergo. It laid them out bare, not as prediction, but as fact. These events, David had been certain, were going to happen exactly as he'd planned.

Jack closed his eyes. He didn't need the typescript to refresh his memory, he'd read it so often. The facts on the pages had filtered through his mind and asserted themselves there with the same potent authenticity as memory. Had he actually been there in person, they couldn't have been more grounded in reality for him than they already were. The events swept him along before them. He found himself an invisible entity, spying on the unfolding narrative, incapable of interference, incapable of doing anything but staring as the drama played itself out before him.

David was losing count. It was the third, fourth, maybe even fifth time this evening he'd greedily snorted his way along a line of cocaine. Was there a limit to how often he could do this? Could this be that one snort too far? He didn't know. He was new to this stuff. Three months of feeding off it, no more. This stuff made him new, brushed familiarity aside. And this was what he liked. It didn't take him out of himself. No escape routes were offered here. Nothing so weak. This stuff offered something better than escape. It offered confirmation of what he already knew. It confirmed that his life was bigger and better than anything anyone else had ever experienced. He could do anything. More. Everything. He'd do everything. Everything was here for him to taste. Everything was his by right. That's why it existed. Nothing was too high to escape his erudite reach and nothing too base to avoid the trail of his primeval knuckles. No matter how glorious, no matter how sick: he was going to do it all. He was going to take and take and take until all that remained of life was a shrivelled husk. He was going to take until he was full. And then he was going to vomit, vomit on the page and publish. They wanted truth. They wanted life stunned for inspection between the covers of a book. He'd given it to them. He'd give it to them so pure they'd wish they'd never asked for it in the first place. Posthumous publication. A book by a dead author.

A noise boxed his ears and he shuffled across to the window. The cab was there in the drive. He looked at his watch. They were here right on time. Good girls. Good girls always came on time. And filling time to its full capacity was essential. What had the doctor given him? Years? Months? He hadn't even been able to pin it down to that. Probably years. Probably years left to live before the virus ate him alive, finished its meal and belched him into the atmosphere. Probably years before he ended up, years before his time, as fragile as his mother had been when the cancer had sunk its teeth into her during her eighties, his strength sucked from his body, his muscles lax and lazy, his eye sockets pleading craters. Probably years, but possibly less. Possibly less before he joined her, left this place behind to people who didn't deserve it. People like Rachel, who'd wasted their lives. People like Jack whose potential for excellence had been stunted from the first. People without worth. The same people who wouldn't discover his condition until he keeled over dead before them with still, enlightened eyes. Let them read his writing then. Let them collapse alongside the media in a stuttering heap when they realised the exact extent to which they'd been duped. David Jackson, the moralist. Suckers. Stupid fuckers. What did morals mean to him? A route to cash. A path to fame. But he had those now. Morals didn't mean shit to him any more. Screw the critics. Screw the public, too. This virus wasn't a curse. It was a blessing. It was a passport out of the conventional world, into a place whose very existence other people were too afraid even to acknowledge. It was the last and loudest laugh of all.

But that was the future. And – he watched the two girls get out of the cab and start walking towards the house – who needed a future when you could make the present pass by any way you chose?

'Thank you, thank you, sweet, sweet, ladies,' he said, downstairs now, taking the women's coats and hanging them up on the stand by the door.

He turned round the surveyed them. Not too bad. Not too bad at all. The blonde was seventeen, eighteen tops; her make-up wasn't thick enough to fully disguise the bubble of acne below her lower lip. The other was brunette and older.

Less make-up. Perhaps thirty. Though who could tell for sure these days? Too many cosmetics on the market. Too many tricks of the trade. But they were younger than him. Much younger. He didn't need to check their faces or bodies to know this. Their eyes said it all. When they looked at him, their eyes said, *Dirty old man*. And when they took their eyes from him and scoped the room, their eyes said, *Filthy, rich, dirty old man*.

'Nice house,' the brunette said.

He took in the fact that the older one spoke first. She was the one he'd be dealing with. The blonde was avoiding his eyes now. Probably new to the game. Far from being a problem, this was a perk. What the brunette would do, the blonde would do too. Controlling her was the key.

He smiled at the brunette and said, 'Indeed. Now names. I want to know what you're both called.' The blonde glanced at the brunette for guidance and so he sped the charade up: 'Not, of course, that you're going to give me your real names. But I do need names. Otherwise, how are you going to know who I'm talking to later on? Eye contact might not be convenient.' He stared hard at the brunette, growing impatient now, and reminded her: 'Names . . .'

'I'm Sam,' she said.

He nodded and turned to the blonde. 'And I'm Sue,' she muttered.

'Very imaginative.' He turned away from them. 'Well, Sam and Sue, follow me. Time is money, so let's not waste it.'

Upstairs, he held the door open and ushered them into his bedroom. They walked to the centre of the room and then stopped, looked around.

'What now?' Sam asked.

He looked them up and down. 'I take it that you're wearing something appropriate under those jumpers and jeans,' he said. 'I was very specific when Alex asked me what I wanted . . .'

'Are you going to keep the curtains open?' Sam asked, staring out at the ink black sky.

'Does it bother you?' he asked with a barely concealed

sneer. 'Have you got something to hide?'

'No,' she said, pulling her jumper over her head, revealing a black latex bra strapped tight across her puckered white skin.

'Good.' He watched Sue walk to the bed, sit down and begin to unbutton her jeans. 'I'll be back in a minute.'

He went downstairs and poured himself a vodka and tonic, then climbed the stairs and walked down the corridor which led to his room. He then halted, turned to the room that Rachel now slept in, turned the handle and entered.

She'd made this spare room hers many months before, left their marital bed to him alone. It had been down to him, of course. She was incapable of making decisions on her own. He'd been drunk, sitting on the side of the bed, clawing like crazy at the dose of crabs – donated by some cheap King's Cross tart – that had made their nest between his legs. Rachel had sat up and asked him what was wrong. And he'd told her, hadn't pissed about, had come straight to the point. There hadn't seemed any purpose in lying. It hadn't been as if she hadn't known anyway. It couldn't have been possible that she'd been ignorant of the homage his hormones had paid to woman after woman during the course of their marriage. So many unaccounted for weekends and monosyllabic explanations couldn't possibly have escaped her attention. Yet still she'd acted shocked, betrayed. He'd watched her walk out of their bedroom. He hadn't tried to stop her. And then she'd gone to the clap clinic, got herself checked out, got the all clear for everything from herpes to AIDS. She'd told him about it, too. Told him as if he'd even cared.

So why hadn't she left him altogether, packed her bags and vacated his life for good, rather than just moving to another room? Because she was weak. Because she realised it was him, by seeking the company of other women, who'd rejected her and not the other way round? Because she thought he'd repent and want her back? Because he'd grow to love her again? What did it matter? She wasn't even here to ask. She was away in London this weekend, visiting stupid friends or seeing her psychiatrist or something. It was just as well she wasn't here, because if she was – he felt the familiar tingle in his nostrils as the membrane continued to absorb the cocaine – he'd ask her why she'd switched rooms. Ask her? Ha! The way he felt right now, he'd show her. He'd sit her down in his bedroom, introduce her to the whores and let her watch, let her witness with her own eyes the hollow charade her life had faded into.

He drained his drink and put the glass on her dressing table, surveyed his pornographic reflection in the mirror, a narcissistic voyeur, as he stripped and stroked his fingers across his skin, silently attended as his mind and body grew hard. He leant down, slowly slid his belt from his trousers, left her room and walked back to his.

The two whores were standing by his writing desk when he opened the door. Sue turned, startled, and walked to the bed. Sam stayed where she was, briefly examining his body, her eyes settling on the belt he held in his hand.

'You're a writer, then,' she eventually said, heading towards the desk and its scattered papers.

'It doesn't matter what I am,' he said, crossing the floor and standing next to Sue. He ran his hand over her shoulder, onto her leather-bound breast. 'All that matters is what you are. All that matters is what you're going to do to me.'

'OK,' Sam said, walking towards him, ending with her face inches from his. 'So tell me what you want.'

He stepped back, turned to Sue. 'Get on the bed. That's it. Right back. Sit on the pillows facing me. I want to be able to see you.'

She moved as he'd instructed and sat with her knees high, reached down to her knickers.

'No,' he said quickly. 'Don't flatter yourself. Keep them on. It's your face I want to see – your reaction,' he specified. Sue glanced at Sam for reassurance and, though he didn't actually see, he knew that Sam had nodded, had let her know that this wasn't something she should worry about, that everything was going to be just fine. He knew more about these people than they knew about themselves. He watched Sue's hands drop to her sides. She was new to all this, all right. It was there in her nerves, in her flickering eyes. It was there on the soft, unscarred skin of her limbs, an invisible tattoo that escaped all eyes but his. Her reaction to what she was about to witness was going to be a repeat from a film he'd already imagined in its entirety. 'Here,' he said, pressing the belt into Sam's hand. He sank to his knees at the foot of the bed, stretched his arms across the bedclothes. 'Use it.'

There was a moment's silence. He watched a smile crinkle across Sue's lips as her eyes looked over his head into Sam's. 'You've been a naughty boy, have you?' Sam said, resting a stilettoed heel on his back. 'Well, you naughty boy,' she continued, removing her foot and flicking the belt lightly across his back, 'Mama's going to have to spank you.'

Sue's smile had grown into a suppressed grin now. He spun round to face Sam. 'Listen, bitch. I didn't ask you to speak. I said use it and I meant it. So, if you want to see a penny of your money, do it. Use it or forget it. Use it. Use it till there's blood.'

There was silence and then he heard the belt flicking back through the air. Pain and pleasure. The buckle snapped down across his spine and his fingers clawed into the bedclothes. This is what it's all about. Finding the difference. Finding that there's no difference at all. The belt snapped down again. He watched his knuckles whitening, felt the tears coursing from his eyes. This was alive. Not just existing. Not the crap he'd written in his books, the crap those stupid bastards had lapped up. Feeling. Extreme. The whole point of being. Pushing back the boundaries. Entering the other places, the places you only imagined existed. The belt landed and he heard someone moaning, realised it was himself. He looked up at Sue. Her smile was gone, her jaw now clamped tight. Her hands were wrapped round her shoulders, holding herself tight.

Behind him, he heard Sam say, 'You're bleeding. That's what you wanted. That's enough.'

His voice was buried beneath a growl when he spoke:

'More. I can't feel the blood. I can't feel the blood leaving my body.'

There was a pause and then the belt whipped down again and this time he did feel it. And again. And again. The sickness and poison was flowing from him now. He stared at Sue. She'd turned away and was leaning over the edge of the bed. Beneath the continual roaring from his own mouth, he was aware of her beginning to retch. Wretch . . . She'd vomit soon. It was only a matter of seconds. She didn't have the stomach for it. A few more strokes and her throat would lose the battle for containment. A few more strokes. And there it was. He closed his eyes and inhaled the scent of fresh vomit. Pleasure and pain. The belt snapped down. He felt his groin begin to tingle.

When his senses returned, he staggered to his feet. The agony in his back was intense. Sam was getting dressed. The warm leather of the relinquished belt was now cooling on the bed. He looked round. Sue was nowhere to be seen. He heard the sound of running water coming from the bathroom.

'What are you doing?' he asked Sam, stumbling to the door and closing it. 'We're not finished yet.' She ignored him, continued to pull her jeans up. Whore. Filthy, disease-ridden whore. Plague-carrier. Just like the others. No different to the one who'd given it to him. He turned the lock. 'Are you deaf? I said we're not finished.'

'I'm going.' She picked up her top from the floor.

'You're going nowhere.' He crossed the room and grabbed the belt, strode towards her and ripped the top from her hands, threw it to the floor and started dragging her towards the bed. 'Not till I'm done.'

As he struck her across the face, sending her flailing onto the bed, his eyes fell on a wrapped condom on the bedside table. Sam must have put it there. Sue was moaning and he clamped his hand over her mouth, his eyes staying focused on the condom. Love was a four-letter word, spelt with an A an I a D and an S. He looked down at Sue and smiled.

'Let's make love,' he whispered, flattening his body on top of hers.

They said nothing as he handed them their coats downstairs and opened the front door. There was a darkness in their eyes that hadn't been there before. Sue was leading Sam by the hand out of the door, towards the waiting cab, not the other way round. Sue was the leader now, not how it had been when they'd arrived. Things had changed in their lives. He'd changed them himself.

'One thing,' he said, stepping forward, stretching out and grabbing Sue's wrist. 'Keep your mouths shut.'

'You fucking animal.' She tried to pull free. 'Alex's gonna kill you.'

He shook his head. 'Alex has been paid. He won't give a shit.'

'Let go.'

He tightened his grip. 'Not a word to anyone.' He nodded at Sam's battered face. 'Nothing to the police. Not unless you want Alex to make you into a beauty queen, too.'

'Look,' she said, beginning to struggle again, 'I won't talk. I fucking swear it, OK?'

He stared at her for a few seconds and then released her. 'OK.' He turned and walked back into the house. 'OK is just fine by me.'

Jack looked down at the writing desk. David had been right. Jack hadn't known about the virus paddling on an unscheduled voyage down David's bloodstream, undecided as to when it would finally dock. And he'd been right again. Jack hadn't discovered its existence until David had been dead. But he'd been wrong, too. His death hadn't been the pathos-ridden swoon that he'd foreseen, but something more deserved than that – a product of the philosophy of exploration he'd followed since the diagnosis of his condition. And he'd been wrong again. This book wasn't going to be published. Not ever.

Jack returned the notebook and typescript to their place beneath the desk. They were staying there where they belonged: out of sight. For something this sick, there was no other way. It didn't matter that this was David's last dance. So what? David was dead. This was Jack's life now. What did David matter now? So he'd had AIDS and it had flipped him out. So what? David had been a shit before all that. What difference did it make if a disease had made him a greater shit? It explained why he'd stopped caring if people saw him for what he really was. But it didn't excuse him. It didn't mean Jack had to forgive him for what he'd become, or for what he'd always been. It didn't mean that at all. And there were other things, aside from the violence and self-debasement, that Jack could never forgive him for. There were things David had written about Rachel in the notebook, things he'd been planning to do to her, mind games he'd been planning to play before she'd upped and left. The only comfort Jack could take from this was that Rachel had never read this and would never know.

When the time came to leave for London, Jack retrieved the article about Mick Roper and Adam Appleton's deaths, read it and made a few notes in his pocket diary. What was the harm in a little revision? Finally, he folded up the article and added it, along with his wash things and spare clothes, to the contents of his overnight bag. He then went downstairs to leave some food out for Gellet.

He took time to viciously kick the Land Rover before he climbed into it. He still couldn't forgive David for having left him with this corroded form of transport. He felt utterly embittered. With all that money at his disposal, what had he been playing at with this rusted antique? It was self-indulgent. Not to mention selfish. Why not make someone else happy? There were legions of salespeople out there whose day would have been made by someone like David wandering into their showroom and purchasing the sports car of everyone's dreams with a speedy signature on a cheque book. But Jack wasn't in a position to do that, no matter how much sense it made to him. Everything that had once been David's was now his. The bad came with the good. That was the way it worked. He couldn't go changing David's way of life just like that. Not just yet, at least. Not until enough time had passed and his role had been perfected, and changes would be considered as unusual, not unnatural. He started the engine and catalogued a lexicon of obscenities as the vehicle shook its way down the drive.

He parked the metallic dinosaur at the station, deliberately leaving it unlocked, vaguely hoping that someone might be desperate enough to want to steal it. Or just plain dense. That would provide him with the perfect excuse to snap up that new convertible, whip through the lanes with the wind in his hair. But the chances of that happening were less than zero. He strolled into the station and asked for a first-class ticket to Paddington, paid cash.

Finding he had some time to kill, he walked into the town centre and wandered around until he found a bookshop. It was quiet inside, and apart from a brief encounter with the proprietor, who recognised him and – oozing enthusiasm – persuaded him to sign a few copies of some of David's books, he achieved the purpose of his visit with little trouble.

Later, reclining in his seat as the train heaved out of the station, he clicked open his briefcase and pulled out the copy of Adam Appleton's *Cold Journey*. As he opened it and began to read, he considered his inaugural appearance on TV and smiled. David wasn't the only one capable of dropping a relevant quote or two into the debating arena, or if confidence failed to reach that height, scuppering the debate altogether with some pretentious stance.

CHAPTER SEVEN

public relations

Two hours of reading later, Jack exited the train at Paddington and entered London.

After all the years he'd ebbed and flowed like a piece of battered cork on the metropolitan currents, he now felt apprehensive, wary of his ability to navigate the hazards and survive.

It was ridiculous and he knew it. He should have been experiencing the opposite emotion. An aura of confidence should have been radiating from him, hooking the attention of those he walked among. Wasn't that the way it was meant to be with the rich and famous? Wasn't the whole point of possessing those two fantastical traits the fact that people could tell from a glance exactly who you were and be able to enviously estimate just how much you were worth? Wasn't that what power was all about? He kept walking, thinking aura, thinking power. He waited for a section of the Red Sea of bodies before him to evaporate with impossible speed and leave a virgin path for him to tread. He monitored people's eyes, hankering after that solution of recognition and disbelief, waiting for a repeat performance of the Soho experience which had led to his arrest, willing that hardback to be produced from someone's bag with David's cheesy publicity photo and two-hundred-word author profile stamped on the inside of its glossy cover. Vague, literary-sounding phrases formed a queue on his tongue, eager to take their first steps into the public arena.

He stopped at the top of the stairs which led to the Underground, closing his eyes in disgust at what he'd been about to do. David had had a phobia about the tube, wouldn't have been seen dead in that subterranean labyrinth, had felt that he would have died for certain down there, trapped in a burning metal carcase in a tunnel a hundred feet beneath the tyres of a useless fire engine. And then there'd been the snobbery, too, the shield of disdain behind which he'd secreted his phobia. The Underground was cheap, designed with the transportation of workers in mind; a practical thing, affording no comfort whatsoever, enough to get people to their jobs and back again, no more.

In *South of the Border*, chapter six, if Jack remembered correctly (he'd reread it yet again at the weekend), David had described his protagonist standing uncertainly, much as Jack was now, at the top of these steps in Paddington. Should he enter the Underground, the bowels of the city, and by so doing join the masses, the corrupt bacteria of the intestine of life, or should he turn away to the streets and, despite his relatively impoverished situation, hail a cab and continue as he meant to go on, elevated from those beneath him?

In the cab on his way to meet Leonora Smiles for their lunch date, after Jack had booked into (according to a series of receipts – not to mention the obsequious grin of the porter) David's favourite hotel, Jack flicked through the budget projections for the current and the next financial year. Smiles knew her stuff. In spite of what he thought of her on a personal level, her ability had never been in doubt. It had been her, after all, who'd caught him out.

She'd already been in place when David had given Jack the job. It had actually been Smiles who'd conducted the interview. What had staked her competence firmly into Jack's mind then was that she'd taken the interview seriously, even though both of them had known that it was a formality, that the job was already his.

But he hadn't forgotten how Smiles had treated him. Nor had he forgotten the fax he'd found that night at David's. Even his triumphant exit from Smiles' office had been unveiled as a sham after the event. He'd got the money all right, but not because he'd won it, but because she'd given it to him, seen it as the most convenient way to neutralise the problem that he'd embodied. He'd come away with not a penny more than David and her had agreed on. Cheap at the price. She must have laughed the moment his back had been turned.

But what to do now? Smiles' case was different to those of Emily and David. They were dead. There wasn't anything he could do to change their pasts, in just the same way that he was impotent to affect the present they'd led him into. But Smiles was different. Smiles' future – like his own – was an organic, malleable entity. Smiles was here with him, alive, though naïve to the shift in power that had occurred behind the scenes. With an effort of will, he had the power to reach into the very core of her life and sculpt her into any shape he wished her to be, any caricature he saw fit.

He locked the sheets of budget statistics safely away in his case and lit a cigarette. He noticed the driver frowning in the mirror.

'Can't you read, mate? No smoking. Put it out.'

Jack flicked soft flakes of ash on the floor by his feet and pulled a twenty-pound note from his wallet and waved it tantalisingly before him. 'How about now?' he asked.

The driver's hand cranked back and snatched the note. He said nothing, pressed a switch. The glass partition rose up, leaving Jack to bury himself in a cloud.

It was a small success, but it was indicative of things to come. Soon it would be second nature. He wouldn't have to think it, just do it, just like David always had. The times were changing. Other people didn't know it yet and, if things went according to plan, they never would. All they'd see, hear and touch, and maybe one day with Gellet, smell, was David. Only he'd feel the changes multiplying inside him. Only he'd listen to the words leaving his mouth, examine himself in a mirror and marvel at the insidious metamorphosis that had taken place.

He checked his watch and rapped his knuckles on the glass divide. Startled eyes in the rearview mirror cut to antagonism and the glass slid down.

'Pull over here,' Jack ordered.

The driver ignored him, ploughed on, replied gruffly, 'We're not there yet.'

'Change of plan. Just pull over.'

The driver negotiated his way out of the traffic and parked at the side of the road. Jack paid him, didn't wait for his change, and got out. A malodorous aroma clogged his nostrils as he walked back down the street in the direction he'd just come from. The unrelenting heat was taking its toll on the city. Or maybe it was just that he was no longer used to this: during his time in the country his immunity system had altered. Or – and this rang true in his ears – maybe this was how London had always smelt and it was only now that he had the option to make a living elsewhere that he realised just how much it stank.

He walked into SlipSlide. There was still some dead time to fill before his meeting with Smiles, and the venue he was meeting her at was only round the corner. It would take him precisely seven minutes to walk there. Precisely, because he was meeting her at the Book Bar, his last place of employ. It didn't have the same extravagant licensing hours that Tommy had organised for SlipSlide. The brief walk here from Covent Garden had extended Jack's nocturnal binges on more than one occasion.

It was quieter than Jack remembered inside. The ubiquitous glut of tourists was still here, consuming cosmopolitan beers and unimaginative bar snacks with an air of excited discovery: the London Experience. But there were no stars or media groupies to be seen and even the Suits were sparse: only a couple of tables, three barstool occupants, segregated from one another by their upheld newspapers. And Tommy wasn't to be seen. That was good. Tommy he couldn't cope with right now.

He went down, through Level 2 without a second glance, and into The Basement. Apart from a solitary figure behind the bar, it was empty down here. The jukebox spun a disc, its volume low, the tune mournful. But Jack wasn't here for company or atmosphere. He recognised the figure behind the bar. Regardless of the state he'd been in when he'd last seen him, his face, like the face of the girl – her name was Zoe, printed on plastic – in the garage where he'd customised his car into a bomb, like everything he'd seen and heard that day, was still startlingly clear; they were unforgettable segments from the day his life had changed.

He felt relieved. The curtailed taxi journey had proved beneficial. The figure behind the bar was Sean. It was Sean that Jack had called in here to see.

'Whisky, please,' Jack said when he reached the bar.

Sean looked up from some calculations he'd been performing on a scrap of lined paper. When he saw who it was who'd ordered the drink, the pen fell from his hand, clattered across the surface of the bar, plastic on wood. 'Mr Jackson?" he asked, swallowing between the two words in consternation. 'But I thought you—'

'I'm David,' Jack interrupted. 'Jack's brother.'

Sean exhaled. 'The writer. Sure. I've heard of you. I'm sorry. It's just that you look so . . .'

'He was my twin,' Jack told him, waving his hand across his face, and sitting on one of the barstools. 'You weren't to know any different.'

Sean nodded and returned with a whisky. 'On the house,' he said. 'Tommy was really upset about what happened.'

Jack drank and lit a cigarette. 'They were close friends. Is he around?'

'On holiday. He left last week. Went to his place in Spain. Said he needed a break. He's coming back today.'

'Right,' Jack muttered. He'd been to Spain with Tommy a couple of times in the past. He could picture him there now. Or rather, he could picture his place, up in the hills, overlooking the vast, shimmering sea. He didn't know what Tommy would be doing at all. All the old references had become blurred. He should have been in bar X or bar Y, living it up. But after what had happened, the way he'd been at the wake . . . He couldn't tell what sort of mood would be smothering Tommy's movements today. How could he? How could he project, relate to that? How could he imagine someone mourning his own death?

'Your brother – Jack – was in here the day he died,' Sean said, avoiding Jack's eyes. 'It was his birthday, wasn't it?' Jack nodded. 'He came in for a few drinks with Tommy.'

'Yeah, Tommy told me.' Jack wondered if Sean knew about what Tommy thought of David, of the person whose name he now travelled under. He decided to test the waters before he waded in any further. 'Tommy said Jack was upset. Do you know anything about that?'

'No,' Sean apologised, 'I just work here. Tommy keeps his private life pretty much to himself.' He took Jack's glass and flooded it afresh from one of the optics on the wall. 'Were you looking for him?' he asked, returning the glass to Jack.

'Not really. I mean, it would have been nice to see him, but it's not him I came here to see. I'm looking for someone called Sean.' Jack made an ostentatious show of flicking through his pocket diary and reading his handwriting aloud, making what he felt was an impressive show of emulating the cops and private detectives he'd seen in films. 'Sean O'Connor. You know him?'

Sean frowned, as Jack had known he would. 'Sure,' he said. 'That's me.'

Jack overdid the surprised expression somewhat. It clung to his face, feeling as artificial as cellophane whole seconds longer than was required. It left him feeling shrink-wrapped. He reached across the bar and shook Sean's hand. 'Good to meet you, Sean.'

'And you,' Sean said uncertainly.

'Anyhow,' Jack said, 'I expect you're wondering what I came here to see you about.'

'Well, yeah.'

'It's not about Jack or Tommy. Something just as sad, though. I wanted to ask you a few questions about the night Mick Roper died.'

Sean's eyes escaped Jack's gaze. 'Tommy told me I

shouldn't be speaking about that any more. Not since they quoted me in the papers.'

'Really.'

Sean lowered his voice. 'He says it's not good for business. You've seen what it's like here at the moment,' he added, looking demonstratively round the empty room.

'It wasn't so bad upstairs.'

'The tourists are still here, sure,' Sean agreed. 'But all the real players have been avoiding it like it's been condemned since all that stuff about Roper was splashed over the papers.' He grimaced. 'I thought Tommy was going to fire me after he found out I'd been speaking to that journalist. Or worse . . . I still feel bad about it. It was stupid. I shouldn't have shot my mouth off.'

'Don't be too hard on yourself. I doubt what you said was what kept people away. It was pretty innocent stuff the way I remember it; just what drink the killer ordered for Roper.'

'That's the thing, though,' Sean broke in. 'It wasn't *just* what drink; it was everything. The killer knew that Roper would be in SlipSlide drinking it, just like she knew that part of the kick people like Roper get from coming here is that we'll cater for any whim, fix them any drink, no matter how weird. She knew it was a way of getting to him. That's why everyone's steering clear. They're afraid that if they come here it's going to be them next.' He paused for breath. 'Nobody's going to want to come here and order some fancy drink if they think that it's the kind of thing that's going to get them killed. No amount of hipness is worth that kind of pay-off, is it?'

'No,' Jack conceded, 'I suppose not.'

Sean came to the side of the bar and lit a cigarette. 'Why are you interested in Roper anyway?'

'I'm appearing on a TV show tomorrow night. *Answer Time*, you know it?'

Sean shrugged. 'I don't get much chance to watch the box, what with working here most of the time.'

'Yeah, well it's no big deal. Just a debate show. They're

discussing the murders.' He tipped his head to one side. 'That's why I wanted to have a quick chat with you.'

Sean groaned. 'Look. I already told you. I can't talk about it. Not if it's for TV.'

'It's not a problem,' Jack reassured him. 'Tommy will never be any the wiser. I'm not about to go quoting you, so rest easy.'

'Yeah? So how come you're here?'

'I just wanted to get a feel for the subject. Murder's not something I know much about. I thought coming here, looking round – just talking to you – might make it more real for me.'

Sean remained silent for a while, enveloped in thought. 'Doesn't it feel enough for you already?' he finally asked.

'What do you mean?'

'You're a writer. Same as Appleton and Roper. Same as those two women killed yesterday. That looks pretty real to me.'

Before Jack could reply, Sean's attention was snagged by the sound of a phone ringing. He walked the length of the bar and disappeared through an open doorway. Jack looked around the deserted room and felt himself subdued by a terrible ache of nostalgia: for this place, for what it had once been and had once meant to him, and for his former self, too. He peered into his glass, into the past, as if some truth might become apparent if he stared long and hard enough. But the whisky remained sepia, the spirit of a bygone age, conveying only a sense of loss and distance travelled. He sipped at it, let it trickle down his throat, fed briefly off the transient warmth it imparted to his cold insides.

From nowhere, a hand wrenched at his collar, jerked him to his feet. The glass he'd been holding fell and exploded on the floor, spattering whisky erratically across his shoes, like a drunk's misdirected urine. His head bobbed down instinctively, wedged between his shoulder blades, but the grip on his neck remained resolute, unshakeable.

'Who let this piece of shit in?' a voice behind him, and behind whoever held him, boomed.

Jack struggled, tried to spin free, but all he got for his efforts was his hand snapped back against his wrist, his arm cranked up against his spine in a half-Nelson.

'Who served this bastard?' the voice continued to demand.

Sean came back into sight and halted, paralysed by the scene before him. Jack looked at him desperately, opened his mouth to cry out.

'Don't even think about it,' whoever was holding him growled, thrusting him forward with alarming speed and ease, so that Jack saw nothing but the surface of the bar against which the side of his face was pinned.

'What's the matter?' he heard Sean asking. 'It's David – Jack's brother.'

'Come here.'

There was a creak as Sean lifted the bar-gate, footsteps as he crossed the floor and joined thc owner of the voice.

'What's he doing here?' the voice asked.

'Nothing,' Sean blurted out. 'Just having a drink.'

'Scum like this never *just* do anything. What else?'

'He wasn't doing anything – I mean it. We were just talking.'

'What about?'

'He was asking questions.'

'Go on.'

'He wanted to know about the night Roper was killed. He's going on some TV show tomorrow night.'

There was a pause, then: 'What else?'

'That's all. I swear that's all. I didn't tell him anything, Tommy. I wouldn't. Not after what you said last time.'

On hearing Tommy's name, Jack's instinct was once again to call out. There must be some mistake. Tommy wouldn't treat him like this. Not even David deserved this. Then he remembered the funeral, his arrogance in the face of Tommy's fury. He wasn't at a wake now. He was in Tommy's club. Whatever rules remained were Tommy's.

'Get upstairs,' Tommy told Sean. 'Close The Basement off. I don't want anyone coming down.'

Sean's footsteps accelerated into a run, moving away, out of earshot. Then the sound of feet mounting the stairs faded. A door slammed and a fire-bar dropped, locked.

'Bring him through to the dance floor,' Tommy said. 'And you, Jackson, keep your mouth shut.'

Jack found himself being driven across the room. He caught a glimpse of the body that locked his arm and almost wished he hadn't. The animal – and animal it was, not just a man, nothing so simply classified – had a flexed waist the size of Jack's shoulders. Jack might as well have been on a leash, muzzled, incapable of autonomous sound or motion, trained and subservient. Tommy walked ahead, barged through the soundproof doors to the deserted dance floor beyond.

'Let him go,' Tommy said, once the three of them were standing beneath the unlit lights and silent speakers.

The bouncer – Jack was now convinced he'd been here when the fight had broken out the day David had died – released Jack, leaving him to contend with the afterburn of the manhandling he'd undergone, steady his feet and quell his shock, feel blindly around for his dignity.

'You've got a nerve coming here and sticking your nose in,' Tommy said, his stare intense, rabid. 'Correction: you've got a nerve coming here at all.'

'What's your problem?' Jack demanded, anger suddenly dashing through his veins like a charge. 'What the fuck have I—'

Tommy stepped swiftly forward and smacked Jack in the chest with the flat of his palm, sending him sprawling back onto the floor. He stood over him and, with a thread of saliva stretching between his lips, released a flash-flood of words, sent them rushing down on Jack.

'What's my problem? I'll tell you what: you – you're my fucking problem. I come back from a holiday I've spent trying to get your sickness out of my head, only to find you sitting at my bar, in my club, drinking my drink and trying to pump information out of my staff . . .' He placed a foot on Jack's hand and trod down. 'And as for who I am, treating you like this . . .' he continued, watching Jack gasp and writhe, attempt to rip his hand free. 'I'm God in here. I can do what I want to who I want and nobody's going to be any the wiser.' He turned to the bouncer. 'Pick this sack of shit up.'

The bouncer whipped Jack to his feet and pinned his arm behind his back as before, leaning him forward in deference to Tommy. Jack craned his neck up, looked into Tommy's face. 'What . . . What are you going to do with me?'

'Whatever I want.'

Jack watched him move back, away from the sphere of his limited vision and listened to the regular click of his brogues as he slowly paced the floor. He heard his own breathing, too. It was weak. It could have been an old man's.

'Be reasonable,' he wheezed. 'I've done nothing to you.'

'You think you've got power,' Tommy's voice echoed. He was behind Jack now, close. Jack could feel his breath as he spoke. 'All that changed the second you walked in here. You haven't got shit any more. I'm the only power here. This is mine and what's mine I protect, got it? One person's already messed with it and if I get her before the cops do, it'll be her lookout. And now there's you. Coming here and making matters worse . . . Only you're easier to deal with.' He moved round in front of Jack, lifted his chin with one hand, and produced a flick-knife from inside his jacket with the other, sprung the blade. 'You're mine.'

'Don't!' Jack screamed, struggling desperately. This couldn't be real. This couldn't be happening. But the undercurrent of violent intent remained in Tommy's eyes, washed Jack's voice away. He felt his arm forced higher up his back, then the pain became too severe. White light speared his mind.

'This isn't business, Jackson,' he heard Tommy saying, horrifically aware that the point of the knife had been stuck against the soft flap of flesh beneath his chin. 'It's pleasure. You've had this coming for a long time.'

Their eyes met, Tommy's manic, Jack's wet, agonised.

'Don't do this!' he choked. 'It's me, Tommy. Can't you see?'

Tommy shook his head. 'You're no one,' he stated. 'Scum.'

'Please . . .'

Tommy increased the blade's pressure. 'Tell me what you are.'

'No one.'

'Tell me.'

'Scum!' Jack heard himself screaming. 'Scum!'

Tommy stared at him for seconds, coldly assessing his face. Then he slowly withdrew the knife, folded it away and put it back in his jacket. He stepped back and walked towards the doors. 'Kick him out,' he called back before he disappeared.

Recovery came slowly to Jack as he sat chain-smoking on a bench in the street next to SlipSlide, insects of sweat crawling down his neck and spine.

He was in a city he'd lived in for nearly twenty years, almost half his life. Now all that had been taken away from him. Even the smell of the streets, the same air he'd thrived on all those years, was causing his throat and nostrils to contract in repulsion. Pouring himself into David had entailed sacrificing far more than his name. Names meant nothing in themselves. They were loose jumbles of letters. It was what they represented that mattered. And his own name had represented many things to many people. It had marked his territory, the places he could and couldn't enter. With his name, his history had vanished. Everything he'd taken for granted – from the man who sold him his cigarettes, to his friends, right through to his closest friend, Tommy – although they still existed somewhere, had ceased to exist for him. The threads of the pattern of his life lay unravelled, meaningless. Until he learnt to claim David's history as his own, all London had to offer him was loneliness, danger, or at best neutrality. It was as if he'd never set foot here before. He got to his feet and began the seven-minute walk to the Book Bar.

Later, after the meeting with Leonora Smiles, standing on the balcony with a glass of whisky in one hand, a cigarette in the other, Jack watched the evening approaching. The heat out here was so intense that he could hardly feel the smoke coursing down his throat. He had to look down his nose as he exhaled to check the cigarette was lit. Even then, when he saw the smoke mingling with the wobbling haze of exhaust fumes cast up by the peristalsis of traffic moving through the gut of the city below, he had to inhale twice more to convince himself that it wasn't just his eyes deceiving him. Taking pity on his weeping skin pores, his brain snapped into action. Memories of the air-conditioned hotel room that he'd stepped out of minutes before burst into his mind. He stayed where he was, remembering also the way the walls of the room had closed in on him, threatened to collapse.

He looked at the ice in his glass. The solid blocks, taken from the mini-bar, had held their form for the few minutes the glass had remained in the refrigerated atmosphere of the room. Now they'd become thin and brittle discs, dissolving towards nothing, suspended in the whisky, itself as lugubrious and golden as syrup. Soon they'd have shrunk away from the light altogether. He swallowed them, letting the acid in his stomach accelerate the sun's work.

Smiles had kept her job. He'd let her keep it. At the end of lunch, when the moment had come for him to act, to drop the security of her job away from her like a trapdoor, he'd hesitated. And then the moment had passed; he'd left the lever alone. She'd got the pay rise, too. It had all gone according to plan. Only the plan hadn't been his. It had been David's. The salary they'd settled on and the increased length of contract had been exactly as David had forecast in his diary under today's date. And all this despite the fact that Jack had known that David would try to reach out from the grave to pull his strings and manipulate his future. The intention had been left there in permanent ink for Jack to read in David's diary. And when the moment had come for him to obey or rebel, when his brother's ghost had tightened the strings and jerked, Jack had danced step-perfect. He'd followed David's lead and that choice had had another sewn into its fibre: in his failure to assert himself, he'd left himself behind.

It wasn't that he'd forgiven Smiles for what she and David had done to him. But his view of the event had changed. The concept of revenge was dependent on perspective. Now that his perspective had altered, he understood that. As the power he'd inherited had elevated his position, his hatred for her had faded into the distance, diminished, moved so far below him that he couldn't relate to it any more. Looking at her as she'd sipped her coffee, he'd felt no emotions towards her. What had gone before had been negated. Only business had remained. She'd become dehumanised, a tool. And she'd been the right tool for the job.

His face damp, lubricated by the sun, he stared across the landscape of roofs and windows which straddled the horizon: grey against blue. Out there somewhere was Rachel. Of the pantheon of characters from his former life, she was the only one he still had a claim to both as himself and David. She was the only mutual friend he and David had ever had in adult life. It was she who'd provided the expanding bridge between the drifting continents of their lives. Stretched tenuously between them, she'd kept them from entirely losing sight of one another.

Despite what had happened between her and David, there was still a chance. Couples had got back together before. It was usually only a matter of settling the differences that had driven them apart. All it usually took was for one of the parties to initiate the sequence of compromises that would eventually escalate until the distance between them was eradicated. And Jack felt no qualms about compromising David's pride on this front. And since compromise wasn't a problem, there was nothing to prevent him starting the healing process. She'd left David because he'd changed into something she no longer recognised nor loved, because he'd treated her so disgustingly. All Jack had to do was reverse that process. Something so clear in his mind surely couldn't be that difficult to achieve. If it was love and change that Rachel wanted, all she had to do was to look into Jack's eyes. Deep down, he was still here, as different from David as anyone could want. And if he was going to come out of hiding and reveal his true self to anyone, it would be to her. All he needed in this city, this world, was one person. Her. If he could have her, London, along with everything else, would be his for the taking.

Flicking the dead butt of his cigarette into a spiralling descent over the balcony, he went back into his room and picked up the phone. He didn't need to look her number up in David's diary. He knew it already, just like he knew the feeling that smothered him as he listened to the phone ringing at the other end. He'd been here before, many times, after she'd split from David. He'd substituted the selfish for the selfless for the duration of their conversations, pretending to himself that he was calling to check that she was all right, denying the truth: that he was actually doing it to make himself feel better.

'Hello?' a voice – her voice – answered.

'Rachel.'

There was a pause, then, 'David? Is that you?'

'Yes.'

A longer pause. 'What do you want?'

He panicked, cornered, didn't know which direction to move in. He'd been rash. He should have planned this out. This was crazy. 'I just thought I'd give you a call.'

'We're separated, David.' Her voice was dull, communicating nothing more subtle than words. 'Separated people don't keep in touch. That's what it means.'

'I know, but . . .'

'There are no buts.'

'I thought we could meet up.'

'There wouldn't be any point. We've got nothing to say to each other.'

'That's not true. There are things I need to tell you.'

'What things?'

'Just things,' he said. 'Let me meet you. There are things I need to explain.'

'No. Not now.'

'When, then?'

'When I'm ready. We'll meet then. We'll meet when the time's right for me.'

'I just thought,' he said quickly. But it was too late. The phone had already gone dead.

Covering his face with his hand, he replaced the receiver, then stayed still for a whole minute, his breathing echoing irregularly off the pristine walls. He picked up the bottle of whisky from the table and crossed the room, heading for the escape of the balcony once more, averting his eyes from his reflection in the mirror on the wall, uncertain if he could face what he'd become.

Do it! He didn't know how long he'd been staring across the cityscape when these two words invaded his head and hurled everything else into oblivion. Do it! He thought back to David's notebook and, letter by letter, a sentence written there scrolled across his mind's eye: *Life never comes to those who stand still.* Do it! David was right. It was only through movement that he was going to break this stasis. He focused his eyes on his watch. A whole evening and a whole day lay before him before he'd make his television appearance. A whole evening and a whole day to stay hidden in this room, to stand still and hide from the world. Or a whole evening and a whole day to fill . . . a whole evening and a whole day left to live. He thought back to the two women Toby Still had told him about who'd been found burnt. It could happen to anyone, any time. The two women, David, and himself – no one should just sit back and wait for it to happen to them.

He fetched David's diary, felt his heart pound as he flicked through the pages, looking for the list of phone numbers. This was crazy. It was a panicked reaction. He shouldn't be doing this. Do something, sure. But not this. Not direct into the deep end. His breathing was falling heavily. He could smell the drink spreading across the room. He put the flicking pages on pause, tried to calculate how much he'd drunk, glanced at the bottle on the balcony: two-thirds dead. What did that make him? Drunk. Not just a fool, then. A drunk fool. But a drunk could always be forgiven for his actions, right? So what about Rachel? Something inside him answered. What about her, huh? You think this is the way to endear yourself to her? Being just like David is the way to her heart? But all he could do was review her voice as it had been on the phone. She didn't want David. For Christ's sake, she probably didn't even know what she wanted. She hadn't wanted Jack when he'd been there for her all those years. Oh no, not Jack. She'd chosen David. She'd married David, left Jack to rot. And then she'd left David. So who was he kidding when he thought they'd get back together? Not her, and that was certain. And now, not even him. He was alone. This wasn't sick, what he was contemplating now. This was what lonely men had been doing since the world had begun. He turned his attention back to the diary, located the correct page.

Some of what was written here was clear – names written next to numbers – but other numbers were bordered by shorthand, meaningless unless you held the key to their interpretation, a key, for example, like the episodes described in David's notebook. There was an evening described there that Jack remembered. No pain. Just pleasure. The establishment David had visited hadn't been named in the notebook, but at the top of the page, where the description of the episode had begun, there'd been a date – some months ago – and next to the date there'd been the shorthand abbreviation of *Srs* that Jack now traced his finger across in the diary next to a phone number.

He glanced from the diary to the phone. In spite of his drunk logic, uncertainty still held him. This wasn't him. He'd never done this sort of thing before. He didn't even know if he wanted to. Do it! The words came again. So what if this wasn't him? What was him any more? He couldn't even answer that, couldn't divide his body and his mind into what was David and what was Jack. And if he couldn't do that, why shouldn't he try to find out, discover? Discovery and experience. One led to the other. He picked up the phone and dialled.

'Hello,' a female voice answered. 'You're through to Sirens. How can I help?'

'I was just checking you were open for business,' Jack said. 'I'm planning a visit.'

'We're always open for business, sir.'

'Yes, of course.'

'Are you a member, sir?'

He didn't know. 'Yes,' he chanced.

'And your name is . . .'

'David Jackson.'

'Oh,' the voice said, brightening professionally. 'Mr Jackson. We haven't had the pleasure of your company for a while. 'How are you? Well, I hope?'

'Very well, thank you.'

'Good. And have you got any preferences, Mr Jackson?'

'I'm sorry?'

'Is there anyone you'd like to be waiting for you?' she explained.

Jack stretched his mind, desperately trying to remember the names mentioned in the notebook. 'Er, no,' he finally replied, his memory having flunked the test. 'Let's keep the options open.'

'Very good, sir,' the voice said. 'When shall we expect you?'

'Half an hour?'

'Fine. Half an hour it is.'

'One thing,' he said quickly before the line went dead.

'Yes?'

'This probably sounds crazy, but I've had a long day . . .'

'Yes . . .'

'And I've forgotten the address. It's ridiculous, I know, but it's entirely slipped my mind.'

'No problem, sir. Have you got a pen?'

Jack stood outside the plain black door wedged between a newsagent and a Chinese restaurant and checked the number on the door against the scrawled address on the piece of paper he held in his hand. He looked around and saw that the cab he'd just exited hadn't yet pulled away from the kerb. A change of mind was all that it would take to whisk him away from this place, back to the hotel room, further away from David's life, deeper into his own. He looked back at the door, focused on the brass knocker. No pain. Just pleasure. He thought back to the phone conversation he'd had with Rachel earlier. There'd been no unity, nothing but desperation on his behalf, nothing but hatred on hers. As they'd spoken, there'd been more than geographical distance between them, something less easily bridged. What was the point in even dwelling on it? He needed pleasure. He needed it now. It would help him forget – and even if that forgetfulness was only temporary, was that so bad? He heard the diesel drone of the cab engine rise behind him as it joined the traffic. Experience. That was the real message contained in David's new work. That was the only part Jack need accept. Not the pain. Not the misery. Not the hatred. Jack could leave all that behind. But what remained after these had been discarded . . . Why shouldn't Jack taste the good side of David's life? He approached the door and rapped the knocker against the wood. There was only one way to find out.

'David!' the woman who answered the door exclaimed. She was in her late-forties, wearing a red trouser suit. Perfume filled his lungs as she leant forward and kissed him lightly on the cheek, took him by the hand and tugged him inside. 'How lovely to see you again. I read about what happened to your brother. I'm so sorry.' Jack didn't say anything. 'We thought you'd given up on us,' she continued, quickly changing the subject. 'Cherry was very upset.' She gave a mischievous smile, released his hand and turned to the door. 'She thought she'd done something wrong.'

Jack walked a couple of paces down the corridor. It was simply decorated: stripped wooden floorboards, white walls. At its end was a doorway, shrouded by two velvet curtains drawn tightly together. An antique lamp with a yellow glass shade on a table by the door threw his shadow onto the curtain, invited him towards it. Smells filtered through as he heard the door being shut and bolted against the street behind him: cigar smoke mingled with the scent of perfume and joss sticks. Mournful music from the ghettoes of 1970s America filtered through the air. The nervousness that had trickled through him as he'd stood indecisively on the pavement outside now left him. Every molecule that joined together to make this place was familiar: it was exactly how David's writing had described it. To all intents and purposes, David might as well have written it into existence to begin with. Jack felt an arm being slipped through his as the woman in red joined him and began to walk down the corridor. 'Cherry?' he heard himself asking. 'Is she here?'

'Oh, yes,' she said, sweeping the velvet curtain back and nudging him through. 'She'll be ready in a minute.'

David's writing continued to speak to Jack on the other side of the velvet. With curtains sealing out the day, there was no natural light and the naked and semi-naked figures which lay slouched across the sofas and chairs were bathed in shadow, causing Jack to peer vaguely around him as he was taken across the room to a bar on the far side. A topless girl wearing a bright yellow bow on the top of her piled-up blond hair beamed at him from across the counter.

'Hello, Mr Jackson,' she said softly. 'The usual?'

He nodded and watched her back arch as she bent down to the fridge and removed a magnum of champagne.

'Peachy?' a man's voice called from somewhere behind. 'Oh, Peachy? Can you come here for just a second?'

'Just a second?' the woman in red whispered to Jack, releasing his arm. 'He's hardly capable of lasting that long.' She winked at Jack. 'I'll leave you to it,' she said, running a hand over his shoulders. 'But don't worry; Cherry will be out in a minute.'

Peachy started in the direction the man's voice had come from and Jack watched the bargirl tear the foil off the bottle and twist the wire free from the cork. 'How many glasses?' she asked, her thumb clamped over the top of the cork. 'Just you and Cherry?'

'Um, yes,' Jack said, trying to keep his eyes focused on her face. 'Unless you want a drink yourself, that is . . .'

She smiled patiently at him and placed two glasses on the counter. 'I've told you before, Mr Jackson,' she said, twisting the cork free and starting to pour. 'I only work the bar here.' She finished filling his glass, then glanced at him, then at her chest, and then back at him again. 'You can look all you want, but you can't touch.' She shrugged. 'Sorry, but that's just the way it is.'

'My fault,' he said, studying the swirling psychedelic patterns thrown by some hidden projector across the ceiling. 'I forgot.'

'So just the two glasses, then? You and Cherry?'

'Yes,' he assured her, looking her in the eyes and managing a smile. 'Two's plenty.'

She nodded her head. 'Two glasses it is. Cash or credit?'

He took his wallet from his pocket and fumbled for a card, handed it over and watched her scan it through the machine. When she handed him the receipt to sign, he nearly gagged. Then he remembered two things. One: money wasn't something he had to worry about any more. And two: what he'd just spent was buying him more than just a bottle of plonk. He stared at the floor.

'Hello, David. Is that for me?'

He turned to the woman who'd appeared at his side. Cherry. The name switched three-dimensional. And now that the name had arrived, there was no mistaking her from David's notebook, or from the completed chapter of the typescript that she featured in. The physical descriptions in both had been paramount, casting her character into the shadows where David hadn't chosen to delve. To David, she'd been dehumanised, a creature of flesh, a creature with only one motive programmed into her mind: pleasure. And not even David had been arrogant enough to think that that pleasure was a two-way process. She was there to give not to take. David had commented that if she'd possessed such a thing as a curriculum vitae, the only things it would have needed to contain to ensure permanent employment in her chosen industry were her date of birth and vital statistics. She was taller than Jack, much taller. He looked down her body, expecting to find her slim legs tapering off to a pair of high heels, but there were none. His eyes climbed again, slowly this time, finding David's detailed anatomical descriptions matched her flesh, right down to the Playboy bunny tattooed on her bare hip.

'Here,' he said, taking the bottle and filling her glass. 'Allow me.'

'Always the gentleman,' she said, accepting the glass and taking a microscopic sip. She stared into his eyes. 'Long time, no see . . .'

He nodded, drank nervously. The bubbles grumbled down his throat, disagreeing with his earlier ingestion of whisky. 'I haven't been in London for a while.'

'Well,' she said, chiming her glass against his, 'never mind. You're here now. That's all that matters.' She nodded at the door at the back of the room. 'Shall we go somewhere more private?'

'Sure,' he agreed, taking the bottle from the bar and following her through the fug of the room, keeping his eyes on her, choosing not to examine too closely the other clients, the ones who presumably – judging from their motions and whispered moans – didn't have privacy on their agendas at all.

Through the door was a corridor, again lit by a single yellow lamp. As Cherry walked ahead, he paused momentarily and viewed his shadow. His shadow? This silhouetted suit wasn't his. It was David's. That's what resided in the shadow, his dead brother. And they were David's footsteps he was following in as he moved to catch up with Cherry. They passed two doors on either side, before she stopped and entered a room on her left. He joined her inside and she closed the door behind them. He looked around. There was a double bed against the wall. Pressed white sheets covered it. In the corner of the room was a washbasin and bidet, both shining wet from a recent clean. Cherry walked past him to the bedside table and put her glass on it. He copied her motions, placing the bottle and glass there, then turned his back to her as she reached for him, allowed her to remove his jacket and hang it over a chair next to the basin.

'Do you want me to undress you?' she asked, walking round to face him and loosening his tie.

He hesitated, unlocked his eyes from hers. So far, this was only fantasy. If he went any further, it would be for real, a memory, his own, not something of David's he'd read, not some secondhand experience passed down from one brother to another. It would have originated from him and that was where it would stay. And that wasn't the only potential hand-me-down that worried Jack. There was the AIDS, too. David had contracted it from a prostitute, hadn't he? Who was to say it wasn't Cherry? Or if it wasn't, who was to say that David hadn't passed it onto her? He thought of the condom in his wallet. Thin rubber. Could he really trust it with his life? Rachel came back at him again. For a second he thought he saw her, sitting there on the chair by the basin, watching him with impassive eyes from a face immunised to surprise. He looked back at Cherry.

'I don't know,' he answered. He backed away from her and sat on the bed. 'Not yet.'

She sat next to him, placed a hand on his knee. 'Whatever you want. Do you want to talk for a while first? Is that it?'

'Yes.' He swallowed, couldn't get the taste of whisky from his mouth. He turned to her. 'Do you mind if I smoke?'

'You can do whatever you want, David.' She walked to the chair and slipped her hand into his jacket pocket and removed his cigarettes and lighter, fired one up for him and inserted it in his mouth. He sucked down a draught of smoke and exhaled. 'I hope you don't mind,' she said, crossing over to the door and taking a silk gown off the peg there, 'but just talking can get pretty cold.'

'I suppose you find it weird . . .' He watched her sit next to him on the bed and draw her legs up. He assumed this wasn't exactly David's style. 'Me just wanting to talk. I mean, I've never really chatted to you before, have I?'

She smiled sympathetically. 'No.' She reached out a hand, saying, 'Can I?'

'Yeah.' He passed the cigarette to her, watched her smoke. 'It's just that I haven't really been feeling myself recently.'

She flicked the cigarette over the ashtray on the bedside table, then returned it to him. 'You don't have to make excuses to me.'

'Yeah,' he muttered. 'It's my money, right.' He shook his head and stared across the room. 'I'm sorry. That was out of order.'

'No, it wasn't. It's true.'

'But still . . .'

'But nothing,' she said, moving across the bed so that she sat behind him. She rested her hands on his shoulders, squeezed hard.

He groaned, feeling his muscles shift and relax. 'That feels good.'

'It should do. I paid a fortune for the course.'

He sat back against her as she continued to work his muscles. 'How long have you been working here? I mean, I've been seeing you for . . .'

'I met you maybe a year ago,' she filled in. 'And I've been here three.'

'A year,' he repeated. 'And this is the first time we've ever talked – properly, I mean?'

She began to work her fingers down his spine. 'Yup.'

'Well, I'm sorry,' he said, closing his eyes. Heat radiated through his body as his muscles relaxed, realigned. He couldn't believe he'd even come here to begin with. He couldn't do this stuff like David had been able to, couldn't just dismiss his conscience with the dropping of his trousers. Do it! Sure. More like, forget it. He couldn't even manage it drunk, couldn't even take what he'd paid for; it simply wasn't in him. 'What about you?' he asked. 'Outside of this place. What do you –'

'Shit!' Cherry said.

He opened his eyes. The ceiling light was flashing frantically on and off. 'What?' he asked, her panic becoming contagious as she leapt off the bed and grabbed his jacket from the chair.

'Quick!' she shouted, throwing the jacket at him and heading for the door.

He got hurriedly to his feet and pulled the jacket on. 'What?' he laughed. 'I don't understand?'

'It's a raid!' She opened the door and looked down the corridor. 'Come on!' she implored. 'We've got to get you out of here. Now!'

He joined her in the corridor and, seeing the panic of bodies tumbling past, hissed, 'Jesus!'

'This way,' Cherry said, running down the corridor with him to the fire exit at the far end, pushing past a fat man desperately threading his suspender-covered legs into his suit trousers, as a naked woman ripped a red wig from his bald head and set about unfastening the lace corset that straddled his girth.

'Now go!' Cherry said, pushing Jack roughly out into the alleyway. 'Count yourself lucky you've got your clothes on.'

'What about you?' Jack gasped, stepping aside to let a man clutching a bundle of clothes against his bare chest get by.

'The front door will hold for a few minutes and so long as you lot aren't anywhere to be seen when they break through, we'll be fine,' she said. 'So get going!'

She turned from him and ran back down the corridor, got to work on some unfortunate with a rubber mask zipped over his face.

Someone ran into Jack and muttered, 'Sorry, old boy, didn't see you there,' then stared into Jack's face and laughed. 'David,' he said, tucking his shirt into his unbuckled trousers. 'Didn't know you were a member.'

'Oh,' was all Jack managed, recognising the face from television, not knowing what else to say.

The man finished buckling up his belt. 'Come on, then,' he said, starting off down the alley, heading for the bustle of traffic at its end. 'Let's get the hell out of here.'

Jack ran with him to the main road. 'What now?' he asked, breathless.

The man grinned at him and waved a hand at a cab. 'Well, I don't know about you, but I think a drink might be in order.' He held the cab door open and motioned for Jack to get in. 'It's not every day you get to avoid the squeeze of the long arm of the law.'

Jack glanced back down the alleyway where uniformed policemen were flooding out of the fire escape and getting to grips with various half-dressed men who hadn't moved quickly enough, or had simply been too tied up to react in time. Jack quickly slipped into the cab and moved along the back seat.

The man slid in next to him, pulled the door closed and said to the driver. 'The Muse Club. Quick as you can.'

'Cigarette?' the man offered, lighting one for himself and passing the packet and a lighter to Jack. 'Sorry,' he continued, reaching out to take them back. 'You don't, do you.'

'I do now.' Jack took one and lit it, passed the lighter and packet back to the man, then wound down the window and exhaled into the passing street. 'God,' he muttered, 'that feels good.'

'Stressful times,' the man concurred, facing forward, idly gazing over the driver's shoulder. 'Still,' he added quickly, nodding meaningfully in the direction of the driver, 'best not discuss it now.'

Jack turned his stare back to the street. Bernard Bennett. He smiled. He was only sitting next to Bernard Bloody Bennett; only sitting next to one of the best comic actors and writers of his generation; only sitting next to one of his heroes. He continued to smile, couldn't get it off his face. And he wasn't even just sitting next to Bernard Bloody Bennett. He was sharing – yes, sharing – a cab with him, going to the Muse Club with him. Christ, they were hanging out. Mates. Bernard (he tried the first name in isolation, rolled it round his mind) had recognised his face. Well, he'd recognised David's face. But Jack was David these days, so yeah, he'd recognised Jack. He'd looked at Jack and – even during the mid-raid rush, a time when most people would only have been thinking of themselves – had thought that this was someone he should hang out with, someone who'd make a good drinking partner. The cab drew up outside the Muse and Jack pulled David's wallet from his pocket.

He glanced at Bernard's face and found himself trying to twist it in his mind into one of the many familiar caricatures that populated his eponymous television series. But the face remained motionless, not even a sparkle of irony in its eyes. 'I'll get this,' Jack said, remembering himself and passing some cash to the driver.

'Good man,' Bernard said, opening the door. 'I'll forge ahead and get the drinks lined up. Something large and stiff. Appropriate, considering recent circumstances, wouldn't you say?'

It took Jack several attempts to finally reach the Muse Club's main bar. Although the room was probably only half full, it seemed that half of that half called out David's name and, of that half, half insisted on not just shaking his hand by way of a brief and superficial greeting, but interviewing him as well on a variety of topics from the progress of his latest book to his opinion on the Thriller Killers.

'Tedious buggers,' Bernard said, pushing his fringe back and walking with Jack to a table by the window.

'Who?' Jack asked, sitting down at the table.

Bernard craned his neck one hundred and eighty degrees, covering the whole room. 'It makes me sick, them going on and on like this, treating it like some tasty morsel of gossip to be spat from one mouth to another.' He glanced at Jack's bemused expression and smiled. 'If you didn't insist on living on that grotty little farm in that grotty little Welsh county, then you'd be as sick of them as I am.'

'I'm sorry,' Jack admitted, 'but I haven't got a clue what you're talking about.'

'The killings,' Bernard said in exasperation, tipping back his drink and drawing a circle in the air for the benefit of a nearby waiter, signalling his desire for another round of drinks. 'I know Wales is backward,' he continued, returning his attention to Jack, 'but really . . .' His television persona flashed into being in the form of a squinting frown. 'They do have newspapers down there, don't they?'

'Yes.'

'Then you have heard of the Thriller Killers?'

'Yes.'

Bernard grinned broadly. 'Well, I just wish everyone else was as monosyllabic about them.'

The waiter arrived and Jack polished off one drink and accepted another. 'You can hardly blame them for talking about it,' he said, after he'd lit a cigarette.

Bernard waved the smoke between them away. 'I bloody well can, you know.'

'But it affects them. It—'

Bernard groaned loudly. 'Don't say it,' he begged. 'Please, David. Just don't. It's not worthy of you.'

'Don't say what?' Jack laughed.

'That it affects us all.' Bernard stared adamantly at the table, his fringe falling in an avalanche over his eyes. 'That's the whole point: it doesn't. It affects Adam Appleton and Elliot and Carrier and even that silly little prick, Mick Roper. It affects them because they're dead and it's a bloody tragedy because they're dead.' He looked into Jack's eyes; there was nothing amusing his face now. 'You knew Adam as well as I did. He didn't deserve to go out like that. So he'd been scribbling porn on the side for a bit of cash . . . Big deal. It's not as if he's the only one.' He lowered his voice, glanced at the ceiling. 'Christ knows, none of us are saints.'

'You don't need to remind me.'

'I tell you, David . . . you'll never believe some of the rubbish I've heard people saying about these murders in the last few weeks.' He sighed and lit a cigarette off the candle on the table. 'You know that vile runt, Hawtrey-Smythe?'

'Presents that book programme, yes?' Jack said, putting the name to another face he'd watched on TV.

'Yes, that's him. Wrote – and I use the word in its broadest sense – a novel last year, too. Has himself down as something of a Renaissance Man. Specialises in reviving other people's opinions and passing them off as his own, you know the type?' Jack nodded, as if this was the type of bore he encountered on a daily basis, too. 'He was in here, last week,' Bernard continued, wiping his fringe behind his ear, 'and – and I swear it wasn't through any fault of my own – I ended up sitting at a table with him and some other people. Heinous situation. I don't know; I must have been paralytic.' He took a swift swig as if to endorse the validity of this excuse. 'Whatever. The point is that someone was rattling on about Roper's death and, inevitably, Hawtrey-Smythe had to stick his oar in.'

There was a pause which lasted a couple of seconds before Jack realised that he'd been cued and cued Bernard back. 'So what did he say?'

'The usual. He pondered aloud who might be next.' He tapped his finger on the table. 'Only he wasn't just pondering, he was accusing. He launched into a list about twenty names long – people he thinks are hypocritical, or whatever. And that's what gets me so angry. People like him don't really give a toss about the fact that Adam and the others are dead. All they're interested in is that the competition is being eliminated. It just gives them a chance to spread rumours, settle scores.'

Jack still couldn't believe he was sitting here with Bernard Bennett, couldn't believe either that the man was confiding in him as if he'd known him for years. 'Did you point this out to him?'

'Damn right!' Bernard spluttered. 'And more. I told him that going on the way he was was just playing into the killers' hands. That's what they want. So long as we keep talking about it, then they've succeeded. They've got their result. Everybody's paranoid. The Thought Police are out on the town, accusing their rivals of God knows what. You see that, don't you?'

Jack nodded, though in all truth he wasn't sure that he did, couldn't honestly say he'd bothered to think about it before now. But there was one thing he was sure of: now probably wasn't the best time to tell Bernard that he was appearing on television tomorrow to join the ranks of the Thought Police in picking over the charred bones of Elliot and Carrier. He nodded again. A nod felt right, a nod kept the conversation lubricated; it kept him here with this man, undetected, masked as to who he really was. 'How did he react?'

'I'm not altogether sure,' Bernard admitted. 'I sort of lost control at that point. He made some smart-arse remark and white rage descended. Tipped a drink over his head. That sort of brought things to a satisfying premature conclusion . . .'

'Sounds like justice,' Jack said with a smile.

'So you agree with what I did and why I did it?'

'Sure. One hundred per cent.'

Bernard frowned. 'Good. In that case, before we get as drunk as lords, can you make me a promise?'

'Of course.'

'Right, when you're on *Answer Time* tomorrow, stick a rocket up Dick Middleton's arse by bluntly refusing to participate. Scupper the whole bloody debate.'

A tide of blood swept through the skin on Jack's face. 'You mean you know about that?'

Bernard sat back, surveyed him with shining eyes. 'Naturally.'

Jack struggled to win back his composure. 'Who told you?' he asked, more out of a need to speak than genuine interest; he doubted he'd know the person anyway.

'Oh, come on, David. You know it's impossible to keep anything secret in this town. Christ, if the Thriller Killers have proved anything, it's that.'

'Who told you?' Jack repeated.

'Hermione Shortbottom.'

Jack had been right; he didn't know her, not in the flesh, anyway. But he knew about her. Who didn't? Hardly a month went by without her kicking up some controversy or other. She was an Anglo-Saxon diehard. Keep England for the English. Keep England Christian. Keep England white. She'd set up some political party to this end, popped up ranting at every by-election across the country. And she wrote books, too. Novels set in the near future, detailing a society where white people were slaves, where Christian churches were burnt to the ground . . . David, though he'd publicly distanced himself from her politics, had been spotted in public with her on more than one occasion. 'Ah.'

'Ah, indeed. She's going to be on the programme, too. Public platform. Wouldn't miss it for the world. Wants to be there to contradict whatever whingeing liberals Middleton's invited on. She said she was looking forward to seeing you again.' He peered into Jack's eyes. 'She was smiling when she said it. Something you haven't told me, old boy?'

CHAPTER EIGHT

candid camera

No sooner had the Probe TV limousine vacated the parking space and silently slid off down the street, than a black transit van pulled out from its vantage point on the corner. It drew up purposely, as confident and as smooth as a cab filing into its allotted position on a taxi rank, and filled the space outside the limousine passenger's house.

A thick-set man, his electricity-board overalls taut as skin across his shoulders, and a woman, slight within the overalls too large for her, animated in their centre, a cat in a bag, stepped in unison from the front doors of the van. With the evening sun bouncing off their sunglasses, they walked to the back of the vehicle. The man slipped the key, turned the lock, and waited for the hydraulics to raise the back door towards the raw sky. The woman skipped inside, slid two metal cases, adorned with the electricity company's new logo, across the van's floor into his grip. He set off up the short path leading to the front door of the house owned by the limousine passenger. His companion jumped out, swung the door shut behind her, and followed. Together at the door, behind the hedge that bordered the garden, she toyed with the lock. Then it sprung and they entered.

Later, a limousine journey away.

After a rehearsed signal from the floor manager, the familiar theme tune – unnaturally fast piano, which could only have been computer-generated, against a backbeat of similarly rapid and dramatic drum loops – asserted itself on the ears of those assembled, as emotive in this environment as a national anthem in a sports stadium.

She was sitting in the fifth row back of the auditorium, her head raised slightly above those of the people on the studio floor below. The back of her seat was uncomfortably vertical, leaving her, along with the rest of this evening's audience, with no option but to lean slightly forward as a measure against potential back strain. She glanced left and right at the people in her row. Their manipulated body language – the fact that they were literally sitting on the edge of their seats – gave them an air of excruciating anticipation.

Cameras stood guard on the perimeter of the studio floor, their operators making final adjustments, focusing on either the audience or the centrepiece of the stage, a mahogany table with a panelled front, still glowing tastefully from its recent, lovingly administered beeswax massage. The table was curved forward in such a way that each of the five people who sat behind it had unrestricted views of one another.

In the middle of the table, the position of command, furthest back from the audience, foremost in the camera operators' minds, was Dick Middleton. His lower lip protruded for a second to direct a blast of relieving breath onto his nose which itched busily where the last brush of make-up had been applied. He peered with distaste down his front at the discreetly placed microphone on the lapel of his Savile Row suit, as if he desired nothing more than to pluck the offending article free and restore his image to its immaculate, classical best. He lifted his head and, with his eyebrows slightly raised in paternal reassurance, looked at the man and woman on his left and the man and woman on his right. He then faced front and, instantaneously, the music cut.

He spoke rapidly and clearly, his voice surpassing the electronic intensity of the music with a human, but equally manufactured, intensity of its own. 'Good evening ladies and gentleman. Welcome to *Answer Time*. I'm Dick Middleton, and tonight we're here to discuss the murderers known as the Thriller Killers, two people who've murdered their way across the literary nation, their most recent victims being

Louise Elliot and Clare Carrier, whose corpses were found in a barn at Louise Elliot's country home in Gloucestershire less than forty-eight hours ago.'

He paused to glare meaningfully at the camera. 'I apologise to those of you at home who were expecting to watch the scheduled debate on the morality of genetic engineering. That programme will be transmitted at the same time next week.' He nodded solemnly to convey that the gravity of this evening's issue for discussion justified this decision.

'But before we begin, let me introduce tonight's panel of guests. To my left,' he said with a demonstrative tilt of his head in that direction, 'is John Rawlings, editor of the cultural analysis periodical, *Icon*. And next to him is Michelle Brand, lecturer in English Literature and Media Studies at Southampton University, and author of the controversial, *Cultural Terrorism: Does The End Justify The Means?*'

He turned to the right. 'And on this side is David Jackson, prize-winning novelist and moralist. And finally, next to him, is Hermione Shortbottom—'

'Fascist!' someone shouted out from the back of the auditorium.

No sooner had Middleton heard this, than his features honed into something less hospitable. It was an expression anyone who'd tuned in on him before knew well. It was the same expression that dwarfed people of a wary disposition in an instant, stripped the years away from them, left them schoolchildren caught with illicit comics cloaked inside their regulation textbooks. He glared at the audience as a whole. 'Thank you for that contribution, madam. You'll be able to have your say after the break. Until then, please don't interrupt.' He paused, waited for a reply, then turned back to Shortbottom. 'Good. Now, as I was saying, sitting next to David Jackson is Hermione Shortbottom, author of the bestselling *Dark Storm* series of novels, and founder of the Island Nation Party.'

He swept his gaze onto Hermione Shortbottom. 'I'd like to begin with you, Hermione. How do you view this recent spate of killings – in a cultural context, that is?'

Hermione collected herself by gathering her brown hair behind her ears. Her eyes flashed combatively, fleetingly competing with the alluringly bright colours of her lens-friendly clothes and accessories: the powerful shoulder-padded blazer, bright lipstick, and shimmering jewellery. 'I don't think it's that simple, Dick. Any attempt to place this series of murders – and that's what they are, no more no less – in a cultural context is a futile exercise. The only comparisons I can think of for these murders are the equally sick acts of other psychopaths. What we're talking about here are people who should be hunted down like animals and treated like animals once they're caught.'

The words flowing from the mouths of the panel members hissed into silence as the woman in the fifth row back closed her mind to them, cut them out. She wasn't here to listen, but to speak. There wasn't anything these people could teach her. What had brought them here tonight wasn't some abstract subject up for debate. This was for real, outside the domains of academic discussion. The time for talking was over. The revolution had already begun. It was coming for them. Nothing they might say would change that. She closed her eyes, waited for her moment to arrive, waited for this dead time to pass.

'Huh-huh,' Middleton was saying with an exaggerated clearing of his throat when she reopened her eyes some time later. 'That's one viewpoint, Michelle. But what about the victims of these crimes? We're not talking about a political act here, are we? We're talking about an attack on individuals.'

'All art is political,' Michelle insisted. 'It's naïve to claim otherwise. If you look back over history, you'll see that art, whether literary or otherwise, has been a defining force behind our cultural development. It's ludicrous to even attempt a distinction between art and politics. Each comments on the other.'

Middleton nodded at the camera-operator opposite him and waited for her to nod in return, zoom in. 'So what we're debating now,' he summarised, 'is to what extent art – or literature, at least – is a political issue . . .'

Hermione looked with transient annoyance at David Jackson, whose failure to contribute to the debate was obviously beginning to irk her, then returned her eyes to Dick Middleton. 'I don't know how many times I have to say this, but we're not here to discuss politics. Nor literature. Murder. The intellectual agenda behind the killers' acts is irrelevant.' Her eyes switched between John Rawlings and Michelle Brand. 'You're acting as though you're discussing an exhibition of modern art. It's disgusting that you should even attempt to contextualise these murders in this fashion.' She turned on David Jackson. 'I'm sure David would be the first person to agree with me on this point.'

David Jackson jolted in his seat at the mention of his name, as if he'd just woken from a surreal and seemingly interminable dream only to find himself in a strange hospital bed. He stared at Hermione in disbelief for a moment and then leant forward and sipped from his glass of mineral water. He then settled back, his eyes wan with disinterest, submerged beneath the gathering currents above him.

Dick Middleton craned his neck in Jackson's direction. 'Well, David?' he prompted.

'Yes,' Jackson said, breaking the surface uncertainly. Then, finding his stroke: 'One hundred per cent. Absolutely.'

'In what way?' Middleton enquired.

Jackson's eyes closed for a moment. 'Modern art. Modern art and murder. The two things aren't the same at all.'

'Which is to say?'

Jackson glanced quickly at Hermione, but she was looking into the audience, apparently oblivious to his discomfort. Caught in Middleton's intense stare once more, he finally resorted to speech. 'I've already said that I agree with the case Hermione has made. She made the point perfectly well. I see little to be gained from making it again.'

'You agree, then, that the Thriller Killers should be treated with the same contempt we reserve for psychopaths, and that we shouldn't lower ourselves to . . .' Middleton's lips squelched together with relish, savouring the turn of phrase before he spat it out. '. . . debate the method of their madness?'

Jackson frowned for a moment, ran his hand beneath the collar of his jacket, but Middleton didn't go away, just kept on staring inquisitively. 'Well,' Jackson conceded, 'naturally, I'm inquisitive. I'm a writer. Much of my life revolves around raising and attempting to answer questions.'

'Which is to say that you don't agree with Hermione at all,' Middleton surmised, scanning the audience purposefully, attempting to encourage a reaction.

'That wasn't what he said,' Hermione said.

'Just what *are* you saying?' Middleton demanded of Jackson.

'I think that motive is an important part of any crime. But . . .' Jackson closed his mouth for a moment, reached for his water and took a sip. Just when it seemed he was going to slip back into the entranced state which had held him earlier, he nodded his head, as if in agreement with a suggestion that only he'd heard. 'But I also think that introducing the motives behind these particular murders into the public forum is doing exactly what the murderers want us to do.' There was another pause. 'I'm familiar with the works – the literary works – of Adam Appleton. In his last novel, *Cold Journey*, he wrote: "Silence has the potential to drown out even the loudest of voices." ' Jackson stared at the camera. 'I think that we should bow to Adam Appleton's wisdom in this case. I don't think we should give the murderers what they want. I don't think we should discuss their motives at all.'

Middleton stretched his arms across the table before him. 'But David, as a writer, can you honestly say you feel no affinity with the writer of the confessions? The murders aside, isn't she, just like you, someone with a voice and an opinion she wants to be heard?'

'*The murders aside!*' Hermione Shortbottom burst out. 'How can you even contemplate drawing a comparison between a talent like David's, which only cares for the improvement of the human condition, and the deranged scribblings of a psychotic murderer?'

A lonely pair of hands clapped loudly in the recesses of the studio. Jackson looked in the direction the noise had come from, as if the isolated support was the cue he'd been waiting for. 'It's not often we can save lives by keeping our mouths shut, but if that's what it takes, then we should do it.' With that, he crossed his arms and sank back in his chair with a look of impenetrable stoicism.

Middleton held back for a moment, assessing the situation, irregular lines appearing on his forehead, betraying his agitation. His mouth opened, then closed again, whatever words he'd intended to deliver apparently having been reconsidered and rejected. Finally, he resorted to a poignant intake of water. When he looked up, his expression was set solid, an actor's mask.

'That this issue has proved controversial,' he boomed, 'isn't something that comes as any surprise.' He surveyed the panel guardedly, then snapped his face to attention in the direction of the camera once more. 'Join us after the break when we'll be taking questions from the floor and seeing just where public opinion really does lie.'

The theme music cut in on cue. Then, as the floor manager's stance slackened and his raised hand dropped to his side, the audience breathed a collective sigh of relief. Conversations bubbled up like subterranean water rising to a spring. Middleton rose and leant his arms on the table, his shirt cuffs sliding out from beneath his jacket, breaking the symmetry of his clothing for the first time this evening. His eyes closed as he exorcised his body of its recent stress with a series of expansive stretches. Hermione Shortbottom curled protectively across David Jackson, secreting him from the world, filling him with words which no one else could hear. Michelle Brand clenched into a cell with John Rawlings, whispering conspiratorially, occasionally scanning the immediate vicinity for signs of illicit intrusion.

Middleton quit the stretches, circled the table and wove his way through the production staff to the central aisle which divided the audience. The audience watched his progress with their peripheral vision, none of them wishing to be caught staring. They all knew what he was up to. Being too obvious would only exclude them from his search. It was part of the Middleton legend. He wanted live TV in every sense. He didn't believe that the people from the audience who got to ask the questions should be those who'd bothered to write in, or whose experiences had been vetted before the show began. Middleton believed in 'live, as in *alive*'. The people who got to ask the questions were the people he and his researchers chose on the night, not because of who they were, or even because of what they were going to ask, but because of how stimulated they looked. He moved swiftly. Time was short, the advertising break brief. He searched the assembled faces, looking for the one that drew him most.

'Pretty impressive, huh?' a wire-framed man sitting next to the woman in the fifth row back of the auditorium commented.

She flipped her knee out like a pinball arm, releasing it from the increasingly claustrophobic pressure, presumably sexual, which he'd applied during the first half of the show. She didn't bother to look, but felt the change her declaration of independence had inflicted. His breath, which had fallen with tediously enamoured regularity on her neck over the past few minutes, ceased, as if he'd been instantaneously suffocated, deprived of oxygen, snuffed out like a candle. He wouldn't be back to bother her again. And anyway, who could blame him if he did? She was beautiful, wasn't she? Even the cotton packs in her cheeks to soften her expression, the heightened make-up and other sacrifices to disguise, couldn't take that from her. Wasn't she just the kind of female stereotype any stereotypical male with reproduction on his mind would pay to sit next to? Lustrous blond hair: the Shampoo Spirit. Supple limbs: the Exercise Video Nymphet. Clothes straight off the catwalk. Eyes so brown they'd make Bambi feel inadequate. Even so, she was right, he wouldn't be back to bother her again. Probably wouldn't ever be able to come to terms with blowing the only opportunity he'd had with the crass line he'd chosen to use as his opening gambit. She rubbed at her eyelids. The contact lenses stung. When she'd glanced at herself in the mirror in the washroom before the show had begun, the whole world had seemed dull. She knew now that if she were to go out and find a mirror, her eyes would appear brown, not the brilliant reflected blue she'd been used to all her life.

She was suddenly aware of the man next to her moving, his leg annexing her personal space, brushing against hers once more as he got to his feet. She flexed her muscles, preparing to rise herself, meet any challenge he was about to make. She turned to face him, looked up his body, saw him smiling ludicrously to his left. She leant forward and saw why. A manicured hand shot out to greet her. She shook it, effortlessly matching its grip.

'Dick Middleton,' Middleton said, as his hand and bony wrist retracted inside his jacket sleeve. He raised an eyebrow flirtatiously. 'I couldn't help noticing how absorbed you looked. I take it the issue we're discussing tonight is something you feel strongly about . . .'

For his benefit, unwilling to upset the status quo of the world as he saw it, she broke into a suitably embarrassed smile, ostensibly flattered by the attentions of such a universally respected star of the small screen. It worked its charm as she'd known it would, just as she'd known that her contrived appearance would act on him like a lure, spotlight her in the sea of mediocrity in which she'd patiently waited. He smiled. She was the one. He was going to invite her to take part in the debate, ask the panel of guests the question of her choice. All that was necessary now was a few words. And words were something she'd never been short of.

'Yes,' she said, feigning nervousness to begin with, then allowing her words to gather momentum and meaning as they linked into grammar, manipulating his expression into one of fascination, 'this is a story I've been drawn to from the first. And the people you've gathered here tonight . . . I couldn't have chosen them better myself. There's so much they've got to tell us. There are so many things I want to ask . . .'

'I thought as much.' He produced a pad and pen from his pocket. 'What's your name?'

'Victoria Stone.'

'Miss, Mrs, or Ms?'

'Ms.'

He scribbled this information down, seemingly pleased. 'Your occupation?'

'I'm an account manager for an advertising firm.'

'That's great,' he said with curdling sincerity. His stare fell briefly from her eyes, devoured her chest and lap, then rose to greet her as an equal once more. 'But out of all these things you want to ask . . . is there one question which stands out above the rest?' His head bobbed encouragingly.

She rolled her head, arrived at a decision with an enlightened click of her tongue. 'Yes,' she enthused, 'it would have to be—'

'Whoah!' Middleton laughed, looking around the turned heads in the immediate vicinity. 'Don't tell me now. Tell me later.' He glanced around again for maximum impact, before looking at her again and saying, 'Tell us all when I throw the discussion open to the floor.' He leant down, bringing his face close to hers, his breath stale against her nostrils, and said in a more private tone, 'I find it more interesting when I don't know what's coming next.'

With that, he reared upright and took his time brushing her thighs gently aside as he continued his progress down the row. She watched the people he passed stand to attention to ease his passage, as if they were on parade. And she watched him habitually smiling for the camera that was no longer trained on him. He made his way back to the studio floor, hung out in the wings briefly conversing with various flunkies, allowing his skin to be pampered by an overweight make-up-wielding woman, and then hurriedly returned to his seat and concentrated on arranging the atoms of his face into a pattern of pugilistic perfection. The theme music was cued. It faded in. It faded out.

'Hello, this is Dick Middleton, welcoming you back to *Answer Time*. And to those of you who've only just joined us:

thanks for tuning in.' He followed up a buoyant smile with a sinking frown. 'Tonight we're debating the recent series of murders which have outraged the public at large and driven fear into the very heart of the nation's literary community. And the people sharing the panel with me are . . .' (He looked at them in turn as he spoke their names, allowing the camera time to emulate the sequence.) '. . . David Jackson, Hermione Shortbottom, Michelle Brand and John Rawlings.'

He scanned the table again with titillating apprehension before switching back to the camera. 'But our experts have had their say. Now it's the turn of the studio audience to ask a few questions of their own, questions which, I might add, neither myself nor the rest of the panel have yet heard, but questions, nevertheless, which I'm sure deserve answers.' He consulted the pad before him, then peered into the audience and called out, 'I believe there's a Victoria Stone who has a question she wants answering.' He smiled comfortingly. 'Victoria?'

'Here,' the woman in the fifth row back called.

Middleton focused on her. 'Ah, yes,' he said. 'Victoria. What is it you'd like answering?'

'Thank you,' Victoria said. 'I've got a question for Hermione Shortbottom.' Hermione inclined her head with weighty attentiveness in Victoria's direction. She smiled winsomely, as if this well-dressed, well-spoken stranger in the audience could only possibly be on her side, as if any other allegiance was absurd. 'About your writing,' Victoria continued, speaking to Hermione now. Hermione nodded approvingly in reply. 'And your politics. About how the two combine.' Strain suddenly began to show on Hermione's face, as if she was bracing herself, suspecting that the weather was about to change for the worse. 'You said earlier that the intellectual agenda of the killer wasn't important. Surely the agendas of all writers should be scrutinised. Surely that's where the real purpose of their writing lies. Take your agenda for example. Wouldn't you agree that you use your fiction as a vehicle for distributing your racist views and that, as a result, your writing's little more than propaganda?'

'Exactly!' someone shouted from behind her.

Hermione composed herself. 'I try to keep my politics separate from my writing.'

'Liar!' the voice shouted again.

'I've warned you before,' Middleton directed at the back of the auditorium. 'Keep quiet.' A few seconds' silence ensued before Middleton gathered himself and realised that Hermione wasn't going to expand any further on her reply. 'Does that answer satisfy you, Victoria?'

'No, not at all.' She spoke to Shortbottom again: 'It's true, isn't it, that you won literary prizes with your first two novels?'

'Yes, which just goes to prove—'

'And as a result of those successes, you're now regarded as part of the literary establishment? You do sit on various judging panels for literary awards, don't you?'

'Yes, I—'

'Your first two novels weren't political,' Victoria continued. 'Only the ones you've written since. The way I see it, you don't care about writing any more. Only how it can help you achieve your political goals. You've abused the position you were entrusted with. You've betrayed the literary community.'

Middleton squeezed the bridge of his nose thoughtfully. 'Well, Hermione,' he said, turning towards her. 'What's your response to that?'

'I can only repeat that I do my best to prevent my politics from dominating my art and vice-versa.'

'No platform for fascists!' the voice came again.

Middleton turned back to the audience, this time choosing to ignore the voice. 'Is there anything else you'd like to ask, Victoria?'

'No,' Victoria replied after a brief consideration. 'I think that's as near to the truth as we're going to get right now. On camera. When she knows she's being filmed. I think it might be a different matter if she didn't know she was being recorded. I think she might choose to be more frank.'

'Thank you, Victoria,' Middleton said, before pointing efficiently to another part of the audience and calling out a name.

Victoria looked one final time at the panel of five seated behind the desk in the centre of the studio floor. Her look had the power of a camera, freezing time, capturing the now, recording it for posterity, knowing that tomorrow, where there'd once been five, there would be only four. She blinked, then quietly rose from her seat and moved along the fifth row to the exit.

She pushed through the door which led out of the studio, conscientiously forcing its hydraulic hinges closed behind her, aware that the ripple of light from the corridor outside was disrupting the calm surface of the controlled environment she'd just left. At an uncharacteristic loss, she glanced up and down the bare corridor which mirrored itself in either direction, uncertain which way led to the lift. She screwed her face up, pressed her eyelids together, wringing fluid from them, lubricating the lenses which scratched her eyes like sandpaper. A draught of air brushed the back of her neck and she turned. With his back to her, pushing the studio door closed behind him, was a well-built man in jeans and a T-shirt with a list of some rock band's tour dates scrolled down its length. He turned his face – a handsome enlargement of a set of distant features which had been locked in intensive communication with Dick Middleton in the wing of the studio floor towards the end of the advertising break – and whispered through a grin, 'Hi.'

'I'm sorry,' she began.

He held a finger to his lips and pointed with his other hand down the corridor. She followed his lead, walking down the corridor which branched off round the corner to the left. He halted conveniently by the lift and smiled warmly.

'It's OK,' he said, his voice no longer geographically inhibited. 'They won't be able to hear us here.'

'Sorry about leaving during the show like that,' she said. 'I know it's probably not the done thing.'

'Don't worry. It's done now.'

'Oh – I thought that's why you followed me out.'

'No, nothing like that.' He scrutinised her face, concerned. 'Are you OK?'

She traced his stare with her hand, felt the moisture around her eyes and she smiled with relief. 'Oh, that. They're not tears, if that's what you're thinking. Lenses. I haven't been wearing them for long.' He nodded with comprehension, and she asked, 'Is that why you came after me?'

'No.' He grinned, embarrassed. 'Dick asked me to find you after the show. Dick Middleton, that is,' he clarified.

'Is that a fact?'

He grinned again. 'Yeah. You made quite an impression on him when he met you during the break.'

'I presume you mean intellectually?'

'Yeah, intellectually. He thought your question was very good.'

'He didn't know what my question was then,' she pointed out.

'No, I suppose he didn't.' He looked up, smirking. 'But you know what I mean, yeah?'

She folded her arms across her chest. 'No. Why don't you explain?'

He exhaled loudly. 'It's no big deal.'

'Well . . .'

'He wants to see you again after the show, that's all.'

'I'm not interested,' she said and turned to the lift.

He placed a hand on her shoulder, gently turned her back to face him. 'Mr Middleton isn't someone who people usually say no to.'

She shook her shoulder free. 'Well, that's what I'm doing now.'

'Look, lady, like I say, it's no big deal. He just wants to take you for a drink, get to know you a little better, you know?'

'No, he doesn't. He wants more than that.'

He shook his head. 'There's no need to be like that. Why don't we just go to the bar upstairs? You can wait for him there. All I want you to do is have a drink with him. What happens between you two after that is your business. Come on. Give me a break, huh? I'm only doing my job.'

'And your job includes pimping for Dick Middleton, does it?'

His smile returned, warped, ugly. 'Don't you think you're overreacting, just slightly? I'm offering you access to the bar. Nothing else. Christ, most people would jump at the chance.'

She looked at the floor for a moment. 'OK,' she said. 'Maybe you're right.'

'Good. That's better.' He held up his hands, shrugged. 'And anyway, like I say, it's just a drink.'

'You'll see him before I will, won't you?'

'Yeah, I'm going back to the studio after I've taken you to the bar.'

'Will you give him a message for me?'

'Sure. Whatever you want.'

She inserted the middle and forefinger of her right hand into her mouth, sucking them sensuously, running them in and out over her lips. His grin spread wide as he watched. She withdrew her glistening fingers and held them up before his captivated eyes. 'Well, pass this on to him,' she said.

Her hand snapped back and then darted forward before he could blink. Her fingernails stabbed into his eye-sockets, sending him wailing to the floor, his hands clawing at his face. She stood over him and dropped knee-first onto his stomach. Air burst from his lungs in a blast, leaving his respiratory system a vacuum, his voice dumb. She looked up the corridor and listened. Nothing but the hum of air conditioners. She got up and pressed the lift button, then looked back at him. He was curled on his side now, biting for air, his hands gripping his sides. Tears of blood ran from the corners of his eyes, obscuring his sight. She licked the drops of blood from her fingers, casually commenting, 'People like you have got to learn that you're not the only ones with schedules and agendas to stick to.' The lift bell sounded and the door slid open behind her. 'See you around some time,' she said, blowing him a kiss and stepping into the lift. She pressed a button, and waited patiently until she disappeared from his sight.

Downstairs, she snapped her visitor card down on the reception desk and walked briskly through the gallery of corporate mugshots which looked benignly down at her from their elevated, evenly spaced positions on the walls. The plate-glass security doors hissed open, activated by her arrival on the rubber pressure pad. As she moved outside, a closed-circuit television camera tracked her down the steps. She held her hand to her face, leaving it an incomplete jigsaw, then thought again. She'd already made it on to national TV tonight. Her zoomed, blurred image would be printed across the nation tomorrow morning. If her disguise could carry her through that unscathed, it was hardly going to flounder in the face of a low-resolution security camera recording which, like tonight's *Answer Time*, would undoubtedly be scrutinised by frustrated police the following day. Let them have two recordings of her. Let them feel twice as stupid, if that was what they wanted. She lowered her hand and set out across the carpark in the direction of the main gates, taking her gloves from her pocket and pulling them on.

Unwatched, unrecorded, on the streets, the transit van's ignition fired the instant her gloved hand touched the door handle, as if the spark of electricity needed to set the engine into motion had come from somewhere inside her.

She settled into the passenger seat and pulled the mirror down. 'Lights,' she said, and waited until her reflection transformed from monochrome to technicolor. The lenses came out easy. She dropped them on the floor. The cheek packs joined them seconds later. She folded the mirror away and killed the map-light.

'Do you remember the address, Tup?' she asked him, crouching forward in the passenger seat, pulling a plastic bundle from the glove compartment.

'Yuh,' he grunted, flicking the indicator on, shifting into first. 'Same road back?'

She unwrapped the pistol, jammed a fresh magazine into its butt and fixed the silencer. 'That's right. Keep under the speed limit. We don't want anyone paying us any attention.'

He checked the mirror and drove.

Answer Time had long since gone off air. Drinks had been drunk in the bar in the Probe TV building. The limousine which had picked Hermione Shortbottom up from her house earlier in the evening now returned and parked in the space behind the black transit van. The chauffeur stepped out and opened the passenger door. Shortbottom moved out onto the pavement, smiling, saying something to the chauffeur. The other passenger door opened and a man stepped out. He joined Hermione and the two of them walked to the front door of the house.

Behind the tinted glass on the back door of the transit van, Victoria Stone turned to Tup and their frowns met.

'The man,' Tup said. 'Why?'

'His name's David Jackson. Another writer. And you're right: he's not meant to be here.'

Tup shifted his position. 'What now?'

Victoria watched the limousine pull out. 'Wait,' she said, looking at the house the couple had entered. The hall light was on. 'Watch and wait.'

She moved back from the window and sat down on the cushions scattered before the wooden bench which supported the monitor and other electronic paraphernalia. Tup settled beside her, silent, expectant, waiting for the film to begin. She turned the equipment on and the monitor lit up. It showed a bedroom, empty, a black-and-white still. She flicked a switch and the view of the sitting room came into focus and, with it, she located life: Shortbottom and Jackson sitting on a sofa, drinks in their hands. Their mouths were moving in rapid, intense mime. Jackson was smoking a cigarette, self-consciously directing the smoke away from his companion's face. Shortbottom leant in, as though trying to drink her way through the cloud that engulfed him. Victoria reached forward, turned on the sound, watched and listened.

'I still can't see what the problem is,' Shortbottom was

saying. 'It's not as if it's the first time. It's not as if we're incompatible.'

Jackson pulled his head back further away from her. 'It just doesn't feel right.'

She held her hand in front of her face, covering her expression. 'I'm offering myself to you on a plate. How else am I meant to take it?' Her hand moved from her face, descended to his thigh. He flinched, but she just leant forward. Her words complimented the pressure of her fingers. 'I want you. You don't know how much I want you. I want you now. Tonight. Why go on denying me? Why else did you decide to come back here?'

He made no move to free his leg, just took a swig from his drink, smoked his cigarette. 'I was drunk in the Probe bar. You asked me back for a drink and I came. I didn't decide anything. I just did it.'

She moved her hand from him in frustration, sat back away from him. 'Why are you taunting me like this? You know why I wanted you to come back here with me. It's not as if I made a secret of it.'

He stubbed out his cigarette, put his drink down. She took his hand in hers and he stared down at it. 'I'm not taunting you,' he said. 'I know that's how you see it, but it isn't like that. I'm just not interested, that's all.' His eyelids drooped. 'I'm sorry, but that's the way it is . . .'

'But why?'

He avoided her eyes. 'I don't know how to say this without sounding rude, so I won't even try. It's you. Your views. The whole racist thing. It disgusts me.' He stared at her. 'It makes me sick.'

Her free hand joined the one already holding his, so that her palms lay flat on either side of his hand, angled in prayer. 'There's no need to lie to me,' she said soothingly. 'You're not in public now. I know you share my views. Is it your brother? Is that what the problem is?'

'No,' he said without hesitation, 'it's not. That's over now. I've used him as an excuse too much already.'

'Well what?' she said. 'If it's not your brother, and it's not me – unless you've gone off me . . . Is that what it is?' she asked, looking away. 'Don't you find me attractive any more?'

'It's not that,' he reassured her. 'You're beautiful. You're stunning. You could have your pick of men. You must know that. I'm just one person.'

She laughed edgily. 'At least you can't tell me it's because of your wife.'

'Why not?'

She smiled to emphasise that she understood that this was his idea of a joke. 'Well, for one thing, you're separated.' She traced his profile with her fingers, making sure to keep her hold on him with her other hand. Her eyes stared hypnotically into his. 'And for another, it never stopped you while you were still together, did it?'

She stared him into speech. 'No, I suppose not.'

She moved closer, dipped her lips fleetingly onto his. 'So if it's not your brother and it's not me – and it's not your wife – then it must be you. But don't worry, I know how to fix that.' She kissed him again, but any reaction he may have had wasn't betrayed in his face when she pulled back. 'That wasn't so bad, was it?' she asked.

He slid his hand from hers and ran it through his hair. 'I'm going,' he slurred, attempting to rise.

'Stay still,' she said, the tolerance gone from her voice, leaning on him as she stood, forcing him still. 'I'll get you another drink.'

She fixed him a full tumbler of whisky and returned and watched in silence as he smoked another cigarette and drank. The moment his lips left the glass after he'd swallowed its last glow of liquid, she took it from him and put it on the table. He mumbled something the camera's inadequately sensitive microphone failed to amplify into sense and allowed himself to be pulled to his feet. She confiscated his cigarette, crumpled it into an ashtray, then half-escorted, half-supported him across the room and out of the door.

Victoria hit the switch, closed in and captured them in the bedroom. Some quick work had occurred. Jackson was flat on his back on the bed. His feet were bare, shoes and socks already discarded. His jacket was gone, too. Shortbottom was crouched over him, unfastening his belt and flies. As she stripped his trousers from him and reached for the elastic of his shorts, he made a weak effort to sit up. But it was too late. He was exposed, flaccid and pathetic. He lay back, closed his eyes, and let her finish undressing him.

Once this was accomplished, Shortbottom left the room. Victoria waited. Shortbottom's return to this scene was inevitable. She just stared at Jackson, unblinking.

'The woman?' Tup asked without looking away from the screen.

'It doesn't matter.'

'Woman?' he repeated.

'I said it doesn't matter.'

Tup's hand darted out and hit a switch. The screen flickered, then reasserted itself in the silent and empty sitting room.

Victoria turned on him. 'Don't.'

'Woman,' he mumbled again, his hand retreating to his side. 'I want to see.'

'You'll see her when I want you to – is that clear?' Victoria asked, correcting the screen to the bedroom view once more. Jackson was still alone, his legs entwined in the sheets. 'I said, is that clear?' she demanded a second time.

Tup grunted incoherently.

Hermione came back into view, her legs sheathed in high black plastic boots, a rubber singlet stretched across her top. But it was the flesh, crowding at the perimeters of her clothing, which engaged Tup's stare. He leant into the screen, poised to topple through the glass that separated him from the cause of his arousal, and watched Hermione walk to the drawers beside the bed and dig out two sets of manacles from beneath her underwear. Jackson opened his eyes as she sat astride him. He watched in confusion as she stretched his arm towards the metal bars of the bedhead.

'What are you doing?' he asked, shrinking beneath her, retracting his arms and legs, curling up like a child.

'Don't play the idiot,' she told him, fighting to get his wrist where she wanted it. 'You've been here before.' She snapped the manacle round his wrist and swiftly fixed him to one of the bars.

Jackson twisted violently, knocking her off-balance, so that she crumpled into a cursing knot of limbs beside him. He sat upright, pulling at the wrist locked to the bed with his free hand. 'You've got to be joking. Get this thing off me. I don't want any part of this shit.'

She sat up, facing him, excitement stretching into a cruel grin. 'It's too late to play hard to get now, David. You're locked.'

He examined the manacle. 'Where's the key?' He spun to face her, flushed, his voice becoming uneven, agitated. 'Give me the key. Come on. Stop pissing about. I'm not into this.'

'You can have the key when we're done,' she told him. 'When I'm done . . . And don't tell me to stop pissing about. I'm in charge, remember? This is what we do. It's too late to go changing the rules now.' Her hand moved quickly, delved between his legs. He yelped, unable to speak as she tightened her grip. 'Good boy,' she petted, keeping her grip solid as she clambered over him. 'It's all or nothing now.' She clicked the other manacle into place, bonding his other wrist with the bedframe, crucifying him. 'But you knew that anyway, didn't you?'

By now, Tup was rocking back and forth beside Victoria, zooming in and out of the screen, his eyes cameras, rapt in focal adjustments.

Jackson gasped as Hermione released him. 'Don't be such a baby,' she said, manoeuvring herself astride his waist and peering down. 'There's no harm done. I wouldn't hurt it for the world. That's something I'd never do.'

'Let me go. Please . . .' Jackson groaned drunkenly.

'You'll have to beg harder than that,' she said, swooping forward, then pulling back, clawing her fingernails across his chest, leaving raw tracks.

'Please. I mean it. I don't—'

She began to gently grind from side to side. 'Harder than that,' she moaned. 'Harder still. Gooood boy. Give me what I want.'

Tup's rocking slowed like a metronome to a halt. 'Love?' he asked.

'No,' Victoria said. 'This isn't love. This has nothing to do with love.'

'Love.'

She turned from the screen to Tup. 'This isn't love,' she repeated. 'This is corrupt. This is the only thing people like this are capable of.'

Tup stayed plugged into the screen, monitoring Hermione's body bucking and rearing. 'Good love,' he said. He wheeled from the screen to Victoria and slapped his hand roughly between her thighs. 'You give me good love now.'

Her hand whipped the air molecules between them into a storm as it cracked into the side of his head. His face fattened with the clenching of his jaw and his hand shifted back, hovering between them like a hawk.

'Get your hands off me!' she hissed. 'Not now. Not ever like that.'

In a flurry of motion, his fists flew, plummeting on to her shoulders, shaking her until it seemed as though her neck would snap, loll forward in a humble realisation of death. He lifted her to face him and greedily scrutinised her, before slamming her onto the floor of the van and pinning her by her head with a hand that covered the majority of her face. Her arms and legs flailed, grasping and clawing at him. He didn't notice. Blood ran freely across his jaw where one of her nails had sliced through only to be halted by the enamel of his teeth. The hand which gripped her head bled too, where her jaw had chattered into his palm. Her wig had slipped, roots growing wild beneath. Air from her mouth hissed sporadically from between his fingers as if she was somehow punctured, would deflate and disappear altogether unless he was quick. He leant forward, increasing the pressure on her skull, until her arms dropped to her side and only her fingers moved, squeezing frantically in upon themselves. He ripped at clothes, first hers, then his. Her body froze.

She didn't know how much time had passed when she pointed the pistol at Tup's peaceful, contented, sleeping face, and pulled the trigger. One of his eyes half-opened as the bullet jolted his head from the cushion onto the cold metal floor of the van, but it was unlikely that he had time to register that his life was ending. His shattered jawline shifted as the second bullet inverted his nose. And then it was over. She regulated her breathing to the barely audible and stretched her hearing into the night, not yet prepared to drop the gun, staring at the silencer, not trusting whether it had accomplished its purpose, her memory of the moment already lost in a rush of hatred, degradation and adrenalin.

The engine of a stationary vehicle chugged like a generator somewhere close. Footsteps, came falling outside with foreboding, carrying the implicit threat of amplification, like a storm's first drops of rain. She pulled her ripped clothes across her bare skin, and watched them fall uselessly like ribbons. A jumper of Tup's lay across from her. Outside, a door thudded shut. She picked up the jumper and threaded herself through it, letting it engulf her body and collect shapelessly over her legs. Her body ached after the movement and she took some time to collect herself before shuffling across the floor to the back door and peering through the glass. She watched the red eyes of a taxi fade away up the street.

The screen was still on. Shortbottom's bedroom was deserted. The bed had been stripped down. Sheets lay gathered on the floor at its foot. Victoria's hand passed through the pool of light the screen emitted. Her fingers were gnarled, deformed by the cramp which had gripped her since the shots had been fired. She stretched and worked them towards uniformity, then switched to the sitting room. Empty. Victoria looked away, adjusted her wig into place, and set about loading the pistol once more.

Shortbottom was soaking in the bath when Victoria stepped silently through the bathroom doorway. The radio was on: opera. Shortbottom's eyes were sealed against the steam which hung like mist around the rim of the bath. There was a waist-high laundry bin against the wall near the bath. Victoria crossed the room and lowered herself quietly, stiffly onto it, laying the gun on her lap for a moment, closing her eyes, listening to the music, momentarily at peace.

When her eyes opened once more, they were lifeless. She pulled her gloves back, pushing her fingers deep into their dead-ends, then lifted the pistol and slotted a finger through the trigger-guard.

'I had such plans for you,' she announced without looking in the direction of the bath.

Water swirled with the motion caused by panicked flesh. 'What . . .'

'It was all meant to connect with what I said to you on *Answer Time*. It was meant to link perfectly. It was going to be thematically and structurally sound,' she continued as if Shortbottom wasn't here and she was indulging in a soliloquy.

'What are you—'

Victoria raised her arm, exhibiting the pistol. 'I'm the killer you were there to debate. I suggest you give that some thought before you open your mouth again.' She waited, but there was no response. 'Now, what was I saying? That's it. Thematically and structurally sound.' She sighed and looked at Shortbottom with passing chagrin. 'Do you remember what we discussed?' She took Shortbottom's gagged horror as a denial. 'No? Let me remind you. I asked you if you used your fiction as a vehicle for distributing your racist views. And you denied this. And I went on to accuse you of lying, saying that in private, in different circumstances – if it were just you and the barrel of a gun, for example – you'd probably be happy to admit that you abused your position as a writer by swamping your fiction with your fascist filth.'

Victoria paused for a moment to half-rise and stretch her legs. She sat back again. 'And I was glad you denied it at the time. It was going to make your later confession all the more immediate. You see, I hid two cameras here between the time you got picked up and taken to the TV studio and the time I got there. I was going to film it all. Your hypocrisy would have been staggering. Saying one thing on camera one minute, confessing the opposite on camera later that same night when I asked you in the comfort of your own home . . . You'd have made my point for me.' She shook her head. 'And then I was going to post copies of the recording to all the mainstream publishers, let them know that writers like you won't be tolerated any longer.'

Victoria walked to the basin and filled a glass with water. She turned and toasted Shortbottom with the glass before draining it and dropping it carelessly onto the tiled floor. It shattered into a loose mosaic of shards.

'Whoops,' she said, returning to the laundry bin and sinking down again. 'See how easy mistakes are? All it takes is one little upset to alter the whole pattern of things. You brought Jackson back for sex. Doesn't sound so bad, I know – even considering what your sad concept of sex is – but the ramifications . . . unbelievable. Someone had to die because of what you and Jackson were up to. Incredible, wouldn't you agree?'

A noise – not a word – seeped from Hermione's lips. It was impossible to distinguish the sweat from the water from the tears on her face. *Clack*: humanity dissolves as death draws near. *Clack*: only art remains constant, because only art cannot die.

'Lost for words. You're not the first. Still, at least you haven't interrupted. I really don't think I've got the energy to cope with another pointless debate this evening.'

Hermione cupped her face in her hands, croaking incoherently.

Victoria smiled tolerantly and then continued, 'And now's the time when you think I'm going to allow you in to create a dialogue, one through which you'll be able to exercise your no doubt considerable negotiation techniques and live to tell the tale. But sorry – it's not going to be that way. I've had a bad day.' Her smile was gone now. 'Things didn't go how I wanted. You fucked things up and now you're going to pay.'

She aimed the gun and fired. One shot was enough. She stood in a trance, observing Hermione's dying gesture of dyeing the water red. *Clack*: red is the colour of blood. *Clack*: blood is the foundation of revolution. As Hermione's head disappeared beneath the water, fronds of hair obscuring her face, Victoria looked away.

She went next door into the bedroom and got the camcorder down from on top of the wardrobe. She'd bury this and the other camera downstairs, along with the rest of the equipment and recordings, in the same unmarked grave she'd dig for Mr Tup Maul. There'd be no point in making them accessible to the public along with this chapter. The ending hadn't been as she'd planned, the denunciation and confession unrecorded. Some skilful editing and – who knew – a different story altogether could emerge. But that wasn't what she was here for. The public would read it how it was. *Clack*: the truth is its own art.

CHAPTER NINE

killing the dead

Three months had passed since Jack Jackson's life had been converted into fiction by the hand of a killer, and now, as a means of coping with the life he found himself living, he'd resorted to fiction himself.

He'd been lucky. He'd been spared the void of unwritten words which other novelists found themselves customarily confronted by at the beginning of a new work. There'd been no confrontational blank page resting between his elbows, no uniform screen between his eyes. He'd been given a head start: one hundred and eighty pages of completed text, eight chapters in all, as well as page upon page of notes in the irregular handwriting he now replicated with perfection, was capable of reading or writing as his own. It was the beginning of what David had very nearly taken to an end.

Jack could have turned away, equated it to a comatosed patient best left untampered with until a suitably qualified specialist arrived to restore it to consciousness.

And there'd been a time when this approach would have suited Jack just fine – if he hadn't chosen to burn the typescript first, that is. But his circumstances had changed, his sensibilities with them. Experience had taught him that it simply wasn't possible to dedicate a period of one's life to learning someone's writing verbatim, being able to contextualise and conjure quotes at will, without appropriating those selfsame words, adopting them as one's own, as if the very idea that they'd ever belonged to another was ludicrous. Like every dedicated academic, he'd become the living receptacle of his subject, a reincarnation. And he'd recognised the unbound sheets of paper of the unfinished book for what they were: foundations, not ruins. Even though they'd been rendered temporarily meaningless by their isolation from the guiding hands of the architect who'd conceived them, they remained a platform upon which he was certain something could be built.

And build it he would. He'd seen things, things he'd been denied in his former life. He'd seen how David was treated by people who previously Jack could only have dreamt of meeting. He'd glimpsed the future from the top, wanted more, realised that it was his to take. He thought back to what had happened after the brothel had been raided, the evening he'd spent with Bernard Bennett. It wasn't what they'd done that had been so spectacular, but the way they'd done it. With style. As if London had belonged to them. Money couldn't have bought the recognition and respect they'd received. Only fame. Only the friendship of people like Bennett. Only Jack's friendship with him. And Bernard *was* Jack's friend now, just like he'd been David's before. He'd sent Jack a postcard, which had arrived two days after Hermione had been found murdered in her bath, expressing his grief, but also saying that, no matter how bad things looked now, what Jack had done on *Answer Time* had been right, had been something he should always be proud of. And Jack was proud. Not because he'd taken Bernard's advice over the silent stance on *Answer Time*, but because it was something he'd done himself. It hadn't been David's actions that had caused Bernard to write; it had been Jack's. It hadn't been David who Bernard had written to; it had been Jack. David's life was over now. Jack's – and he understood this to his core – had only just begun.

He stared at the computer on David's writing desk. It was simple, then. If he wanted to continue to make that life his own, then he had to finish David's book. Either that or become a recluse, throw it all away and return to the ranks of anonymity from which he'd only just gained promotion. And in the days following Hermione Shortbottom's death,

Jack had discovered that not only did he need to finish the book, but also that he was more than capable of doing it.

Shrinking from the trauma which had tracked him from London, he'd skulked fearfully around David's room, a wraith, shrouding himself in shadows, listening to the sound of his feet padding across the floor. The normal devices of communication with the external world – the telephone and the television – had filled him with dread: they'd offered only further predictions that the killer was coming for him next. He'd severed their lifelines, pulled their sockets from the plugs in the walls in two separate but similar fits of panic. It had taken him three days even to be able to face the clogged answerphone downstairs and its series of strangled, distant voices. For comfort, there'd been nowhere to turn but in on himself. And for words, too.

His writing had begun with reading. The alienation which had mocked him with increasing fervour had meant that only the familiar had been able to provide him with the sense of security he'd so desperately needed. His thoughts had moved to the incomplete typescript, the autobiographical work whose completion had been terminated at the same time as its subject's life. Even when he'd read it for the first time and the nausea had crawled along his throat, he'd found the style so familiar, it was as if he'd written it himself. He'd caught himself anticipating first words, then whole sentences. And, more recently, as he'd stared down at the printed words, he'd been able to detect passages which had only reached this stage after pedantic and exhaustive editing sessions. Checking what was before him against David's notebook had only shown him to be correct.

And then there was the blueprint for the design, the notebook. The unwritten chapters which would carry the work to its conclusion were all here. All that was needed to expand this skeletal frame into a vigorous and complete lifespan on the page was time. And Jack had time to spare. Already he'd completed a chapter in addition to those left behind by David. It wasn't yet perfect, but that too would come in time. The more he'd written the more he'd become convinced that he could write, that it was his vocation, something he'd been born to do, something that the genetic link between himself and his brother had ensured had been there from the first. In the nights, when fresh ideas and sentences had chased him out of his bed, across the room to the writing desk, and only allowed him to return to sleep once they'd been set down to await his attention in the morning, he'd wondered how he'd avoided this addiction up till now. As with smoking, he'd wondered how he'd previously coped.

And when he wasn't working on the new chapters, he was working on the old, editing out the more glaring of the autobiographical strands, replacing them with more imaginary flights, keeping matters firmly off what was now his own doorstep. He wasn't David, didn't have the same viral get-out clause that had endowed him with the courage to go through with this ritualistic self-exposure. No, when this was published, Jack was going to be very much alive. And so, with this in mind, he'd worked on changing what was already there. This wasn't as difficult as he'd first imagined. The majority of what David had written (what he'd done) was distantly removed from how the public perceived him. Aside from names and places, a gratifyingly small proportion needed alteration. And once these links had been broken, what had been fact, became fiction.

The physical abuse had been erased. It had been sick. It had been symptomatic of a sickness that only a shrink could have cured. But there was more to the notebook than sickness. There was life. There was the captured elation of what life could be like when taken to extremes. It was only because he'd known that the book was fact that he'd reacted against it when he'd first read it. Now that he'd doctored it, wielded the surgical tools of computerised cut and paste across the body of words, it was sanitised. All that was left was a story, a story about a man who decided to live life to the full, a story – and he was keeping the end as David would have wished – in which the man died for the simple reason that he'd lived too much. No critic or reader in their right mind would deduce that this had been culled directly from reality. A radical departure from David's usual? Certainly. Designed to shock? Again, yes. Prize-winning material: Who could tell? . . . But whatever the reaction, who was going to be anything but impressed by the phenomenal generic range this author was capable of? No one. No one at all.

He looked up from the computer and checked his watch. It was lunchtime. He saved the morning's work, backed it up and quit the word-processing application. Routine was an essential ingredient of success. Eating regularly. Sleeping regularly (where ideas allowed). The temptation was there to go at it one hundred per cent. But Sally Scott-Thompson had reassured him on the futility of that course of action. She'd faxed and phoned him several times in the week following Hermione's murder. He'd plugged the phone in and rung her in return from the isolation of his bedroom, claiming, when pressed, that he was out of the country and her messages had been forwarded to him by a friend, knowing he shouldn't be telling people where he really was, knowing that the police had fed the newspapers the story that he'd gone into hiding abroad. The repeated concern she'd expressed for his well-being had been ordinary considering the extraordinary circumstances he'd been subjected to. But that hadn't been the only reason she'd rung. He suspected that someone like Sally rarely, if ever, made contact on purely sociable grounds.

The real reason, the solid wood beneath the veneer, had been that the delivery date for his next novel was rapidly approaching. Although his editor was fully aware that he hadn't had the easiest of times recently (Sally had made sure of that), he must understand that a deadline was still a deadline. There was a substantial advance waiting to be collected for the delivery of the typescript. But more than that, Sally had stressed, it was a matter of timing.

Sales in David's backlist had rocketed following his appearance in the account of Hermione's murder published on the Internet by the remaining Thriller Killer. His role as survivor and possible next victim had empowered him with guru status across the country. And the sex thing. He shouldn't worry. That had been greeted with sympathy and intrigue by his current readership. Had he participated willingly? Had he been raped? Or was that what he was really like? And it had cracked the market wide open to those who might have considered him too conservative for their tastes before.

The next novel was the most eagerly awaited book since . . . (And here, Sally's considerable powers of hyperbole had failed her.) Suffice to say, the whole thing was unprecedented. So long as he was OK (And he was, wasn't he? she'd checked) then he should still be aiming for the original delivery date. Now was the time. Bestseller. Best-ever-seller. There was no telling how far this one would run . . . Only don't burn out. She'd stressed this time and time again, as if she'd feared she'd ignite alongside him if this were to occur. Keep your routine. Eat regularly. Sleep regularly. And between those, keep the words coming.

He switched the computer off and Gellet left his place by his master's feet and followed him downstairs.

All six foot four of Simon was folded in an armchair watching television when Gellet trotted into the room. Jack entered seconds later and watched the dog fussing over the other man's leather boots. Not so long ago, he would have been jealous of the bestowed affection. But Jack had earned his own place in the dog's heart. And now that he truly felt master of this house, the dog felt it, too. Simon, despite the easy comfort he displayed in these surroundings, was a guest, someone to be inspected and fawned over, stung for an illicit morsel of food slipped surreptitiously from the dining table, or someone to be bullied into animation, as now, forced from his armchair to his feet. Jack was different. Jack was here to stay.

'OK if I take him with me on the rounds, David?' Simon asked, gently pushing the dog down and pulling his denim jacket on, concealing the side-arm which never left the holster strapped across his back.

'Sure. I'll fix some food while you're gone.'

'Great,' Simon said, opening the door on to the garden, half-turning to face Jack as Gellet squeezed around his legs and dashed erratically off into the sunlight. 'Half an hour OK?'

Jack nodded and walked through to the stove, listened to Simon shut and lock the door behind him. Human whistles and animal barks faded around the side of the house. He turned the stove on, lifted the lid of the saucepan and stared into the thick broth, waiting patiently for it to boil.

Simon was someone Jack suspected he had a lot in common with. They were both more used to having their lives cast into relief by tower blocks than trees, were single, and alone. But David wasn't like Jack. So that was that. The opportunity to discover whether his intuition was correct was not one that it would have been appropriate for Jack to take. Simon was here to do a job, to conduct an operation as per his superiors' instructions. It would have been unprofessional for him to have been the first to relax in the other man's company. It wasn't what he was here for.

The phone rang and Jack left the stove and strode through to the answerphone in the hall, counting the rings, feeling his pulse match their rhythm. He knew the routine well now. Six rings. A click. A whir of spinning tape. Simon's voice explaining firmly and politely that David Jackson was on holiday abroad, but that he, Simon Kent, the housesitter, would ensure that any urgent message would be forwarded to him at the first available opportunity. Jack stood watching the machine as the message finished.

'Hello,' a voice crackled through the poor-standard speaker, 'this is—'

Jack snatched up the telephone receiver. 'Rachel? Rachel, is that you?'

'Yes, David. It's me.'

He gripped his hair, told himself to subdue the excitement which highlighted his voice. 'How are you?'

'Good. You?'

'Still alive,' he said with a wheezed laugh.

'And still smoking, by the sound of it.'

'Afraid so.'

'I got your letter this morning. It sounds terrible.'

'Yes, things have been better.'

'Was that the policeman on the answerphone?'

'You mean Simon. Yes.'

'Are you both still getting on all right?'

'Yes. Keeps to himself and I do the same.' His words ran out on him. He didn't want to be communicating this way, resorting to small talk. But he was too apprehensive to do anything else. 'Gellet thinks he's fantastic. Simon takes him on the rounds he does every hour or so.'

'Rounds?'

'He checks the outbuildings and the surrounding fields for – well, anything or anyone suspicious, I suppose.' He laughed. 'The only success they've had so far was finding a freelance photographer who'd got his foot jammed in the cattle-grid at the bottom of the drive. Didn't I tell you about that in the letter?'

'No.'

There was a pause. 'Listen,' he said. 'Are we going to meet up some time? To talk . . . To talk things through. Only I'd understand it if you didn't want—'

'Yes.'

'Yes?'

'Yes.'

'But I don't understand.'

'What's the matter?' she asked. 'Have you changed your mind?'

'No.' He laughed nervously. 'Christ, no. Nothing like that.'

'What then?'

'I just can't believe you've changed *your* mind.'

'Well, I have.'

Disbelief still held him. 'But the last time we spoke . . . When I was in London. The same night . . .'

'That Shortbottom was killed,' she said. 'The same night you went home with her.'

'Look, I can explain all that. It wasn't how it seemed.'

'She's dead, David. It doesn't matter now.'

'It matters to me. You don't understand. She made—'

'Let's not talk about it,' she stopped him. 'If you want to tell me about it, you can tell me to my face. Things like that are never very good on the phone.'

'OK,' he said, calmer now. 'But when shall we get together? And where?'

'When are you next coming to London?'

'I'm not. Not in the immediate future, anyway. I can't.'

'Oh.'

'Simon says I shouldn't be moving off the property unless it's vital. It's a controlled environment here. No contact with the outside world. Officially abroad, like the papers say.'

'Yes. I believed it myself until I got your letter.'

'Well, if I was to meet you in London, no matter how safe we thought it was, who knows who might find out? I'd be compromising myself horrifically.'

'OK then. If you can't come to London, why don't I come to you?'

'To Wales?'

'Why not? I can't see any other way. Or are you having second thoughts?'

'No,' he said. 'No, it's not that at all. It's you. I don't know how safe it would be. It might not be wise for you to be here at the moment, what with the way things are. And I know what Simon would say. I haven't had anyone round since this whole thing began. That's how he wants things played. His people made that clear right from the start. If they're going to protect me, they have to isolate me. For the time being, they said. Until they catch her. Until it's all over.'

'Fine,' she said. 'I understand. You're probably right. We'll just have to meet up some other time.'

He felt her pulling free, couldn't tolerate the thought of cutting the line, no matter how much sense it made. 'No,' he protested. 'Here's good. It doesn't matter. Simon will be here. If he can protect one person, I'm sure he can protect two.'

'Are you sure?'

'Certain.'

'So when should I come down?'

'I don't know. I hadn't really thought about it.'

'What about today?' she suggested.

The immediacy of the proposal threw him. 'Today?' He looked at his watch for confirmation of what he already knew. 'But it's lunchtime already.'

'Dinner then. I can come down for dinner and travel back to London tomorrow.'

'You mean spend the night?'

'Well you're not suggesting I sleep in the car, are you?'

'Of course not. But—'

'But what? The spare rooms are still there, aren't they? I know Simon's staying in one, but that still leaves me with a choice of two.' She concluded hesitantly, 'Or wouldn't you feel comfortable with that?'

'It's not that. It's just, like I said, I haven't cleared any of this with Simon yet.' A moment's silence followed his frown, then he said, 'Never mind. I'll run it by him this afternoon. I'm sure he won't mind.'

'Good. I'll aim to get to you around seven. Does that sound OK?'

'Excellent. But one more thing before you go . . .'

'What?'

'You still haven't told me what made you change your mind about seeing me.'

'Do you really need to know?'

'Yes, it's important.'

'Because I'm scared for you, David. I read about you in the papers every day. And now that I know where you are, I don't think I can stand by any longer.' He heard her sigh. 'Until seven, David,' she said, and the connection was cut.

It was like a death. He continued to hold the receiver to his ear, as if some latent trace of her spirit, an aura, was trapped there. He closed his eyes and sensed her close. It was the same as it had been with his mother. The doctor had had to unfasten his hand from hers after she'd gone. Holding her, feeling her temperature change, he'd been convinced that the physical link provided by the union of their skin would somehow continue to graft her to life.

He replaced the receiver and exhaled. This was life, not death. This was an opportunity to make his life complete. Rachel was inside him, just as she'd been inside him from the day he'd met her. He now had the chance to free her from the prison of his imagination in which she'd unwittingly slept all these years, breathe dimensions into her, make her corporeal, his. But this – now, tonight – was so close.

He hadn't wanted it to be this way. The letter was meant to have been an opening. Riddled with calculated ambiguities, he'd sweated over it more than any part of the novel he was completing. The invitation for her to meet up with him which it had contained had been carefully framed, intended to be read as an open invite, a gesture of reconciliation. It was something he'd imagined her taking up probably never, at best in the distant future. Other letters were to have followed first. Then phone calls. Only then, once the ground work had been laid, was the meeting destined to occur. She wasn't meant to have pounced on it this way, not the same day it dropped through her letter box. It didn't make sense. History was against it. He should have remained spurned, his letter vindictively burnt. His love should have continued unrequited. It was his persistence, the inner change that he'd have projected and gradually focused into clarity on her mind over the coming months, that was meant to have won her over. Not this. Not this simple. Not this sudden stamp of pressure cast down upon him.

He wedged a cigarette into his anxious mouth, retreated to the practicality of the stove and stirred the shifting liquid. He was going to have to be on his guard tonight. Not to convince her that he was David. He no longer had to try to do that with anyone. He was going to have to be on his guard, not against his personality, but against his emotions.

He had to ensure that he prevented himself from rushing in and attempting to condense the reconciliation into a matter of hours. She wouldn't buy it. She knew David too well. She'd just think that there was something insidious lurking behind his unlikely declarations. For this to work, he'd have to allow a bit of the old Jack back to the surface. A controlled measure. A glimpse of his skull. He'd have to let her see the longing in his eyes. That way, when she went away the next day, he might be inside her, just like she'd always been inside him. Then it would just be a matter of patience and persistence.

'Simon,' he said, as they sat at the table after they'd finished eating their lunch. 'There's something I want to run by you.'

Simon raised his eyebrows. 'Shoot.'

'You understand that my wife and I have separated?'

'You've mentioned it.'

Jack smiled. 'And you already knew. Just like you know most things about me.'

'It's my job,' Simon apologised.

'I know. It's not that I want to talk about, though. Our separation is a fact. It's something that happened, something that was reported in the newspapers at the time and then dropped. The public eye closed once the articles had been written and read. But that doesn't mean the matter ended there. Life goes on independently beyond the tabloids' copy. Do you understand?'

Simon nodded. 'Meaning that the tabloids got it wrong.'

'No, meaning that the tabloids might have reached a premature conclusion.'

Simon drew his own conclusion. 'Are you telling me that you're getting back together?'

'No. I don't know. Not yet.' Jack blinked heavily. 'It's complicated.'

'So what are you telling me?'

Jack recalled the rehearsed sentence – the opening gambit, designed to snag sympathy – in his mind, then recited it: 'There's a possibility that things still might work out between us.'

'And that's what you want?'

'Yes, of course. That's why I'm telling you.'

'Sorry,' Simon said, picking up the stump of baguette from the table. 'You've lost me. What's all this got to do with me? Do you want my opinion on what you should do? Is that it?'

'No, not on what I should do. I already know what I want to do.' He steadied his gaze. 'But I do need your opinion, or your cooperation, anyway. It's a professional matter rather than personal.'

Simon tore some bread and held it to his mouth. 'Go for it,' he said, inserting the starchy swab into his mouth and biting down.

'Rachel – my wife – called while you were out with Gellet doing the rounds,' Jack confessed. 'I wrote a letter to her. I told her about what was going on down here. About you being here. Pretty much everything. And she rang me. In the letter, I asked her if she wanted to meet up some time and talk things over, try and sort things out. That's why she rang.'

Simon continued to chew meditatively until his mouth was clear. 'Did you name a date?' he finally asked.

'I didn't actually say. It was more an open invitation. Nothing specific. Nothing immediate.'

'And what did she say?'

'She said yes.'

Something must have been written on Jack's face, because Simon asked, 'More immediate than you thought, then?'

Jack rolled a cigarette across the table surface. 'She said she wanted to come down today. Tonight, in fact.'

Simon sucked his lip pensively, drew breath. 'And you said yes. That's why you're telling me now.'

'Yes.' Jack surveyed Simon, attempted to decipher his expression. All he registered was discomfort. Not anger. Anger was something he could have fought against. Anger would have given him the opportunity to state the case he had mapped out in his mind, encourage Simon on a specific route. But anger wasn't there. And so he had no option but to compromise their relationship further, to explain. 'Believe me, if there'd been another way, I'd have taken it. I know she shouldn't be coming down here. I know it doesn't make sense for either of us. It puts us both in danger.' He frowned. 'And I know it's something we agreed I wouldn't do.'

Simon reached down to stroke Gellet's prone form. He avoided Jack's eyes. 'You do realise that you've put me in a difficult situation, don't you? It's something I should've run by my bosses first.'

'I know. That's why I feel so bad about it.'

Simon looked up, rested his broad forearms on the table. 'This psycho we're dealing with isn't going to give up. You know that, don't you? She's got you marked. The way that last confession read, it could have been you or Shortbottom who got it. Who knows, if things had worked out differently – if she'd been able to move in quicker and you'd still been there – she might have capitalised on the opportunity and killed you as well. That stuff you were saying on *Answer Time,* slating the killers the way you did. It put you in the same camp as Shortbottom. It made you as much of a target as she ever was.'

'But so much time's passed. There hasn't been another killing since . . .'

'People like her don't stop. Believe me: she's coming for you. That's why there's been this pause. It's you she wants next. It's only because she thinks you're hidden abroad, out of her reach, that she hasn't come for you already. Inviting your wife down here is just increasing the danger. People talk. How do you know your wife won't mention her visit to someone?'

'She won't.'

Simon leant forward, closed in on Jack. 'But how do you know? You're separated now. We suspect the killer's an insider. Chances are she's some publisher or author with a grudge to bear. It could be someone you and Rachel are friends with. It could be anyone. How can you be certain who Rachel confides in these days?'

'Because she understands how serious all this is.' He stopped toying with the cigarette, lit it, rose from the table and walked to the window. He stared out across the garden. 'Because I told her in the letter. Because I told her everything and the only reason I was prepared to do that was because I know what she's like. I know she won't tell anyone else.'

Simon got up from the table and joined him. 'I'm sorry, David, I really am. But I'm going to have to make a few phone calls. And I can tell you – right now – what the answer's going to be. She can't come down. We just can't risk it. We can't risk her life as well.' Simon looked around the room with professional contemplation, his mind a computer, accessing files, performing complex calculations, passing judgement on just how bad the situation had become. 'And after you calling her, telling her where you are, I don't think they're going to think it's a good idea that we stay here any longer either. It's too dangerous.'

Instinctively, Jack moved back a pace, blocking any potential movement by the bigger man towards the telephone. He'd intended this to be intimidatory, a tool to aid the imposition of his will. But instantaneously, he realised the futility of such a proposition. Gravity, in the face of Simon's size, crushed his confidence, diminishing his ego, shrivelling his stature. He felt weak, ineffective and emasculated. He suspected that men like Simon could detect weakness in the air. He had to keep it together. Be David. Be David. David would tell Simon . . . David would bring him round to . . . David would sort everything . . . David . . . No. No, he wouldn't. David wouldn't have even wanted Rachel down here in the first place. He wouldn't have written the letter. He wouldn't even have picked up the phone. That was why no words came now. This mess was all down to Jack, to his buzzing mind and sweaty loins. No one else. What did David care for this? It was only Jack who cared. Only Jack could speak up for what only Jack wanted. Rachel burst into his mind. An injection. A rush.

'If it's me or Rachel you're worried about, don't,' he tried to reassure Simon. 'It's what I want. It's what we want.'

Simon shook his head. 'It's not up to me. I can't go making decisions like this blind.'

Jack switched tack, desperate to find a way to navigate this obstacle. 'Well, if it's you you're worrying about – if you think they'll hold you responsible if anything were to happen – then I'll put it in writing for you that this is what I wanted. I'll let them know that you tried to change my mind.' The rush was beginning to evaporate against the contrast of Simon's solidity, become invisible, a gas. 'I need this,' he mumbled. 'I need this chance with her. You're here to keep me safe, to keep my life intact. This is it. Rachel is my life. Don't you see? All this hiding means nothing if . . .' The last remnant of nobility cowered in his eyes, then shrank inwards, became inverted, and in its place desperation burned. 'I'm begging you,' he said soullessly, his eyes closed. 'If you block this . . .'

His failings drew together and synthesised into silence. He walked away, slumped into the armchair, knowing there was nothing else to say, knowing he hadn't the energy even if there was. Unattended ash collapsed onto his trousers as his cigarette receded towards the skin on his fingers.

Then came words: 'One night. But I'm telling you, David, that's it. She comes down tonight and I make the phone calls tomorrow.'

Jack looked up at Simon's apprehensive face. He said nothing, because there was nothing he could say that could come close to conveying the gratitude he felt.

After he'd prepared dinner for the evening, Jack left Simon downstairs and returned with Gellet to his writing. But as the hours passed, the words he sought failed to materialise. His fingers, stabbing with habitual determination down at the keyboard, lost their rhythm and aim, stumbled. Their order didn't even seem to matter any more. The fatigue affected even Gellet, who left his post by Jack's feet and sloped out of the room.

Jack got to his feet and wandered into the corridor, passing the door of the first guest room, stopping at the second, opening it and entering. He'd been in here often over the past three months. Silence held it. It radiated peace. He looked at the hexagonal antique clock on the wall. It was this which had triggered his memory, telling him whose room this had once been. Rachel had told him about how she'd finished sleeping with David and sharing a room with him some time before she'd finished with him altogether. This place had become her refuge. Jack removed his shoes and lay on the bed, staring at the clock, listening to its mesmeric sound. It was wrong that someone like her should have been contained in such a way, that David should have driven her from him into the solitude of these four walls. Jack could picture her here as she would have been then, lying on the bed, watching the seconds flick by, wondering how much longer she could last, watching her life drain away. He rolled over and pulled a pillow between his arms, nuzzled it, breathed it in, searched for her.

When he woke, he returned to David's bedroom. But his mind was elsewhere, wandering towards Rachel once more, clawing her back from his dreams. He managed a couple of strenuous paragraphs, but soon his fingers left the keyboard altogether. Instead, they nursed cigarette after cigarette. He deserted the desk and channelled the smoke out of the bedroom window. She was a drug. The thought of his next injection, like an approaching zeppelin gradually annexing the sky, loomed larger by the moment, until it was all he saw. His breath became saturated, hormonal, and his eyes watched the progress of the sun across the sky.

And then, with the silent reduction of the light, came another source of illumination: headlights, shyly dipped, roamed up the drive, halted in the yard, then blanked. The door of the car opened and she stepped out into the dusk, her face a segment of her silhouette, impenetrable. From his vantage point, he continued to observe, a voyeur, seduced by the animation before him. She removed the bag that held her clothes, her make-up – all the things he wanted to touch –

and swayed beneath its weight past the Land Rover, through the herb garden, towards the door. And there – below him – she looked up and tentatively smiled.

He reached the front door and slowly drew it open, savouring the moment, as though he were revealing an exhibit for the first time. Close now, thrown from the blur of silhouette to the intricacy of cells, he could only marvel at her. Her hair was shorter than he remembered it at the funeral. And her face had altered, too. The bitterness which had chilled her eyes, cast them in an unalterable glare, had vanished. There was only openness now. Innocence.

'Come in,' he said, cracking the frozen moment with the sound of his voice.

She stepped into the hall, brushed her lips against his cheek, and allowed him to take her bag. Then she looked beyond him, saying, 'And you must be Simon.'

Simon walked over from the kitchen doorway that he'd been leaning against. 'Rachel, yes?' he asked, briefly enfolding her hand in his.

Rachel looked away from the larger, younger man to Jack and said with a smile, 'Well, he certainly looks capable of looking after us.'

'I don't mean to be a nuisance,' Simon said, 'but there's a couple of things I'd like to get clear.'

Rachel looked to Jack for guidance.

Jack closed the door, then said, 'We might as well get this out in the open. Simon isn't exactly pleased about you being here.'

'It's nothing personal, you understand?' Simon intervened.

'David?' Rachel queried. 'I thought you said it would be all right . . .'

'It probably is,' Simon equivocated. 'I just want to be certain.'

'What he wants to know, Rachel, is whether you spoke to anyone about coming down here today.'

Simon added, 'Or whether you spoke to anyone – I mean anyone at all – about David's letter to you, about him being in this country, anything.'

'Of course not,' Rachel said. 'David made that clear in his letter. I haven't told anyone. I wouldn't be so stupid.'

'There,' Jack said. 'What did I say?'

'I just wanted to be sure,' Simon said with a nod to Rachel.

'And are you?' Rachel asked.

Simon shrugged. 'As sure as we're going to get, I guess.'

Jack moved forward. 'So we're all happy now?'

'Yep,' Simon said, some of the afternoon's stress gone from his face. He smiled broadly at Rachel. 'How was your drive? OK, I hope?'

'Good. No problems.' She smiled back, joking, 'And before you ask, nobody followed me, as far as I was aware . . .'

Before Jack or Simon could react to this, Gellet came sprawling into the hall and thundered into Rachel, his tail a blur of excitement.

'My God!' Rachel cried out, crouching down and letting the dog nuzzle her face. 'Gellet. You're all grown up.' She looked up at Jack, laughing. 'I can't believe it. Last time I was here, he was . . .'

'Smaller?' Jack guessed. He didn't know how old the dog was.

'Yes,' she agreed. 'Much smaller. I'm amazed he still recognises me. He only knew me for a month or so.'

'Gellet!' Jack called and the dog came to him. 'Simon, will you keep him with you for a little while, till I get Rachel sorted out?'

'Sure,' Simon said, taking Gellet by the collar and leading him through to the kitchen.

'Come on,' Jack said to Rachel. 'I'll show you to your room.'

He led the way through the hall and up the spiral staircase, conscious of the fact that this whole host and guest relationship was little more than a charade, that she knew the way as well as him; in all truth, she probably knew it better. She'd lived here with David for years. Jack knew the nostalgic sequence which must have been going through her mind right now. It would be similar to the one which had gripped him in the Book Bar before his meeting with Smiles. Only this would be more profound. Not just nerves, but loathing, too. It was she who'd left David, not the other way round. This tour she was making now would be the same as if she was visiting a prison she'd once been held captive in. She'd escaped, grown a fresh life, and only now was she strong enough to retrace her roots. Jack was relieved that she was behind him, that he wasn't able to see her face and attempt to decide whether the hatred she'd once held for this place – and, indeed, for David – was still blazing in her eyes. One step at a time, he told himself as he reached the top of the stone stairs. Follow her lead. Don't attempt to take her anywhere she doesn't want to go. He paused at the top of the stairs and looked ahead to the corridor which led off the far side of the room.

'Simon's staying there. I put him as far away from me as possible. Not to be antisocial,' he explained. 'Just the sound of my typing. I didn't want to keep him awake.'

'So you're still writing. I'm surprised you've been able to concentrate what with all that's happened.'

'It takes my mind off it.'

She nodded sympathetically. 'Is it the same novel you were writing when I left? Or did you give up on that?'

'The same.'

'How's it going? You never let me see it. Not like you used to with the others.'

'Fine. Good.' He stared at her, wanting to erase everything David had done to her, wanting it desperately. 'I'm so sorry,' he said. 'I don't know what else to say. I'm just so sorry.'

She lowered herself onto the arm of the chair behind her. 'What you wrote. In your letter. About the cocaine. About how much you'd been taking. About how addicted you were. About what it did to you. Is it over now? Is it finished?'

He looked at her steadily. He'd rehearsed this moment in his mind more times than he could remember. This was it.

Get it right. This was the only way to get her back. Blame it on the drugs David had taken. Exaggerate. Do anything necessary to wipe the past away and start afresh. 'I haven't touched it for months. It's dead. I swear to you, Rachel. It's over.'

She didn't need to reply. Her unchanged expression said it all.

'You don't have to take my word for it,' he continued. 'Christ knows, my word doesn't mean anything to you any more. But you'll see. You'll see. All you've got to do is look.'

'I never even guessed,' she said quietly. 'If you were as dependent as you say you were, you'd have thought I would have noticed.'

'It was hardly something I was going to brag about, was it?'

'No,' she admitted. 'I suppose not.'

'But I'm back to normal again now. I'm as normal as anyone you'll ever meet.'

She stared at him for a moment, then said, 'I didn't marry you because you were normal.'

'I'm not saying that.'

She propped her elbows against her knees, cradled her head in her hands. 'I married you because you were different to everyone else. You had something to say. I wanted to be the one there to listen to you say it.'

He couldn't bear this, couldn't stomach the regret in her voice. 'I know. I let you down.'

Her eyes gripped him. 'You can't imagine how your writing made me feel, even before I met you. I thought you wanted to make a difference to the way we lived. I thought you wanted people to become decent again.' She blinked heavily. 'I used to sit at work, editing junk day in day out, because it was low-risk, because it was what would sell. Page after page of mediocrity and formulaic drivel. Can you imagine what that was like? Someone with my mind. Someone who knew they could probably write better than any of them.' She looked away, and slowly, uniformity returned to her face; her frown flattened out, disappeared. 'And then you came along and it suddenly made sense.'

'And so you married me,' he said.

She gazed past him. 'Yes, I married you because I loved you and I loved what you wrote. They were the same thing back then, indivisible.'

'I can bring it back,' he said, and he meant it. 'Things can be different. I can make things right again.'

'It's not that easy, David. I don't love you any more. I haven't loved you for a long time. I hardly even remember what it feels like to love.'

'You can't mean that. Why else would you have stayed with me all that time? You must have felt something for me.'

'I did.'

He pounced, 'Then there's a chance that we can work things out.'

'No, David. You're not listening. I did feel something for you, but it wasn't love. It was regret. That's what I felt when I looked at you. And hope – hope that you might change back. That's why I stayed.' She lifted her head back, stared at the ceiling, heaved air powerfully into her lungs, then faced him. 'But it got to the point when I couldn't take it any more. The abuse. The things you wanted me to do to you . . . Your affairs. My breakdown. But even then, I still thought the man I'd married was inside you somewhere. But he wasn't. He wasn't coming back. That's why I left. Do you see that, David? It was the sickening waste of it all. You threw your life away.' She got to her feet and stood awkwardly, waited for words from him. But his lips failed to part. 'And you destroyed me along the way,' she said. 'You left me dead.'

'I'm' sorry,' was all he could say.

'And now you want me back . . .'

'I love you,' he said, and as he did, he understood that these words were his and not David's. This was where David's input ended and his own commitment began for real. His voice continued in a croak. 'And that's why I've got to have you back.'

She stared at the floor. 'If you're lying to me, David . . .

If this is another one of your games . . .'

'It's not,' he said. 'Believe me, it's not.'

'I don't know, David,' she said, breaking the silence that his words had disappeared into. 'I just don't know.'

Not now, he told himself. Too early. Leave it for now or there won't ever be another time. 'Come on,' he said, setting off down the corridor which branched off next to them, the one which led to the two guest rooms and the bathroom, and which terminated in his bedroom. 'It's too soon for us to be talking this way.' He paused outside her old room and, when he spoke again, his tone of voice was artificially vibrant, censorious of the conversation which had preceded. 'Which room's it going to be?'

'This one,' she said.

He handed her her bag. 'I'll leave you for a while. There are clean towels in the bathroom if you want to take a shower.' He turned to go. 'I'll see you in the drawing room in a little while.'

Jack was waiting in the drawing room. The scents of nocturnal flora spun through the open window, blending into a narcotic mixture with the fumes of his whisky and the smoke of his cigarette. He heard her steps approaching and self-consciously resumed the pose he'd taught himself over the preceding minutes of swirling apprehension. Look natural and you'll act natural. Basic logic: act natural and nature will take its course. She entered the room and came and stood beside him at the window.

'What can I get you to drink?'

'Just water. I'm parched.'

He nodded and went through to the kitchen to fetch it. As he poured it over the snapping ice cubes in the bottom of a tall glass, he tried not to read significance into her choice. So what if she didn't want anything alcoholic? What did it matter? What had he been expecting? A night of drenched flirtation, capped with a shared bed? It wasn't going to be that way. From what she'd said upstairs, it wasn't going to be that way at all. Maybe he shouldn't be drinking either.

Whatever they had to put straight wasn't going to be simplified by drink. There was enough confusion already. He returned to the drawing room and put the glass in her hand. She didn't turn from the window to look at him.

'I've missed this place,' she said. 'I didn't think I had. Not till your letter arrived and I read about it again. And even after that, it didn't really hit me until I pulled off the motorway and made my way here.' She finally looked at him. 'You're very lucky, you know – having all this here, all the time.'

'You had it once,' he told her, picking up his cigarette from the ashtray he'd left it in. 'And it wasn't enough to keep you here.'

'It wasn't the house that made me leave, David.' She was watching him for a reaction now, but he couldn't think of anything to say. He didn't even know what to think. She walked away from the window and settled into one of the armchairs.

He stubbed out his cigarette and sat opposite her. Although he knew he should be telling her what they were having for dinner, discussing the weather, anything to keep her at ease, avoid a return to the antagonism of upstairs, he heard himself saying, 'Do you believe in fresh beginnings?'

'That depends.'

'On what?'

'On who you're talking about.'

'I was going to say us,' he admitted. 'But perhaps I really mean me.'

Her eyes shifted from him, concealing her mind. 'Go on,' she told him.

'Do you remember when we were sitting in the car at the cemetery?'

She nodded. 'It's not a day I'm going to forget.'

'No, I don't think either of us will.'

She stared into his eyes. 'I don't—'

'No,' he interrupted, 'hear me out first. Jack's death made me think about a lot of things. Not even just about him.' He bit his lip deliberately, attempted to summon the sensation of mourning inside himself. 'About myself. About where my life was going. About my priorities. When we were in the car, I told you that you didn't know the first thing about me any more.'

'I remember.'

'It was premature. I can see that now. But I meant what I said: I'd changed. Even then. But it was still premature. I couldn't have understood just how permanent the change was going to be. And it wasn't just that I wasn't taking drugs any more. It was me. It was my whole life I wanted to change. I wanted to cut out all the bad bits. All the hatred. All the hatred I'd always reserved for people like Jack. Do you understand? It's only now that I know that what I said to you back then was completely true.'

'You said all this in your letter. I didn't know whether to believe you. That's why I agreed to meet you.'

'Do you believe me now?'

Her eyes closed for a second or two. 'I'm confused. I don't know what to think any more.' She looked at him again. 'But you have changed. I can see that. But I don't know how much. I hardly know into what.'

Jack left his seat and went to the window. He stared out into the evening, counting the first visible stars. 'You were right to hate me for what happened to Jack. It was my fault.'

'I know.'

'But he's not gone. He's with me now.'

He said these words and turned to gauge her reaction to them. They'd leapt from his mouth and now he waited to see if they were going to swim, or flounder and gasp for air. But her profile gave nothing away. He held his tongue, pinned it to the bridge of his mouth, waiting for a reaction from her, waiting for analysis, waiting for pity, still waiting for love.

When she turned to face him, her eyes glistened. 'It's funny, but I almost wish I could believe you. I wish it was that easy.'

Before Jack had time to formulate a reaction, Simon's voice mugged the silence, subduing any reaction other than the practicality of the here and now. He told them that the food was ready. They stood up and followed him from the room.

As the meal wore on, Jack felt the pressure rush down. It should have been natural, a regular social exercise, even graceful. But it wasn't. His mouth was arid with apprehension. All he could register with assurance was the passing of precious, wasted time. Food cloyed in his mouth, stodgy and barely palatable.

It wasn't the cooking – his planned and perfected meal – that was to blame. He, like Rachel and Simon, had no complaints there. And it wasn't the company. How could it be with her here? And even if it could have been improved by Simon's absence, he had no cause to resent the other man; without him there wouldn't have been any Rachel here at all. But still, he was inadequate to the task. He needed to go back to the moment they'd sat down, review the deal and change the current outcome.

In an effort to instil some sense of order into the mess he was making of the evening, he rearranged his food yet again, lifted a fork towards his mouth, then recoiled. He returned the implement to the plate and reached for the bottle of wine.

He was counting the glasses. This was number three. And then there was the whisky before. He wondered if Rachel was counting his intake, too. He left his glass half-empty. He had to be careful. It was essential that he remained sober within reason. He pointed the neck of the bottle he was still holding at Simon's glass and tilted it, watching the liquid conform to its confines. An intonation dragged his concentration outwards and he returned the bottle to the table and asked Rachel to repeat the question he hadn't heard the first time round. But by the time she'd said it again and Simon had launched into a reply, Jack had already forgotten what the question had been. Resigned, he picked up the bottle and filled his glass to the brim.

The meal was over and Jack was drunk. He was standing outside Rachel's room. His memory of the evening was incoherent, a jumble of disconnected, overheard phrases, moving eyes and mouths. But what did it matter? She was here with him now, in his house, late at night, standing in the open doorway of her room, only paces from the closed door of his own, staring at him. And if she was looking at him with disgust, he couldn't be sure. Caution had deserted him some time around the eighth glass of wine, around the same time his silence had graduated into noisy, alcoholic banter and, by necessity, flirtation. Now he felt high, soaring, a plane bursting through a cloudbank into the unadulterated sunshine above.

'You can't go to bed now,' he was saying. 'It's only . . .' He made a fumbled attempt to shake his watch from beneath his cuff, failed. 'Who cares what the time is anyway? I don't. I could stay up all night.' He looked at her coyly. 'All I need is someone to keep me company.'

'It's late, David. And I'm tired. I'm going to bed.'

'But why? I'm having fun. This is fun, isn't it?'

'It was a nice evening,' she conceded.

'Well there you go, then. You've had fun. I've had fun. Why leave it there?'

'Because it's over, David. It's time it came to an end.'

He was suddenly aware of the absence of a smile on her face. 'And that's it? You're not going to change your mind.'

'No.'

Her abruptness took him back. The anger in her voice. She was cold, the kind of cold that would strip the skin from his fingers if he tried to touch her. 'Please.'

'Goodnight,' she said, beginning to close the door.

He stuck out a hand, grabbed the door. 'Wait.'

'What?'

'The way I was with you before. The things I wanted you to do. It's not what I want any more. It disgusts me.' He leant forward instinctively. 'I want you to believe me. I'd never . . .' Hermione came to him, writhing across him. Wine rose in his throat. He couldn't think about that. Not now. Not ever. 'The thought of it makes me want to vomit . . . Believe me – you've got to. It's the truth.' The fear of losing her over this, for the things that David had done to her . . . He lurched back against the corridor wall. 'Jesus,' he pleaded as she closed the door on him, 'how can I prove it to you when you won't even look me in the face?'

Drunken minutes later, when he eventually managed to extricate himself from his clothes and crawl into the warm cocoon of bedclothes in his room, the image of her face as she'd left him engulfed his drunken mind, plummeted with him into unconsciousness.

Later – he had no idea how much time had passed – he woke to the sound of his bedroom door closing and feet stealing softly across the floor to the bed. The back of his head was aching. It felt sticky against the pillow. His eyes opened, but all was black. He felt the cool of air across his body, fleetingly wondered where the bedclothes had gone. The back of his head was throbbing. But what did it matter? He heard breathing next to him. Rachel was here. She'd changed her mind. She'd come to him. This was it. Everything. This was the full circle, the completion of things . . .

What? Fresh pain cut across his face and he opened his mouth to scream. Only his lips wouldn't move. Gagged. Air snorted from his nostrils and he found himself struggling to swallow. Close by, a shadow moved swiftly. A dream? The pain was settling across his face, expanding through his head. Nightmare? He needed out. He needed out now. He made to move his arms, to reach out and touch this solid silhouette rearing over him, convince himself that it was nothing but the darkness of his imagination. But his arms were fixed in place, paralysed behind his back. 'He kicked out wildly.

'Stay still,' the shadow hissed. He felt something flat and cold slapped down on his throat. And then the object slowly turned and he sensed its flat surface switch to a thin edge which rested lightly against his skin. 'Stay still, or I'll cut your throat.'

He froze, alarm bells in his head now ringing, loud enough to rip the most hideous of nightmares to shreds. Oh Christ. Oh Christ. Oh Christ. She'd come for him. Oh Jesus, no. Not Rachel. Her. Skreen. He knew it. Killer. Cleo. She was here. Diana. Oh Jesus, please. Victoria.

Holding a knife to his throat. Please be wrong. How could this have happened? Where was Simon? Simon! He was screaming in his head now. He was screaming in his head, but he was too terrified to even move.

'How does it feel to be struck dumb, David?' the shadow whispered. 'What does it feel like to be denied a voice?'

She pulled back and climbed off the bed. From where he lay, with his head raised on a pillow, he followed her progress across the room to where she stood against the window, barely discernible from the silent night sky. His breathing was coming in a rush now, raging like wind around his ears. Don't quit. Simon's here. In the building. Rachel, too. Only a corridor away. Someone's bound to hear. Think of Simon's gun. Think of it under his pillow. Think of him creeping down the corridor, coming closer, listening at the door, bursting through, pulling the trigger, dropping her cold. Think of him bringing this to a close. Any second. Think of him doing it any second now.

'You knew I was coming for you, David,' she said quietly. 'You're guilty. As guilty as any of the others. You knew that the only reason I hadn't come for you before was because I was saving you for last.' She walked to the door and leant down, returned with a bag. The sound of motion, scrabbling hands, cut through his hissing breath. 'The first shall be last. You should feel flattered. It's not just anyone who gets to feature in the dénouement. Only the key players get that far. Only you and me.'

He watched her cross the room, pick up the chair from where it stood in front of the writing desk and carry it to the centre of the room. She climbed onto the chair and her silhouette showed in full against the backdrop of the window. Something hung from her side, trailed down to the floor. Long and thin, it shifted position as she stood to her full height, trailing to the floor like a tail.

'I wonder,' she said, the tail vanishing momentarily, detaching itself from where he'd imagined it had grown, rising instead, loose now, in her hands, 'have you guessed yet? Have you predicted the future this time, calculated the way things are going to go?' Her arms reached up and her fingers knitted closely against the ceiling for a moment, then released, and the rope she'd been holding dropped to the vertical. He watched her fingers grasp it and concentrate once more in compact industry. 'Let me give you a clue.' She climbed down from the chair. 'There,' she said, the black shadow of her head tipped back, staring at the empty noose which swung back and forth beneath the ceiling, wiping across the sky. 'You must have guessed by now.'

He watched her return the chair to its former place and slide something smaller, something below his line of vision, across the floor, beneath the noose. Then she leant down over the end of the bed. His legs twitched as fingers entwined themselves around his ankles, settled in a sweaty grip. Then he was moving forward, shunting across the mattress. He thought of spinning, rolling across the floor, crashing to the ground, startling Rachel and Simon from their dreams with the sound, bursting them into consciousness, hounding them into his room. But his legs were hanging in space at the end of the bed now. He felt his ankles released and then she was at his side. Her fingers crawled through his hair, yanked his head and torso upright in one smooth motion. His legs dropped down, fell against the floor.

'Time to get dressed,' she said, reaching into the bag and picking something out. She lifted his left foot and inserted it through the knickers, then the right. The now familiar sensation of the cold metal returned, as the point of the blade was pressed against his neck below the back of his skull. 'We're going to get you to your feet,' she whispered into his ear. The pressure of the blade increased. 'Fuck with me now and you'll see this ripping through the other side.'

He slowly rose and, once he was upright, she reached down and pulled the knickers up over his knees and thighs. His legs were shaking now, threatening to give way. She searched the bag behind him and then he felt her arms around his waist as she wound the corset around him and fastened it. She nudged him onto the footstool and stood behind him, the blade still poised, and he felt the noose lowered over his head, jerked tight. Then the blade moved back and she walked around, sat on the bed and faced him.

'There are no excuses,' she said. 'Even if you could speak, there isn't anything you could say to make me change my mind.'

Jack's breath was coming out in groans now. He felt the snot slumping from his nostrils onto his face. He felt light, felt as if a gust of breeze from the window, even the draught caused by the opening of a door, would be enough to tilt him from his tiny platform, signal the contraction and subsequent collapse of his throat as the tips of his toes scraped like David's had against the floor, never quite finding support. No, he was repeating, over and over. You're wrong. But his lips were locked and the letters which made up the words stayed glued on top of one another, incomprehensible, without form. It's Jack. Jack Jackson. You don't know me. You can't do this. I'm not the one you want. For Christ's sake, let me speak!

'You probably can't believe this,' she was saying, 'but I know exactly how you're feeling. I know because I've been there, too. I know exactly what it's like to be controlled and manipulated and written off by someone else as dead. You can hear yourself breathing, feel the thump of your heart. All the signs are there that life still goes on. But, deep down, you know it's just an illusion. You know it because that's what you've been told so many times that you've come to believe it yourself. It was the same for me. Only I got lucky. I got away. I found a way to change things, a way to change myself. I found a way to prove to people – people like you, David – that I was still alive. I found my voice again, because I found out how to make people pay attention, make them listen.' She got to her feet. 'But that isn't going to happen to you, David. Your voice has gone. It's gone for good.'

She started to cross the room towards the door. His eyes were adjusting to the dark now. There was something familiar in her gait. And her voice, too. There was something there that spoke to him from the past.

'No excuses. You can't blame it on the AIDS. You were

sick before that. And as for the cocaine . . . Let me tell you something about coke David: it just exaggerates what's already there. It just lets the demons out of the cage.' She paused at the door. 'Oh, yes, David. I've read your new book. You don't honestly think you could have kept that secret from me, do you? Husbands and wives shouldn't keep secrets from one another. You should have learnt that a long time ago.'

As her sentence switched off, the light switched on, and Rachel walked through the glare of the bulb towards him. Rachel. The name that flashed neon through his darkest and loneliest moments. Rachel. The face he saw every time his eyelids drooped. Rachel. The face of the woman he loved, the only woman he could conceive of loving. Rachel. The same woman who was married to David. Rachel. He was begging with his eyes now, pleading through the tears. You can't do this. Not David. David's dead. Jack. Don't. Sweet Jesus, just don't.

'Don't tell yourself it doesn't make sense,' she said, her eyes alight. 'Don't tell yourself that it wasn't you who made me this way.' She rested her foot on the edge of the stool. 'Self-asphyxiation. Fucking death itself. Snorting coke. Inflicting pain. Bringing pain on yourself. You actually thought it meant something, didn't you? You thought it made you someone. Well, let me tell you, you never even came close. What you started with your pathetic whore and wife beating, I've done for real. How does that make you feel, David, knowing that I've gone further than you were ever capable of?'

She reached up and gripped his face. 'I want to leave you with a question, David. Whose life's useless now? Yours or mine? Who's going to be remembered more when they're dead?'

Her blue eyes stared into his and then she released his face and kicked the stool away.

The next morning, with the curtains closed, Rachel sat huddled at David's writing desk, David's dressing gown wrapped tightly around her. There was noise outside: a commotion of footsteps and barks. She put down the typescript she'd been reading, rose and walked to the window, pushed her head through the join in the curtains. Simon was there, setting out on his morning round with Gellet. As he closed the gate of the herb garden behind him, he glanced up and spotted her. Even from that distance, even though the alteration in his expression was negligible, she witnessed the knowing look in his eyes. Then he smiled and turned and whistled after Gellet, following the animal down the drive. Rachel then turned herself and looked towards Jack, hanging from the ceiling, oblivious to her conscious state and the new dawn, motionless. She returned to the writing desk and switched the computer on. It blipped obtrusively. She loaded up the word-processing application and stared at the blank screen. Crouched forward, intent, her fingers straddled the keyboard and she began to type.

Outside, the sun climbed higher in the sky. Inside the bedroom, the computer screen continued to scroll down, weighted with words. Finally her fingers stopped moving and her head swivelled, turned to gaze lingeringly at Jack. Her blue eyes froze in a stare, as if blinking would somehow signal the end of something. But eventually she did blink and, fixing her eyes on the screen once more, she resumed typing:

Clack: *the past finds its place in the future.*

She stared towards the centre of the room where David Jackson hung, then glanced down at her hands. It felt good not to be wearing gloves, to have nothing left to conceal.

In a few moments, she'd save the file and dump it onto the Internet. It wouldn't be long afterwards that the phone would ring to inform Simon of the state of health of his charge. He might wait for back-up, or creep upstairs alone. It didn't matter which; it was over now. She meant him no harm. He'd find her standing by the window, waiting patiently for him. He'd bring his gun, but he wasn't going to need it. All she wanted to do now was talk.

The last full-stop she typed, like a domino falling to rest, made a sound: clack.